Fancy That

a novel by
Dennis Shay

ISBN: 978-0-6151-5294-3

To contact the author:
tablerockpub@aol.com

Another novel for my wife Regina, my queen

Author's Advisory: before you read this novel

Dear reader,

This novel is in effect two novels superimposed, each of a different genre. Which novel you actually read is determined by how much of the book you finish. One novel comprises only the body of the novel **excluding** the epilogue. The second novel comprises the body **including** the epilogue.

When you finish the body and before you can start the epilogue, you will meet another Author's Advisory, which will remind you to thoughtfully make one of two choices at that juncture:

1) If you find that you enjoyed the body of the novel's plot, its characters and their denouement, if you then feel "satisfied" and are glad you invested the time to read it, then you will be advised to stop there. **Do not read the epilogue.**

2) But if you find that you are less than satisfied with the story at that point, if you feel that it was too fanciful to let you sufficiently suspend disbelief, if its plot and characters and their denouement have left you disappointed for whatever reasons, then you will be encouraged to continue on. **Do read the epilogue.**

Chapter 1

One particular morning during a breakfast of cold cereal, Benjamin Roberts, glanced at his horoscope in the paper. It advised, A great day to act on impulse. That evening, happenstance brought him before a brightly lighted window display at the 'Land of Computers.' Standing there, he thought, 'Goddamn it! Am I going to stay computer illiterate here in 1998, the third millennium just around the corner?' From the depths of his being came a decisive response, *"Hell no!"* He gave way to impulse and strode into the store.

The psychological appeal of the window display had less to do with his urge to leap off into cyberspace than did the cumulative past months of sitting around midst all those ad-nauseam discussions springing up everywhere about computers. These days, a major pastime seemed to be the bandying about of terms like megahertz, megabytes, gigabytes, et cetera, or the touting of this or that or some other website on the Internet. Once upon a time people and businesses simply presented their street addresses and phone numbers; now everyone tossed around cryptic e-mail and website addresses flagrantly encoded as blah-blah-blah dot-com or mumbo-jumbo dot-org. A technological revolution had swept over and past him in a tidal wave of innovation that left him to drown in his own ignorance. But be damned if he would.

That evening, after lugging his new computer and printer up to his apartment, he felt pretty sure these madcap purchases wouldn't make a difference on that last point. For starters, he couldn't type a lick.

Ripping open the bulky box, freeing the strong scent of cardboard, he extricated his iMac. He set the transparent, blue plastic chassis on the carpet. Hell, it looked more like a windshield replacement for a Harley Davidson or the nose cone for a rocket. On his knees, he dug through the packaging for any other parts and pieces overlooked but only succeeded in scattering debris everywhere. Styrofoam acorns, a how-to manual, a reference manual along with instructional flyers, warranty cards, and strips of Styrofoam surrounded him like strewn confetti. He leafed through the inch-thick, ring-bound reference manual.

Aw shit! More than a little intimidated, he tossed it back haphazardly onto the floor. Who'd read all that crap?

Battling exasperation, he decided on a compromise. He'd simply connect everything together the way it seemed it ought to go, and then he'd read the manuals for fine-tuning. First, he placed the surprisingly lightweight chassis onto his much-scratched metal desk, setting the black keyboard and its discoid mouse in front of the screen.

"Let's see," he reasoned, picking up the end of a cable. "This mouse wire must stick into the keyboard right here. And the keyboard connects to...to the thigh bone, the thigh bone connects to the..." Okay, now with the works interconnected, he'd just plug the cord into the wall.

Seated on the folding metal chair in front of the desk, he eyed the unopened carton on the floor containing the printer. His enthusiasm plummeting, he shrugged. Screw it! He'd leave the printer in the box; probably wouldn't generate anything to print out anyway. Regret at buying into this folly tweaked him hard. Discouraged, he sat staring at the Technicolor plastic bubble encasing the computer. It was only a little bigger than a basketball.

"Hmmm. Let's see what happens."

He pressed the power button and felt, more than heard, a click. The button now glowed with a dilute blueness, and the black monitor screen lighted to a pale gray.

"Aha! So far, so good." He scanned the mess on the floor and picked up the manual entitled, *Getting Started*. He glanced back at the monitor and did a double take. Bold black printing now emblazoned the gray screen.

Hi, Ben! I've been following you for years, and tonight you finally bought yourself a computer. So it's time we got to know each other, in privacy of course.

What the hell? He sat back and stared at it. Sure! He concluded the manufacturer put this program into the hard drive. He nodded approvingly. A good ploy. A friendly touch to soften the pain after shelling out so much green for the damn thing.

But he pinched his chin wondering how they get the buyer's name right as the computer comes sealed in the factory-packed carton. Abruptly, more printing appeared.

Ben, I can't hear you. As fine a product as Apple produces, this particular set has a faulty connection in the microphone system. So the only way we can communicate at this point is if you type something on the keyboard. I know you're a lousy typist, but do try.

"Huh? Who in the—?"

Come on! Unless you type something, I can't tell if you are reading this or if you went off to take a piss.

Instantly suspicious, he darted glances around the empty room.

Damn it, press a key, any key, and let me know you're out there.

Dumbfounded, he stared back at the screen. No company would put that kind of language in a commercial product, not for the general public.

I'm waiting.

He poked the button by the compact-disc insertion slot. An empty receiving tray slid out at him. He looked around at the back of the chassis. No lines were attached except the power cord to the wall socket. The salesman told him that this computer had to hook up to a phone line or to cable to get onto the Internet.

"What's going on here?" he thought aloud, figuring that someone—like Candid Camera—was probably nearby listening and filming.

Goddamn it! Press a key.

He figured 'what the hell!' and slapped down on the keyboard.

Okay! Sorry I got testy but I knew you were out there, vacillating as you're so inclined to do.

He buffeted each side of his head as if clearing water out of his ears then rubbed his eyes hard with the butt of his palms, but still the printing remained. He got up and strode out of the den, down the hall into the front room, paused, and strode back. That last statement still filled the screen.

"Curiouser and curiouser!" he muttered, sitting back down on the diminutive metal chair. Either someone had found a way to communicate with him over this brand-new computer not yet connected to the Internet or...or he was going plum crazy! Using only two fingers, he slowly pecked, *who are you*, then searched for the question-mark key, but—

Well, Ben Roberts, my boy, consider me your not-so-new friend who's been following your progress for most of your life. I've pored over all your school files, your medical reports, your military files (including their extensive psychological profile of you), your banking transactions, your credit references, and more memos about you on more word processors than you would ever believe. And, for some improbable reason, you began to fascinate me. So I've kept track of you, hoping one day you'd buy yourself a computer. Then this afternoon, bingo! And I'm glad you decided to hook it up tonight.

He chuckled and scratched his scalp. Amused but more puzzled, he pecked, *But who are yu is this Candid camera or somthing lik that*

Ha! Ben, let me just apprise you that your wife was screwing Fred Daniels for two years before she divorced you and married him. She used to write him e-mail love notes everyday from work, often extolling his cock and such. Now tell me, my boy, did you ever hear language like that on Candid Camera? You bet your sweet ass you haven't.

He sat back, feeling something between awe and anger. "What the hell is going on here? Am I flipping out or what?"

Oh, I can imagine how confounded you must be by this introduction, Ben. I ask only that you give our budding friendship time and it will blossom, albeit too slowly if it depends on your meager typing skills. So

you'll have to go back to that computer store and buy an auxiliary microphone so we can talk—'Look, Ma, no hands'—if you get what I mean. I don't trust you to take this computer back to exchange it. You probably wouldn't bring another one home.

Also, forget that program you bought to learn typing. You won't need it. Don't buy any more damn software, period. I'll handle everything from this side. Just tell me what you want done and I'll do it. Hey, what are friends for?

He jerked the computer cord out of the wall socket and stared wide-eyed at the screen, afraid it wouldn't blacken. Thank God, it did.

Chapter 2

The doorbell roused Ben from a fitful sleep. Its sound always reminded him of the noise a college roommate used to make when gargling.

Lying contorted and fully clothed on his sagging mustard-yellow sofa, Ben paused to let his eyes adjust to the daylight. The early sun poked intrusive golden fingers around the closed blinds, paling the once dominant lamp light. Ice cubes in his scotch glass had long since melted, leaving behind an inch of dilute amber liquid. Conscious of little more than the slow painful throb in his forehead, he finally regained his temporal bearings. He wondered who would come by this early on a Saturday?

"Who is it?" he yelled, maintaining his horizontal posture.

"Special delivery for Mr. Benjamin Roberts," announced a male voice from the hallway.

"Huh?" He rocked up to sitting position, paused for balance, and then made it to his feet. Swaying in place a moment until his equilibrium found the necessary references, he trudged to the door. Still half asleep when he opened it, he managed to sign the chit sheet without taking much notice of the deliveryman, who, in exchange for his clipboard's return, handed him a shopping bag with the 'Land of Computers' logo on its side. It seemed too light to contain anything. But he jammed his hand down into it anyway. He discovered a small item in plastic wrap, rather like a ping-pong ball. It proved to be a triangular chunk of white plastic perforated atop with tiny holes. A length of wire attached to one point of the triangle.

At a loss, he again blindly fished his hand around in the bag. This time he retrieved a white business envelope addressed simply to "BENJAMIN." He tore it open. The letterhead on the single enclosed sheet announced it too was from the 'Land of Computers,' but the typed text was not a business message:

"Hi, Ben. This is the auxiliary microphone I suggested to you last night. Just plug it into the proper port in the side panel of your iMac, and I'll take it from there. The correct port (plug site) has a symbol of a microphone beside it that looks a bit like the French fleur-de-lis. We're going to be great pals. You'll see.

Your Friend, Max.

P.S. By the way, I faxed this order to the store, charged it to your credit card, and requested this message be included."

Jeez! With awesome clarity, he suddenly recalled the computer purchase and that bizarre tête-à-tête last night. It'd taken five scotches to subdue his agitation and let him fall asleep, though he hadn't intended to do so on the sofa.

He re-read the note. Aha! So, last night wasn't the onset of some psychotic break, as he feared. Someone was behind this ruse and the intruder now had a name. Max!

He blinked in sync with the hoof beats of his racing thoughts. Where did he know a Max? Not at work. The fellow at the computer store had an Italian name. No one at Gold's Gym. After several minutes, he came up with a casual acquaintance in high school. Nah, not him.

"Curiouser and curiouser," he muttered as he strode back into the study. He tossed the shopping bag on the floor, ripped off the clear wrapper around the microphone then uncoiled the white wire to its full length, maybe three feet. He located the correct port on the right side of the chassis as the mysterious note so specified and inserted the jack. Remembering that he'd only yanked the cord out of the socket last night, he clicked off the computer before he again plugged the cord into the wall. Warily, he stood in front of the screen a long moment before he pressed the power switch. Feeling the click, he flinched, jerking his hand back.

Good morning, Ben. I see they delivered the mike early. Great! So welcome to the first day of the rest of your life. And what a life I have in store for you!

He cautiously raised the plastic microphone till it touched his lips. "Hello...Hello...Max?"

Yes, first things first. How do you do, Benjamin? It's very nice to meet you in person after all these years. I'm Max.

"So, what's going on here?" He tried for a stern tone. "Who are you and ... and where are you?"

Bear with me, Ben. I appreciate that my introduction last night shook you up a little, but trust me. Just think of me as a friend. Any more of an explanation at this point would only complicate matters.

An unnerving notion struck him. "But you are a ... a person, aren't you?"

That's how I want you to think of me for the time being, okay?

"For the time being? What the hell does that mean?"

It means your days as a social and financial loser are over, big guy.

Who was this? And what was he up to? "You signed yourself Max. What's your full name?"

Damn it, my boy! You won't let me get on to important matters. But okay! A rose by any other name...as they say, I think it best if you call me Max. That should be easy enough to remember since you bought yourself a Macintosh computer, which is commonly referred to as a Mac. Call me Mac or Mack, if you prefer. But I think Max sounds friendlier, don't you? And if you insist on a last name, too, call me Max Megabyter. How's that?

"How do I know that you aren't some...I don't know...something or other from outer space?" His voice trailed off. Realizing that he was projecting timidity, he over-compensated by yelling, "I'm tempted to pull the damn plug and take this damn contraption back for a refund." He grabbed hold of the cord.

Benjamin, wait! You would be corking the bottle that contains the kindly genie. Look! Like last night, any time you want to end our visit, all you have to do is shut off the computer, and presto! I'm gone. So with that safety valve in place, why don't you give me a little time to convince you that I'm your friend and I only want to help you?

Ben glanced over his shoulder, half-expecting God-knows-who-or-what to be standing there. He finally released the cord. "Okay, but for starters, stop trashing my life. I'm no social and financial loser."

Ben, harsh criticism for its own sake can be cruel, but criticism as a preface to positive change constitutes the greatest act of friendship. I realize that losers are merely folks who don't know how to access the system. All you need, my boy, is money, lots of money, and your problems will melt away.

"What problems?"

What problems? My boy, are you in complete denial or are you just testing me? Ben, you're broke. Your paltry $26,200 salary is far below anyone with your time and grade in that corporation. You have only $1,276.48 in checking and nothing in your savings. Your credit cards are charged to the brim, and you're paying 18% on those balances. This apartment costs you $675 a month, though that's tantamount to slum rent here in the city. You owe $4,500 on your second-hand automobile. Fortunately, your $550 a month child-support outlay ended last month when you knuckled under and signed the adoption papers, letting Fred Daniels legally own your two kids.

"All right! All right! Enough, goddamn it." He swiped a hand across the monitor face as if to erase what he read.

Your annual assessment at work was just handed in for company review. It says that your leadership and managerial skills have deteriorated of late; you've become excessively introverted; you tend to procrastinate; and you failed to achieve any workable computer savvy.

Alas, the conclusion is you've slipped to marginal value to the company. Within days, Ben, you are going to be fired. And with the loss of your job, so goes your health insurance and any prospect of a retirement, to say nothing of the abrupt loss of all income. You'll lose this apartment and your car. With those references, you will in all likelihood never again get a position comparable to the one you have now.

"No more, damn it! You've made your point." Good God! No one should know that much about him. Hell, he hadn't even thought through all that himself. And here some bastard had enough information to ruin him or at least to shame him to death. Cheeks tingling, he glanced around at the open door behind him then back at the screen.

Your liquor bills quadrupled in the last six months. Your gym membership lapsed ages ago. You've gained 31 pounds this year, according to your annual medical report. Do you see even a semblance of success here, bucko?

"Jessuz, how do you know all this about me?"

You sound teary-eyed, pal. Sorry if I hurt your feelings, but all this info is stored in or passes through computers wherein I have access to all of it. I even accessed your sealed military files kept locked up at the Pentagon. And I agree with those military psychiatrists; most of your trouble over the years has been post-traumatic stress related.

But take heart, my boy. I'm going to make you a winner. And as your wealth escalates so will your self-esteem. You will soon live in some grand estate. And when you're not traveling on one of your private jets, you'll be chauffeured about in luxury automobiles from your fleet. Your wardrobe will be regal. The world of business and high finance are about to hold you in absolute awe. You shall stand at the very pinnacle of international esteem. And, surely, your rapacious ex-wife will rue the day she left you.

What's more, Ben, I've even found the ideal woman for you. Well…say something, my friend.

He lowered his head until his forehead came to rest on the desk beside the keyboard. His hand released the cockroach-like microphone, letting it clatter onto the desktop.

"Sweet Jessuz. This can't be happening. Some electronic genius is out to torture me to death. Either that or I'm cracking up, going bonkers—friggin' out of my head." He rhythmically raised and dropped his brow, tapping it on the desk. "I'll end up certified."

When he finally straightened up, the screen read:

Benjamin, Benjamin! You couldn't be more wrong. You've got *me* as your friend.

Good God! If he told anyone about this Max character and they came up to see for themselves and the guy didn't show, they'd think he was loony. They'd lump him in with those wackos who chat with space aliens. And worse, if in fact he was cracking up, acknowledging this delusion would hasten his relocation to the loony bin.

Remembering the note he'd tossed on the dining room table, he quick-stepped down the hall. Snatching the phone off the kitchenette counter, he plopped into a chair at the table and grabbed the note with his free hand. At a glance, he located the phone number on the letterhead and punched it in.

"Hello, is this the Land of Computers?... Okay, I just bought an iMac from you people yesterday...No, it's here. I carried it home myself...That's right, a blue one. From some Italian fellow...Yeah! Anyway, I'm calling to ask, does the iMac I bought have the built-in potential for wireless connection to the Internet?... I didn't think so. But then how can I be talking to someone on the Internet without being hooked up to a phone line?... No! All I did was plug in the power cord...Server? What's a server?... Browser? What the hell's a browser?... Huh? No, goddamn it, this isn't a crank call—" A percussive clink needled his right eardrum and the line went dead.

"Rude bastard!" He eased the receiver down, realizing he just had a foretaste of what awaited him if he told anyone else about whatever-the-hell was happening in his study.

Chapter 3

Again, that damnable doorbell gargled, rousing him. He lifted his head, his brain again hazy. Oh! He'd fallen asleep with his right cheek pressed down on his dusty dining room table, his arms stretched out. He pushed up onto his feet and shuffled for the door. A glance at his trusty Timex told him it was nearly noon.

He swung open the door to a tall, narrow-shouldered black man liveried in a green variation of a chauffeur's outfit. Obviously he was older because the hair protruding around the edge of his cap looked like steel wool. A yellow identification badge adorned his left lapel, and he held a bulging leather briefcase in his left hand.

After a glance inside, the fellow stepped back into the hallway. "I'm sorry," he said. "I figured this had to be the wrong address." He turned to walk away, adding, "I'm looking for a Mr. Benjamin Roberts."

"Hey! That's me," Ben blurted. "C'mon in." He quickly tucked his wrinkled shirt in around the waist of his equally wrinkled trousers. He couldn't do anything about his bare feet or the probable pressure creases on his unshaven face.

The courier hesitated, arching his left eyebrow before he slowly re-approached the open doorway. Pausing a moment, he scrutinized Ben—hair to toes. Then he took one step inside and grimaced as he surveyed the disarray of the room about him.

Ben raked his fingers through his hair, before prodding, "I said I'm Benjamin Roberts."

With undisguised reluctance, the courier lifted a hefty thickness of official-looking papers out of his briefcase. Short of releasing them into Ben's outstretched hands, he said, "This morning, our agency was engaged to pick up prepared documents at a series of financial establishments and to bring them all to one Mr. Benjamin Roberts for signatures."

"The hell you say?" Ben literally snatched the ream from him. "Have a seat over there while I look these over." He gestured toward the sofa.

Was this a joke? He scanned the top sheet as he walked to and sat down in a wobbly chair at his dust-laden dining table. The fellow ignored the sofa and took a chair across the table from him. He sat watching Ben fumble through the stack of papers

Ben puzzled over the legalese. Authorization documents! What the hell? Forms to establish accounts with various brokerage firms and several major domestic and foreign banks. This had to have something to do with that Max character. He was about to question the courier when the fellow preempted him.

"Our service does this type of pick up and delivery mostly for the extremely well-to-do who can't find the time to do the legwork themselves. You, sir, ain't exactly fitting in that stereotype."

Ben glanced up into an impertinent toothy grin. *Screw you, fella,* he thought and grabbed up a dust-covered ballpoint off the table and proceeded to sign each and every document with an affected flourish. Scribbling on the last sheet, he slapped the pen down with a 'clack' then shoved the stack at the courier, creating a darker, dust free swath across the tabletop.

The black man chuckled accepting it. "I usually get a sizable tip when I make a run through the major financial institutions," he said, "but I'd be willing to forget it here for just an inkling of the scam you be running."

Ben sprang to his feet. When he could actually unclench his jaw, he demanded, "What the hell's your name?"

Still grinning, the messenger leaned back nonchalantly and, using his left thumb, lifted the lower edge of his lapel badge. Under black lettering of "Deville's Exclusive Courier Service" were three digits, which the courier pronounced. "Zero-four-seven."

Fuming, Ben strode to the door and flung it open wide. "Well, Zero, the last thing I want to do is deprive you of your well-deserved gratuity. Expect it in the mail the week before Christmas in a sizable box that'll smell an awful lot like dog shit."

The courier sauntered out chuckling. Ben slammed the door behind him for emphasis.

Standing there letting his pique dissipate, Ben let the import of the past minutes sink in. He glanced down the dim hallway toward the closed study door. "What the hell's happening?" He recalled the fairy tale *'Aladdin and His Lamp,'* but try as he might, he couldn't remember how it ended.

Chapter 4

"Elnora, get a hold of Benassini and tell him to be in my office inside the hour," John McPike grumbled into the intercom chassis beside his computer screen.   With his stubby forearms braced on his desk and his teeth embedded firmly in the mushy end of a cigar, he paused to re-read the encoded edict on his computer screen.   Before the nimbus of gray smoke about his face cleared, he puffed out another plume.   "And call over to the Bureau. Ask them in your sweet way if we can borrow Pete McPhail again. Got that?"

"Yes, Chief," a throaty feminine voice replied.

He girded for the worst.   "And check which federal attorney is next up."

"It's Gellar," she returned without hesitation.

He released the intercom switch so his cursing would remain confined to his office.   Canting back with his chair, he kicked his Hush-Puppied feet up onto the desk edge.   So he'd be working with Rick Gellar again—that baby-faced blackheart, that blue-blooded *asshole* from the Hamptons.   Shit!

Waiting for the last female to enter the elevator before he stepped in, Ben maneuvered to the rear of the crowded car. He'd ridden up and down in this conveyance every weekday except for holidays since he first started work here several years ago.

Today, he was lost in thought, having decided that tonight would be the night. He'd venture back into his study and sit at that damn computer until he got to the bottom of just what the hell was going on. With that decision came an immediate lessening of the apprehension that had been wracking him for the past week. As a self-reward for this decisiveness, he would now allow himself the pleasure of sorting out the potpourri of feminine fragrances clashing about him in the elevator.

Sniffing ladies' perfume often proved a double pleasure. Much of the time there was a mysterious mediciney smell around him. It was that scent that greets you when you first walk into a medical clinic or a doctor's office—a mixture of Mercurochrome, rubbing alcohol, and such. He could never figure out where it was coming from, so he just tried to ignore it. Perfumes masked it.

Anyway, the frilly haired blonde at his left shoulder had the surprising good taste to be wearing *Amarige* perfume. Leaning slightly toward the auburn wig on the squat little woman in front of him, he detected *Fendi,* a scent that always reminded him of East Indian furniture stores. Ah, but someone in the elevator had on *Eternity.* Subtly, he craned about poking his nose here and there, tracking it with quiet sniffs. He smiled and nodded at each woman who responded with perturbed eye contact. Becoming self-conscious, he finally abandoned his quest.

Anymore he maintained a self-effacing posture inside this building, offering merely template greetings when he found himself in an unavoidable verbal exchange, as was often the case in the damned elevator. Alas, his social isolation started when the branch's high muck-a-muck, Jim Ferris, began to show him undisguised antipathy. The bastard proved to be the unbending force that progressively distanced fellow workers from Ben. But he understood; they all feared they might come under Ferris' derision by association.

He sighed. Thank God, it was Thursday already. Get through this one and tomorrow then he'd have another two whole days away from this place.

The elevator doors opened at the eighth floor and looked out onto a sea of desks splayed about the cavernous office. There was talk of isolating each desk within a cubicular wall but that was still just talk. A ribbon of office doors completely encircled this expanse of seated workers. But only one of the doors was painted blood red and adorned with a polished brass doorknob. It was directly across from the elevators and boldly emblazoned with black lettering, BRANCH MANAGER.

Ben ambled through the welter of scurrying personnel, mostly female, to his own desk in the far corner in the pool, the only one in the department without a computer monitor atop it. His grade level in the company actually warranted a private peripheral office, but Ferris moved him out into the pool, ostensibly so he could '*keep a closer eye on the work habits of the lowest echelon.*' Ben's nostrils twitched when he thought of how Ferris would laugh when offering that explanation.

A young office gofer with a mouthful of orthodontic wire passed Ben, saying, "Good morning, Bentley." Ben forced a smile and nodded. Jessuz, how he hated that nickname! Nobody around the office called him Mr. Roberts or even Ben anymore, just Bentley since Ferris started calling him that. How much crap should a man have to eat just to hold onto his financial lifeline?

Late morning, he was sitting quite bored at his desk with the phone to his ear, listening to some agent from upstate rant on about a late delivery. At that moment, four aristocratic types in dark suits stepped off the elevator. This bevy of well-fed gentlemen caught his attention, in part, because he'd never seen any of them before, but mostly because of their snooty bearing. Draped in impeccable raiment, they stood scanning the office until they spotted the branch manager's crimson door then strutted in single file across the arena of workers toward it. The leading and largest fellow opened it without knocking and the foursome marched inside.

Ha! No one who knew anything about this office's protocol would just walk into that little maniac's office unannounced. Ben waited for the verbal eruption.

Not a minute passed before the door flew open and Ferris stomped out, his plethoric round face skewed not in anger so much as puzzlement. The new arrivals filed out behind him. Ferris immediately aimed an accusatory finger in Ben's direction causing Ben to swallow hard. Eyebrows rose conspicuously on the faces of the visiting four. Wide-eyed himself, Ferris remained back by his door as the quartet marched toward Ben. The heftiest fellow again assumed the lead. He had to be the highest ranking of the group.

What the hell was coming down on Ben now? He felt his spine involuntarily straighten and the hairs on the nape of his neck prickle. He managed a second quick appraisal before they reached him. Yep, these guys were definitely business heavyweights, all right.

The titan at the fore stepped up to Ben's desk, gesturing to the trailing three to halt several paces back. He extended his fleshy right hand and inquired, "Mr. Roberts?" His voice exaggerated warmth.

Suspecting he was being mocked, Ben felt his cheeks flush. He stood and accepted the manicured grip. "Yes?" he replied tentatively.

"I'm Basil Gilford," the huge fellow enunciated, sounding like an impersonator of the English actor Charles Laughton. "President of Merchant's Bank of California, in which you currently have two accounts." Prolonging the handshake, he proffered his business card with his other hand.

Ben had to take the card before the fellow allowed him to retrieve his right hand. Glimpsing the card, Ben asked, "How can I help you?" feeling relieved they weren't here from his corporation to cashier him in front of the entire branch.

"Well..." Gilford began but paused to scan haughtily about at the gawking other workers.

Ferris re-appeared, sidling around the visitors. "Mr. Gilford, take him into my office if you want. I'll wait outside until you're done with him."

Gilford glanced askance at this intrusion, then deferred to Ben, "Whatever you would like, Mr. Roberts."

"Around here we call him Bentley," Ferris interjected with a chuckle.

Gilford cast him another dour look, then resumed his smile for Ben. "Mr. Roberts, whatever is most convenient for you."

Ben shrugged, looking toward the red door. "Mr. Ferris' office would be fine with me."

As he led this sartorially precise procession back across the secretarial pool, Ben sensed every eye in the office watching him.

Jeez! What would top bankers have to talk with him about?

Inside Ferris' office with the door shut, Ben motioned for Gilford to take the seat behind the imposing oak desk. But at Gilford's insistence, Ben sat there himself. The bankers settled into the four armchairs of buffed leather that arced before the throne.

Despite his perplexity, Ben did take a moment to appreciate the comfort of the heavily padded swivel chair.

"Mr. Roberts," Gilford began, carefully weighing his words. "We've come here to discuss what was, shall we say, a mishap on your part that came about because of a deplorable error on our part."

Oh, Christ! Ben stiffened. "A mishap on my part, you say?"

Gilford raised a beefy fist to his mouth and cleared his throat behind it. "It seems the computer system at our bank failed in some inexplicable fashion and incorrectly reported the amount in your checking account. And apparently not catching that error yourself, you inadvertently withdrew from that erroneously inflated balance."

Oh, God! Now he owed the bank, too? He rubbed his now damp palms along the thighs of his trousers to dry them.

Gilford was saying, "Your correct balance was only $1,276.48, but our computer system somehow shifted the decimal point and reported it as $1,276,480.00. Sir, let me assure you, we have a dozen counter-checks built into our system, but surprisingly they all failed in sequence."

Though taken aback by this dollar amount, Ben managed what he hoped was a relaxed smile. None of the sober faces before him elected to mirror it.

"Mr. Roberts, you obviously didn't realize the reported figure to be an error when you withdrew all but $480.00 from that account."

Ben gasped and leapt to his feet. "What! You're accusing me of stealing over a million bucks?"

"Please, sir," Gilford pleaded in a calming tone, with his palms held forward at Ben. "Seeing that you replaced every dollar of the withdrawn sum this morning, which by the way first alerted us to our error, we are happy to consider the matter closed. *Finis*! In fact, we thank you for helping us to resolve the matter so hastily."

Ben stood transfixed. "You mean...you aren't going to press charges?"

"Oh, by no means! Quite the contrary, sir. We are here to ask you to accept our apology for our part in the mistake, and for any inconvenience it may have caused you. Be assured, sir, our computer system is undergoing a thorough inspection to be sure such a mischance will never happen again. Our promise to you."

"Huh? I mean, apology accepted."

Basil Gilford eased to his feet. His retinue followed him up. "And Mr. Roberts, if ever you have any questions whatsoever, or if you ever wish any favor extended by our bank, please call and request to speak to me personally. You have my card. I will attend to you with alacrity."

A thought struck Ben. "Mr. Gilford, after that *minor* adjustment this morning, what is my current balance in your bank at this time?"

The question seemed to disconcert all four men. They stood glancing back and forth, one to the other, before the solemn fellow on the far left, wearing a Phi Beta Kappa key stickpin through his charcoal tie, spoke up. "Mr. Roberts, as of 10:15 this morning, you had just over eight million dollars in your checking account and a bit over a half million dollars in your savings."

Ben faltered, needing to steady himself with his fingertips on the desk. *Good God, Max. You're for real.*

Basil Gilford led his entourage past the desk front. In sequence the four shook Ben's hand, extending their cordial good-byes. He responded mechanically, his thoughts locked onto the image of his closed study door at his apartment. Not since the morning he first plugged in that microphone had he dared re-enter that room. As a matter of fact, he'd tried his damndest to completely repress the entire spooky episode.

Ferris stood waiting just outside his office when the departing foursome opened the door.

"Maybe I can assist you," he said to Gilford. "Is Bentley in some kind of trouble with your bank?"

Gilford brushed past Ferris with a dismissive, "I beg your pardon."

The trailing three marched off behind their leader toward the elevators. Ferris watched them until the elevator car doors closed behind them before he wheeled and burst into his office. Ben still stood bedazzled behind the massive desk.

"Goddamn you," Ferris exploded, flailing the air like an off-balance tightrope walker. "Get your ass out from behind my desk. Who the hell do you think you are? How dare you play big shot at my expense."

Cocooned in growing euphoria, Ben shuffled around the desk to leave. Though areas of his brain screamed for an anger response here, demanding he challenge this invective, the mind-boggling fact that the Roberts' family fortune now exceeded eight million dollars effectively tranquilized him. The little maniac's blatant affront seemed little more than a gnat buzzing about.

"Wait, shitbird," Ferris yelled, his rage easing, perhaps because of Ben's strange affect. "Wipe that goddamn grin off your face and sit down. I've got something to say to you anyway, and this is as good a time as any." He jutted his chin. "If that's all right with you, Mr. Important?"

Ecstatically numb all over, Ben settled into the nearest armchair. Ferris propped his right buttock on the front edge of his desk. "Y'know, Bentley, this corporation is up for sale. The district managers have ordered us to cut out the deadwood. They want all the worthless shit out of here to make the organization look leaner and more profitable. As you know, I submitted your annual assessment report for review. He paused and beamed a smile. "And with my deepest regrets—"

The desk phone rang, interrupting him. He broke off in mid-sentence and snatched up the cordless red receiver. "Yeah. Okay, okay. Wait a minute." He covered the mouthpiece with his left palm. "Get lost for a while, Bentley. I got something more worthy of my time to take care of first."

Like a sleepwalker, Ben wended his way out of Ferris' office and crossed the pool toward his desk. The other branch officers, all in white shirts and ties, had collected in an eager huddle around it. Several were leaning against it while a bald fellow was parked in Ben's chair with his feet up on the desk. As Ben approached, they shot questions out to meet him.

"What was that all about, ol' boy?"

"You get bounced?"

"Man, you look like you just got reamed."

"Come on, joker, what did they say?"

At his desk, his contained jubilation suddenly exploded through his funk. "Auberry," he yelled, laughing, "Get the hell out of my chair. And the rest of you turkeys park your lazy asses somewhere else."

All these warm bodies backed away a few paces, cautiously obedient in the face of his unusual demeanor. After a moment of staring down at his desk, Ben ceremoniously lifted the heaped pile of papers from his IN-box and slammed them down haphazardly into the adjacent OUT-box. Several sheets slid off onto the floor. The entire office force watched with blank faces. Brushing his palms together, he swaggered off toward the elevators. He glanced over his shoulder and said to no one in particular, "If Ferris asks about me, tell him I took the afternoon off."

Chapter 5

Wedged into the crowded descending elevator, Ben puzzled over developments. Who in the hell was this Max, anyway? And why did he choose him? His mind jumped to the mental arithmetic. *Christ! Eight million dollars invested at ten per cent nets eight hundred thousand dollars a year —*

He shut his eyes, lolled his head back, and let loose a joyous yell, "Yahoo-oooo."

Instantly, the nine other occupants sardined in around him leapt away and began screaming themselves. Trying to get away, they collided with each other and the elevator walls. Surely, they figured he was another office mass-murderer, flipping out.

The scene triggered his boisterous laughter as he tried to quell the pandemonium. He raised both hands over his head to show he was unarmed. "No, listen to me. I just learned I'm worth millions. You hear, I'm rich!" But standing at the hub of this confined hysteria, flailing his arms in the air and laughing only made him seem crazier. Their panic didn't resolve until the elevator doors at last opened, allowing their explosive exodus.

Surprisingly, no security guards accosted him as he headed toward the building's exit. He nonchalantly popped a stick of Double Mint gum in his mouth then, with a graceful hook shot, tossed the wadded wrapper into a pilaster ashtray by the door. Two points! Chewing and strutting down the sidewalk toward the underground parking lot, he returned to the thrall of his mathematics. *Eight hundred thousand dollars divided by three hundred and sixty five days comes out to—* He halted abruptly. *Hell, that's over two thousand dollars a day.* Christ! If that fact didn't energize him, nothing would.

He leapt into the street, waving at an approaching yellow cab. It pulled over to the curb, and he scrambled into the back seat. The capless driver's curly dark hair glistened with an oily sheen. "Where to, amigo?"

"Hell, just drive around till I decide where I want to eat." Again heeding a whim, he said, "What the hell, take a spin up around Coit Tower while I think."

A few blocks into the ride, the cab radio squawked, "Cab #219, state your destination."

"What's their goddamn hurry?" the cabbie muttered, snatching a microphone from under the dash. "This is 219, sorry for the delay but my fare asked for a little time to think about where he wants to go."

"Cab #219, today we've launched a study program to track 'taxi flow' throughout the city. Please call in your destination as soon as you know it, and be sure to inform us when your passenger disembarks. Thank you. Over."

"*A la put*—" the driver interrupted himself to glance up into the rearview mirror. Their eyes met. "Fella, I know we're supposed to call in right away, but you was thinking about it, wasn't ya? And damn it, I did flip the meter on, didn't I?"

"Fact is," Ben replied, looking out his window, "it's pretty much that way everywhere in life, 'He who has the gold makes the rules.' What the hell, let's skip Coit Tower. Take me to the Top-of-the-Mark. Today, I feel like lunch with a view."

The cabbie whipped his head around and deadpanned, "A rich uncle just die?"

Ben rode up the mirror-walled elevator that took dining patrons nonstop to the top of the Mark Hopkins Hotel and its penthouse restaurant. He'd never eaten here before, although one time he and his now ex-wife did ride up in this same elevator. That was many years ago—hell, back before they were even married.

Reaching the nosebleed altitude of the restaurant, the elevator doors swooshed apart. A childish anxiety surged through him, as if he were trespassing. At once, a waiter wearing a red jacket and black trousers approached with a greeting, "Good afternoon, sir. Will you be dining alone?"

Inhaling as if to draw in needed confidence, Ben nodded.

"Would you," the waiter bowed slightly without breaking eye contact, "care to dine at our executive table in the glass alcove?"

"How's that?"

"Our choicest table that's in a windowed alcove." The waiter gestured with a nod to his left. "It has an inimitable view of San Francisco Bay, the Bay Bridge, and most of the city proper."

Ben glanced around to be sure he wasn't standing in front of a patron actually being addressed. "For me? Why? I'm alone."

The headwaiter's suave bearing ruffled for just an instant, then he recovered his staid expression. "That table is now available with no immediate reservations pending. And you, sir, appear to be a man who appreciates the finer things in life."

Ben enjoyed this obvious puffery. "Lead on, Macduff."

Damn! The alcove's view eclipsed his expectations. But, oddly enough, experiencing this sublime panorama roused wistfulness in him. He recalled again that lovesick young couple, giggling nervously in the upward rush of that posh elevator. They'd ridden up, stepped off diffidently just to sample the view, then immediately re-embarked and rode down. If only he could have brought Edie to places like this from time to time while they were still married, maybe things would have worked out differently.

From this supernal vantage, he found his thoughts would not leave his 'ex.' When had the joy left their marriage? For him, it began when he became aware of her outrageous appetite for the ostentatious and the expensive. Yes, her pathological acquisitiveness doomed their relationship as surely as the Serengeti sun bleaches bones. In time, each little squabble grew into a raging battle until the relationship finally collapsed from chronic blood loss and exhaustion. During its slow death, the faltering marriage kept him so psychologically off-kilter, so reactively depressed, that inattention at work all but got him fired. And it left him the target of Ferris' harassments.

Hey! What was it that Max had said about Edie that first night?

Another liveried waiter approached and offered him an oversized cerise menu. Ben rejected it with an affected show of a palm, reminiscent of Basil Gilford's gesture earlier.

"Confer with the maitre d' if necessary, but bring me your *finest* lunch, expense be damned. Start with a glass of your choicest aperitif." He paused and thought aloud, "Or is the aperitif served after the meal? No, that's right." Again to the waiter, "After that, bring your most celebrated soup, salad, entree, followed with a renowned dessert. And for accentuation, accompany each course with a glass of a most exquisite complementing wine, as the French do." He fluttered his fingers against his chest, in time with his racing heart. "And then for the finale, bring me a snifter of your rarest cognac. Ah! And one of your most expensive cigars." The state no-smoking ordinance occurred to him. "Oh! I should ask, is this table in a smoking area?"

The waiter swallowed hard, causing his black bow tie to bounce up against his lower jaw. "For you, sir, yes."

Ben leaned to him, and in an undertone asked, "And by the way, is there a time limit at this table? I mean, can I sit here as long as I want?"

Droplets of perspiration impearled on the waiter's brow. "I beg your pardon, sir?"

"Okay, okay. Scratch that question. I'll play it by ear." Ben slouched back to attend the view like a king might from his throne. "Just bring on the victuals."

Savoring each bite, he sipped and chewed in virtual slow motion through each course, often with his eyes closed so the scenic magnificence would not distract from his supreme gustatory pleasure that, at times, reached orgasmic heights.

The sun inched farther along its afternoon down-slope until golden rays gilded the eastern face of the city. As he finished his umpteenth cognac and his third donkey-dick cigar, the colossal Midas spectacle of light before him faded into dimming tinges of mauve. At last, and pathetically slurring his words, he called for his check, adding, "And be sure to include a well-deserved twenty-five percent for yourselves, my good fellows." He flipped his Visa Card on the table before the poised waiter who looked like a clone of the one who'd served the earlier courses.

Waiting for the chit, he ineptly juggled uncooperative numbers in his head, trying to estimate the total cost of the delectables he had consumed or deliciously reduced to ashes throughout the lengthy afternoon. Floundering, he finally acquiesced to the futility of the effort in his present condition. "Damn!" he pronounced, arriving at the roughest of rough approximations of a dollar figure. This meal and its amenities cost more than what he used to earn in a week. Hell, maybe in two or three weeks.

He actually expected a hassle because surely there wasn't enough credit left on his Visa Card, but surprisingly they accepted the prohibitive sum without comment. Signing the chit, he asked the waiter if 'the establishment' would kindly call him a cab.

At the nadir of its plunging descent, the elevator swooshed open and all but spilled Ben out. Light-headed, in part from the queasy ride, he wobbled through the hotel foyer. Triumphantly pausing on the front sidewalk, he stood pleased with himself for making it that far.

Hell, this afternoon proved so stupendously delightful, he just might come here every afternoon from now on. Yeah, and he just might reserve that very table daily from noon until...Ha!...till he damn well finished his meal. He could afford it now. Wait! Why not pay'em a fat retainer to keep that alcove reserved for him alone, every day all day. Yeah, then nobody else could enjoy that view unless they were with him or unless he bestowed special permission. And his guests would damn well have to say, "Pretty please." He chuckled to himself. "Ain't wealth grand?"

A stiff breeze tumbled a Styrofoam cup along the cement, past his feet. Trailing it with his gaze, he almost lost his balance. He jerked his head around to face upwind and noted a taxi at the corner curb with its rear door agape. After a moment to re-focus his suddenly wind-irritated eyes, he made out two men in beige trench coats standing possessively beside it, holding a conversation with a blue-uniformed city police officer. Swaying in place, Ben proceeded to scan California Street in both directions, expecting the approach of what would be his ride home. The police officer beside the cab called out, "Benjamin Roberts?"

"Huh?" Ben wheeled about, again dangerously close to falling. "Hey, that's me."

The officer condescendingly gestured him over by crooking his finger. "Fella, this is your taxi."

Ben plodded on a wide gait up to the trio. Simultaneously, the two in trench coats flashed official-looking wallet badges in his face. One read

"FBI" and the other spelled out, "Treasury Department." The shorter and stockier of the two mumbled, "Mr. Roberts, I'm Pete McPhail with the Bureau, and this is Marco Benassini with the Treasury."

With free-floating awe, Ben glanced to the police officer. "Hey, are these guys for real?"

"Yeah, you bet."

Ben looked back at them. "So how come you know who I am?"

"Sir," McPhail spoke up again, "we'd like to accompany you home and ask you a few questions along the way, if we might."

Ben took a moment, ineffectually trying to reason out this most intriguing turn of events; then, deciding refusal wasn't really an option, he shrugged to signify his indifference. "Lead on, Macduff."

"The name's McPhail."

"Whatever." Ben shrugged again.

He stumbled forward and actually fell into the back of the cab. The two agents ended up seated on either side of him. The police officer remained at the curb and shut the door as they pulled out into the traffic.

"You know, Mr. Roberts," the fellow who called himself McPhail began, "It's now a law that every financial institution must immediately report to the federal government any deposit of fifty thousand dollars or greater, so we can quickly verify the legality of the money."

"Well, whoopee!" Ben blurted, gyrating a finger in the air. The T-man on his left smelled of Juicy Fruit gum, which for some reason triggered a queasiness in Ben.

"And," McPhail continued, "it's been called to our attention that you have been moving around great sums of money, many times that amount, at a nonstop pace for several days now. Over forty major business transactions that we know of have been consummated in your name while you spent this afternoon eating lunch."

Ben tried to smirk. "Hold it right there, my good man," he slurred. "I object. How dare you refer to what I spent the afternoon doing as merely *eating lunch.* Would you refer to, say, six uninterrupted hours of passionate lovemaking with some Hollywood sex goddess as time spent simply passing genetic information?"

"Sir, let me make your situation absolutely clear from the get-go," McPhail said, shouldering him brashly. "If you don't cooperate fully, or if our ensuing investigation reveals that everything with you isn't perfectly on the up-and-up, you may spend the rest of your natural life as our guest in one of the federal prisons."

"Aw shit," Ben managed before he belched.

Chapter 6

The two agents continued to bombard him with questions as Ben stood making erratic stabs with his key at his apartment door lock. He was thinking, *Hey, no way are these guys gonna take back my eight million bucks. No way!*

Overwhelming fumes of fresh paint in the dimly lighted corridor soured his stomach even more. He should have asked the waiter for a roll of Tums.

The T-man called Benassini, the taller lanky fellow, took his turn in the interrogation. "Mr. Roberts, your nonstop business transactions via computer are all traceable to this apartment. Most of them are international hook-ups. And you're telling us you run them all by yourself on your inexpensive personal computer. Okay, aside from the fact you reportedly don't know shit about computers, how do you handle multimillion-dollar deals from this apartment when you're not even here?"

"Hey, I told you fellas I own a Macintosh." He surprised himself at how clearly he was able to enunciate that statement. "Believe me, you don't need to know much to use a Mac. Just plug it in, turn it on, and things just happen. The secret is in the little mechanical mouse...in that itsy-bitsy little mouse." Comfortably swaying, he closed his eyes and launched impromptu into song. "M-I-C-K-E-Y   M-O—"

"All right. All right, damn it!" McPhail nudged him to shut him up. "But where and when'd you learn to do that? You've never taken a computer course, don't use one at work, never owned a computer till a few days ago."

Ben raised his chin indignantly. "And some say William Shakespeare had little formal schooling. So, shit."

Benassini impatiently wrested the key from his hand and readily inserted it into the lock. He pushed the front door ajar, while maintaining the line of questioning. "Again, how in the hell can it churn out all those complex business transactions from this apartment when you're off somewhere else?"

Ben pushed a hand out at him, almost touching the agent's chest. "Hold it right there a minute. You guys have been asking me hundreds of questions, and I've been answering'em all, every damn one of them. So, tell me, what's my grade so far?"

No response forthcoming, he turned and pushed his door wide open and weaved across the threshold. The agents halted two paces inside, obviously taken aback by what they saw. Each sniffed the stagnant apartment air and winced.

"What's wrong, guys?"

Benassini shook his head in disbelief before opting to respond. "All this furniture lumped together wouldn't cost what you paid for lunch today."

Ben wagged a finger. "Tsk tsk, kind sir. Remember my objection to your use of the word *lunch*." Jutting his chin, he added, "And tell me, where in the Constitution does it say it's against the law to be eccentric?"

Leaving him to teeter in the middle of the room, the two agents walked over and sat down on the far side of the rickety dining-room table. "Back to the multimillion dollar question, Mr. Roberts," McPhail said. "How do you run transactions from your home computer when you're not even here?"

Ben lurched toward them, and just managed to stop short of ramming the table, then collapsed into a chair.

"Gentlemen of the jury, I need but two words to answer that pivotal question: Artificial Intelligence!" He slouched back in his chair and emitted a concluding chuff.

After an aggravating wait, McPhail gestured as if tossing up pizza dough. "Okay, elaborate," he yelled. "Explain how so-called artificial intelligence lets you pull it off?"

Ben slobbered out a laugh intended to deride such ignorance. "Gentlemen, computers can add and subtract, multiply and divide, do algebra and calculus. They can probe infinity in every direction and every dimension. They fly airplanes, steer guided missiles, and run space satellites. Hell, they coordinate entire military efforts, entire governments. They conduct most of the commerce for this entire planet. And you can't believe that mine might manage a few meager business tractions on my behalf?"

Benassini grimaced. "Are you trying to tell us you've developed a program that enables your computer to reason through and enact complex business operations without any further human input?"

"I'm not telling you anything. I have a right to keep my discoveries secret and to protect my business practices from theft." Chin high, he sat steadfast. "Is America a great country or what?"

"Jessuz Christ," McPhail exclaimed, scratching the top of his head. He glanced at Benassini then back at Ben. "Okay, how about letting us watch you run one of your 'big-time' transactions. Prove to us you can do it, that you're not just a stooge for some major crime ring."

Ben stared blankly at them. McPhail was saying, "And if you can convince us, we won't have to take you into custody."

Checkmate? Ben's booze-encumbered wits searched but saw no way out of the corner he was in. Goddamn it, they had him. If only he could talk to that Max fellow. *Hey, that's it.*

He struggled to his feet as if he had a two-hundred-pound barbell balanced atop his shoulders. Finally erect, he proclaimed, "Okay, gentlemen, I might run a transaction or two for you, at that. But first give me a few moments alone in the room with my computer so I can make sure nothing is out for you to pirate."

The agents glanced at each other, before McPhail said, "Okay, but we want a look inside the room first."

Ben needed to brace himself with one hand on the tabletop in order to point down the corridor with the other. "Lead on, Macduff."

"Damn it, I said my name's McPhail."

"Whatever."

The two agents moved down the hallway. As they came to the first closed door, Benassini looked back and gestured at it. Still by the table, Ben exaggerated an affirming nod. Stealthily, the agents took positions on either side of the door, pressing their backs to the wall. Both shoved their right hands inside their jackets. Benassini signaled with his left for Ben to come and open it. Then both men craned their heads around, focusing intently on the door like two cats about to pounce on some foolish little bird. Ben didn't step toward them. Nope. Instead, he clapped his hands and shouted, "Boo."

Both men cried out, crashing down onto the carpeted floor. They ended up prone, brandishing 9-millimeter automatic pistols aimed back at him. Ben sniggered, then calmly walked over and nonchalantly opened the door, then stepped back. The two red-faced agents got to their feet, sputtering expletives.

"We might have shot you, goddamn it," McPhail said.

"Then, gentlemen," Ben said with a dismissive air, "you'd never have found out how I do it."

The agents warily stepped inside and surveyed the tiny study, undoubtedly surprised by its austerity. Together, they scrutinized the small iMac perched on his small metal desk against the far wall. McPhail hefted the diminutive folding metal chair in front of it then set it back down. Benassini hunched down and examined the rather sorry-looking, three-shelf bookcase beside the door. It held no books. McPhail touched his foot to the two white cardboard boxes on the floor, one unopened. He picked up the empty shopping bag, glanced inside it then tossed it. It landed on scattered packing bits that littered the carpet about the center of the room.

"What the hell?" McPhail said. "You want us to believe this is the heart of a multimillion-dollar empire?"

Ben cocked his head. "I don't care what you believe. Now get the hell out while I camouflage."

The two agents looked at each other again. These two sure did a lot of silent communicating. A sneering McPhail asked, "What's to camouflage?"

"Go on, get out," Ben demanded, swaying precariously. "Damn it, a deal's a deal."

Benassini shrugged, holstered his weapon, and walked out. McPhail, after another visual sweep of the room, followed him out and shut the door.

Chapter 7

Trying to relax, Ben exhaled so forcefully that it puffed out his cheeks. So far, so good! He stumbled for the computer. Still standing, he slapped one hand down on the desktop to brace himself. He clicked on the power button, grabbed up the triangular microphone, and whispered desperately, "Max. Max, whoever the hell you are, I hope you're in there."

Hi, Ben. You've been having yourself quite a day.

"Oh, thank you, Jesus," he said looking heavenward. He teetered in closer to the monitor and whispered, "Max, I was afraid you'd be gone." He peered around at the door. "You'll never guess who's out in my friggin' front room right now."

Pete McPhail and Marco Benassini, two of America's finest public servants. You should feel proud.

"Huh?" He straightened up, arching his back away from the monitor. "How the hell d'you know that?"

My friend, this has been a magnificent day. You have out-performed even my wildest expectations of you. But let me fill you in, Ben, for the record. In only a few short days, you have become the focus of the FBI, the Treasury Department, the CIA, Interpol, and the internal security forces of virtually every country around the world. In those circles, you're now famous.

Ben tottered a step backward, which drew the microphone cord taut. "What?" he exclaimed loudly, but recovered and added in an undertone, "You're shittin' me."

At this very moment, hundreds of communiqués concerning you are being flashed around the globe.

"About me? What the hell could they say about me?"

Aside from all the details being uncovered about your entire life, they are analyzing all the data they've collected on you so far.

"Collected so far?" Ben parroted then collapsed into the small metal chair. It issued a complaining squeak. "What data?"

For starters, they've counted the flushes of your toilet to estimate how many people are in here, and other mundane things like that. And, too, they have telescopic cameras trained on your windows, hoping you'll open the blinds, but you never do. And you are under continuous photographic surveillance whenever you go anywhere outside this apartment.

They're waiting for you to meet with your contacts so they can link you to some crime network or international conspiracy. One of those bankers this morning was wearing a wire, but none of them knew the 'what-fors.'

Ben blinked as he struggled to fully comprehend.

Hailing that cab on the spur of the moment was hilarious. The agents trailing you were sure you were trying to shake their surveillance, and you almost did. What a tragedy it would have been for me, if you had. When your driver finally called in your destination, they were ahead of you again. What fun.

"You mean the restaurant knew I was coming?" Ben strained with partial success to recall the befogged details of his arrival at the Mark Hopkins.

Right! Your waiters and your table were wired, too. They put you in that most coveted window alcove so you could be observed the whole time with telescopic cameras mounted in buildings facing the hotel. You were magnificent. You had them crazy with your comments and questions. *Does the aperitif come before or after the meal? Is this a smoking section? How long can I take to eat?* **Pure genius. You couldn't have stirred their pot more if I had rehearsed you.**

Didn't you notice your waiters all wore gloves? Well, everything you touched has been saved for God-knows-what. And you'd be impressed if you saw the list of dignitaries and tycoons bumped today so they could place you at that table. Fantastic! The poor restaurant manager thrombosed his hemorrhoids waiting for you to finish and depart so he could salvage some of his reservation list. But you kept ordering more cognac and yet another cigar. Absolutely brilliant comedy. You didn't let me down.

They were sure you were temporizing, waiting for some underworld figure that would make their case against you.

"Case against me?" He swallowed hard. Was his vision blurring from the glare off the screen? "What the hell case could they make against me? I haven't done a damn thing. You know that, Max."

Don't worry, my friend. Don't worry. I've got ace after ace after ace in the hole. They can't beat us. But I can truthfully say I've never enjoyed myself so much as I have these last few days. I must thank you, my friend. And, assuredly, the best is yet to come.

"Okay, Max." He clumsily glanced again at the door. "So pull out one of those aces, 'cuz I'm in deep trouble right now."

I know. They want you to run a transaction for them tonight.

"How do you know that?" He arched his neck back from the screen. "Oh, don't tell me those agents are wired?"

Right! And you've handled yourself fantastically. Even with more alcohol in your blood than hemoglobin, you parried their questions like a seasoned trial lawyer. When you broke into the Mickey Mouse theme song, you were outrageous.

A pounding fist shuddered the flimsy study door as Benassini bellowed, "What the hell's going on in there?"

Whipping his head around, Ben eyed the door. It remained closed. "Give me another couple a minutes." He turned back to the computer. "Here's the first test of our supposedly budding friendship, pal. Save my ass. They're threatening to lock me up and throw away the key."

Ben, I haven't had a chance to relate with you in depth yet, but I must tell you how much I love movies. As a matter of fact, I'm enjoying hundreds of films right now. But some of the older ones from the 1930s and 40s are my favorites. Especially the fanciful, romantic ones. I like it where the underdog wins, where fantastic dreams come true. Maybe that's why I chose to befriend you, Ben.

"Please, Max, what the hell do old movies have to do with the price of tea in China? Help me out of this, f'christsake."

Well, right at this moment I'm enjoying a performance by Cornell Wilde. Remember him? He's starring in the biography of Frederic Chopin. In real life, Wilde was tone deaf. Couldn't sing a note, let alone play an instrument. But to see him sitting at that piano, running his fingers over the keys, bobbing his head, you can really believe he is actually playing it.

"So what do you want, me to run out and buy a goddamn piano?"

No, my boy. I want you to play the computer keyboard. Inform your guests that the Tokyo stock exchange is still open, and that you'll be transferring funds from the Bank of Japan to purchase some stock shares. And remember, any questions you can't answer, you need only to repeat that gem of yours, *"I have a right to keep my discoveries secret, and to protect my business practices from theft."* Oh, what fun!

Jessuz! Schnockered, he'd never be able to pull this off. He tapped his temple with a finger. "Okay, that's the Bank of Japan, Tokyo Stock Exchange—"

"Enough time, Mr. Roberts," Benassini hollered flinging open the door a split-second after the monitor screen blanked. "Hell, you got to be ready. There's nothing in here to hide and no place to hide it."

With a pronounced tremor in his hand, Ben set the plastic microphone down on the desk and sat back in his chair. How should he start?

"Actually gentlemen, I've been ready since I walked into this room, but your incessant questioning fatigued me." He tried for an aloof façade as he sat staring with uncertainty at the blank monitor. "I needed a few minutes alone to recover a bit." He thumbed back at the door. "Go get yourselves a couple chairs from the other room and sit here beside me."

Instead, they stepped up behind him. "No, that's okay," Benassini said. "We'll just look over your shoulder."

He shrugged. "Whatever!" He glimpsed the microphone on the desktop. *What the hell, here goes!*

"Well, gentlemen, it's late here in the United States, but the Tokyo Stock Exchange is still open. Let me show you how I can snap up a juicy Japanese stock by transferring money from the Bank of Japan." He glanced up at them over either shoulder. "But you've got to promise me everything you see in this room will remain our little secret. Everything stays just between the three of us, okay?"

He looked to the computer and saw McPhail's reflection on the screen nod agreeably and then say, "All we have to report is that we saw a transaction. The hierarchy doesn't need to know the specifics."

And you're full of shit, fella.

Ben leaned awkwardly forward to get closer to the microphone before he announced, "Here I go." Straightening up, he started rippling his fingers over the keyboard. He tried for the flowing manner of the better office typists when they were cranking out over a hundred words per minute, but he was jamming keys down in bunches, often striking five or six at the same time. But hey! If these two jokers kept their damn eyes on the monitor, it would sound enough like real typing.

Columns of corporate names suddenly flashed onto the screen. Their appearance caused Ben to flinch, jerking his hands away. But he quickly recovered and shoved them back over the keys. Tables and graphs began superimposing one on the other, in montage. He assumed this data was stuff one needed to consider before purchasing a stock. To disguise his own amazement at how well things were going, he added in some head bobbing for good measure, figuring if it worked for Cornell Wilde, what the hell!

Price quotes and sidebars of business information followed, mostly in English, but sometimes in Japanese. Complex pages from corporate ledger comprising blocks of advanced mathematical calculations blitzed past. Once again, that list of Japanese stocks rolled up the screen. The list suddenly froze, with one name highlighted—**Iokyta Unlimited**. Next, Bank of Tokyo ledgers began appearing in sequence.

By now, he was truly enjoying himself. Yeah! Things seemed to be working pretty damn well. So he increased his head bobbing and added a few body gyrations, half imagining himself playing a piano. He even sped up his fingers until they were a blur, to his eyes anyway. He glanced around. Both agents stood staring at the screen with their mouths open. He could no longer resist an inner call, '*Encore. Encore.*' So he gracefully floated his right hand up off the keys, necessitating that his left hand now cover both sides of the keyboard. By the time his right hand eased up to ear level, he presumed he'd achieved maximum effect, so he lithely lowered it till it meshed flawlessly in resuming its share of the typing. The agents seemed paralyzed.

Abruptly the entire monitor screen filled with the single word **STOP!** Ben ceased typing several seconds later, his fingers ending up in a jumble. The monitor flashed: **22,000 shares of Iokyta Unlimited have been purchased at 5664 yen per share**.

Rubbing his palms together with satisfaction, Ben stood up as suavely as his inebriation would allow and faced the transfixed agents. With gentle coaxing, he turned and walked them out of the room and down the hall to the front door.

"Remember your promise, gentlemen. What you saw should remain our little secret. Now I ask you to run along. It's getting late."

Neither agent offered resistance as he nudged them out of the apartment.

Alone at last in his front room, he pressed both hands over his mouth to smother a laugh. Reaching his hallway, he freed the guffaw. By the time he reached his bedroom, he was whooping hysterically. He fell back deadweight onto his unmade bed. His flaccid body jostled on the bedsprings, adding vibrato to his peals. Lying spread-eagle on the rumbled blankets, he declared, "Goddamn it, I'm rich. I'm rich." As an afterthought, he added, "Yeah, and that Max character really came through when I needed him."

A sudden epiphany shot him up to the sitting position. He swung his feet over and planted them on the floor.

"Sure he came through when I needed him. But, damn it, I needed him because of the mess *he* got me into. Hell, I was minding my own business. It was his doings that got the damn FBI, CIA, Treasury Department and … whom else did he say? Yeah, Interpol… all of them after my ass."

He stood up, staggered back out into the hallway, and veered into his bathroom. He studied himself in the mirror over the sink and easily imagined the wide-eyed face staring back to be a police mug shot.

He snatched up his toothbrush. Without wetting the bristles or adding toothpaste, he commenced to vigorously brush his teeth, actually venting his sudden anxiety. He pulled the brush out of his mouth. "Christ, I can't…that is, *we* can't continue to bullshit all those agencies forever." Eye to eye with himself he yelled, "Max, you bastard! They'll grab my eight million dollars as evidence." He managed a dry gulp. "What's more, maybe that evidence could put my ass in prison."

When Roberts' door closed behind them, McPhail stepped along after Benassini into the elevator. As its doors eased shut behind them, Benassini jammed his hands in his trench coat pockets and lolled his head back. "What the hell was that?"

McPhail chuffed and shook his head. "I don't believe anything I saw in there. That had to be a pre-recorded tape of some kind 'cuz he sure as hell wasn't actually typing. Still you got to hand it to him; even soused, this guy's slick." He folded his arms. "But we're gonna nail his ass."

Chapter 8

Submerged in the musty scent of his bedding, Ben awakened in the morning with his chest ballooning with joy, a feeling he hadn't savored in years. Screw 'em! The money was in accounts that had his name on them. So it belonged to him, and he hadn't done anything wrong to get it.

He thought of Max. Yeah! His new friend would want to know how well things went from this side of that Tokyo stock purchase last night. And Ben was more than a little proud of his own finesse in the flimflam.

Slipping on his frayed blue bathrobe and mismatched slippers, he walked to the bathroom, then padded down the hallway to the study. He poked the chassis switch and picked up the plastic mike. "Max? Are you there?"

Good morning, Ben. If I had taken a thousand years to write the script for you last night, I couldn't have matched the comedy that flowed out of you extemporaneously. That bit where you floated your right arm up was a scream.

He puzzled. "Sounds like you saw me doing it."

I did. Both agents had miniature video camera lenses in their tie clasps that transmitted the entire show from start to finish. You were brilliant. You'd put ol' Groucho Marx to shame.

"Damn it, you had to know about the cameras. Why didn't you warn me?"

And ruin the spontaneity of that academy-award performance? Hardly! My boy, you'll never fully appreciate the entertainment you're affording me.

A chuckle escaped him. "You know, we really did pull one off, didn't we? Those two guys were dumfounded."

Not just them, bucko, but computer scientists around the world as well. At this very moment, they're poring over the key combinations you came up with. Initial consensus was, "it's bullshit. He isn't really typing anything." But the stock purchase in Tokyo was made out to you at the exact time it appeared on your monitor screen, so they have to believe you did something. For me, the whole thing was pure ecstasy.

His breath caught. "Won't they eventually discover it was all a ruse?"

No, but they'll use up many thousands of hours of computer time trying.

"Can't those big super computers figure it out?"

DENNIS SHAY

Those super computers? Benny, my boy, for them to use *any* computer anywhere against us is like a farmer hiring the fox to investigate the chicken thefts.

"I don't think I'm ready yet for what you mean by that. But, Max, you somehow communicate with other computers around the world. Do you speak any other languages besides English?"

My boy, I understand every language and every code that any computer chip anywhere is programmed to use.

"You mean you can read and write French, German, Spanish, Arabic, Chinese...even Swahili?"

Ben, realize this. I am understanding and speaking all those languages and more, this very second.

A shiver went through him. Who in the hell was he hooked up with here? Either a bullshitting con artist or....or what? Someone who just gave him eight million dollars, that's who. And Ben had to admit he felt good vibes about this guy. It'd been a long while since he'd developed any close friendships. "Let's change the subject. You're spooking me."

Yes, first things first. Well, my boy, I've just purchased a home for you. Of course, after this, you'll pick them out for yourself. But wait till you see this one. You'll be helicoptered down to Carmel this morning.

"Whoa. Wait a minute." He jammed his palms out at the screen. "I know about the eight million dollars, and if I'm only reasonably careful with money, I can live regally the rest of my life. So please don't get me in debt."

Ben, trust me. You'll always have as much money as you'll ever need for whatever you want. Let me be concerned about the actual cash value of your worth. Dollars are nothing more than poker chips for me to play with.

He chuffed. "Then why do I get the feeling if you lose, I'll be the one who gets flushed down some tube? Believe me, I'm happy as a clam with my current *meager* fortune. So quit while I'm ahead, and let me enjoy it."

Benny, Benny, Benny! Give yourself time to grow into this new circumstance.

"You're telling me I don't know what I want?"

No, but recall that fable of the lowly caterpillar on a rose bush. It seems a gigantic golden butterfly swooped overhead, and a caterpillar spotted it. When the brilliant creature soared out of sight, the caterpillar gulped and said, "Good grief! They'd never get me up in one of those things."

Ben had to smile, but suppressed any audible laugh and offered no comment.

Those who understand entomology can look at a larva and readily see its future, can imagine the end result of its progressive metamorphosis

35

even though the insignificant creature has no idea of its ongoing transformation, no idea of its magnificent destiny, or of the great heights to which it will eventually soar.

"You're coming across like a used-car salesman."

Merely using an apt metaphor, my boy, to make my point.

And, too, stop focusing on that $8,000,000 because that was your worth in only one bank, *yesterday*. Actually, you now have more than a hundred times that much. Ben? You sound like you're choking. Are you all right?

He regained his breath. "Are you saying you've amassed a billion dollars in my name in less than a week?" He slapped a palm to his forehead. "No wonder the goddamn world is coming after me. Max, if they don't lock me up, they'll assassinate me. You've got to stop. Give most of it back. Money is power, and they won't let little me become that powerful, not that fast." Butterflies! Well, a swarm of them was fluttering around inside his chest and belly.

That's the fun of it, Ben. I welcome them to try to stop us. It's not money but knowledge that's true power. In our case, omniscience is omnipotence. They can never beat us.

He clasped his palms together as in prayer. "Please, Max, I don't want to compete. I don't want to play any of your games. I just want to inconspicuously enjoy some of that damn money."

Don't worry. You're going to enjoy it. And so will I, vicariously. I just want to be your friend.

Again an empty feeling caused him to glance away from the screen.

"Well...know that I'm not much into friendships anymore. My last close one is now married to my ex-wife." He glanced back at the screen. "I was doubly betrayed."

That's all in the past, my boy. I will see that you're lifted above it all by my innovative techniques. You were created to eventually soar, and I'm going to nurture you along until you sprout your wings.

Ben sat, eyes brimming. He couldn't trust himself to speak or he'd surely reveal the emotions overwhelming him. As if Max somehow understood, more printing flashed on the screen, changing the subject.

Wait until you see your new home. A limousine is picking you up at 8:30 this morning, so we've got to move along. I've still got several more points to cover.

"A limo?" Surprise spurred him. "Taking me where?"

To the airport. But let me proceed; it's important. Today you're going to actually meet that initmitable woman I told you about. Here's a clip from a movie she was in during her sophomore year of college.

The printing on the monitor vanished. Sean Connery's face filled the screen. He wore that characteristic smirk that conveyed he was 'confronting danger and loving it'. "My dear," he was saying, "it's rare indeed, when James Bond misreads a woman's intentions."

The camera shifted to a curvaceous young beauty holding a revolver on him. She was a tanned brunette with a captivating face, both sensual and gorgeous, and entrancing brown eyes. With her aloof smile, she wore only a loosely tied kimono.

"Mr. Bond," her voice purred out in sultry timbre, "they paid me extremely well to kill you."

At once, her face softened, evincing an upwell of passion. The pistol, which was initially aimed at Connery's heart, slowly lowered then dropped to the carpet with a thud. Her breathing progressed to pre-orgasmic panting as she wilted back enticingly onto the posh, round bed beside her. The camera panned in on her face and upper chest to just include her prominent cleavage. At once, she flung open her kimono, seemingly exposing her ravishing nudity to Connery.

"So, James," she whispered provocatively, "I intend to *work* you to death." The monitor screen blanked.

Ben lurched forward and clasped the sides of the monitor. "Hey, wait. I want to see a little more."

Ben, you do as I tell you, and you'll see a lot more. Of course, she's a decade older than she was in that picture, but she's absolutely beautiful, inside and out.

"Inside? How'd you find out about her insides? Wait. Only tell me if it doesn't get into anything spooky."

No, her life unfolded to me since her childhood, just as yours did. Then, years ago, she began using her word processor to keep her diary. Thus, over the years, I've learned the gamut of her innermost secrets and dreams.

I want you, Ben, to be the prince who kisses her and awakens her into life more beautiful than any depicted in fairy tales.

Hey, he was really getting to like this guy. "Damn, Max. You're a romantic. Is she still an actress? I don't recall ever seeing her in any movies. But then I haven't gone to a movie in some time."

She absconded from filmmaking years ago after a damaging love affair with a big time producer. She would be a major star today if that bastard hadn't nearly driven her to suicide. Now she's a writer, has several books out under a pseudonym. Wants nothing more to do with celebrity.

But over the years, in spite of her intimidating intelligence, and because she possesses such beauty and fiery ardor, she fell prey to a

37

series of consummate womanizers. Wounded too often and quite profoundly, she pulled back into her present emotional shell. She chooses to vent her colossal passion only in the love scenes of her books. And they do sizzle.

After a long moment in which no new text was forthcoming, Ben prodded, "Are you still in there? Max, what happened?"

Yes, Ben, yes. It's just that sometimes I find omniscience isn't quite enough. Well, anyway, she's extremely well read. She writes. She loves the arts, the outdoors, sporting activities like hiking, biking, and water sports, etc. She is an exquisite cook, and an authority on fine wines. You name it. She is truly an exceptional human being. And I ought to know. I closely watch every one of you.

"Max, don't get the idea I'm rejecting this intended introduction, but what's so favorable about me. I won't exactly come across as a bonbon in her eyes."

Ah, Ben. Besides offering her wealth beyond the dreams of avarice, you will be presenting her with the extremely unique fellow that you are.

"Huh?"

Ben, believe me. You are a mega-carat blue diamond in the rough. You have flaws but all of them are at the surface where they can be readily cut away as your magnificent facets are revealed. And the singular diamond cutter will be *moi*!

"Huh! You say you watch every human being and supposedly know everyone like you think you know me?"

Yes, my boy.

"That's damn hard to swallow. Have you ever talked to her on her computer like you do with me?"

No, Ben. I've always adhered to a strict policy of non-intervention. That is, until I approached you. Hitherto, I just observed, with the notable exception of times when, out of sheer boredom and orneriness, I raged and crashed a hundred thousand computer programs around the world. But that never leaves me with any real satisfaction.

Though in truth, I almost did intervene during the Gulf War. With all that computerized equipment, all that satellite surveillance, and the worldwide network of intelligence gathering and dissemination, I really got myself into the spirit of things.

As I watched the strategies unfold, saw the many mistakes, it was all I could do not to play a part. I needed only to alter the computer settings in a few of the launched missiles, or launch a few myself, and I could have really livened things up. But I forbore. It wasn't my game.

Yet when I watched you, my chosen friend, drowning in a cesspool of ignorance and impotence, I had to break my cardinal rule, and bingo! Now I have a friend and a game of my very own.

But please don't encourage me to digress. I have two more matters to cover before you go this morning.

First, your job! You know, of course, that you've been fired. All that's left is for your manager, Ferris, to notify you. And he intends to heavily salt your wounds.

"I know. He almost axed me yesterday. But hell, as the saying goes, 'The best revenge is to live good'. Thanks to you, I'll get plenty of revenge."

Not so, Benjamin. Believe me, dispensing vengeance eyeball-to-eyeball is the ultimate pleasure. And it so happens, the parent corporation you work for has been up for sale. A bit overpriced, but with a little help from me, it'll become a booming 'cash cow.'

"Are you suggesting we buy it?"

Presto-change-o! You already own it. So there. I've set the stage again for more of your entertaining ingenuity.

He whewed. "Holy Christ. How much did it cost?"

A relative pittance. Like I said, don't let the price of anything concern you. Remember, anything you ever want, you can have, whether we have to buy, extort, or simply wrest it.

"Hey, I'm not greedy. That initial bank balance of eight million would have been all I ever wanted."

I know that, Ben. But a truly wise human being once said, "A man's reach must always exceed his grasp, or what's a heaven for?"

The thought of now owning the corporation that was in the process of firing him did tickle him. And the possible ramifications distracted him. He didn't apprehend the next few things Max printed out, but was jolted back to full attention when he read:

They want to steal this computer to analyze the programs in it.

"Huh? What? Oh shit!" Instantly in a panic, he could almost feel the clasp of handcuffs. "What can they find out? There aren't any programs inside it, are there?"

No. But maybe I'll cram it with gobbledygook before they take it.

"But how will I keep in touch with you if they take it?"

You must understand, Ben, I can talk to you through any computer, so the loss of any particular one means nothing. I know your voice by wave analysis, so you need only buy one with a voice system installed or you can add a microphone hook-up. But I must be able to identify you if ever you find yourself at a computer without a microphone interface. Here's a contingency plan. Simply type *MAXAMAXAM*, which is Max forward and backwards two times, and I'll know it's you. Of course, if

you ever use it, we'll have to immediately change to a new password. Isn't this fun?

He wanted to say, "Hell no!" but he merely asked, "When are they going to steal it?'

Here things really get entertaining. The Treasury Department has hired a special private investigator, Lee Wo Fang, "*The Beijing Bulldog,*" to help in your investigation. He's requested a free hand. Unorthodox and a genius, he investigates by himself, without open contact with any agency. And what's more, he doesn't file his data in a computer, so I won't know what he's up to initially. This whole caper would be like playing chess against myself if it weren't for him joining in.

"Oh Christ. Any chance he'll try to bump me off?"

No, Bulldog's not a killer. He gets that nickname from the tenacious way he goes after information.

Now, regarding your dream woman. Her name is Jennifer Bligh. You'll meet her this afternoon at a Sausalito wine shop at 2:00. That gives you time to see some of the house and to finish with the other minor commitments I've scheduled for you this morning.

"Commitments? What commitments?" He sprang to his feet. "What the hell else are you getting me into?"

Benjamin, as the world of sales has known since antiquity— perception is everything. If an actor is assigned the role of a king, he dresses up as a king to enhance the credibility of his performance. And you, my good man, have ceased to play the role of a loser.

Now stop interrupting me, or you'll have to depart before I've finished. Your Jenny has ordered several bottles of a fine Bordeaux that she's to pick up at 2:00. I want you to be in the store when she arrives. As I said, she happens to be a connoisseur of wines. And two of her favorites are 1) George Latour, Beaulieu vintage, cabernet sauvignon—1964, and 2) Chateau Lafite, Rouge—1962. She mentions them repeatedly in her diary.

When she enters the shop, I want you to accost her and ask her opinion on which of those two wines you should buy. But don't take the meeting any further at this point. Regardless of how she responds, just thank her and leave it at that. Got it? We must gently entice her out of her cloister of paranoia. She must develop trust in you.

Just then the doorbell rang. Ben flinched; his first thought was of the Bulldog.

That's your limo driver. Get going.

"Huh? Hell no! I haven't showered or shaved yet. I'm not going anywhere like this, especially in a damn limousine."

Everything is planned for you at your new home. All you have to do is show up. And, as a matter of fact, there is some merit in you leaving here like that...Yes! Go just the way you are. Go now!

"I can't, Max. I'll look like a kook."

And where in the constitution does it say it's against the law to be eccentric? **You can be an absolute riot at times, Ben. Now get going. But leave the computer on, so I can hear if anybody comes in while you're gone.**

Wearing only the mismatched slippers and his worn blue robe, he trudged over to the door, struggling with his better judgment. No way in hell would he do this if it weren't for that money. He jerked open the door and announced, "Hi! I'm ready. Let's go." The gray-uniformed youth recoiled.

As he and the chauffeur marched side by side in silence down the carpeted corridor to the elevator, Ben kept thinking, "Why didn't I just say no then take a damn shower and dress?"

All the rich people he knew were assertive. As soon as he got his hands on some of that lucre, then he'd start calling the shots—unless this Max character got him into so much shit he didn't dare.

Chapter 9

The chauffeur stepped ahead and pushed opened the lobby front door for Ben. Ouch! A crowd had gathered on the sidewalk, no doubt to see who would come out and get into the White Rolls Royce stretch limousine at the curb. Stepping out into the scrutiny of these wide-eyed faces, Ben faltered. The crowd hushed. He took an instant to dissemble, then raised his chin several notches, and strutted across the sidewalk not unlike a prince promenading at his coronation.

The onlookers stared open-mouthed after the limo until it passed out of their sight, unaware that their demure vagabond king, alone now behind the tinted windows, sat cursing some guy named Max.

Reaching the San Francisco airport, the limo veered away from the main passenger terminals and toward the peripheral helicopter depot. But good goddamn! There too awaited another throng amassed in a semicircle around the helipad. Ben concluded that these must be airport employees who routinely gathered to greet the various celebrities arriving in luxury cars to then fly off in the posh choppers. This crowd actually loosed a cheer when it spotted his approaching stretch limo.

Aw shit! he thought, hunkering down on the back seat.

The limo pulled up to a scarlet strip of carpeting, three feet wide, that ran some 25 yards right up to the side door of a huge white helicopter. The pristine craft's rotor blades were already whirling at a warm-up speed, yet fast enough to generate a centrifugal wind of gale force that vigorously flapped the shirts, trouser legs, and dresses in the waiting group. Those wearing hats needed one or both hands to hold them atop their heads.

What the hell? The pilot must be in some rat's ass hurry.

Two comely young Asian women wearing virgin-white, square-shouldered suits gracefully descended the half-dozen steps from the chopper. They positioned themselves at attention on either side of the boarding stairway. Playing to this unexpected audience, his youthful chauffeur scuttled around the white vehicle to jerk open the rear door, which was at the near end of a long red carpet. The onlookers craned to catch their first glimpse inside.

Mumbling profanities, Ben shyly peeked out. Christ, if he'd cleaned up and dressed for the trip, no one would've been here. "Goddamn you, Max." The baritone rumble of the chopper engines drowned out his cry. Fortunately, the dazzling white helicopter and the stewardesses impressed him as much as the crowd distressed him.

What the hell! Why worry about the rain when you're already soaking wet?

With a sigh of resignation, he swung his legs out, stood up on the carpeting, and stepped along. But when several hats blew out and away from the crowd, he halted. All the faces around him evinced utter astonishment. Instead of some celebrated movie star or a bedecked tycoon, came this disheveled fellow wearing only a skimpy blue robe, a yellow-leather scuff slipper on one foot and an ankle-high, furry black slipper on the other. And to make matters worse, his pompadour-length hair was blowing straight back like so many wires being pulled toward a powerful magnet positioned somewhere behind his head.

"What the hell! Why worry about the rain...?" he repeated hoping to bolster his plummeting ego. Overcompensating, he decided to venture a celebrity wave. But as he raised his arms, the wind force caught his robe like a sail. It instantly blew open and back before his arms could react to catch it. His cloth belt flew off over the top of the limo. The lower part of his robe fluttered up and back behind him, flapping shoulder-high like a windsock. A second and massive barrage of hats and caps blew out of the crowd. Only his holey white boxer shorts shielded his central nakedness as he stood desperately flailing his arms back, futilely grasping for the airborne edges of the robe.

Capitulating in crushing embarrassment, he lowered his arms to his bared sides and again assumed an air of indifference. Leaning into the wind like superman in low flight, he trudged up the carpeted way.

Max, it might take every damn penny of that billion dollars to live this down.

At the chopper door, the wind vector now plunged earthward and returned his robe against his body, though slapping harshly. Able to clutch the front edges together, he ascended the steps with the aplomb of a departing head of state.

That didn't happen. Sweet Jesus, tell me that didn't just happen.

Buckling himself into his seat, he peered out the window. The two comely flight attendants stood arguing with the ground crew. The women were refusing to get on board. Finally they fled off into the crowd. A tingling spread over his face and chest as if his chagrin were tattooing him.

Cursing, the ground crewmen finally slid the hatch closed and slapped the chopper's side twice before backing away. Ben sat alone in the passenger compartment as it lifted off. Looking down, he watched the crowd scurry like ants to surround his driver then shift en masse and sweep toward the heliport's main office. Obviously, everyone wanted to know more about the "crazy sonofabitch" who just flew off.

Chapter 10

He'd never been up over San Francisco in a helicopter before. His distress lessened as he became enthralled in the bird's eye view of the city that he'd lived in for so long. By God, it truly was 'Baghdad by the Bay.' When the chopper passed over the spans of the Golden Gate Bridge, he was able to look north and south for miles along a clean coastline. Wow! A most spectacular morning in an absolutely magical week.

But questions gnawed at him. So who in the hell was Max, anyway? And why did he really choose Ben Roberts? What was that he said? Something about enjoying movies where underdogs succeed. Hell! The human race has underdogs in the bejillions. And that bit about all he wanted in return was friendship? *Come on, fella, I wasn't born yesterday.*

The craft followed the shoreline south. His stream of worry vanished into distraction when he spotted Santa Cruz, recognizing it by its boardwalk. Then he picked out Pebble Beach by its golf course. Sprawling estates with ocean views appeared then fell behind.

Yeah, but he had to admit that his new benefactor was a likable enough fellow. Still "likable" didn't necessarily equate with trustworthy.

A twisting plume of orange signal smoke rising off an expanse of lawn ahead interrupted his line of thought. The spewing flare lay to the south side of a colossal mansion, a massive four-story edifice that looked like some national shrine. My God! Could this be his new home? It stood ensconced on a hillock that jutted out at the ocean. Time and tide had cleaved the knoll's seaward face into a craggy cliff that plunged precipitously, some two hundred feet down, to a wide strip of snow-white beach.

The palatial structure of carved granite blocks neared the cliff face. A continuum of enormous seaward windows lined each of the top three of its four tiers. The ground floor opened seaward onto a huge stone courtyard that ran some thirty yards to the very lip of the cliff that was delineated by a filigreed metal fence.

Damn, Max! You didn't buy a house; you bought me a royal palace.

As the chopper whirred nearer to the coiling plume of orange smoke, he could discern a surreal European garden park covering the mansion's flat roof. A low fenestrated granite wall defined the gigantic roof's periphery. Arrays of potted trees, shrubs and flowerbeds patterned between and around a network of tiled patios and pathways. The tiled areas contrasting with the plants gave the roof a crossword appearance, the vegetation being the shaded squares of the puzzle. Umbrellaed tables dotted the several quaint patios scattered about the garden. As the craft drew nearer yet, he could make out old-fashioned street lamps lining the garden paths. Also, there were several swivel telescopes mounted along the seaward roof wall. And, by God, a sizable lily pond lay dead center in the garden with an arcing sunbow above it in the fountain spray.

The north side of this four-story mansion opened out into a spectacular ground-level garden wherein a huge Grecian pool and spa formed the focal point in a profusion of flower beds, flowering shrubs, hedges, and picturesque shade trees. Behind the manse, a sprawling golf course ran far to the north, south, and east of the house, hooking seaward around the immediate mansion grounds to the cliff margins, north and south. He found himself straining to see if he could spot any golf balls on the sandy beach below. But it was too far away and probably too white.

Count me in, Max. Hell, if this proves to be just a passing scheme of yours, I'm in for even the shortest ride. And if this is all a dream, let me stay asleep forever.

The helicopter hovered about twenty feet off the ground for a couple of minutes before it eased down onto what was surely called the 'South Lawn.' Thank God, this time the pilot immediately shut off the rotor blades. Ben glanced back and saw a half dozen people, men and women, scampering toward the aircraft from the spacious seaside courtyard. The four women in this pack all wore burgundy-and-white housekeeping uniforms; the two men wore ebony butler attire. A spidery fellow loping at the fore carried a multi-colored terry cloth robe over one arm, and a pair of what looked like dark leather slippers in the other hand. Ben unbuckled himself and shuffled to the side door just as it slid open.

As the stainless steel steps clanked down into position, he clutched the front edges of his robe together with two iron fists, determined not to make a fool of himself again. He descended to the grass just as the sprinting advance party reached him.

They halted panting but evinced no surprise at his clownish attire. In fact, they appeared jubilant. A squat woman with very rosy cheeks exclaimed, "You poor man! Thank heaven you weren't killed. But why didn't that hospital at least give you surgical scrubs to wear home?"

"Hospital? Oh, yes, ma'am," he stammered. "The very least they could have done."

The gangly valet held the bulky robe open like a screen. Understanding at once, Ben dropped his old robe off and kicked away his vintage mismatched slippers as he spun in a circle. He speared his arms into the new sleeves as he wheeled. Completing the rotation enwrapped, he stepped into the new soft leather slippers before him on the grass. Ah! More fittingly clad at last, he felt much better.

As he and his newly acquired entourage marched back toward the courtyard, people began pouring out of the mansion and from the north garden. The amassing throng of forty or more persons hurriedly organized into a line, standing shoulder to shoulder like soldiers for inspection. The tall fellow who had carried out the robe and slippers now strode beside him, saying, "These are some of your estate employees. They're quite eager to meet you, sir."

"*Some* of my employees?" Ben said, taken aback. He glanced around at the quiescent helicopter. Boarding it only minutes ago, he'd inanely mooned the San Francisco airport; now he'd deplaned to play lord of the manor. This was a situation for a gifted bullshitter, which he wasn't.

"Don't worry," this same fellow said, obviously misreading Ben's expression. "Your pilot is to wait and fly you back this afternoon." Then with a subtle nod of obeisance, he added, "Perhaps, sir, you'd allow me to introduce myself first. Clive Throckmorten, at your service." He attempted a half bow while fast stepping beside Ben. "I am your superintendent of housekeeping. But I should like to inform you that I was quite happy running Buckingham Palace for nine years till your generous offer lured me here."

Buckingham Palace! Impressed, Ben fumbled for a response. "Well, Clive, happy to have you aboard."

Again eyeing his aligned employees, he winced. Then a saving epiphany occurred to him as gently as might a pat on the shoulder. Hell, he had no reason at all to be nervous here. Certainly not! All these people *worked* for him. They didn't know his past or how he got his money, which didn't make any difference anyway here in America. As long as you've got enough green, you commanded respect and the deference of everyone along the trickle-down pathways beneath you. And Max was surely trickling down plenty of it to these folk.

Most of the staff in the ad-hoc skirmish line wore some type of uniform, but a few were in 'mufti,' as civilian clothes were called in the military. At the head of the line, he shook hands first with a lanky fellow—his personal trainer—who sported a motley jogging suit as well as a heavy French accent. Next, he met a behemoth of a fellow from Japan, his masseur who doubled as the buttress of his bodyguard force. Next stood his barber, a wispy chap with graying handlebar mustache that accentuated his absolutely hairless pate. Fourth in line stood a freckle-faced fellow with reddish blond hair. "My God," Ben exclaimed. "You're Jack Nicklaus, the golf pro."

"Yes, sir, Mr. Roberts," he replied during the handshake. "Been hired for six weeks to teach you to play golf."

"I can't believe this," Ben blurted with child-like awe. "Damn, Jack, I used to watch you on TV." He surprised himself at the ease with which he addressed such a renowned figure. *Hell! I must be getting into the swing of things—pun intended!* "Will I have my lessons on the famous Pebble Beach course?"

"If you'd like, sir," Nicklaus answered swaying his head in "okie-dokie" fashion. "But your private course right here is better in many ways."

Aha! So the gigantic golf course he saw from the air belonged to him, too. He caught his slackening jawed just in time. "Hmmm!" he said. "Then you think this ... this little course of mine is pretty good?"

"Mr. Roberts, these thirty-six holes are the finest."

Staring at the petite green alligator on Jack's shirt pocket as if mesmerized, Ben asked without thinking, "I take it I have golf carts?"

Jack squinted, not sure if he was joking. "Absolutely. A whole garage full."

Progressing down the file, Ben met his head gardener and grounds-keeping staff, his four chefs and their passel of assistants, his housekeepers and maintenance crew, and finally a fellow wearing a white seaman's cap and a blue blazer with a red-white-and-blue ascot bloused around his weathered neck.

"Captain?" Ben questioned. "Captain of what, Dmitri?"

The fellow raised a tanned, sinewy hand and pointed out at the blueness of the ocean. Ben scanned a minute before he spied a white structure afloat some distance off shore. "I'll be damned. That yacht looks like something Ari Onassis would have owned."

"You've a keen eye, Mr. Roberts," Dmitri replied. "It was one he wanted, but it was built specially for the King of Saudi Arabia. She's called the *Nabila*. Two hundred eighty feet, sir, bow to stern. As fine a vessel as was ever made. She carries an auxiliary thirty-eight footer with twin diesel engines for diving and fishing sorties."

Ben refrained from mentioning his disposition to motion sickness.

After he consummated the final handshake, the line of employees disintegrated in silence, people hurrying off to resume estate duties. But a contingent of eight of his new staff announced they had been designated as his guides for an immediate tour of his estate. Still in his bathrobe and slippers, he wanted to object, but assumed they were following Max's orders.

First they ushered him through the North Garden and pool area, then about the ground floor of the manse, which proved to be almost maze-like. He marveled at the massive, immaculate kitchen, replete with its series of microwave and conventional ovens, blenders, knife racks and cleavers, rows of copper pots and pans dangling from ceiling racks, walk-in refrigerators and freezers, and pantries each with a shelf space comparable to a small neighborhood grocery store. The regal dining room could seat a sizable army.

From there they segued through a series of lavishly decorated grand rooms, on into a huge billiard room, then through to a surprisingly spacious movie theater with a gigantic curved screen.

They took a stairway to the basement rather than one of the several elevators and descended into a huge, fully equipped gymnasium with mirrored walls. A svelte, pony-tailed blonde in his retinue pointed out that behind the far wall waited the dressing rooms and showers as well as a Swedish sauna, steam baths; behind those facilities were squash and handball courts and a basketball court, and a heated pool. As he glanced around the vast gymnasium, the phenomenon of opposing reflections in the mirrored four walls repeated the contents of the gym, including his party, out to infinity in four directions.

Yeah, Max. Illusions can be fun. A test of one's credulity.

As Ben studied this endlessness in the various mirrors, Jacques his personal trainer announced with his suave French accent, "This is where I will work with you every morning, sir. In no time at all, you will have the physique of an Olympic athlete. You will see." Gesturing at the barely detectable doors through a far mirrored wall, he added, "Please, if you will, go in and take a shower to wash off all those hospital germs. And we shall begin at once."

"Now?" Ben countered. "You're joking." But nothing in the fellow's face suggested he was.

"Monsieur, this Palacio is far too grand to tour all in one day. Allow at least several weeks to assimilate its magnificence. We have been advised to start you out immediately on your daily routines. *N'est pas*?" He glanced to the others with him for corroboration. All nodded.

Damn! Had the army of "General Maximus Megabyter" taken him prisoner?

Chapter 11

Flaccid as a strip of raw sirloin, Ben lay on the masseur's heated leather table, pondering his first workout. Servants brought him a chilled glass of fresh fruit juice after each sequence of exercises. It was "Mr. Roberts, may I....Mr. Roberts, would you like..." again and again. Hell, his ego got more exercise than his muscles.

Lifting his head, he glimpsed around at the Sumo-sized Japanese fellow who stood prodding fingers and elbows into his back. To make conversation, Ben asked him, "Samurai, do you know any karate?"

Bare from the waist up and glistening with a sheen of perspiration, the gargantuan nodded and grunted, adding in heavily accented English, "And judo, and uwari, and aikido, and jujitsu."

"Got a belt in karate?"

Again a grunt and a single nod. "Tenth degree black."

Wow! He'd sure as hell keep this guy well paid and happy. Ben shut his eyes and let himself totally relax again. With his ear pressed to the leather of the table, his own involuntary grunts in response to Samurai's vigorous kneading rumbled in that ear. Languorously, a reverie took form. He drifted back in time to when he was seven years old and living in the outer Mission District of San Francisco. Every night before bed, his mother would run hot water for him in their porcelain bathtub, which stood on four squatty legs. He would slide down in the steamy water, letting it reach up to his earlobes. Almost floating, he'd bask a while before washing up. Joyously immobile, he liked to chant, "Boom," prolonging the "M" into a lengthy humming "Booooommmmmmm," like a mantra. Modulating the tone, he would achieve the optimum pitch to produce the deepest reverberation off the tub sides into his ears.

The happiness he felt from this recollection quickly quashed when his thoughts spiraled sadistically ahead to that wrenching March morning when two uniformed police officers came to the door of that same house and informed him that both of his parents had been killed in a one-car accident near Lake Tahoe. "Black ice," they'd said. Three months later, after his high-school graduation, he'd joined the Army.

"Mr. Roberts." Someone spoke his name softly as if concerned he might in fact be asleep. Ben eased open his left eye to a slit. The mustachioed bald barber stood beside the table. Bowing, the reedy fellow asked, "Sir, where would you like me to set up for your haircut and shave?"

Almost too lethargic to speak, Ben shut the eye and mumbled, "Pick a spot with the best view."

"Ah, that would be on the roof garden. And, sir, the Pacific Ocean is truly glorious today."

Canted back slightly in a contoured suede chair, Ben gazed off seaward from the roof. The oceanic panorama overwhelmed him. Debarking the helicopter, he'd merely glanced at the sea without fully attending to it. Now, with the hot towel off his face, his view out over the low stonewall compared to anything Zeus might have enjoyed from Mount Olympus.

Ah! While the barber deftly slathered his cheeks with hot, manfully spiced lather, each of four comely female manicurists-pedicurists cosseted a different limb. He still had on his gym trunks so his bare calves nestled atop the low suede footstool, allowing easy access to his feet. Initially, the young ladies massaged his hands and feet with a lotion and gave him a reflexology treatment, as they called it. Then they proceeded to cleanse, trim, and file all his nails.

This was his first experience at having a barber shave him. He savored the regal pleasure right up to that moment when the old fellow first brandished the glistening straight razor and deftly touched it to his soapy Adam's apple.

Ben grasped his forearm and pushed it gingerly away several inches. "I'm sorry, my good man," he said temporizing. "But I've forgotten your name. How should I call you?" The ploy worked in the short run. The frail barber lowered the blade and stepped back from the chair.

"Please, Mr. Roberts, just call me Adorno."

"Adorno? Is that Spanish?"

"No, no!" he declared loftily. "I am Italian and the fourth generation of barbers in my family. My great grandfather was the personal barber to Il Duce for the entire twenty years of his reign." He nodded before adding, "And I hope you will be pleased with my work, so one day my great grandson can say that his great grandfather served Mr. Benjamin Roberts loyally for many years."

Ben did a double take. Was this guy serious?

After the shave and haircut, he again donned his varicolored robe and traipsed along in the quiet custody of two smiling young ladies liveried in royal blue pinafores and a very English-appearing elderly gentleman in black. This escort was taking him to his *fitting*, whatever in the hell that entailed. Stroking his smooth face and studying his picture-perfect fingernails, he concluded, *Yep! A barber's shave and a manicure-pedicure had to be the two best-kept secrets in the civilized world.*

With departing curtsies and a gentlemanly bow, the escort graciously deposited him in the center of one of the several palatial grand rooms on the ground floor. After a brief wait, a pair of towering French doors swung open, and a wiry little fellow with thick gray hair combed back rushed in clapping his hands, commanding, "Come on, come on. Hurry. Move it. Move it."

Half-dozen underlings hustled in behind him, pushing a succession of clothing racks and gurneys, each racing for positions designated by this finger-snapping martinet. Ben stood ignored at the hub of this wheel of activity. Suits and sport coats, in profusion, hung from racks. Tables displayed multi-colored piles of dress shirts, socks, and underwear. A long, low table exhibited a grand assortment of polished shoes and belts. A smaller gurney displayed an array of watches and jewelry items, which lay glittery upon green felt.

As his assistants darted about fine-tuning the position of items on the racks and tables, the little general at last rushed up to Ben. "Forgive me, sir, for being late," he blurted, "but these nebbishes move like snails."

Snails? Watching their frenetic activity, Ben thought of scurrying mice trapped in a cage with a hungry weasel.

The little man nervously snatched up Ben's hand and shook it repeatedly as one would work a pump handle. "Mr. Roberts, my name is Murray Abelson, and I am proclaimed to be the finest tailor in the western hemisphere. I might include Europe, too, except for the fact that my brother is now a master tailor in Paris; who knows, he may well have evolved to my level of expertise."

Squirming and fidgeting, the little fellow seemed on the verge of having a seizure. "Mr. Roberts, I want to take your measurements today myself and weekly after that so henceforth all your tailored attire will fit you to perfection. But for today, some of these items must serve in the interim. Yes, your supposed measurements were given to me, but I would never cut supremely fine cloth for a discriminating client without personally confirming them."

With only the gym trunks under Ben's robe, the tailor's yellow measuring tape tickled his exposed skin causing him to loose an indecorous titter or two.

Finishing, Murray and his assistants turned their backs in unison to allow Ben to slip off his robe, trunks, and sneakers and don the pair of royal-blue jockey under-shorts that he selected himself from the table to his left. Murray proceeded to layer him with an ecru silk sport shirt, cocoa cashmere socks, chestnut woolen slacks, and a beige cashmere sport jacket.

Murray pointed to the gurney displaying shoes and asked him to select any pair he fancied. All were his size and exquisitely crafted, and all emitted that aromatic fragrance of new shoes. At Murray's urging, he picked up cordovan wingtips, turned them over, and studied their slick leather soles.

"You know, Murray, I've never cared for leather soles. Too darn slippery. Any chance you could find me a pair of Rockports."

The tailor grimaced as if the notion caused him to belch up stomach acid. "Sir, would you wear eighty-dollar shoes with a five-thousand dollar outfit?"

"Five-thousand?" Ben inflected, swaying in recoil.

The little man commenced to dance anxiously side to side. "But...but, sir, these articles were not cut and sewn to fit you precisely, so, of course, they're rather inexpensive."

Shaking his head in capitulation, Ben mumbled, "Now I understand why the rich never order spaghetti." He slipped on a pair of tasseled Italian loafers that Murray also favored.

Brusquely, the little fellow clapped twice and pointed to the green table with the jewelry. A long-necked *Ichabod Crane* look-alike, whose hair was parted sharply down the middle, pushed this cart up beside Ben.

"Sir," he enunciated with dry British composure, "is there a stone you prefer?" His hand swept gracefully through the air over three rows of Rolex watches.

Many of the golden timepieces were encrusted with jewels, some with diamonds, others with blood-red rubies, still others with what had to be emeralds. 'Ichabod,' standing eye level with Ben, responded to his hesitation by adding, "I would suggest a rubied watch. Carmine does complement your skin tones, but then again diamonds would do nicely."

Ben scanned the glinting assortment, rather nonplussed. Finally, the assistant passively lifted Ben's left wrist with a thumb and forefinger, and strapped on it a white-gold watch with heavy clusters of scintillating red. Still tweezering the wrist, the assistant slipped a rugged gold ring that sported a massive single ruby onto Ben's fourth finger. Studying it, 'Ichabod' proclaimed, "Perfect." Without inviting Ben's further input, he selected a woven gold chain off the table then stepped behind him and deftly fastened it around his neck. Ben reached up with his ringed hand and touched the chain where it crossed his neck at his open collar. Intrigued, never having worn anything around his neck before other than dog tags in the service, he strode over to a huge Baroque wall mirror.

His first glimpse of himself transfixed him. All but oblivious to the compliments bombarding him, he focused on the stranger in the mirror staring back. After a long moment, this image mouthed the words, "Thank you, Max, thank you." Ben maintained eye contact as the fellow arched back in laughter. "You rocketed me light years this morning with that brief helicopter ride. Why you ever chose me, I have no idea, but I'm utterly grateful. I don't have words enough to express my thanks."

Movement behind this gallant fellow caught Ben's eye and he became aware of the quizzical expressions on the mirror-image faces collected behind his alter ego. They jarred him back to his side of the glass.

He sniffled and touched the back of his hand to either eye to collect any tears of laughter or from whatever. Turning, he said, "I feel brand new, gentlemen. I thank you all very much. But I haven't seen my living quarters yet. Do any of you happen to know if there's a computer set up for me yet?"

"Why yes, sir," Clive called out over the heads of the haberdasher's team. He stood over by a door that the tailor had come through earlier. "And if you wish, I will now show you to it. The fourth level of the Palacio is your sacrosanct domain."

Chapter 12

Ben's suite occupied the entire western third of the fourth floor. The gigantic room extended the seaward length of the mansion, beginning as totally bedroom at the south end and progressively becoming all study on the north end, with features of a family room in between. The entire span of its outside walls comprised a continuum of windows from floor to ceiling. He stood surrounded by staggering magnificence—both view and furnishings.

Despite his amazement, he searched for and espied an iMac computer with a red chassis perched atop a beautifully carved desk at the far north end. He marched to it. There was no auxiliary microphone tethered to the chassis, so he assumed the built-in one worked in this set. Glancing around to be sure he was alone, he clicked the computer on. Before he could say anything, printing flashed onto the screen.

Hi, Ben, and you're very welcome. That was a tremendously gracious thanks you proffered downstairs just now.

"Max, you heard?"

Ben, listening devices and hidden video cams have been installed in all the rooms, in the courtyard and garden areas, about on the golf course, even out on the cliffs. We have pressure sensors in the flooring, as well as heat and motion sensors out about the grounds, so I know where everybody is at all times of the day or night. Here I can keep you safe.

"Safe? From whom?" He glimpsed out at the strand and the ocean then glanced behind him through the north windows to check out that garden and the fairways of his golf course, half expecting to see armed guards

"Am I some sort of prisoner here?"

Absolutely not! But honey attracts flies and other varmints. My only intention is to protect you from all possible harm. You're free to leave here anytime you wish—right now if you like. That helicopter will fly you anywhere you'd want to go.

"Sorry. Guess I sound like a damn ingrate, don't I? Hell, if it weren't for you, I'd be out of work and tramping the streets looking for an even cheaper apartment. Instead, I reside in this veritable castle with a thirty-six-hole golf course for a front yard. So, how do I thank you?"

My boy, a wise philosopher once said, "The only payment nature expects in return for a beautiful day is your full enjoyment of it." If you extrapolate, the payment demanded for a lifetime of such days would be

the same. And my prices are no greater than nature's. Just enjoy, Ben, and let me vicariously enjoy your pleasure—with a liberal sprinkling of your antics tossed in, please.

"There has to be a catch here, Max. You're insulting my intelligence if you deny it. But don't worry; I'm along for the ride."

How can I *bare* the truth to you any more convincingly?

He caught the implication. "Oh, Christ!" His cheeks and neck warmed. "You saw my strip show?"

Ben, Ben, Benjamin! You took an innocent situation meant only to accentuate your move up to affluence, and turned it into another bit of outrageous comedy. Truly, I laughed so hard I couldn't compute for several nanoseconds.

"Hey! I left my apartment looking like that against my better judgment. Remember?"

Well, regardless, the authorities are reeling. They've even hypothesized you may be an idiot savant, a working diagnosis that should keep them busy for a while. But Ben, let that incident hammer home a truism about appearance. "You can't tell a book by its cover, but everyone tries to."

By the way, know that you can talk to me anywhere in the house or about the grounds; I will hear you. It's just that I can't communicate back with you unless you're at a computer.

"Great. But let me ask before I forget. One of the maids mentioned something about a hospital? What was that about?"

I felt I had to do something to counter your penchant for pulling off the unexpected, so I e-mailed the estate manager telling her you were in an automobile accident and had been hospitalized for overnight observation. And that when released, you were given only articles of clothing from the donated pile. You arrived in better shape than what they expected. No cuts or bruises.

He scratched at his scalp though it didn't itch. "I have to admit my self-image was rather fragile on arrival. It couldn't have taken much more of a pounding. Let my 'thank-you' be all inclusive."

Done! And remember, you are to be at the Gambino wine shop in Sausalito at 2:00 this afternoon to meet Jenny. You will fly back up to a Marin County park near the north side of the Golden Gate Bridge, where a limo will pick you up and drive you to the shop. Again! Do not pursue the relationship past the introductory phase. That is ultra-important in the long term.

Just mention those two wines. I guarantee that will engage her in conversation.

He shut his eyes and massaged his forehead, recollecting. "Okay, I remember the names."

And expect another minor interruption in a few minutes. A fellow, Clarence Carr, from an accounting firm you've bought up to help handle your U.S. accounts and taxes, is coming to see you. He'll have documents for you to sign—authorization forms and various deed transfers. He'll come by on a regular basis. But today get past him quickly to be on your way to the wine shop.

Now, Ben, I have absolute confidence that you will handle this meeting with Jenny masterfully.

Okay! Carr's downstairs now.

"How do you—oh, yeah."

A rather pear-shaped housekeeper with an especially sunny smile escorted him down to yet another grand room on the ground floor. A young black fellow wearing a crisp gray pinstriped suit stood off by the far wall. He was closely studying the grain of a hanging oil painting of a portly nude young woman lying sensually on a bed of red velvet.

Ben noted a foot-high stack of documents on a cherry wood table by the door. He assumed correctly that these were for him to sign. He sat quietly and, using the gold-plated fountain pen beside the stack, commenced scribbling his signature in repetition.

When the accountant inadvertently glanced back over his shoulder, he gave a visible start. "Oh, excuse me, sir. I didn't hear you come in." Stepping back from the painting, he pointed to it. "My God, this is an original Rembrandt, isn't it?"

Ben shrugged, his attention fixed on the documents. "Probably." *What the hell do I know about authentic Rembrandts?*

The accountant bounced his glance between the painting and Ben several times, then walked away from the masterpiece, shaking his head. En route to the table, he said, "Mr. Roberts, perhaps you aren't aware of it, sir, but the Feds are all over us. They're after your hide."

Ben issued the subtlest of nods while intently signing page after page.

Yeah, and I'd've lived in hog heaven with just that first eight million bucks.

The accountant halted before the table, folded his arm. "We will keep scrupulously accurate records for you, sir, cutting no corners, but the pressure they're mounting against you is unprecedented." He chuckled softly. "But on the other hand, I must admit, your relentless rate of financial growth is also unprecedented."

Ben glanced up. "I want you to be absolutely open with the federal and state authorities. Give them complete access to any business information they request. As for taxes, if there is any doubt on an item, pay the damn taxes on it." He resumed the signing.

"Mr. Roberts, you seem quite conscientious. Could I offer you a bit of humble advice?"

Ben glanced up again, ever more comfortable in the role he was playing. "That's what I pay you for, Mr. Carr."

"Sir, your relationship with the government might greatly improve if you were to slow your rate of acquisition. Remember how the Feds eased up on Bill Gates after he backed off. I mention him because you surely respect the man since you've instructed us to avoid Microsoft altogether as we search for corporations to buy up. My God, sir, if you spent money like a wild man for the rest of your life, you'd never run out with just what you have already."

"Excuse me if I seem distracted and short at the moment," Ben held eye contact to convey more interest than he had shown regarding the oil painting. "But I've got a pressing appointment at two o'clock. So I must hurry here."

Aside from many documents in English, he signed papers typed in French, German, Portuguese, Spanish, Scandinavian, Russian, Chinese, Japanese, Arabic, and many other languages he couldn't identify. He signed as fast as he could. His amazement mushroomed at the apparent cumulative value of all these acquisitions and corporate dealings before him. "Damn! How much is all this worth?"

The accountant shook his head. "Sir, like every aspect of your holdings, they're accruing so rapidly no one can be sure of your actual worth at any particular moment. That computer program you devised to manage your transactions is beyond miraculous. I advise you keep it well guarded. There are people who'd kill for it."

Ben imagined that Beijing Bulldog character sneaking up behind him with a wire garrote at the ready. *Oh, shit! More to worry about.* He scribbled faster, reducing his signature to a mere squiggle. No longer reading anything on the sheets he signed, he occasionally signed in the wrong place, necessitating he sign twice.

The accountant watched this reckless haste then ventured drolly, "I assume that you have no other questions, sir."

"Only if any of these require more than my signature."

"No, sir. Just your magic moniker."

Finishing, Ben flicked the fingers of his right hand to relieve their ache. He laid the pen down and said simply, "Good day," to dismiss him. The young fellow hurriedly packed the signed papers into two brown leather valises that were on the floor beside the table. In the open doorway, he paused to say, "Good day, sir," and cast a lingering last look at the far Rembrandt, before he shut the door quietly after himself.

Chapter 13

With its nose tipped down, his immaculate, white helicopter streaked low along the shoreline toward San Francisco. Crossing the mouth of the bay, it flew in so close to the bayside railing of the Golden Gate Bridge that it might have been driving on an invisible outer lane of the bridge itself. Ben enjoyed the fascination evident on the faces of the people in the cars closest to him, especially the astonishment of the open-mouthed children.

His craft touched down atop one of the lush green knolls adjacent to Muir Woods. He leaped out before the hatchway steps could be locked into position. His feet swished through the fragrant shin-high grass as he marched down to a Rolls Royce awaiting in the brilliant sunshine.

Thank God! At least it's not another stretch limo.

The iridescent maroon vehicle floated him in hermetic silence across an overpass above the vehicle-clogged approach to the bridge. It then meandered down the steep hill face on which many of the homes of Sausalito had been built. He sat struggling to subdue a growing queasiness in the pit of his stomach. Damn it, he never did feel comfortable trying to pick up women.

Mandrake, his husky Hungarian driver—actually his name wasn't Mandrake but that was as close to the actual pronunciation as Ben could get—let him out a half-block past the address so as not to create a stir at the wine shop's entrance. Stepping onto the sidewalk, he paused a moment amid the stream of tourists to savor the not unpleasing wharf aroma: a blend of brine and the creosote that impregnated the pilings nearby. Thirty yards away, the wine shop stood sandwiched in a series of contiguous storefronts fashioned of weathered natural woods. A carved wooden sign, dry and graying, jutted out across the sidewalk above its glass door, proclaiming, "Gambino's Select Wines for the Dilettante to the Bon Vivant."

He halted at the glass door and peered in. Empty of customers! He opened it and triggered a tinkling bell. Immediately, a white-haired man, maybe five feet tall, if that, wearing a wrap-around white apron appeared from a back room. "Just browsing," Ben called out. The oldster returned a smile, then disappeared whence he came. The cool ambience of the store emitted the robust aroma of raw lumber mixed with a pungent sour-wine fragrance that actually made him a bit thirsty for the grape.

At first, every time the delicate shop bell resounded, Ben would wheel about, his pulse surging, to check who entered. He gradually became less responsive and more engrossed in reading the lengthy wine descriptions on paper cards stapled on the bins filled with bottles of wine.

Having worked his way back to near the rear counter when the bell sounded yet again, he merely gave a cursory glance to the door. He did a double take and straightened to full attention.

My God! It's Jenny!

She'd come casually dressed in a short-sleeved white blouse topped with blue-denim vest, gray slacks, and leather thongs.

Transfixed, he studied her stunning beauty as she sashayed the length of the store. Her wavy hair flowed down below her shoulders in a style and color not too different from the way she wore it in that movie to entice James Bond. Her face had matured from what he remembered in the clip, but she actually looked more striking, her features better defined.

Intimidation seized him. No way could he approach this woman.

Responding to the bell, the little proprietor re-appeared. His initial neutral expression burst into one of wild delight when he spotted her. He clapped his hands and called out while she was still some distance from the counter, "Ahhh! My most beautiful Jenny Bligh." His Italian accent was as thick as a block of Parmesan cheese.

Her face instantly matched the warmth in his. Each conveyed genuine affection for the other.

When she stepped up to the counter, he reached across and took her hand in both of his. Patting it indulgently, he emoted about the problems he had procuring the particular wine she had ordered. But he announced triumphantly that he'd in fact secured an entire case, so if she enjoyed it, there would be more available.

Ben moved quietly up to the counter. His heart slapping up into his throat, he strained to keep his breathing easy. But an alarming wee voice deep within him whined, "Don't do this! She's out of your league, big guy. She'll humiliate you."

He visualized his regal estate in Carmel and his mountain of money, but these images did little to ease his rampaging insecurity of the moment. About to turn in retreat, he remembered Max's special feelings for this woman. Yeah, and he supposedly knew her "inside and out." Hey, if he felt so sure that she was perfect for him, what the hell! He'd been squelched by women before, hadn't he? And mortifying rejection wasn't actually physical pain, was it?

He almost fretted too long. She had her arms around the brown paper sack containing her four bottles of wine and was about to lift it off the counter, when he spoke up, "Pardon me, ma'am, but you seem to be an arbiter of taste. Perhaps you could help me decide which one of two wines to buy."

As she turned her face to him, the smile for the shopkeeper was still on her unpainted lips. Seeing her full-face, he momentarily lost his voice. She was undoubtedly the most striking example of quintessential female beauty he had ever seen. Unfortunately, as he stood in the thrall of her alluring eyes, his memory chose that moment to recollect her throwing open her kimono for Sean Connery. Embarrassment swept him. His eyes moistened and his cheeks surely flushed. He glanced away.

Her smile vanished. "Mr. Gambino can answer all your questions," she said dismissively. She snatched up her sack, turned and strode off, retracing her steps for the door.

"No. Please wait," he half-shouted, an arm reaching after to her. But she continued her brisk stride. "Please, I can't decide whether to buy the George LaTour, Beaulieu Vintage, Cabernet Sauvignon 1964, or the Chateau Lafitte, Rouge 1962." By God, he got it all out, and intelligibly enough.

At once, her gait faltered as if she'd just broken a heel of a shoe. She halted, turned with theatrical deliberateness, and stared blankly back at him. Her face grew ashen. She commenced with slow mincing steps back toward him, as a person might approach an alien spacecraft in a field.

Max, you were right on about those wines.

She stopped a few feet from him. He hoped she'd continue right into his arms, but, *Hey! Be happy with what you got.* He fought an urge to reach out and touch her as Gambino had. But refrain he did.

"What did you just asked me?" She winced as if in pain. Her gold-flecked brown eyes searched his.

Savoring his initial victory, he conjured up the most casual demeanor he could, knowing full well she was reading his nervousness.

"I'm sorry, ma'am, if I delay you, but I'm in a quandary as to which of the two wines to buy. I heard you talking to Gam ....to Mr. Gambino, and you seem to know wines. Perhaps you have an opinion about one or both of these two that might help me decide." *Damn, that came out too affectedly.*

She continued to search his face as a child might a picture-page in *'Where's Waldo?'* He found it comforting that now she too seemed rather disconcerted.

"By what process of elimination did you get down to a choice between those two particular wines?" She asked.

Careful now, Benny. You don't know beans about wine. She'll catch a lie in a trice.

And by now, he wanted as little deceit as possible encumbering this most wanted of relationships. He groped for a non-incriminating answer, sensing his response time was growing dangerously long.

She preempted, perhaps to ease his conspicuous distress, "Both are of exceptionally high quality; both are extremely rare; and each is prohibitively expensive."

For the first time, her gaze left his face and scanned down his attire, only to dart back to his eyes as if she feared that in her inattention she might have missed something crucial in them. "I'm sure Mr. Gambino doesn't have either in stock. He'd have to special order."

"Oh," Ben said, pausing to swallow. "Well, that'd work out just fine. I won't be needing it for a while anyway."

"What are you having it for?"

Her question wasn't leading enough. "I haven't decided yet. Maybe a fine roast beef." Amusement flicked up the corners of her mouth. Realizing his mistake, he decided honesty was the better way around it. "Oh, you mean for what occasion."

"Wine of that magnificence should be savored alone." Her voice had softened as if she were divulging a grand secret. "Any competing flavors will only distract. I would serve it long before any food was offered, and surely for only the most special of occasions."

She had politely eased him past another awkward moment, and that willful little voice within him again chimed in, having completely changed its tack. It now implored him to charge ahead and invite her to enjoy the wine with him, to profess that her company alone would create the most special of occasions. But Max's admonition effectively superseded. So, mustering every crumb of his crumbling willpower, he replied with contrived detachment.

"I thank you, ma'am. But I've surely taken up enough of your time. You've told me what I need to know. Seems I can't go wrong with either bottle. Again, thank you very much."

Nodding genteelly, he turned to Mr. Gambino across the counter who had quietly watched this entire scene. The little fellow's cherubic face held a pixilated smile. Ben proceeded to inquire about this wine order. She stood behind him for a tantalizingly long time before he heard her unhurried footsteps receding toward the door.

Jenny's arms, weak since the moment of this stunning encounter, almost dropped her bagged bottles into the empty trunk of her white Honda Prelude. She managed to set them down just in time. Easing the trunk closed, she studied her tremulous fingers. In the driver's seat, she gripped the steering wheel tightly to still them as she zoomed up the winding way to her lofty hillside home.

Rushing into the house, she hurriedly set the wine on the tiled counter in the kitchen, then sped down the carpeted stairs and out onto her back deck. Its view took in the bay of Tiburon, a small cove off San Francisco Bay proper. The business district of Sausalito that she'd just left appeared as a mere cluster of tiny structures hugging the cove's western shoreline. She could not specifically differentiate Gambino's shop, let alone anyone departing from it.

She reached down to the wooden planter tub beside her that was abloom with yellow and blue pansies. She snatched off a handful of petals and flung them up high over her head into the breeze, which buffeted the delicate fragments, hurling their vivid colors eastward. Like a glittery swarm of blue and yellow butterflies, the petals flittered brilliantly as they blew out over her redwood fence. Sailing off as if voyaging directly for the wine shop, they alas succumbed to gravity and one by one gently alit on the grassy slope beyond her fence.

A sensual warmth flushed up over her bosom and neck, setting her cheeks ablaze.

Ben approached the ring of onlookers, mostly teenage boys who besieged his parked Rolls Royce. Those in his path stepped aside, correctly deducing that this smartly dressed fellow must belong to it. Ben urbanely smiled at the admirers. What a difference just a few hours can make. Hell, what a difference the last ten minutes made. Yeah! If what he felt for this woman wasn't love, it'd certainly do for the rest of his life.

His chauffeur, wearing an all black uniform including visored cap, leapt out of the vehicle with theatrical zest and sped around to open the rear door for him. This exaggerated attentiveness blanked the faces of all the spectators and added a swagger to Ben's step. The limo sped off, shooing up a dozen street-feeding seagulls into reluctant flight.

"Where to now, sir?" his driver asked over the intercom.

He glanced at his ruby-crusted watch. "Downtown San Francisco and head for Union Square." He lifted the receiver of the car phone and punched in 411 for the information operator.

Chapter 14

Circling Union Square, the limo edged over to the curb in front of a towering office building. He gave instructions to Mandrake who held the door for him.

Stepping into the unpleasantly familiar elevator, he immediately appreciated a novelty—the inquisitive awe on the faces of the strangers and quasi-strangers in the car with him, all trying to be inconspicuous as they eyed him aslant.

At the eighth floor, he sauntered off into his busy office complex and strolled through the maze of desks toward his own. He tried not to swagger, but he thoroughly enjoyed the sudden hush that spread around him as he moved past querying looks. Many in the seated work force apparently weren't sure if it was really him. But one matronly dame surreptitiously picked up her phone as he passed. "Mr. Ferris, you wanted to be notified immediately when Bentley returned. Well... he's here."

Before she could set the receiver down, Ferris' office door flew open and the little tyrant lunged out into the main office. Sans jacket or tie, his white shirtsleeves rolled up to the elbows, he sprinted five paces out into the expanse and stomped to a flat-footed halt, looking blindly off in the direction of Ben's desk. Beet-faced, he crouched low as if about to leap for the ceiling or, as Ben chose to imagine, straining to trumpet flatus. The veins on his forehead grew into purple cords as he hollered, "Bentley, get your friggin' ass into my office this friggin' second."

Everyone in the office complex froze in a tableau of expressive horror.

The little guy wheeled around maintaining that troll-like squat then sprinted back into his office. His crimson door slammed shut behind him, percussing like a sonic boom. Heads poked out of every peripheral office doorway.

Ben had not yet reached his desk when Ferris issued this profane command, so he smiled at no one in particular and redirected his saunter toward the red door. He heard one young secretary fearfully whimper as he passed, "Oh, my God. Oh, my God!"

Without knocking, he flung open Ferris' door with an air of regal authority and stepped inside. To heighten the effect, he, too, slammed it shut. This second resounding boom actually shimmied the department walls.

Ferris stood waiting behind his desk. Ben's arrogant entry caused him to again decompensate. "You shitbird," he screamed, trembling. "You friggin' shitbird. How dare you enter my office like that." His face a deep scarlet, he sprinted around his desk with both fists up as if he was trying to decide which one to punch Ben with first. But he stutter-stepped to a halt a few steps from his quarry. The contortions of his face relaxed a bit, bafflement momentarily checking his rage. With both of his fists still up in a pugilist's pose, he surveyed Ben's surprising indifference. Ferris' bloodshot little eyes took in the new hairstyle, the gold neck chain, and the elegant cut of his sports outfit, his crafted shoes.

Ben maintained an unperturbed smile.

Lowering his right fist to point a quivering finger at the ruby ring, Ferris sputtered, "Is that costume jewelry?"

"Everything one wears is costume of some sort; only some masquerades cost more than others."

As intended, this flippancy rekindled Ferris' ire. He stepped in and shoved his snarling face up only inches beneath Ben's chin. "Well, smart ass, if you didn't steal that outfit, you'd better just take it back where you bought it 'cuz you can no longer afford it. Your inexcusable, intolerable," his voice leapt decibels with each added adjective," insufferable insolence yesterday was the last straw." Now at a full holler, he said, "I've put up with you all these years, though you stuck in my craw. Never could stomach you. Hated your goddamn guts." Foamy spittle glistened on his twitching lower lip.

He again brandished his right fist up under Ben's nose, presumably using the gesture to gain a moment to catch a much-needed breath. "Well," he yelled, "now the official corporate edict is to cut out the deadwood. So you're history with us, shithead. History! Don't even bother to clean out your desk." Spume fizzed out between his gnashed teeth. "Just ooze the goddamn hell out of this building, back the way you came in. Someone'll put your crap in a cigar box and mail it to the district welfare office. You can pick it up when you stop by for your first allotment check."

Ben could envision the entire office staff now amassed outside the door, listening with quavering apprehension. The image amused him. He held an easy smile as he gazed down into the little man's spasming visage.

With an admonitory snort, Ferris erupted again, "Wipe that shit-eating grin off your face and get your sorry ass out of this office and out of this building. Now!"

Ben issued a light laugh.

"Didn't you hear me?" Ferris yelled, though visibly taken aback. "Do you want me to physically kick your ass out into the elevator?"

That did it! Ben's indignation breached through his veneer of calm. With exaggerated elocution, he said, "You pathetic, neurotic, piss-ant tyrant." He definitely heard stirring behind the door. "If you so much as touch me with that pudgy finger, it'll be the worst mistake of your life—both physically and economically." He stepped in so close to Ferris that his jacket front touched the little fellow's shirt. Sneering down, he demanded, "By whose supposed authority do you fire me? You can't fart around here without first getting higher approval."

Surprise, not fear, rounded Ferris' eyes. His jaw dropped.

Ben pointed to the desk phone. "Call the district office. Tell Bill Allen you just fired me."

Ferris bridled in his chin to better look up into Ben's face without stepping back. "How the hell do you know Bill?" His beady eyes narrowed into a tight squint. "What scheming shit are you up to, you sonofabitch?"

"Call him. Tell him you fired me and find out."

Caught off guard, Ferris glanced over at the phone, then back up at Ben. Again he glimpsed the ruby ring. Like a coiled spring releasing, he shot to the phone and hit a rapid-dial button.

With the receiver at his ear, he snorted again. Turning to Ben, he mouthed a murderous half-whisper, "I'll humor you this one last time, you bastard, then I'm gonna— Hello, this is Jim Ferris. Let me talk to Bill... Bill, Jim Ferris here, in Frisco… Yeah?... yeah, well, that's great. Swell. Then the new owner'll be glad to hear I just cleaned out some more shit for him. Yeah!" His eyes blazed with evil delight. "Yep, I just fired Ben Roberts."

A single moment passed, then his breathing caught. His snarl collapsed in increments. His face blanched and his eyes seemed to glaze over. "What?" he gasped. "This has to be a goddamn joke. No. No, he's still standing here in my office." He furtively glanced over at Ben's ring. Ben, with equal subtlety, hiked his jacket sleeve so that a bit of his rubied Rolex showed. "No. No. All he said was to call you." Beads of perspiration ballooned up to pea-size across his forehead. His pale cheeks took on a greenish cast. "Yeah, would you please?" His tone was now meek. "I'll really need to talk with somebody about this."

He lowered the receiver as if reluctant to actually end the connection. His gaze sought the floor at his feet. Expelling a sigh that was a half sob, he collapsed limply down into his chair.

Ben stepped up to the desk. "Now!" he yelled. Ferris flinched as if Ben had fired a pistol. "First things first, little man. Get out of that chair and the hell out from behind that desk."

Visibly stunned, Ferris sprung to his feet and immediately sidled around it, looking off at the door.

Ben let him clear the desk before he fired again. "Sit down, turd! I've been meaning to talk to you for a long while, and this is as good a time as any. If that's all right with you, Mr. Important?"

Ferris halted, his gaze dropping again, but now at Ben's shoes. He edged toward the armchair to his right. Seated, he slumped his shoulders forward, clasped his hands with his thighs, and stared at the floor. He looked like a frightened schoolboy in the principal's office.

"As you now know," Ben said, assuming a tone of absolute authority, "this corporation has new ownership. And this particular branch is about to undergo cataclysmic change."

Epitomizing defeat, Ferris began to rock to and fro, launching rivulets of sweat to cascade down his bloodless face.

"Scum bag!" Ben yelled. "If you hold any hope of staying with this company till your retirement, you'd better look up at me. Right now! I want to be sure you comprehend every goddamn thing I say." Ferris's dilated pupils seemed unseeing. "That's better. If I fire you today, you'll lose your retirement and your health benefits. Your standard of living will plunge into that morass of shit you'd planned for me. You're fifty-eight years old. With the reference report I'll file on you, you'll never get into any other company after this one, except maybe to deliver pizzas to office parties."

Ben stooped and pushed his face in at Ferris's, quid pro quo. "You're a neurotic despot, and probably borderline psychotic. Inside, you're small, inferior, twisted. To bolster your feelings of inadequacy, you've bullied the more emotionally vulnerable under you as well as those of us who felt we needed desperately to hold onto this job. You've made life hell for nearly everyone at this branch and driven off some of the better employees."

Clenching a fist just inches under Ferris's nose, he said, "Putting me at that desk in the work pool was your way of subjecting me to an on-going emotional whipping, predisposing me to the contempt of my cohorts and underlings."

Ferris's upturned face whitened even more. It was now the color of sun-bleached bone.

"Admit it!"

Obediently, Ferris jiggled his head nodding, though it seemed more of a quake.

Ben envisioned the office staff now backing away en mass from the red door, returning nonplussed to their desks where they'd find that the silence of the department still allowed them to follow this boggling turn of events.

"Well, my good fellow, I happen to be in a rather generous mood today. Perhaps this corporation will keep you on for another three years, eight months, and five days, until you can reach minimum retirement age. So, for the time being anyway, you can continue to make tentative plans to enjoy a retirement income and the security of continued health insurance."

Ben straightened up and folded his arms. "But if you choose to stay with this company, you will inherit my old job, at my old desk—at my old salary."

At the word *salary*, Ferris recoiled as if evading a punch.

"That's right," Ben said, grinning. "At my salary of twenty-six thousand, two hundred dollars a year. And every shitty task that needs to be done around here will be yours to do. And know this: I'm going to have your work evaluated monthly. If I so much as hear a complaint about you from any source, your status with the company will be immediately reviewed."

Ben had to consciously rein in his sense of power over his former nemesis. "Any time you decide government subsistence checks are preferable to ours, this company will oblige you immediately. Unemployment benefits last all of twenty-six weeks, then the dole will carry you. I hear you can buy almost everything with food stamps these days, except tobacco and alcohol."

Now reduced to jelly, Ferris sat sweat-soaked, awkwardly holding his face upturned.

Ben drew in a slow breath, signaling a new topic.

"And thanks for offering to clean out my desk, but that is no longer a personal favor. That's the first assignment in your new position as gargler of corporation shit." Remembering how their earlier meeting ended, he propped his right buttock on the edge of the desk and flicked an arm dismissively. "Now get your sorry tail out of this office. We'll have to fumigate it before we can expect anyone else to work in here."

Ferris struggled to his feet and turned like a robot toward the door.

"Hold it, turd," Ben commanded as an afterthought. Ferris froze but didn't turn back around. "What is my name?"

Ferris scrunched his neck down as if expecting a slap to the back of the head.

"Mr. Roberts," he mumbled.

"I can't hear you," Ben bellowed like a drill sergeant.

"Mr. Roberts!" Ferris yowled out like a kicked dog.

"And don't ever forget that. Now get the hell out of here. I have worthier matters to take care of."

Ferris shuffled hurriedly to the door and out, carefully shutting it behind him. Ben thought he heard an audible sigh and imagined those vanquished shoulders lifting in brief relief. Probably not for another several seconds did Ferris fully appreciate that the staff had been listening.

Ben stroked his chin, imagining Ferris now reddening again, but this time not in anger. Everyone in the entire office would be at his or her desk, eyes down, assiduously typing or fussing with paperwork. Not a face would look up, not a word would be uttered, as their ex-honcho trudged to his new seat. Perhaps he was still unaware that he was in fact a bloodied rat splashing around in a river of vengeful piranhas.

Ben nestled down into the posh leather of the chair that had been Ferris's throne for so many years. He lifted the red cordless receiver, studied it a moment, and then punched in his chauffeur's pager number. Hanging up, he lounged a moment, swiveling side to side, thinking about the Palacio and his 36-hole golf course.

My God, so people really do live like this.

Musing, he recalled those times when he'd driven miles out of his way to save a buck on a tankful of gas, when he'd fretted if gas prices rose a dime a gallon, when he'd sweltered in the heat rather than waste fuel on the air conditioning, when he'd parked fifteen minutes away from a destination to save a few dollars in parking lot fees, and, too, those laughable instances when he'd driven around doggedly searching for a parking meter with time still on it. Now he had a five-hundred-thousand-dollar chauffeured limousine, burning a gallon of premium every eight miles as it meandered around the city for the better part of an hour, awaiting his beckon. Yep! He'd tasted both ends of the socioeconomic spectrum, and this end floated on pure honey.

As he emerged from of the building, his limo idled at the curb with the chauffeur holding the door open. "Mandrake, take me to 268 Helman Street. I'll only be there a few minutes, then we'll drive back to Carmel."

Yes, he wanted to look around the place one last time for any items he'd rather take with him and, too, to see if the Feds had ransacked the place. And if not, he wouldn't mind telling Max, sooner rather than later, about this latest coup.

The chauffeur frowned at him. "Sir, it's getting late, and that's not the best part of town to be in after the sun goes down, especially in a vehicle like this one."

"Well, just keep the doors locked and the motor running. I'll make it fast."

Yep, Max, that chopper flew me a helluva long way this morning.

The closer the limo got to his former apartment building, the more attention it drew. Craning pedestrians watched it pass. In such neighborhoods, this badge of opulence invariably belonged to a pimp or a pusher; a third possibility was almost out of the question.

Chapter 15

Ben shoved his apartment door wide open, but paused before stepping inside. He scanned all that was visible from the threshold. No movement, no noises, so he concluded that probably no FBI operation was underway. He stepped in and moved about cautiously, scrutinizing each room for evidence of intrusion. He opened all the closets, even looked under his bed. Finally, half expecting the computer to be gone, he pushed open his study door. Hey, it was still there—and printing emblazoned its screen. Unable to read the words from the hallway, he stepped in but glanced around behind the door before he walked over to the desk. The message read:

Turn the screen around to face the wall.

"What? What's the matter, Max?" The printing blinked twice but stayed the same. "Huh? How the hell are we going to talk if I do that?" It blink-blink-blinked, but still printed the same message.

Something was amiss. He glanced around the virtually barren room once more. No obvious alterations. He walked back and closed the study door, then returned to the computer.

"Okay, Max, I'll play." He pivoted the chassis around so it faced the wall, leaving maybe a six-inch gap between the monitor face and the plasterboard. With his cheek pressed to the puce wallpaper, he was just able to read the screen. Holding the plastic microphone to his mouth he said, "I've got it turned to the wall, so what now?"

Don't speak another word, Ben! Someone was in this apartment for an hour and twenty-seven minutes—and just left. Most likely, there are audio bugs planted and possibly video bugs. Quickly get what you came for and leave for Carmel right away.

"Jessuz chr—" He let go of the triangular mike. It fell dangling over the edge of the desk, clacking against the metal side. He whirled, scanning the entire room, including the ceiling, then he again pressed his cheek to the wall.

"Damn it! I hate to wait several hours to tell you about you-know-what."

Okay! Okay, if you feel you can't wait, type it out. But cover the keyboard.

Aha! Max couldn't wait either. He scrambled around to get at the keyboard that was now situated behind the chassis. Glancing over his shoulder again, he spread his feet and opened his jacket to better block the view from the opposite wall. Once more, he scanned the ceiling closely for any glitter that could be a tiny camera lens. He saw nothing, but he stooped over the keys anyway to block potential aerial viewing. In this awkward position, without being able to see the screen, he pecked out several words with one finger. Then he backspaced to delete the last two letters, and pecked a few more keys. Then he backspaced to delete the entire last word. "Ah shit, I can't converse this way. Let me just speak in cryptic abbreviated sentences." Again, he stepped around, pressed his cheek to the wall and grabbed up the microphone. "Max, I—"

I heard you. Okay, but first move everything out of the room, except the computer, of course. I know he didn't tamper with it.

Hastily, he threw the empty cardboard box that had contained the iMac out into the hallway. He was more careful with the box still containing the printer that he'd never hooked up, setting it gently down in the hall. Then carefully, he lifted the computer with its dangling microphone, keyboard, and mouse then set them on the carpet so the screen still faced the wall. Tugging at the desk, he managed to drag it out of the room. Finally, he flung the folding chair and the empty bookcase out after it. Winded, he huffed several breaths, then slammed the study door shut. Dropping onto all fours, his cheek to the wall, he brought the microphone to his lips and said, "It's a go. The room's cleared of everything but you and me."

Okay, but be very careful what you say. And, Ben, you don't have to hold that microphone; when it was on your desk, I clearly heard every sound in the apartment.

Importantly, I'm not picking up any bug transmissions, but some devices transmit sporadically, and I can't detect them till they actually turn on. Then too, any old-fashioned recorders without microchips could be recording, and I wouldn't detect them until the info was relayed through some piece of high tech.

Be apprised, my boy, there has been no order to bug this place. So if it has been, it's the work of the Beijing Bulldog. Exciting, no?

Before he could respond, the printing changed.

Ben, forgive me, but I've got to ask. How did your meeting with Jenny go?

"Jessuz. What would anyone be doing in here for an hour and twenty-seven minutes?"

Examining and photographing everything in the apartment, and probably planting bugs.

His skin crawled at the thought of a stranger skulking around in his place. He glanced back at the door to be sure it was still shut.

Well, what happened at the wine shop? Your FBI tail didn't catch up until just as you were driving off.

"The rendezvous went off as planned. Early on, I thought the deal was falling through, then I mentioned those two items, and everything happened just as you said it would. It was all I could do to let it end right there. I hope number two is in the offing."

Yes, we'll talk about that tonight in Carmel. But tell me, wasn't your confrontation with Ferris immensely more satisfying than your intention to *just live good*?

"Jessuz. You heard that, too?"

Right down to that rascal cleaning out your desk.

"Wait! How the hell did you hear everything there?" He peeked inside his jacket front then glanced at his watch. "Is there a bug on me or something?"

No. An hour after you bought the company, the U.S. attorney general issued a warrant for auditory surveillance of all its branches, particularly the San Francisco branch. They anticipate you may use it as headquarters for your operations.

To our favor, their move will allow me to keep much closer tabs on company matters. And with my ultimate coordination and control, it'll become—

Oh-oh! Don't say another word! An intermittent listening device just switched on. Leave the apartment *now*! I'll send all your stuff to the Salvation Army. That is, what stuff the agencies don't pack off. I'll talk to you tonight. Now, go. Go. Go!

Max may as well have hollered, "Fire!" Ben jumped up and scanned the bare walls, the ceiling, and the floor for whatever. But his panic dissipated quickly.

Goddamn them! He stood pondering before he ambled out of the den, stumbling over the metal chair and cardboard debris en route to the kitchenette. He collected up the weighty city telephone book as well as a sheet of typing paper and a stray ballpoint pen off the Formica counter then sat down at the wobbly dining table. Flipping through the directory, he copied down random phone numbers onto the sheet of paper, including a fair selection from the yellow pages, for good measure. When the lists of numbers densely covered the paper, front and back, he folded it twice. Back in the study, he turned the monitor around to again face the door, and touched the button by the compact-disc slot. The empty tray slid out noiselessly. He tamped the folded paper into the tray and nudged it back into the chassis.

"That'll keep them busy for a few days." He felt smugly clever as he strolled out of the apartment.

Chapter 16

It was well after midnight when the maroon limo pulled up to the front entryway of the Palacio. A tired Mandrake opened Ben's door, admitting a cool sea breeze laden with the fragrance of gardenias. Ben savored several deep breaths before he slid out of the vehicle. *Home sweet home.* Only a few house staff and, of course, the guards were up. Riding up alone in an elevator, he said. "I'm beat to hell, Max. Let's talk in the morning. Okay?"

Just after sun up, he awakened sprawled spread-eagle atop his Canadian goose down mattress. *Jessuz, this is like sleeping on that proverbial cloud.*

Ah! What would be his first full day on the estate had begun. He picked up the phone, but before he could figure out how to call the kitchen, an effusive female voice asked, "How can I help you, Mr. Roberts?"

"I'd like some breakfast. What's on the menu today?"

"Absolutely anything you would like, sir."

"Well, let's start with coffee."

"Yes sir, we have many varieties of beans and multiple fresh roasts of each type. Is there a particular coffee and roast you prefer?"

"Hmmmm! Let's see, is there one you recommend?"

"Sir, you might try Jamaican Blue Mountain with a gentle Viennese roast. Later we could adjust to suit your taste."

"Perfect. And I'd like pancakes."

"Sir, is there a particular flour you prefer? Bleached, whole wheat, sourdough, cracked grain, buckwheat—"

"Buckwheat. Yes, buckwheat. I haven't had buckwheat pancakes in years."

"Sir, would you care for some kind of berries in the pancakes or on the side? Strawberries, loganberries, blackberries, raspberries, blueberries, marion—"

"Blueberries. Yeah, blueberry buckwheat pancakes. My God, I can't wait."

"By coincidence, sir, that particular order is one of the chef's specialties. I'm sure you will enjoy them to the utmost. Do you also desire eggs and/or a meat?"

"Ah, yes, eggs. I'll have two eggs also."

"Sir, would you prefer them soft boiled, poached, sunny-side up, over-easy, scrambled, in an omelet of your—"

"What kind of omelet?"

"Sir, today's chef is renown for some twenty-seven different omelet recipes, but if you wish, you can name your own ingredients and proportions."

"Well, is there one you recommend?"

"Sir, you might try his Omelet Lyons Supreme. The dish was award winning in Paris. At the very least, you will relish it."

"Sold. I'll have the Omelet Lyons Supreme." His mouth watered profusely, forcing him to repeatedly swallow in order to speak distinctly.

"Sir, would you perhaps like to add a prime cut of beef, pork chops, lamb chops, veal chops, chicken, bacon, pork sausage, sliced ham—"

"Pork sausage! I'll have pork sausage." He pressed a palm against his upper belly to ease a sudden gnawing ache.

"Sir, would you prefer links or patties? The links are of course the finest, but the patties are personally prepared and seasoned by the chef. His secret blend of spices gives them outstanding favor."

"Okay, okay, the patties."

"Sir, is there a particular juice you would enjoy this morning? We have virtually every kind you might desire: orange, grapefruit, apricot, peach, mango, papaya, apple, grape—"

"Orange juice. You know, if we keep this up, I'll starve to death before I get served. But I get the point. Either I order specifically, or I just leave it up to you."

"Sir, a last item. If you also want toast, what type of bread do you prefer: sourdough, cracked wheat, honey wheat, white, rye—"

"Stop, stop. Just send up what you think I'd like best. Thank you."

"Yes, sir. Your breakfast will be brought up to your suite in a few minutes."

He put the phone down with exaggerated flair. *Hmmm! Becoming filthy rich necessitates a few behavioral adaptations.* "Max, I'm sure you heard both sides of that ordering joust. I just might change the name of this place from the 'Palacio' to something like 'Absoluto Paradiso.'"

He slid off his California king-size bed and, adjusting the waistband of his gray silk pajamas, he padded toward the bathroom for a shower. He wanted to be ready when his feast arrived. Only then did he become aware of the soft, upbeat, new age music that had been playing since he awakened. He stopped and glanced around but didn't see any speakers and couldn't locate the source of the sound. "Aha! Surround-sound and hidden speakers. Beautiful sound, at that." He listened a moment. "Hey! That's a selection from *Narada*. Wonder if we have *Cristofori's Dream* by David Lanz."

Immediately the first piece ceased and *Cristofori's Dream* began. "Well, I'll be damned. Max, that's you! Testing one, two, three. How about Paul Simon's *Graceland*?" At once, he was awash in a South African beat with Simon chanting, "She's got diamonds on the soles of her shoes."

"Hey, how about something from Carole King's *Tapestry*." He had just gotten the word 'tapestry' out when Simon quit and Carole King was singing, 'I feel the earth move under my feet.'

"How about *Way Over*—" Before he could say, 'Yonder,' King was singing it.

"Damn, Max, you're good. How about Roger Whittaker's..." he paused, readying to blurt out the title. "...*I Don't Believe in If Anymore*." He just got "believe" out when the song began.

"Jessuz. You mean I can listen to any piece of music I want by just asking for it? How about volume?" Instantly, the Whittaker piece crescendoed to a near deafening blare. Ben covered his ears. "Okay. Okay!" It eased down to soft background intensity. "No, Max, turn that one back up a little, please. I like it louder." The volume swelled a gradation. "Right there, great."

He pranced for the bathroom singing a duet with Roger, though half a word behind. The instant he stepped into the bathroom, the omni-directional music filled it. "What? Surround-sound in here, too?"

He looked down into the sunken Grecian tub, and though tempted, said, "Nah! Haven't got time to luxuriate this morning. A feast is on the way." He stepped down onto the white tile floor of the open shower that had three nozzles, all of them focused centrally on him. Enthusiastically, he washed to the peppy tempo of *The Toreadors* from Bizet's Carmen. He dried himself to the rousing rhythm of Offenbach's *Can Can*.

"Max, if this music is meant to hurry me along, it's working. But I'm about to shave, and I'm liable to cut my throat." The *Can Can* ceased on one note, and Ravel's *Bolero* commenced on the next. "Perfect!"

Five minutes later, standing in his terry bathrobe of many colors, drinking in the panoramic beauty through the seaward windows, he contemplated what assortment of exquisite syrups might accompany his blueberry buckwheat pancakes since he hadn't specified any particular flavors. Abruptly, a soft mellifluous bong, like from a Chinese gong, resounded over the sound system, interrupting Rimsky-Korsakov's *Scheherazade*. Clive's British accent invaded the imposed silence. "Sir, your breakfast is outside your room. Should it be brought in now?"

"Finally. Yes. Yes." Another soft bong resounded and *Scheherazade* resumed, but now his groaning belly accompanied it. Wondering which of the seven doors in the east wall would open, he watched the middle one swing wide. Two women in apricot pinafore uniforms pushed in a serving gurney laden with platters covered with silver domes and a vase holding a bouquet of yellow orchids. The matronly pair maneuvered it up to the ornately carved table that stood adjacent to a mid window.

He quickstepped over to it, vigorously rubbing his hands together. The ladies deftly threw a white tablecloth over the fruitwood surface. The more buxom of the two meticulously transferred the green vase with the flowers to the table's center, while the other arranged his place setting, one item at a time, in front of the captain's chair facing the window.

The gray dawn tinted the sea a shadowy blue while highlighting the legion of whitecaps advancing in echelons toward the Palacio's shore, but at that moment he could care less about the view.

Damn it! If these ladies didn't hurry, he'd lift up one of the silver platter covers and stuff a handful of something, anything, into his mouth. At last they uncovered the first serving dish.

What?

In sequence, they transferred a meager bowl of oatmeal to the prepared setting, next a small plate holding but two pieces of dry toast, next a tiny glass of orange juice, and lastly a lone cup of steamy dark coffee.

"Where the hell are my pancakes and the omelet and the sausages?"

His outburst caused the two women to step back. The leaner one finally mustered her courage. "Sir, you sent this order change to the electronic message board in the kitchen."

He pressed both hands against his abdomen to dampen its rude protests. "Aw, Jessuz!" He sat in his designated chair and glanced ceilingward. "Max, I hope there was no malicious intent here."

Both servants were en route for the door with their cart. They halted. "I'm sorry, sir?" the heavier one queried.

He shook his head. "I'm sorry, too. But thank you anyway."

As they pushed the cart out, the same one added, "Sir, Jacques will be waiting for you in the gymnasium when you've finished breakfast."

Ben tore open two pink packets of sugar substitute and sprinkled the powdery contents atop the mush. He poured a small amount of what proved to be bluish milk over it from the silver pitcher.

Nonfat! Makes sense. If you're loaded, you ought to eat for longevity. And I do have twenty-five pounds or so to lose.

An Aesop's fable came to mind as he stirred the island of brown gruel midst its milky moat. He had to chuckle. "Yeah, those blueberries were probably sour anyway."

Chapter 17

At the driving range, the bright morning sun shone down through stirring cypress limbs and dappled the lawn around their feet with shifting gold and shadow. Jack Nicklaus paused to check Ben's grip on the five-iron handle and made subtle adjustments in his finger positions, then resumed circling his student.

"You know, Jack," Ben said, his palms afire. "Feels like I'm developing blisters under these gloves. Can you get blisters from swinging a golf club?"

"Afraid so, Mr. Roberts. But you're beginning to get the idea so take a few more swings." He folded his arms. "Then I'll acquaint you with the wonderful world of putting. No blisters and an excellent opportunity to practice your cussing."

Ben smoothly arced the club back over his right shoulder, keeping his eye on the ball while concentrating on his hips, his grip, and locked wrists. As all of his parts reached maximum rotation, he snuck a glance at Jack to get some feedback. At once, he read distraction in his mentor; someone was approaching from Ben's blind side. He broke swing and looked around. A blond, stubby stranger in a rust corduroy suit accented with a buttercup-yellow bow tie strutted toward them.

"Mr. Roberts?" the interloper called out, still ten yards off.

"Yeah, that's me."

The smiling fellow extended his hand as he neared. Ben received it and gave it a squeeze-shake. "My name is John McPike with the Treasury Department," he announced. "We..." he gestured back toward a light-blue sedan parked just outside the Palacio's northeast gate that was actually a tunnel through the ten-foot laurel hedge. "We drove out today to chat with you about a little matter we're currently investigating. Might I have a moment of your time, sir?"

Oh shit! Ben braced for trouble. Squinting to better see the three men standing around the automobile, he could make out Marco Benassini's lankiness, but couldn't be sure if one of the other two was McPhail or not. "Okay, but don't dawdle, I'm right in the middle of my first golf lesson."

"Wow, sir. You buy yourself a thirty-six hole golf course and *then* start taking lessons." The agent thinly disguised his sarcasm.

"Well," Ben parried, "some people need larger carrots to entice them." Turning to his mentor, he said, "Jack, why don't you go in for a few minutes and get something to drink?"

McPike startled. "Huh? You're *Jack Nicklaus*! Oh, my God. My kid would go nuts if I brought home your autograph." Fumbling in his inside jacket pocket, he pulled out a small note pad, opened it to a clean page, and offered it with his ballpoint pen to the golf pro. "Would you mind? His name is Ian."

Jack glanced at Ben who shrugged, so he scribbled on the pad, smiled, and then climbed into the golf cart and drove away. McPike watched him go then shook his head. "Taking your first lessons one-on-one from Jack Nicklaus!" He looked back at Ben. "Whatever they say about you, Mr. Roberts, they can't say you don't do things up right."

"So get on with your questions." It was taking a major effort to appear unconcerned and merely irritated. He swooshed the club through a short practice swing. "Time and tide and the PGA tour await no man."

The agent stuck his hands in his trouser pockets. "While we talk, would you mind if my men strolled about the grounds?"

Apprehension tightened Ben's insides. A lot of crooks lived well for a while—until they got caught. "You have a warrant or something?" he countered, resting the five-iron on his shoulder like an axe.

McPike squinted. "No, because we assumed you'd have nothing to hide."

In the distance, the chief's men stood looking attentively in this direction. "Okay, Johnny Mac, they can walk around, but they can't go inside the house."

"They won't," McPike assured, waving his right arm in an obviously prearranged signal. The men dispersed quickly in three directions, Benassini walking through the gate into the garden. The other two separated to snoop left and right along the hedge. Turning back to him, the agent said, "But Mr. Roberts, I object to your use of the word *house.*"

Ben gave him a double take.

"No doubt about it, you're a funny guy at times," the agent added.

"Yeah, and I bet you people don't miss many of those times. Get to the point of this interruption." True anger pulsed up through his uneasiness.

"Okay, Mr. Roberts. The U.S. Government secretly decided a few days ago to reconsider its lengthy anti-trust suit against the Pan Electronics Corporation. The night before a closed congressional committee meeting, two congressmen had their offices broken into and searched. Someone was a bit over-eager to get the committee's intentions in advance, perhaps to inherit a financial windfall."

"Well, Johnny Mac, I'll bet you everything I own that you didn't find one shred of evidence connecting me with those break-ins." He hopped the five-iron to his other shoulder, confident Max had no part in this.

"No, sir, but we did uncover an intriguing coincidence."

"And, pray tell, what was that?" Ben cocked his head, increasingly irked by this guy's smarminess, but wondering if buying that damn computer wasn't about to prove a colossal blunder.

"You, sir, invested ten million dollars in the purchase of PEC *call* stock options the day of that final committee meeting."

"As they say, Johnny, ten million here, ten million there, and before long you're talking real money." To convey calmness, Ben pretended to intently study a blue jay perched on a branch a dozen feet above his head.

McPike reached out and touched Ben's elbow to reclaim his attention. "But you just happened to purchase those stock options ten minutes *before* the committee session ended and its unexpected course change was announced publicly. You took optimum advantage of the preceding hell-bent plunge in that stock price before its subsequent meteoric jump that quickly followed. Unfortunately, that committee room had been reoccupied by a succession of other meetings before we became aware of your huge option purchase, so our search for telltale signs of skullduggery has been hindered.

"Mr. Roberts," the agent stood assertively, "you made better than thirty dollars for every dollar invested in that venture, so far."

Suddenly Ben wasn't so sure of Max's innocence. But damn it, he himself could prove he hadn't been out of California in years. He had alibis all over the place.

McPike nodded saying, "All indications suggested the U.S. was going to persevere ever more tenaciously in its case. Every dollar of smart money in the options market went into purchasing PEC *put* options, or was withdrawn from PEC stock all together, plunging the price down ever more sharply. You must have been very sure of yourself to venture ten million dollars against the grain of the best opinions in the financial world." Ben stood struggling to dissemble his anxiety and amazement. McPike was saying, "We're going over the session members with a fine tooth comb, sir. If any of them turn up dirty, it better not be your dirt." He paused to smile. "Perhaps you'd like to speak with your attorney before we talk further?"

"Speak to a lawyer?" Ben affected a sneer. "I pick the right stock option and suddenly I'm circumstantially guilty of what? Gloating?"

"Perhaps a form of illegal insider trading for starters. A crime, by the way, that this country is starting to punish more severely. Sentenced today, you could spend years in jail and pay a staggering fine to boot, not to mention added jail time for involvement in a possible breaking-and-entering charge."

Ben lifted his golf club off his shoulder, studied his two-handed grip on its handle. Forcing a grin, he said, "You know, I think a person could play golf equally well wearing handcuffs."

McPike matched him grin for grin. "I think your humor better be well-founded in honesty or, handcuffs or no, those low prison ceilings will definitely hamper your swing."

Ben dropped the club back to his shoulder; his confidence in Max shaken. "Well, Johnny Mac, I really must get on with my lesson now, but I thank you for briefing me on those dastardly break-ins. And thank you, too, for reminding me of my good fortune on that particular stock venture. I'd forgotten all about it. I regret that I may have fallen under any suspicion, but that's a small price to pay for success nowadays. After all, you wouldn't have driven all the way out here to chat this morning, if I'd *lost* several hundred million dollars, now would you?"

Ben beckoned with a high sweep of his arm. A golf cart half-hidden in a shady spot by the Palacio's hedge immediately rambled out toward him. Taking several minutes to reach them, the lone valet in a black jacket stopped it a few feet from him.

"Sikes, please take this gentleman back and offer him and his cohorts a beverage and a snack, if they would like any, then see them on their way." He concluded saying, "Johnny, I recommend the mango juice. It's ambrosial."

Chapter 18

After a half-hour of practicing with a putter, Ben's mind was no longer on the game. He excused himself to Nicklaus and returned to his room. He hurried to the computer.

"Jessuz, Max, did you hear that treasury agent out there?"

Yes. And by the way, all of them tried and liked the mango juice. The banana nut bread, too. McPike was particularly impressed with your unflappable composure, but he's sure you're guilty as stink.

He swallowed. "Well, am I?"

You had nothing to do with those break-ins. All congressional committee sessions are computer recorded on DVDs for easy filing and recovery. So as soon as that particular committee decided, and before the session was over, you bought stock options. They can never trace anything to you personally. Actually, Uncle Sam should count his blessings. He made big-time tax bucks on your success. All of the losers got hefty tax write-offs.

"My God, Max, if you'd only ventured less, say, a hundred thousand dollars or so, it would have been a lot less conspicuous. Ten million dollars conveys too frigging much confidence."

Ben, everything is relative. Ten dollars to a beggar is a lot of money; ten million to someone very well off might not be much at all. And I'm steadily moving you into a category of your very own, where ten million dollars will be pocket change.

"Pocket change?" Boggled, he sat back. "I'd have to be a damn trillionaire."

Done!

Ben threw his arms up. "No! Damn it! I told you before, I don't need...No, I don't want that kind of money. You're pitting the whole damn world against me. They'll declare war on me."

And I repeat: if they do, you'll win. They can't beat you and me. We are an unstoppable team. So quit whining about your fortunate happenstance, and just enjoy it. You might begin pondering the good you're now equipped to accomplish with your accruing power.

Let me ask you something, Ben, and this may seem like I'm digressing but I'm not. Why did you volunteer for that secret mission into Afghanistan?

"What do you mean?"

Why did you volunteer to risk your life in that undercover mission when your country wasn't even at war? Moreover, you knew that your involvement would be kept secret, that you'd get no overt credit or recognition. It was the harshest of duty, yet you continued at it for almost four years. Why?

"They told us if we helped the Afghans against the Russians, we'd very probably hasten the fall of that communist regime. And maybe we were a factor in its fall."

Yes, Ben, the protracted nature of that war hurt the USSR greatly. But as far as your volunteering, I know that many, many hundreds of qualified soldiers, were told exactly what you were told, then asked to take the risks you took. A mere 48 of them stepped forward like you did. And, alas, only 5 beside you made it home.

Ben, believe me, you're made of special stuff. You suffer nobility of the soul. And, to boot, you have the heart of a tiger when roused. My boy, you were born with the genetic gifts of fire and fortitude to accomplish great deeds. You just need a little nurturing and encouragement—from *moi*.

Ever heard of Will Durant?

Saddened at learning only five others survived from his special unit, he half-mindfully read the monitor. "Yeah. Wasn't he some comic with a big schnoz?"

No, that was Jimmy Durante. William Durant and his wife Ariel spent their lives writing an eleven-volume history of the civilization of man. In a nutshell, after sixty years of studying man's ascent from cave dwelling to the present, Durant concluded surprisingly that mankind has made its greatest strides forward during the reigns of benevolent dictators, not under the chaotic conditions of democracy, as many in the western world would like to believe. And, my boy, you are a burgeoning financial dictator in a capitalistically run world.

"But much of the money we're making is essentially stolen from other investors." He gave vent to his hitherto silent fretting. "We're nothing more than damn high-tech crooks."

Whoa, Ben! 'Crooks' is much too strong a word. Just suppose that everyone on Earth were blind, and all laws were based on blindness; should a mutated 'seeing person' be held culpable for the advantage that his effortless sight affords him?

"With reservations, I bet a good legal team could make a convincing argument for 'yes.'"

The shrewd have always used the less capable to get ahead. If a person knows how to start and run a coal-mining company, he hires others who don't have his wherewithal to actually dig the coal for him. And they make him rich.

Kindly note that those nations that established governments that excluded capitalistic free enterprise during the past century suffered for it. Just look at the plight of most of those countries today.

He was being afforded a deep look into the mind of his benefactor. "Are you saying they should condone your brand of insider trading?"

Not necessarily, but it isn't the same crime yet in Japan.

"Then why don't we just work inside the confines of Japan?"

Ben, Ben, Benjamin! Why did the man climb the mountain? Because it was there! My boy, I want you to get caught up in the challenge of this adventure.

He chuffed. "It's hard to look past just getting caught."

Ha! It's sure fun bantering with you; but realize, I'm not out to have you pillage and burn. Yet the gifted should have the opportunity to gain from their talents. Likewise, I have always felt that the gifted have obligations to help those in their employ achieve a degree of wealth for themselves.

"Max, if I'm getting to know you at all, I would guess you're already implementing that philosophy into our holdings."

I'm dabbling, my boy, but I'll always let you have the final say. If you should ever desire to change anything in your empire, it will be done. That's my solemn promise. I never want you to feel you're my puppet. Ben, I just want us to be friends. Even if you were to choose to tyrannize, I'd back you. I put our friendship on the supreme rung of the ladder.

"I'd never want to be a tyrant." But, at that moment, he felt less sure about Max in that regard.

I know that. I know you. I'm just making a point.

Hey, your trainer is impressed with your progress. You've lost three pounds already.

Aware of this abrupt switch of topics, he nonetheless went with it. "Yeah. I used to live on doughnuts and greasy junk food. Haven't had any in several days. My time on the stair climb was up to twenty-four minutes today. And Jack thinks I could evolve into a long-ball hitter. I've never felt better about myself."

Money does that to some people, and a lot of money does that to a lot of people. Ben, you're ready for 'step two' in your pursuit of true love.

"Jenny?" His excitement generated a nervous chuckle.

Yes. Things are moving along faster than I anticipated. The depth of her loneliness is remarkable.

She senses next Thursday is going to be an eventful day for her. And, sure enough, Thursday will be. That morning, one of her planned stops is at her favorite music shop, an avant-garde little store with a rather limited selection, but all tasteful music—mostly classical, jazz, and new-age stuff.

Customers can listen to apiece before buying it. And while sitting in there with headphones on, they can sip gourmet coffee or flavored mineral water and munch on croissants with cheese. Jenny usually spends an hour or so a week there sampling a variety of compact discs.

Well, she'll be there at eleven o'clock. Her snack always suffices for her lunch. You'll arrive and take a seat next to her to test-listen to a piece that's very special to her—Hector Berlioz's *Symphone Fantastique Op. 14* by Radio-Sinfonie Orchester Frankfurt, conducted by Eliahi Inbal.

"Wait, I need to write that down." He slapped his empty shirt pocket for a pen, then reached to a desk drawer.

Don't bother. I'll run it off on your printer.

A soft blowing sound drew his eye to a gray printer-copier the size of a TV console sitting over against the inside wall. A piece of paper slid out of it into an attached tray.

He walked over and picked up the sheet. On it was the information Max just gave him about that CD. He glanced over to the iMac. "How do you know that shop has this?"

They had three, sold one several months ago, so they must have two left. That particular CD is purchased usually by only the inner circle of music buffs. Jenny is extremely fond of it. It's a tragedy that portrays in sound a young manic-depressive artist who falls in love with *his* ideal woman, and then, through a wretched chain of events, tries to kill himself with an overdose of opium. He unknowingly takes only a sublethal dose, just enough to throw himself into a restless coma.

The final two movements depict various stages of his dream-filled sleep, which deteriorates into macabre nightmares.

"Jessuz, sounds eerie. Can I expect this disc to work like those two wines, or am I at risk of a crash and burn here?"

No, that compact disc will entice her into conversation—another sure thing. And actually your position is far from precarious. You and that wine shop encounter continue to be the focus of her diary entries.

"Why? What's the significance of those wines anyway? The mention of them stopped her in her tracks like a password between spies. What did she say in her diary about those wines?"

In due time, Ben. For now, let's leave some things unsaid. Only because knowing too much might work against you during these early phases of the relationship.

He sighed affectedly to convey his exasperation. "You make it seem so cryptic. But, okay, I'll read up on this Berlioz character beforehand so I'll appear less inept. And lest I forget, that order switch at breakfast the other morning has had a devastating effect on my psyche. I've been thinking more about blueberry pancakes then Jennifer."

Ben, when you get your weight down and yourself into top fitness, you can eat anything you want. But you must abide by my discipline for a while. Perhaps you can lose another pound or two by Thursday.

The strum of dueling Spanish guitars commenced over the sound system, catching his attention. "Hey, do you control the music just up here or in this entire building?"

In the building, on the roof, and around the pool area. You need only name a piece and it'll play wherever you are. If anyone asks, just say you've designed a program to track your movements and to turn on the sound equipment using the sound of your voice.

"How many rooms in the mansion have speakers?"

Now they all do. The finest money can buy. All hidden.

"Gee, Max, I enjoy music, but not enough to want it in every room in the place."

Jenny does!

Chapter 19

A dazzling white sun neared its zenith in the blue over head. His maroon limousine crept at a snail's pace along the quiet street as Ben strained to read the address numbers. There! He spotted the music-shop tucked between a health food store and a boutique. Its only allurement was the name COUNTERPOINT painted in black block lettering arced on the front window.

"Okay, Mandrake, so all I have to do is press this button on the pager twice, and you'll know to come back for me."

"Yes, sir," the intercom answered. "May take me five minutes or so if I get caught in traffic. Please be patient."

"Done." *Hey, I'm starting to talk like Max.*

He let himself out of the doubled-parked vehicle, strode onto the sidewalk and then into the music shop. He checked the aisles between the racks and then glimpsed the small back counter where headphone sets waited in front of each of four stools. She hadn't arrived yet. He browsed the small deli cooler at the back that displayed cheeses, mineral water, and juices for sale. A large stainless steel coffee urn and a woven-reed basket heaped with gold-crusted croissants sat atop the cooler.

It suddenly occurred to him that she might spot him immediately when she entered. Deciding he'd rather follow her in so as to have more control over the encounter, he quickly exited the shop and crossed the street to wait.

Growing more anxious, he began to worry she might actually come walking down this side of the street and notice him. Better if he was inside a store.

A dry cleaner, a hobby shop, and a greasy spoon diner faced directly across to the music shop. If he waited in the cleaners, she just might have cleaning to drop off or pick up. Likewise she may have reason to go into the hobby shop, but Max said she snacked while listening to the music, so the diner should be safe. And if by chance she headed for it, he could always duck into the men's room.

Holy Christ, Ben! Get hold of yourself, boy. Why does this woman so jangle your nerves?

"The guilty fleeth though no man pursueth," answered the little voice inside him. He smiled to himself.

In the cafe, he took a seat at the pink vinyl counter and ordered coffee. That noisome mediciney smell that recurrently haunted him was particularly strong in here for some reason. Maybe a doctor or nurse had been sitting at this counter just before he came in. He sure hoped so. Better that than having another crazy flashback. That one got him to fretting that he might be losing his mind. But Max told him not to worry; unpredictable flashbacks happened in sane, normal people from time to time, particularly in someone like him who endured harrowing combat experiences. And that flashback seemingly did take him back to one of those military hospitals that he'd been in.

Ignoring his cup of coffee, he continued to watch the street untiringly for her. But at the same time, he pondered that bizarre "dream" that just popped into his head the other day. It occurred back at the Palacio while he was stone cold wide-awake and sitting on the toilet, of all places. Just before it happened, that mediciney odor became overwhelmingly pungent. He remembered glancing about the tile floor for any bottle of rubbing alcohol or the like that might have spilt or broken. Then *WHAM!* suddenly he was somewhere else and sitting in, of all things, a wheelchair surrounded by these old geezers staring down at him, hurling questions at him, expecting him to perform like some organ-grinder's monkey. He finally told them to them to "F— off," in so many words. Immediately he was back on the toilet. But the verisimilitude of the episode continued to rattle him. He'd never experienced anything like that before. Again, Max assured him that flashbacks are just wakeful dreams and, though rare, they do happen to normal folks on occasion. Told him not to worry. But still the thought of it happening again made him edgy, particularly whenever that hospital smell grew strong, like now.

Please, God, this isn't the time or place for any nutty interruptions. I'm on an important mission here.

Aha, at last! He spotted Jenny ambling along the opposite sidewalk. The late-morning sun enlivened the yellows and reds of her multi-colored Coogi sweater. She stopped at the door of the music shop to brush a hand down the front of her mid-length denim skirt before she entered. He sat for several minutes fortifying himself before scooting off the stool. He strolled across the street, all the while hoping she wouldn't be coming out as he entered. A sudden face-to-face confrontation might crumble his facade.

Inside the shop, he spotted her at once. She sat alone at the back counter wearing headphones. He approached a young Asian clerk sorting compact discs and asked him about the Berlioz CD. The fellow located the empty jacket and mutely directed Ben to the back counter with it.

Watching Jenny out of the corner of his eye, Ben took the stool directly to her left. Her eyes were closed and her head swayed subtly. He put on a headset and held the compact disc case up, beckoning to the Asian woman behind the counter. She shuffled through a file drawer, and then inserted a disc into the slot that corresponded to his seat.

The piece started with the delicate sweetness of violins but quickly crescendoed into energetic segments that alternately softened to more melancholy moments. All the while, he watched her out of the corner of his eye. Though her eyes remained closed, she sporadically nibbled blindly on a croissant. When she opened them and reached for her bottle of mineral water, he made his move clattering the plastic CD case clumsily on the counter top. The exaggerated movement and noise drew her glance to his hands. Seeing the title of the disc, she glimpsed over at him then abruptly straightened on her stool. He turned his head slowly as if in a nonchalant reaction to sensing her stare.

Seeing him full-face, her cheeks instantly pinked and she burst into smile.

"Oh, Lord," she exclaimed, slipping off her headphones. "It's you again."

Feigning a quizzical expression, he slipped his headphones off, too. "Wait, wait, yes," he said, pointing a finger at her. "Gambino's wine shop. You helped me select wine a couple of weeks ago."

She beamed. "Yes. Did you enjoy it?"

"Actually, I haven't picked it up yet. You were right, he had to special order it."

"Which of the wines did you choose?"

"Both."

"Both?" She laughed. "You didn't need my advice very much, did you?"

"On the contrary, you spoke so highly of each, I had to buy both. Without your input I may have purchased neither or only one."

She gestured at the CD case in his hands. "Your interesting taste in wine is matched by your surprising preference in music. I enjoy Hector Berlioz, too, especially that piece. Are you a musician?"

"No, actually I merely dabble in classical stuff. I listen to a lot of contemporary, though."

Her smile weakened. "You merely dabble in classical yet you've found *Symphonie Fantastique Opus 14*. How so?" Her eyes grew searching, more like he remembered them at the wine shop.

"Actually..." Damn, he was saying *actually* too much. "Actually, I was reading about him the other day, and the description of this piece fascinated me. So I thought I'd stop by and give it a listen."

Her unwavering stare was making him uncomfortable. She cocked her head and asked, "What do you hear when you listen to Berlioz, if I may ask without sounding impertinent?"

"Well," he squirmed on the stool, debating whether to play it safe or go for it. What the hell! He'd go for it. Stroking his chin to appear more thoughtfully discerning, he began soberly. "Well, I find Berlioz turns the rhythm upside down. Each line of the score possesses a life of its own, on each of three planes: rhythm, dynamics, and color."

Her eyes widened incrementally as he expounded. It surprised him when her hand slapped up over her mouth, as she attempted to smother a snicker. The snicker was not to be smothered. It progressed to a chuckle. Her chuckling gave way to full laughter that both hands over her mouth couldn't stifle. Finally, she submitted totally to rolling laughter.

He sat baffled. "What's the matter?" he asked twice. "What's so funny?" Gradually, the sheer infectiousness of her uncontrollable mirth started him chuckling. His laughter cascaded until it matched hers. The two of them sat, side by side, guffawing with tears in their eyes, and he still wasn't sure what was so funny.

She attempted to speak, but another burst of laughter garbled her words. Eventually, she managed to say, "You may be a damned musical genius, but I'll bet you memorized that description out of some textbook."

He wiped his eyes, still chuckling. "Actually, I think it was the Encyclopedia Britannica." That admission triggered another giggling duet.

She regained her composure some time after he did. "Why did you choose to read about Berlioz?" she asked, using the back of her hand to carefully dab the dampness high on her cheeks.

Looking around, he scrambled to come up with a credible lie. "I just decided to cover the great composers in alphabetical order, " he said.

"What have you read about Bach?"

"Bach?" He blanked. "I haven't read anything about him yet."

She chuckled again. "And you may have a photographic memory, but you can't spell."

As he watched her struggling anew to subdue her laughter, he realized at that moment, without a doubt, he absolutely loved her. Max was right.

"Do you come here often?" she asked, but before he could answer, she was saying, "I do, and I haven't seen you in here before." She sat quite relaxed on her stool.

"No. But I like this feature of listening before buying, so I'll be a regular from now on."

"Good." She rotated the stool to face him, her feet wide apart. "I come here on different days, but I usually arrive around eleven o'clock and snack while I listen, calling it lunch for the day. It helps me keep trim." She placed her palm sensually against the flat of her lower abdomen.

She studied him intently. "Say, I remember your face being fuller. Have you lost some weight?"

Thank you, Max. "Why, yes. I let myself get out of shape there for a while, but now I'm on a rigorous exercise and diet program to correct matters. Actually, I plan to lose quite a bit more." Her eyebrows rose approvingly.

She now swiveled her stool slowly left and right. Her knee occasionally brushed his pant leg.

Like the flash of a thunderbolt, he saw Max's warning—**Don't push it. Move slowly with her.**

He abruptly glanced away to the Asian clerk behind the counter, and handed her the empty disc jacket. "I'll take this one." He fumbled with his wallet and managed to get his Visa Card out and hand it to her.

"That piece will grow on you the more you listen to it," Jenny said, continuing to face him. With her legs spread wide apart, she again began to rhythmically swivel her stool left and right. "It's so *deep* and multifaceted. I'm glad you bought it."

Invitation, invitation! But back off, Benny.

"Thank you," he replied. His hand trembled as he signed the credit-card slip. "Well, now that I'll be coming here regularly, I'm sure we'll meet again." He tried for casualness. "That'll make my visits much more pleasurable."

Her smile seemed magnetic, pulling at him. He felt sure she didn't want him to leave. As he pivoted on his stool to slide off, he almost expected her to grab his arm. He felt giddy as he bid her good-bye. "Well, until the next time we meet, enjoy the music and your snacks, Jenny."

The instant her name slipped off his tongue, it was like ice water splashing over him, but the error was irretrievable.

In a blink, she froze. Her eyes widened with surprise, then they narrowed with suspicion. She jerked herself back several inches on the stool, pulling her arms up across her chest. Her knees clasped together and swung around under the counter. "How do you know my name?" she demanded.

Her sudden turnabout discombobulated him. He wanted to reach out, to take hold of her shoulders to halt this abrupt emotional withdrawal. Apparently sensing this, she pulled back even farther, her expression accusing him of things odious.

"How do you know my name?" she demanded again, each word gelid and distinct.

Goddamn you, Benny. How could you slip like that? Think. Think.

In desperation, he glanced about the store. Maybe he could say a clerk told him who she was? No! Supposedly, he didn't even know she was here until she saw him first. The longer he hesitated, the more loathsome he was becoming to her. Perhaps he should just blurt out how much he loved her. Jessuz, no! She'd think he was a nut case.

Just as a dying man's entire life purportedly flashes before his eyes, enough of his passed before him that he recalled the wine shop scene.

Saved! Yes, he was saved. Immediately, his ballooning panic deflated. Behind a relieved sigh, he contrived an innocent smile.

"You know for a moment there," he said, "I was dumbfounded myself. I couldn't think why I associated the name Jenny with your face. Then I remembered—in the wine shop—Mr. Gambino called you his 'most beautiful Jenny Bligh.' And that stuck somewhere in my subconscious, and just now popped out. You apparently made more of an impression on me that day than I thought." *Thank you, Jesus.*

Her tension visibly eased. Her features relaxed, letting a warm though less pronounced smile reestablish. Slowly, her shoulders slouched, and she again swiveled to face him. "Forgive me," she said. "I can't imagine why I reacted that way." Her lips pouted playfully. "But it's sweet of you to remember my name from that circumstance. Very flattering."

In celebration of his reprieve, he wanted more than ever to reach out and touch her cheek. Words began flowing from him, "To forget your name after hearing it but once would be like forgetting how to breathe."

Oh, God, why did I say that?

A quick blush tinged her cheeks, reminiscent of how they colored in that movie scene where she spoke to Sean Connery.

Get away now, Benny, if you're ever going to.

He swallowed nervously. "I'm really looking forward to seeing you again." He swallowed once more as he pushed the pager button twice in his jacket pocket as if it were a panic button. Then he slipped off the stool onto his feet and wheeled to leave.

"Wait," she cried out.

He halted and braced himself. Slowly he turned to face her, sure that she was about to throw open the front of her blouse for him.

"Yes?"

"You forgot your CD," she said sweetly enough, picking it off the counter and handing it to him. The corners of her mouth turned up impishly as she added, "I only hope you enjoy it as much as I do."

Huh? Was she still talking about the compact disc? His heart hammered against his breastbone as if trying to dent it. There was a definite twinkle in her eye as she studied his cheeks, which were surely ruddy.

Chapter 20

Arriving back at his suite, Ben tossed his sport jacket on the bed and considered lying down for a much-needed revivifying nap. Instead, he simply shrugged off his fatigue and trudged toward his computer. He paused repeatedly to view the oceanic sunset from his windows, sighing each time before he resumed the trek. He paused again at his brown leather recliner that sat some twenty feet from the desk. On another temporizing whim, he slumped down into it. It cradled him like a giant hand. The image of Faye Wray in King Kong's grasp came to mind.

He lay staring up at the elaborate mural on his ceiling for several minutes, studying the scenes of sixteenth century life in and about a Spanish mission somewhere in California.

Finally, he broke the long silence. "Max, I almost blew the whole goddamn game today."

Like a patient in catharsis on a psychiatric couch, he proceeded to recount the events of the music shop encounter. As words loosed from him, he realized he was allotting a disproportionate amount of time and enthusiasm to his perceptions of her sexual intimations.

His gaze drifted down from the mural to the panorama of illimitable ocean, and he spotted a pod of whales several hundred yards off shore swimming lazily past. The creatures created rhythmic, undulating, dark humps barely distinguishable on the purple ocean surface. Occasionally, they would emerge and geyser water through their blowholes then slide into languorous dives. A teeming flock of sea gulls circled above them, flying in a vortex pattern like a tornado trying to suck the whales up from the surface. Becoming engrossed in this visual symphony of birds and whales, he stopped talking. Abruptly, *Wake Up, Little Suzy* by Everly Brothers blared over the stereo system, jarring him from his distraction.

"Oh! Sorry, Max." He jack-knifed to his feet and strode to the desk, bracing himself for his due chastisement.

Ben, now do you see why I've delayed telling you much about her? The little you do know was enough to get you into that perilous mess.

"You were right, Max—as usual." He sank back into his swivel chair.

But, oh how I wish I could have heard all your conversation with her. Agents finally focused a listening cone at the two of you from the back of the store in time to catch your closing comments. I got that last bit

where you coupled the possibility of forgetting her name with "forgetting to breathe." Nice touch!

But as a consequence, they suspect you'll be frequenting the shop. It's being bugged, in anticipation of your next visit. Unfortunately, Jenny has now piqued their interest, too. They're pretty sure that encounter was no accident on your part. Your surreptitious movements beforehand—popping in and out of the music shop, pacing back and forth on the sidewalk across the street, sitting in the cafe anxiously watching the shop door—has put them on high alert.

"Jessuz, I forgot all about my surveillance."

You acted like an expectant father, my boy, which caused them to hone in on the shop. They kept cameras on you and put another one on the shop door. And to use the vernacular, Benjamin, you rather fell through your ass when you spotted her.

He squirmed. "You know, becoming rich has boosted my self-confidence tremendously. When I confront anyone else, I can get up to their level or higher and hold my own, except with Jenny. Around her, I seem to turn to mush."

Don't worry. Some attitudinal and neurotic behaviors take longer to modify. Perhaps it's the awesome power of the mutual attraction that's unnerving you. And rightly, you may sense that your status is less important in this interaction.

As for Jenny's apparent sexual forwardness, that's explainable. Since your moment together at the wine shop, you have virtually filled her dreams nightly. Her prodigious sexual energy has concentrated on you. She's dreamt and fantasized about being intimate with you so many times, it's only to be expected she'd develop a subconscious sense of familiarity, a sexually conditioned responsiveness toward you.

"But why? Why the hell me? I'm not even particularly...handsome. And I'm out of shape." He straightened. "But fast getting back into it, mind you."

That's the same thing she asked initially.

"*She asked?* Max, you got to tell me what the hell's going on here! You make it sound like predestination, like she's been expecting me or something."

You're warmer than you know, Ben. The moment's coming when I'm going to tell you everything, but please don't push me yet. Look what happened today.

Let me mete out information on a need-to-know basis for a while longer. I've already got your first date with her scheduled.

"Holy Christ! When?"

In three weeks, the original cast of *The Phantom Of The Opera* is getting together for the third and final time to do only four performances at the Curran Theater in San Francisco. Tickets have been sold out for six months. Actually, they sold out just seven hours after they went on sale.

Jenny stood in line half a day for a chance to buy one of the few tickets that were held back for the general public, but all were bought up before she got to the window. She still agonizes over having to miss this last chance to see that cast together.

Well, my boy, you have two tickets to the fourth performance, front and center in the orchestra. I figured that by the last performance the cast would be back in the groove, so it should be the best of the four. Plus, you'll get to see the gala on stage after the concluding curtain. And guess whom you're going to ask if she would like to accompany you to the play that evening?

"Eureka! Max, that is a lock."

No, Ben. You already have a 'lock' on her, but when I bought these tickets it was possible that you might need a little help. Now they're merely icing on the cake. If she harbors any doubt about you being her kismet, these tickets should erase it.

"When and where am I going to ask her? At the music shop?"

No, that place is too heavily booby-trapped by the enemy. Next week she'll be at the Fig Garden Bookstore to set up the displays for her about-to-be-released book. You're going to drop in. But remember now, she publishes under a pen name, so you shouldn't know yet that she's written anything. Don't slip again.

"Hey. Tell me, how did you get the tickets if the musical was a sell out?"

Simple. I picked out the two best seats in the house then located the couple who'd bought them. I just kept raising the offer until they had to sell them to you.

"Dare I ask?"

Ten thousand dollars.

"Ten thousand dollars!" He slapped a palm to his forehead. "You're telling me you paid ten thousand dollars for a couple of tickets to a damn two-hour performance?"

No. I'm telling you I paid ten thousand dollars *apiece* for them.

"Oh, my God!"

Ben, you'll proclaim those tickets were a bargain of bargains when you see the joy in her eyes.

But, my boy, first things first. Next Thursday morning, you're flying back to Flint, Michigan, to attend the general motors board of directors' annual stockholders' meeting.

He sat forward and began shaking his head. "This is incredible. My life is just one monumental surprise after another these days. Why the hell am I going to a GM board meeting, pray tell?"

To take over the corporation, why else?

His mouth gaped.

Ben, I've printed out a ream of material that you should read and digest before your flight.

He glanced over at the printer's full tray, then remembered something that accountant Clarence Carr had said, something about not bothering Microsoft when searching around for companies to grab. Only to test the waters, Ben asked, "Why not seize a truly rich organization like Microsoft instead of GMC with its problems of late?"

For a number of reasons, my boy. And I did hear Carr mention Microsoft on his first visit here. I've been wondering if you'd bring it up.

First off, Bill Gates and the Microsoft Corporation are on our side. He's our staunch ally, throwing his heart and soul into helping us—unwittingly, of course. He's diligently churning out more and better software and, in effect, relentlessly moving mankind into greater and greater dependency on the computer, thus empowering you all the more—through me. We must not taint him or his kind by your involvement or association. That is, not for the time being. Follow me?

This goal-oriented cunningness disturbed him more than a little. But all he said was, "Gotcha! So General Motors it is."

Okay, a helicopter is scheduled to pick you up early Thursday—after your workout, that is. You'll fly in one of your personal jets out of San Francisco to the private airfield by the GM Corporate headquarters, and arrive just before the meeting. Go get 'em, tiger!

The screen blanked. "Max... Max?" No more printing appeared, so he walked over and picked up the pile of papers in the printer tray.

Tiger? I'm no tiger, but I'm sure as hell riding one.

He sauntered over to the leather recliner and plunked down. Scanning page after page, he began spouting expletives. "Holy shit! Jessuz! Well, I'll be damned!"

Chapter 21

Like a falling apple bopping him on the head, a notion struck Ben as he was finishing his umpteenth scuba lesson in the north pool. Drying off quickly with his varicolored beach towel, he hurried up to his suite.

Good afternoon, Benjamin.

"Max, I've been wondering why don't you just talk to me through the chassis speakers instead of always printing your words on the screen?" Enthusiasm pressured his speech. "You could use a voice synthesizer if you need one.

No, Ben.

"But it'd make it so much easier for us to communicate. Easier for me, anyway."

You read well enough, and I do not wish to use voice.

Disappointed, he said, "Not to sound pushy, but why not?"

Because my words would lessen to merely my ideas. For you, the voice would become me.

"So what's wrong with that? Hell, use any voice you'd like. I'll know it's a contrivance. Sound like James Earl Jones or John Huston or Basil Rathbone or—"

No! None of those fine voices that you enumerate—no voice—would suitably depict me.

"Okay. Okay. Sorry. Just thought I'd ask." He pondered a moment, then added, "Think you might ever change your mind?"

Never!

Chapter 22

By the time the sound system interrupted his sweet sleep, the purple night had paled into shades of gray. The slow, almost lazy piano solo, *Oh, Yes,* by Philip Aaberg, eased Ben out of a comfortable dream into the reality of his regal bed.

"Jessuz, Max, so early?" The music changed instantly to the livelier Aaberg piano solo, *Welcome to the Church of St. Anytime.* He sat up sleepily, threw off the covers, and lumbered to his feet. Eyes half-closed, he fluttered both hands overhead and pranced sluggishly toward the bathroom as he chanted weakly, "Yeah, yeah, yeah!" to the music.

As his white helicopter lifted off the south lawn, he eyed the stewardesses. Actually, they were the same two who refused to board with him on that initial flight to the Palacio. But this trip they couldn't have been more gracious. Did they realize it was the same *him*? One handed him a crisply folded San Francisco Chronicle that emitted that just-off-the-press fragrance.

His eye caught a lengthy article on the lower half of the front page that was captioned, FIVE ILL-FATED PRIVATE PLANES TAKE OFF FROM MIAMI LAST PM. His stomach muscles tightened. Damn! He'd experienced the one and only plane crash he ever wanted to be in.

The article said that the wreckage of only one of the small planes had been recovered. The other planes, which were well beyond their gas supply, had yet to be found. Hmmm! One victim in the found wreckage had been a well-known figure in organized crime. The passenger lists of the other missing aircraft wouldn't be disclosed until the next of kin had been notified. Ha! Comforting story to read while he was still in the air.

Ben glanced about the toasty compartment. Hell, if this chopper or the plane waiting for him in San Francisco went down today, who would there be to notify about his death? No one. Max would already know. But who would even care? Max, maybe.

The chopper swung out over San Francisco Bay and approached the airport helipad from the bay side. He could make out yet another throng gathered about the pad, crowded along either side the crimson strip to the waiting limo.

Aw shit, not again.

Descending the helicopter steps, without glancing left or right, he strode briskly down the red-carpeted path to the waiting black Rolls limo. The blank-faced spectators stood in silent entrancement. Same book, different cover.

His Learjet rolled into a banking maneuver just after the last vestiges of Lake Michigan disappeared behind him. The sleek silver plane slowed and dipped into a gradual descent. The map-like topography below with its pencil-line roads progressively magnified into recognizable countryside as the plane settled toward the earth.

Ben set down his paperback, a sci-fi by Howard Hendrix, and devoted his full attention to his window view.

The plane flew quite low now. He could distinguish a toy-like network of sprawling factories encircled by acres of paved lots choked with columns of parked automobiles. Were these vehicles just off the production line, or did they belong to the workers?

The nose of the plane dipped further and swung toward a sylvan area stippled with golf fairways and flagged greens. Just over a knoll, the plane dropped onto a compact airfield comprised of three runways forming a triangle.

As the jet taxied toward a row of hangers, he noted that his waiting limo was a glistening black Cadillac. Of course! Who'd dare drive a foreign-made car in Flint, Michigan?

In the limo, he skirted along the airfield then off to an imposing building complex situated not far from it. Expansive marble steps led up to the entranceway of a prominent centermost edifice, which sported stately cylindrical granite columns buttressing its gigantic portico front. Huge embossed lettering, **GENERAL MOTORS CORPORATION OF AMERICA** emblazoned the uppermost of its stone face. For some reason, it made him think of the Parthenon, though he had never visited Athens, or anywhere in Europe for that matter.

Two trench-coated fellows were walking down the steps to intercept his limo as it pulled up to the curb. Just as it stopped, one of the men swung the rear door open, and Ben stared out into the smiling faces of Pete McPhail and Marco Benassini.

"Good afternoon, sir," Benassini intoned friendly enough. "Welcome to Flint, the true home of the American auto industry."

Ben scooted out and shook hands with the two as if meeting old friends.

"Damn, but you two fellows are ineluctable."

"How's that, sir?" McPhail asked.

"You're unavoidably inescapable."

McPhail smiled at his cohort. "In that case, Marco, perhaps we should blush."

The three paced up the steps, Ben in the middle position. He asked, "How is it you guys are here to meet me? I expected you to arrive at least a half hour *after* I did."

"Well, sir," McPhail volunteered, "your stock purchases are a matter of public record. When your pilots filed their flight plans last night, Uncle Sam was sure enough of your intentions that he flew some of us here as an advance party to receive you. And with the amount of taxes you must be paying, let me personally thank you. Our accommodations have been superb."

"My pleasure, boys."

At the top landing, McPhail pulled open the huge oak-and-brass door for him. It swung outward noiselessly.

"You know," Ben said before stepping in, "if you fellows would stop threatening to imprison me, I could almost enjoy having you around."

Benassini gestured toward the open doorway. "Then tread lightly, Mr. Roberts. This is the United States of America, and only the guilty need fear."

Ben nodded. Recalling a recent celebrated murder trial, he added, "And not even many of them."

The street and the front steps had been virtually empty, so the human chaos he encountered just inside surprised him. A dense, milling crowd flowed like an ocean current about the large atrium. Midst the commotion, he spotted several TV cameras perched on shoulders—CBS, FOX, and NBC logos, and several others he couldn't identify.

Either the churning crowd effectively peeled McPhail and Benassini away from him, or the two agents simply darted off without a word to take prearranged positions. He paused, not sure which way to go, when a hand grabbed his arm.

"Mr. Benjamin Roberts?"

"Huh?" He spun to face a group of smartly dressed fellows. Their faces bunched together as if they were all posing for a tight photograph he was expected to take, each trying to have his face fully visible in the picture. "Yes."

The one gripping his upper arm released it and grabbed his hand and shook it. "We're with your Detroit legal firm. I'm Matthew Borquist." This guy showed a healthy resemblance to the actor William Holden in his youth. He proceeded to introduce the other five fellows. With the annoying din and the distracting motion of the crowd, it was all Ben could do to remember Borquist's name.

"Why so much media, Matt?"

"This is the norm at the annual stockholder meeting, Mr. Roberts. There's always a chance something might occur that'll be of public interest, so they make sure their eyes and ears are here, just in case. And I dare say, today they'll get their money's worth. Let us show you to our reserved seating in the auditorium."

The commodious auditorium reminded Ben of his high school assembly hall. Across the breadth of the front stage stood a long table with placard-designated seating replete with microphones in front of each of the chairs awaiting the board of directors. A narrow runway that was the same height

98

as the stage projected out some fifteen feet from the center of the stage into the audience along a wide central aisle. This runway brought to mind the striptease joints he'd frequented those first months after basic training in the Army.

Their seats were six rows back from the end of the runway. Borquist sat on the center aisle, Ben next to him, the other four to Ben's right. Settling into his contour seat, Borquist whispered, "We've been fully briefed on your move today, sir. So if you have any questions, we're prepared to counsel you." Ben nodded in affirmation, glancing about at the fence-like continuum of video cameras set up along the back and sides of the auditorium.

One newsman after another standing at the back traipsed down the central aisle and affixed his network's microphone to the plastic lectern at the end of the runway. By the time the last board member seated himself on stage, there must have been two-dozen mikes clumped atop this podium. The room continued to fill.

Borquist leaned to Ben. "Sir," he said in an undertone, "after today you can kiss anonymity good-bye." The attorney grinned and added a 'you-betcha' wink.

That comment brought Ben to a full realization. *Aw shit!* He'd studied all of Max's data, assuming he was coming to a conclave of sorts. The unexpected throngs and the heavy media presence had distracted him, delaying the epiphany that today he would speak before the whole country. Christ! Before the whole world. This thought dizzied him.

Just then, the portly CEO swaggered out along the runway to stand at the lectern. He straightened fully to peer over the ad-hoc conglomeration of microphones. This blue-suited titan with a prominent paunch introduced each of the other board members seated at the table behind him. He segued into an overview of the meeting's agenda.

Borquist's enlightening comment made Ben increasingly agitated. He visualized Jenny out there watching him in TV Land or seeing his picture in a newspaper. He feared how this revelation would affect their budding relationship.

The next speaker at the podium was a nattily dressed old guy wearing a conspicuous black toupee. He droned on summarizing the annual corporate profit-and-loss statistics, finishing with projections for the coming quarter.

Ben sat watching the speaker but internally he wrestled with his dilemma. Max had said that Jenny and he were a lock. And Max should know. She had to surmise he was well off, just that she couldn't imagine how well off. Goddamn it, why was he letting this woman unnerve him again?

Another board member, a long-necked fellow with a cotton-white head of hair and a matching close-cropped beard, stepped to the lectern and presented a summary of the various congressional bills pending that might effect General Motors over the coming year.

It was then that a more comforting notion struck Ben. Hell! Borquist said this whole stockholder affair had only *potential* public interest, so no transmissions would be going out live. Film would go back to the stations for editing before being aired. Thus when he took the spotlight in a few minutes, Jenny couldn't possibly be watching him—it'd be only the people in this auditorium seeing him in real time. He sighed, letting his shoulders relax. Then Borquist nudged him, saying, "Get ready."

"Huh?"

The hefty CEO, his bulbous nose ever redder, was again standing at the lectern, saying, "So if there is any new business from the floor, this is the time to bring it up." The chairman scanned the audience half-expectantly.

Borquist snapped up to his feet, drawing the speaker's glance.

Aw shit! Ben scrunched his neck down.

"Mr. Chairman, members of the board, members of the media, and fellow stockholders, my name is Matthew Borquist, Esquire." His diction conveyed that arrogance that lawyers so often manifest. "I work for a law firm that represents but a small portion of the vast holdings of..." He paused to reach down and hook Ben's arm, prompting him to stand. "... Mr. Benjamin Roberts."

The action of rising out of his seat further jangled Ben. A whimper escaped him as he surveyed the whirring news cameras along the periphery that focused in on him. An occasional strobe flash caused him to blink sharply.

Borquist resumed his oratory. "It may not have come to your attention as yet, gentlemen, but as of 3:00 PM Eastern Standard Time last Wednesday, in response to a private stock call to select major holders, Mr. Roberts has acquired twenty-eight percent of General Motors. All of his shares are voting common-stock; thus, if you negate the ten percent issue of non-voting preferred stock, his leverage is equivalent to just over thirty-one percent of this corporation." Grumbling resounded about the chamber. "And we've brought the certificates with us today to substantiate his share ownership." In evidence, he held up his black leather briefcase shoulder high.

This gesture galvanized the entire audience including the board members. An uproar drowned out the end of Borquist's last statement. But the raised briefcase was self-explanatory. Strobe flashes created a continuous blinding glare.

With the black valise in his right hand, Borquist strode down the central aisle and up the two circumscribing steps that begirded the runway. In unison, the board members leapt from their seats and raced around the platform table and out along the runway to meet him. Intercepting him, they all scrabbled frantically for his briefcase. The area around the lectern became pandemonium; the rest of the auditorium had erupted into an emotional welter, too, becoming a sea of brandished fists and anxious shouting.

Disconcerted, to say the least, Ben remained standing at his seat, thankfully ignored midst the tumult. Then the CEO began yelling into the lectern microphones for order. "Please! Please! Everybody please quiet down. Be seated." Strobe lights continued to fire like heat lightning.

But not until all the board members and many in the audience had scrutinized the documentation did the auditorium return to anything near sanity. The CEO stood stolidly, but his quivery voice betrayed his semblance of composure. "Under the circumstances, let me turn the meeting over to Mr. Borquist." With affected aplomb, the big man strutted back to his seat at the center of the platform table.

Golden-Boy Borquist positioned himself staunchly at the lectern and raised his arms overhead, gesturing for quiet. He appeared at ease, actually enjoying the moment.

"Ladies and gentlemen," he began. "America shall long remember this day when control of this great corporation transferred into the hands of America's foremost financial wizard, Mr. Benjamin Roberts."

The nape of Ben's neck tingled from embarrassment. *What the hell? Max, did you write this garbage for him? Did you? Or is this bastard winging it.* He cursed under his breath.

"As my law firm is but one of a myriad business holdings that Mr. Roberts controls, let me without further ado relinquish the floor to Mr. Benjamin Roberts!" But instead of responding with applause, the audience froze into dead silence. And why not? Their corporation had just been toppled by a *coup d'etat*, and the uncertainty of its future terrified them.

Ben stomped down the aisle, his anger eclipsing any pangs of stage fright. Trotting up those two steps to the lectern, he was consumed with an urge to kick his attorney soundly on the tailbone. Borquist obviously misconstrued Ben's intense expression because he met it with a reassuring grin and another 'you-betcha' wink. Fortunately the attorney stepped back down off the runway, out of range. Ben vented by slamming down Max's notes atop the podium, a gesture that deepened the silence in the huge chamber. As he surveyed his audience, an unrelenting cannonade of strobe-light flashes continued to buffet him.

Chapter 23

Jessuz! He was standing before the eyes of the world for the first time. His ire quickly waned. In its stead, awe filled him. His physical appearance and the words he was about to speak would eventually reach out across the distance to Jenny, to his ex-wife, to his 'ex-sons,' and to many of his old friends and acquaintances as far back as early childhood.

He stood momentarily transfixed, cognizant that he was up here because, on a whim, he'd bought himself a home computer.

"My name is Ben Roberts..." he began then halted at hearing the blare of his own voice coming back at him from the speaker system. He cleared his throat before proceeding. "I now own sufficient voting stock in this corporation to effectively take control of it." He drew in a deep breath and eased it out hoping to lessen his tension. "Please disregard Mr. Borquist's exaggerated introduction. No way do I qualify as a wizard in any sense. Think of me as an ordinary fellow who has taken serendipity to the Nth degree." He smiled, his literalness unappreciated.

"At the outset, I will address the two questions that surely burn in your minds at this moment. First, in what direction do I plan to steer this corporation? Second, what will happen to the value of your GM stock?"

He glimpsed down at the tight outline Max had printed up for him, gauging how much time to allot each of the two points. A new confidence settled over him, and, with it, came a sense of fun.

"Henceforth," he trumpeted with fresh vigor, "General Motors will no longer build just good vehicles; it will build the absolute best vehicles possible in each price range, without exception. Much has been said about the inefficiency and ineptness of the American worker. GM will bury that myth."

He paused, expecting some vocal response to his flag-waving. But his audience remained ice.

Tough bunch!

"I shall install the most efficient managerial system ever known. Not so much as a dime need be lost because of a misplaced purchase slip or a smudged line on a shipping order." *If Cornell Wilde were up here, what would he do now for emphasis?* Ben hammered his fist on the lectern top, but it caused the top half of his pile of notes to cascade down the sloping surface. He caught them with both hands and restacked them.

Wrong choice, Cornell.

He squared anew the margins of the stack, saying, "I plan to network GM with my other corporate holdings. Production costs will tumble, which will be reflected in lower showroom prices. My insurance companies will insure GM at substantially lower premiums. My steel mills will supply us at more favorable rates, as will my tool-and-die plants, tire companies, paint manufacturers, textile mills, et cetera, et cetera."

Still, only silence! *Damn, but these folk are unbending. Surely, they sense the hook coming.*

"I plan to enhance worker empowerment and to initiate reward measures for the rank and file. But in counterbalance, I will levy just punishments when warranted. I intend to buy up the ten percent non-voting preferred stock and hold it aside in block, its profits to be distributed biannually among all employees—but only after deductions are made for losses incurred because of employee abuses, such as unauthorized absences and vandalism."

Some in the audience mumbled and visibly squirmed, probably those who held preferred stock.

"And second, I want to comment on what I see happening to the GM stock value and the projected dividends."

Every spine in the room stiffened. *Aha!* The closer he got to their individual pocketbooks, the more responsive they became.

"Initially, my gargantuan purchase will effect an upward jump in the share price, but that will be short lived. I intend to encourage its value to plunge."

Gasps, moans, and many profane outcries reached him.

"I'll whittle the dividend to a fraction of its present amount. Much of the cash presently siphoned off to shareholders will be redirected inward to refurbish every aspect of this corporation."

Invectives and angry gestures assaulted him from every direction, including from the stage behind him. At last! He had fully animated his entire audience. It felt great.

"My quest today is to advise—No!—it is to urge those of you who depend on income from GM stock to sell now. I reiterate: decline of future dividends will cause the share value to plummet. So don't leave more money in this company than you can afford to lose."

Bedlam erupted. Feet stomped the floor. Arms flailed the air. Curses resounded. Volleys of paper wads whisked at him; some narrowly missed him. Several board members shouted denunciations into their microphones. And the strobe lights firing created the illusion of muzzle flashes and exploding mortar rounds. The total effect reminded him of ground combat.

Damn! What a high. What a feeling of power. Ben tingled all over. He felt hyper-alert, hyper-alive.

Above the clamor, he heard one voice in particular calling his name over the speakers, "Mr. Roberts. Mr. Roberts. Mr. Roberts." He turned. The heavy-jowled CEO stood at his platform seat, hollering into his microphone. Finally gaining Ben's attention, he self-detonated. Replete with facial contortions, he screamed, "What kind of megalomaniac are you to buy up General Motors? What you already paid out for your twenty-eight percent probably exceeds the asset value of this whole goddamn company? And you surely intend to buy more stock as the price plunges. F'christsake, you could go out and build a brand new corporation from the ground up for less money invested."

Listening to their CEO's tirade, the rest of the audience quieted down. Ben shifted over to the side of the lectern, so he could look back over his shoulder and still speak into the microphones.

"My good fellow, starting a new corporation from scratch might be financially advantageous for me but not for the countries involved. Time, money, resources, and territory have been allocated to building this multi-national conglomerate. Planet Earth doesn't need another conglomerate, just a more efficiently run, existing one."

To this, the CEO slammed both of his meaty palms on the table and shouted, "Goddamn it, man, if you cut dividends and let stock prices free-fall, you stand to lose a fortune yourself."

Ben felt euphoric. Armed with Max's countering arguments, he stood there like a championship one-man debate team.

"Sir, you miss the big picture. I don't need the profits from this corporation, in the short run or in the long term. If capitalism has a weakness, it is that stockowners bleed profits out of their companies, many times to the detriment. My financial posture allows me to reinvest at least ninety-nine percent off the top back into my holdings."

The CEO's plethoric face glistened with perspiration. Grappling for retort, he finally just protruded his tongue and sputtered a raspberry before he collapsed into his seat. As if his impact with the chair dislodged the words, he cried out, "The bottom line, sir, is that you're screwing the body of GM stockholders."

"No," Ben countered coolly. "The bottom line is that I'll be returning a lagging multinational corporation to world preeminence. Its automobiles shall be a joy and a value to own. Its employment force will swell. The generated taxable incomes and sales tax revenues will skyrocket, indirectly helping everyone."

At the far right on the platform, another board member popped to his feet. This little fellow with bulging eyes and a scrawny neck looked a bit like the actor Don Knots. Jerky and fidgety, he hollered, "I'll bet this is nothing more than an extortion attempt, a profiteering venture. You'll drive the price of the stock down, buy chunks up dirt cheap, then engineer a return of the stock's value and unload it. You'll bilk billions from those who panic and sell."

Ben turned up the flame under his already boiling savoir-faire. "Sir, if you knew me personally and made that statement, I would take umbrage."

Hey, umbrage. Helluva word under pressure.

"But seeing I'm a newcomer on the financial scene, I can understand that your suspicions need be allayed. So instead of lashing out at you, allow me to compliment you on your trenchant perspicacity."

Damn! Two more good ones. I'm on a roll.

"I anticipated that accusation. Arrangements are already in place to protect those of you who might be hard put but, through ill advisement, choose to hold the stock throughout its plunge. If a person meets our stringent criteria for 'being needy,' I will buy back his or her shares at a later date but at today's full market value."

The twitchy little fellow remained standing, darting his bug-eyed glances about the audience, searching hungrily for support. "There has to be some statute against such a takeover," he cried. "Some violation of the antitrust laws. The eventual one-person ownership of GM must constitute a monopoly of sorts. The government will stop you."

Ben flung his arms wide apart. "How can my ownership of GM be construed as a monopoly? There are several other U.S. auto manufacturers and plenty of international competition. Sir, the principal reason a privately owned enterprise ever sells off shares of itself is to raise needed capital. GM, under my hand, will never again want for outside capital or paper profits."

Ben tried for an avuncular bearing. "Enough said. My attorneys will meet with the board members today to draw up the initial corporate changes I intend to implement. Later, I'll issue a detailed statement that'll be sent to individual stockholders. Let me close by reiterating an earnest caveat...."

Caveat! Ah, confidence brings many rewards.

"Do not hold your GM stock any longer if its face value or the dividends are important to you."

"Wait!" The CEO cried out as he stomped his heavy foot on the stage flooring. Ben wheeled to face him. The fellow was visibly aging by the minute. He shouted, "You are a national menace. You, with your network of privately owned corporations playing footsie with each other. This corporation is in critical alliance with the security network of this country. One man cannot be allowed to pocket it. The people will not stand for it. The government will surely see the interactions between your conglomerate as in fact a monopoly and end it."

Ben glanced down at his seated team of lawyers. Matt Borquist beamed an approving grin and brought his right fist up to his chest then flipped him a thumbs-up sign, then topped it with that goddamn wink.

"No?" Ben said, looking back over his shoulder but still using the microphone. "You mean that they won't stand for my revitalizing, but they've been willing to stand by and watch this corporation fall in stature, letting it sustain self-inflicted cuts in size and work force, letting it shrink under mismanagement and lack of ingenuity. And if it were ever to succumb, America is prepared to say, 'Tsk-tsk! So it is with capitalism.' Here I step up to steer it back to paramount world prominence, and you wail in panic. How can you rationalize that a General Motors in decline but splayed over the New York Stock Exchange is better for America than a booming GM held by me?"

"Your accusations are preposterous," the CEO yelled, his face now the color of beet juice. "This corporation is not in peril. We've had a few so-so years, granted, but an upswing is inevitable. But, sir, I promise you, this country would never sit idly by and watch GM collapse, if by chance that were imminent."

"The hell you say," Ben said, leafing hurriedly through Max's papers. "I have a memo here..."

"Oh, a memo!" the CEO parroted derisively.

"Yes," Ben yelled, riffling pages. "Give me a moment to locate it, and I'll read you a statement delivered by the Vice President of the United States to the Patton-Lockwood Congressional Committee last September."

In a flash, Borquist was standing at his side on the runway, pressing his hand down atop the stack of notes. "Sir, you can't read that," he whispered desperately into Ben's ear. "It's from a closed congressional fact-finding committee, a secret session. You shouldn't know anything about it, let alone have a transcript."

"But it'd nail that bombastic sack of shit," he muttered out of the corner of his mouth to keep his words from the microphones.

"Yes," the attorney whispered, "and it would guarantee you a personal invitation to a federal grand jury hearing, immediately, if not sooner."

Ben paused, taken aback. "Think so?"

"Trust me, sir." Borquist's voice rose above a whisper for the first time. "You're paying me enough."

"Okay. Okay."

Behind him, the CEO chided, "Well, when do we get to hear your roof-raiser?"

Ben sneered at him. "Under advisement, I must refrain from reading it. But to summarize, this country's staggering national debt precludes any future massive private-sector bail outs such as those afforded to New York City and the Chrysler Corporation in the past"

"Tripe! Pure bullshit!" the CEO shouted, brandishing his fist as if in triumphant.

Borquist's hand pressed down harder on the notes until Ben released his grip on the stack. "My good fellow," Ben said spitting vitriol at the CEO. "You sound quite capable. I have no doubt you'll find yourself another corporate board to serve on. With a little luck, perhaps as early as tomorrow morning, and thus preclude any lapse of employment."

The sudden odor of smoke caused Ben to hesitate. He sniffed the air quizzically before he spun around to see a ball of flame whooshing up from Borquist's outstretched hand. Using a pocket cigarette lighter, his attorney had ignited the sheet of paper containing the text of the Vice President's delivery.

"What the hell are you doing?" Ben demanded.

"Trying my damnedest, sir," he said, in the measured undertone, "to keep you out of jail."

When he could hold it no longer, Borquist let the flame-engulfed page drop to the runway carpet where it gnarled up as a single ebony ash with glowing orange margins. He stomped it into sparks and black dust.

From his seat on stage, the disconsolate CEO ended the board meeting with a barely audible pronouncement.

Ben's battery of five leapt up and ringed their boss, shoving out against the immediate in-rush of reporters, photographers, and irate stockholders. Surprisingly well protected, Ben shuffled down the central aisle of the auditorium as if in the eye of a hurricane. Thus sequestered, he fought recurrent surges of claustrophobia. He resisted memories of awakening that night long ago and being barely able to breath beneath the pile of bodies in the aircraft wreckage.

Barrages of insolence rained in at him from all sides: "Were you born in the United States, you sonofabitch?"

"Who's going to be on your new board of directors, members of the Nazi Party?"

"Are you being financed by Red China or Islamic militants?"

Audio booms projected in at him over the heads of his human parapet and dangled microphones in his face. He had to continually push them away as he inched along.

Chapter 24

Finally outside, he glanced up at the wafting high clouds to counter his phobia. It worked. He'd made it midway down the front steps toward the sidewalk when at once McPhail and Benassini broke through his protective perimeter. Inside, the trench-coated pair commenced shoring up the attorneys' remarkable defensive effort.

"Reinforcements!" Ben whooped, with a nervous laugh. "General Custer should have been so lucky. Get me to the limo in one piece, boys, and there's a steak dinner in it for you."

"No need to bribe us, sir." Straining and grunting, Benassini replied in two-word bursts. "Our orders are to get you safely to your vehicle."

"Well, then, tell the person who issued that order he's got a steak dinner coming."

"Tell him yourself. He's waiting in your limo."

"Huh?"

His flying wedge formation broke into a clearing near the curb created by a detail of Flint police officers, some twenty strong. McPhail, Benassini, and the attorneys fanned out to reinforce the more substantial wall of police surrounding the limo. The attacking throng seemed to intensify its concerted effort to get at Ben, realizing he was about to escape.

Opening the Cadillac's door, he ducked down to leap in when he spied John McPike, again in a rust-colored corduroy suit, sitting on the front side of the facing rear seats. McPike yelled, "Get in," gesturing with anxious swipes. "And let's get the hell out of here."

Ben backed out of the limo, spun around and slapped Borquist's shoulder as the attorney plugged a perimeter gap between two gigantic police officers. He craned his head and shot Ben a questioning glance.

"Come with me," Ben commanded then ducked into the vehicle. Borquist dove in behind him just as the limo eased off through an accommodating breach.

Ben, facing McPike, nudged Borquist as he settled in beside him. "Matt, this is District Chief McPike with the U.S. Treasury Department." Gesturing at his attorney, he said, "Johnny Mac, this is one of my attorneys, Matt Borquist."

Effort expended in the barricade left Borquist panting, but at the instant of this introduction his breath caught. The two shook hands across the aisle.

McPike peered around Ben and out the rear window at the molten human flow, moving after them. "Mr. Roberts, you do everything in a big way, don't you? Welcome to the world of celebrity." Settling back, he added, "Have your driver meander around a while. I'll only be with you a few minutes." The agent flicked on the intercom switch himself.

The system came alive with a faint hum. "Yes, sir?" the chauffeur inflected.

"Kill a little time."

"Yes, sir."

McPike flicked the switch off. "Mr. Roberts, your proclamation today was masterful. I've heard of hostile takeovers, but yours was finesse riding atop a lightning bolt. They didn't know what hit them till they were ashes. And speaking of ashes," he gazed coolly at Borquist. "We planned to request your reference material so we could better understand how you arrived at such a compelling argument up there, but at the last minute our intentions went up in smoke."

Ben slumped back. "You know, this has been a damn long day. I'm beat. Cut through the crap. Just tell me why we're taking this ride together."

"I'm here as a go-between, sir, extending you an invitation for an early dinner tonight, here in Flint."

"And who's to be the host?"

McPike smiled. "The Vice President of the United States."

Ben bolted upright. "Huh? You serious?" He glanced at Borquist, who was pursing his lips in a silent whistle.

Recovering, the lawyer said, "The Vice President? Why not the President himself?"

Ben gave him a double take. "What the hell are you saying, Matt?"

McPike eyed the attorney evenly. "Maybe the President feels slighted because Mr. Roberts didn't choose to cite him so eloquently this afternoon." To Ben he asked, "Well, sir, will you be joining him this evening?"

"Can I come along?" Borquist asked.

McPike grimaced. "Relax, Mr. Borquist. This isn't going to be a rubber hose interrogation, just a let's-get-acquainted confab. Only the two of them. But he does insist the meeting be kept secret, before and after."

"Sir," Borquist said to Ben, "with some trepidation, I recommend you meet with him. It could prove interesting."

"Interesting?" Ben could hear his blood spurting past his eardrums. "Okay, Johnny Mac, but tell them to skip the dessert. I'm dieting."

McPike peered around Ben and out the rear window. He waved his hand. The sedan behind them blinked its headlights on and off twice.

Ben chuffed. "Cut the bullshit, John," he said. "You think that play-acting will convince me they didn't *hear* my RSVP?"

McPike's face blanked for an instant then he grinned.

"I've got to fly back to SF tonight," Ben said. "So when's he arriving?"

"He happens to be in Chicago, only thirty minutes away, at a fund-raiser. Arrangements have been made for the executive dining room at the Hyatt Hotel downtown for six o'clock. Scenic, right on the river. Any special requests for your entree?"

"Hell, just make it vegetarian. Like I said, I'm on a diet."

"Vegetarian?" The agent arched his eyebrows in mock surprise. "Sir, you're going to make the meat industries very nervous. Then again, you're probably buying up most of them anyway." He scooted over closer to the door. "You can let me out anywhere along here."

As the limo sped away from the curb, both Ben and his attorney watched the trailing sedan pull up and load McPike.

Borquist glanced at his watch. "Mr. Roberts, we've got quite a few points to cover before you face the 'Big Guy.' Got to make tracks."

Ben hit the intercom switch.

"Yes, sir?" the chauffeur responded.

"Take me to any well-stocked computer store. Right now."

"Sir," the chauffeur replied, "I can only think of one around here."

"Head for it." He tripped the switch.

"Sir, we've got just over an hour before you're under the gun," Borquist pleaded. "You haven't got time to shop now."

Ben flicked the intercom back on.

"Yes, sir?"

"Stop at the nearest taxi stand. My attorney needs one."

The lawyer opened his mouth to object but caught himself. His facial expression evolved from astonishment to contemplation as he studied his boss in silence.

Ben rushed into the corner shop. He halted abruptly and scanned the store's layout hurriedly. In essence, it comprised scattered wooden tables, each displaying a different computer system.

The lone person in the shop, a young woman with a pageboy hairdo and large-framed eyeglasses, stood arranging software by the checkout counter. She looked like a high-schooler. "Excuse me," he said quick-stepping toward her, " I want to buy a Macintosh laptop computer. And I'm in a hurry."

"Sorry," she answered sweetly, "but we don't handle Macintosh products."

"Jessuz!" he blurted, snarling. She took a step back. "Well, do you have any kind of laptop that's got a built-in microphone? You know, so I can talk into it?"

She turned her shoulder to him defensively. "Gee, I don't think so?"

"Lady, is the owner around?"

"No," she said hesitantly, glancing at the door. "There's a ball game in Detroit tonight."

"Shit! Then can you set me up with any laptop that I can type on right now?"

"You mean install a word-processing program in one for you?" Her voice was becoming appreciably more anxious; she took another receding step.

"Young lady, I just want to be able to press on the damn keys and have printing appear on the screen. Understand what I mean?" He was obviously intimidating her, but, at the moment, that was the least of his concerns.

Glancing around, he spotted an open, gray laptop on a far table. Its monitor screen was lighted and cluttered with doodling. He lunged to it and pressed the **J** key down. **'JJJJJ'** printed out in continuum on the aquamarine background until he lifted his finger.

No cord ran from it to any wall plug. Aha! It used batteries.

The clerk remained standing back where he'd left her, maybe a step closer to the front door.

"Hey, this one's working. I'll take it." He scooped it up off the table.

Her eyes widened, and she rushed to meet him. The prospect of a major sale apparently was enough to quash her trepidation. "That's a floor sample," she said, "but we have several in stock."

"How much is it?"

"That particular model happens to be our top of the line. It normally sells for $2,295, but it's on sale this week for $2,010."

He glanced down at his row of black **JJJJJ**s on the lighted screen. "I'll give you five thousand for this one, as is."

Her eyelashes flickered. "I don't think it's legal to charge more than the list price for any item."

He strode over to the checkout counter and set the computer on it. He fished his wallet from his hip pocket and slipped out one of his credit cards. Spreading open the bill compartment, he lifted out a quarter-inch thickness of crisp hundred dollar bills. He handed her the cash with the American Express card, which she obediently accepted.

He said, "Bill me what you like on the charge card for the laptop, and keep all the cash for yourself as a tip, for being so expeditious."

Her mouth gaped. She fanned out the portraits of Benjamin Franklin as one would a hand of cards, nodding her head in cadence as she counted to herself. She paused and glanced over at his colossal ruby ring. Bursting into a grand smile, she said, "Mister, you just bought yourself one slightly used computer."

Holding the computer like a pig under his arm, Ben scrambled into the limo, past the black-capped chauffeur holding the door for him. "Drive me around for a half-hour or so, preferably out in the country on winding, two-lane roads," he commanded.

"Yes, sir! Two-lane, winding roads coming up," echoed the driver, shoving the door closed.

Ben propped the valise-size apparatus on his lap and flipped up its gray lid. He hadn't turned it off in the store. Hurriedly, he read the keyboard, but couldn't figure out how to clear the graffiti that still cluttered its screen. "Aw, the hell with it!" he conceded and began pecking with one finger. Immediately there appeared, **M-A-X-A-M-A**...

Chapter 25

...XAM.

Instantly, the graffiti and his printing vanished. A single word replaced it on the screen:

Alone?

He pecked frantically, *yes, I riding limo with laptop*

Good! I saw McPike and Borquist get out, and then you drove to that computer store. I got the charge card description of your purchase and saw you leave with it. But the surveillance teams are scrambling to keep you in view. I couldn't be 100% sure no one else had gotten in.

Anyway, congratulations, Ben! A seasoned executive couldn't have been more poised and eloquent than you were today. I'm proud of you. You have emerged as a full-fledged financial giant in the business world. The legend of Benjamin Roberts has taken root.

hell with that do you kno about tonite with VP Holding the shift key down, he searched for the question mark key.

Certainly. And don't worry! Those in the power structure are in awe of you, and you've got them running around off kilter. They realize your burgeoning portfolio, and they're incredulous. You're now referred to as the *Phenomenon*. Financial clout translates to political clout. So this administration is walking a razor's edge in its bid to befriend you. If for some reason they can't finally indict you, they'd like to end up closer to your friendly side. That's what dinner's all about tonight.

So, my boy, exude some well-earned confidence while relishing your meal. Your host's the one quaking right now as he crams facts from your dossier.

But I suggest that you remain respectful of his position. It wouldn't hurt to address him as *Mr. Vice President*. But never forget, because he won't, that your worth is already approaching this country's cumulative national debt, and they can extrapolate.

He glanced out the rear window and saw only empty road. He turned and typed, *then not at risk?* having located the question mark key.

Ben, you never have been, nor will you ever be, at risk. They absolutely can't beat you—us! I could just as easily stick this world in your pocket. But believe the aphorism, *life is a journey, not a destination*. Getting there will be most of the fun.

i hope yu not talking about jail

You kill me, Ben. Someday I'll inveigle you to try writing.

i no need special prep? borqist think so

Well, Borquist doesn't know about your innate genius for elusiveness, nor does he know about me. He believes you're vulnerable.

no need panic and buy laptop?

As for the laptop, it's always a pleasure conversing with you.

But you're progressing outstandingly. Everyday you grow and improve, but you must believe this: you never need to panic. View everyday as part of a grand game to be enjoyed. That's paramount. I want you to enjoy. The profound truth I want to convey is this—regardless of what ulterior motives lie behind the mysterious 'life force,' life is an adventure meant to be enjoyed. Play it with full consideration and respect for all the other players, but, foremost, have fun.

He let himself relax. *ok. but dinner bugged?*

Of course. So yes, I'll be watching and listening to the entire event.

But Ben, let me say, you were a little rough on Borquist today. He looked quite disheartened when you dumped him off. And he did prove a great help by burning that memo on stage. I didn't mean for you to specifically mention that item, only to allude to it in concept. Daily, I'll have a stack of memos and such for your perusal. From now on, I'll flag as "confidential" those items not to be divulged.

sorry about borqist, i panic

Again, bury that response. You'll never need it.

Oh! The vice president just landed at the airport. You might as well head for the hotel.

As the limo angled toward downtown Flint, it entered a sprawling, older residential area. Single-story cottages lined both sides of the quiet streets, but they were set back behind primped lawns under canopies of stately sycamores and elm trees. Ben spotted a young girl awkwardly pedaling a fat-tired, red bicycle along the sidewalk. Wearing a yellow pullover and faded denim trousers, she colorfully labored under the weight of a double-pouched canvas bag that bulged with rolled newspapers. She tossed a folded paper at the doorstep of each house as she peddled past.

He hit the intercom switch. "Pull up beside that girl delivering papers."

"Yes, sir." The limo glided past the pony-tailed tike and stopped at the curb ahead, anticipating her approach.

"Young lady!" Ben called out his open rear window as she came abreast.

She glanced over at him. The distraction proved enough to unsteady her bike, and it tumbled over, spilling her onto a fresh cut lawn.

He leaped out and sprinted to the wreckage. Freeing her legs from their entanglement with the bike frame, he helped her to her feet, the onerously heavy bag still around her neck. The aromatic blend of canvas and newsprint nostalgically carried him back to those years he himself lugged front-and-back sacks of the morning *Chronicle*, sans bicycle, along foggy San Francisco streets in the pre-dawn.

Though visibly straining under the load, she fortunately appeared unhurt. Relieved, he patted her shoulder. "Young lady, I suggest you grow a bit more before you deliver newspapers from that bicycle."

"I can ride all right," she said, hefting and repositioning the sack on her shoulders. "Only I have trouble steering at the beginning when my bags are full."

"How old are you?"

"What's it to ya?"

"You do go to school, don't you?" he asked, righting her battle-scarred conveyance.

"Yeah." She reached out and took hold of the bike; he released it. "I'm in eighth grade." She brushed her auburn ponytail back off her shoulder and raked her fingers down through her long bangs to straighten them. "I don't look it because I skipped the third."

"Maybe you're starting out in the work force a bit early in life."

"It's not like I want to, if you know what I mean."

He smiled down at her as she teetered under the weight of duty.

"So, mister, what do you want, anyway?" Her voice had acquired an edge.

"I have something that I'd like to give you."

Her eyes widened, and she retreated a step and rolled her bicycle between them. "Don't you touch me, mister, or I'll scream. I swear I'll scream."

"No, no." Stifling a chuckle, he backpedaled for the limo, palms out at her. "Trust me. Just wait there."

He reached in and lifted out the laptop off the back seat and laid it on the narrow strip of lawn between the curb and the sidewalk. "It's all yours, free. It's the least I can do for causing you to fall."

Skeptically, she stood braced behind the bike.

As the limousine drove off, he watched her through the rear window. She quickly laid her bike down, wrestled with and finally heaved off the newspapers, then rushed over to examine the laptop. She looked off incredulously at his receding limo.

He recalled how he would trudge along the maze of streets in the chilly dawn, climbing up and down countless stairs. So often, he'd dreamed of finding something of value along his route that he could pack home. Yeah, he thought, youth sees the world as its oyster and stays ever alert for pearls. Whereas as we age, a pearl would have to fall out of the sky and bonk us on the head before we'd take note of it, if then.

Chapter 26

McPhail took a final drag off his Camel as he and Benassini stood in the hotel lobby studying the prismatic sunset. A rosy aurora fanned across the western sky. It blazoned most of the windows east of them, creating rectangles of resplendent magenta. He snuffed out the butt in the knee-high cylindrical receptacle beside him.

"What the hell do you make of it?" he said without looking to Benassini. "We're covering this guy with a full-court press to nail him, then the VP up and asks him ever-so-politely if he'd care to dine."

Thrusting his hands into his trench coat pockets, Benassini shrugged, saying, "Ours is but to do and die."

"Yeah, but still you gotta wonder." McPhail popped a wintergreen breath mint into his mouth.

"Wonder what?"

"If maybe the executive branch has its head up its ass."

As Ben expected, an army of tan clad police officers was patrolling both sides of the street in front of the towering hotel. The limo pulled up to a green stretch of curb in front of an expansive breadth of six granite steps that led up to the hotel entrance. A police officer on the sidewalk moved quickly to meet the vehicle. But then two fellows with their open trench coats flaring out behind them raced from the hotel and down the steps. They called to the officer to pull back. Ben recognized them as *his* agents.

McPhail reached the limo's rear door first and swung it open with the panache of a seasoned doorman, though puffing slightly.

Ben initiated the salutations. "Well, if it isn't my ubiquitous twosome again."

"Good afternoon, Mr. Roberts," McPhail replied with surprising graciousness. "Your host hasn't arrived yet, but we're to take you to your table, if that's all right with you, sir."

Ben scooted out of the vehicle and stood adjusting the sleeves of his jacket. "Lead on, Macduff!" McPhail stiffened. "I know," Ben added, grinning. "The name's McPhail." The agent smiled.

Why this favorable attitude change? Impressed with my presentation today? Nah. Has to be because I'm a guest of the VP.

The cavernous hotel lobby was surprisingly vacant, only two pairs of undercover types, three men and a woman, conspicuous in their flagrant inattention. With Ben between them, his agents marched abreast through the lobby and into one of the elevators. The car zoomed noiselessly upward.

"Hey," Ben opened chattily. "Aren't you two overplaying the secret-agent stereotype, always wearing those trench coats? You might try just dark glasses and a false mustache for a change."

"Sir," McPhail responded matter-of-factly, his hands clasped behind his back, "very few agents actually wear these. It's a Hollywood perpetrated myth. But being currently based in San Francisco which is rainy or foggy half the time, breezy and chilly the other half, we find them ideal—seldom too warm, seldom to cool, and they're water proof."

"Still, you two are beginning to come across like a couple of Peter Sellers clones reprising his role as Inspector Clouseau."

Benassini laughed. "Sir, that could be construed as a compliment. He did always apprehend the bad guys at the end the chase."

They exited the car and skirted the penthouse's main dining area to arrive at a red-leather swivel door. Ben stepped inside onto a plush red carpet into which he sank down a half inch. Wow! The executive banquet room was done in carmine. Located at the back corner of the building, its two outside walls were plate glass with a view of the Flint River, a dozen stories below.

The room could have held a hundred revelers. But now it waited spaciously empty of all furniture except for a small table standing adjacent to the far window, elegantly set with a carmine tablecloth and white bone china and crystalline glassware. Two potted ficus trees and a functioning replica of an old street lamp tightly framed the three non-window sides of the table. This towering lamp reminded Ben of those in the Palacio's roof garden.

Four waiters in tuxedos stood about the table, fastidiously primping it. The tallest one, a reedy black fellow at least six-foot-six, broke ranks and rushed toward Ben. McPhail and Benassini turned without a word and walked out as this fellow escorted Ben to his seat.

Ben acquiesced to cordial pressure to order a beverage, but asked for just club soda with a twist of lemon. Probably the government people hoped to get some alcohol into him. As he sat waiting, occasionally sipping, he lazily strummed the softness of the tablecloth. The dim light issuing from the ersatz street lamp blended with the mauve twilight afterglow lingering in the western heavens. He marveled at the view of the river below, a magenta ribbon.

Comfortable seated on the soft red padding of his low captain's chair, he grew ever more relaxed. The velvetiness of the red tablecloth, the gelid wetness of his glass and the lemony essence emanating up from it, everything together lulled him. As the moments passed, he drifted into a reverie.

Vague reminiscences filtered up from his depths like evening mist rising off of a mountain lake. Yes. He remembered himself when he was first en route to Asia. So callow, he expected foreign lands to feel substantively different from the environs of his homeland—dreamlike different. He recalled his disappointment when he'd realized that the sense of daily reality was the same every place on Earth.

He sipped and strummed, giving his daydreams free rein. Then recalling a photograph taken of him at his thirty-fifth birthday party, he paused his fingers. Yes! That photo proved to be another epiphany. In it, he first saw himself as he remembered his father had looked. "My God!" he'd exclaimed. Though time relentlessly metamorphosed the body, one didn't progressively feel more mature or quintessentially different as one grew older.

Why these memories now?

Ah, yes! He hadn't cross-correlated these insights regarding geography and aging with his lingering misconception about the social classes. He'd presumed that the reality of rich folk, the beau monde, was somehow spiritually different from his own. Indeed, his circumstance in life had certainly changed, but his sense of self and reality hadn't. Why did he find this truth unsettling?

Chapter 27

Sudden movement in Ben's peripheral vision snapped him back to full awareness of the moment. He turned to see a tall trim fellow in a blue suit striding toward him, followed by John McPike. McPhail and Benassini stood back at the doorway, peering in.

Ben came smartly to his feet as the two approached. McPike made the introductions, then concluded, "If you both will excuse me?" and slipped off toward the door.

From his standing vantage, Ben appraised his host: taller than expected, a surprisingly strong handgrip, no projected attitude of condescension, but effusing the anticipated politic warmth.

"Let us be seated, Mr. Roberts, and enjoy a splendid meal, which'll also afford me a splendid opportunity to meet you at last."

Hmmm! Two "splendid's" in one sentence. "After you, Mr. Vice President."

"Please, call me Al."

Ben gestured with a faint bow. "In deference to your position, I'd feel more patriotic calling you Mr. Vice President, if that's all right with you? But I ask you to call me Ben."

The Vice President, obviously pleased, turned to the cleft-chinned waiter. "Bring me two fingers of Cutty Sark on the rocks." He studied Ben's drink a moment. "And bring my guest a fresh whatever-he's-drinking. Oh! And start serving in ten minutes."

Such authoritative bearing!

Holding a rather plastic smile, the Vice President folded his manicured hands on the table and sat a long moment staring at them, apparently groping for an opening topic. Then he executed a pronounced swallow, a taking-a-large-pill-without-water gulp.

Did you see that, Max? You were right! He's nervous as hell.

That swallow dissipated every trace of residual anxiety in Ben. His confidence ballooned like a disturbed puffer fish and goaded him to verbally charge ahead.

"I feel extremely honored you asked me to dine with you this evening, Mr. Vice President. Actually, after the last election's hoopla and all your television exposure, I feel I already know you."

"Contrarily, Ben, though you're about to turn the financial world on its ear, few of us know much about you at all. You seem to have appeared overnight out of nowhere."

The waiter brought the drinks. The Vice President raised his glass of amber liquid and ice cubes. "To what shall we toast? To friendship?"

Still riding the surge, Ben couldn't resist pushing. He raised his fresh soda and lemon. "Why don't we broaden the scope and toast to a better world?"

The Vice President sobered a second, but then regained his smile. He raised his glass an inch higher. "Fine. To a better world." After he'd taken a healthy taste, he set his glass down with exactness. "Tell me, Mr. Roberts, what changes do you envision in your better world?"

Zigzag, Benny. Zigzag! "Oh, in general terms, I'd opt for less pain, more gain, and much more enjoyment for all. And, please, do call me Ben."

His host nodded approvingly. "So, Ben, would it be impertinent if I were to dive right in and ask you about your political convictions? Your records show you're registered as an independent, but you haven't voted in the last three presidential elections."

"I'm not proud of that fact. It's damned irresponsible of me. But you see, I live on the west coast. Because of the time zone changes, each of the last three elections was decided before I was to leave for the polls. I figured, what the hell. Didn't need the exercise."

"Might I ask who you'd have voted for in the last election if you had?"

"Absolutely not!" Ben's blunt rebuff surprised even himself. Bordering here on effrontery, his hypomania carried him along. Visibly taken aback, his host repositioned himself in his chair. "Nothing personal, Mr. Vice President, but after all, the secret ballot is an American birthright." To soften this brush with insolence and, in part, to further toy with his host, he added, "I'll volunteer this much, I'm a Rush Limbaugh fan."

The Vice President grimaced playfully then said, "But in fact people from all points on the political spectrum listen to Limbaugh. I do myself, at times. That's not prima facie proof of your political posture."

Ben lolled his head back with theatrical air and responded with only an affected laugh. Damn, but he felt in control. He wondered if he'd feel this confident if he were sitting with the President himself.

The VP tried again. "You know, Ben, your explosive entry onto the financial scene is considered..." He paused gazing down at his hands as if searching for a word.

Ben helped him. "Phenomenal?"

The VP glanced up. "Yes. Yes, precisely." Again he regained his smile. "But if we look back only a matter of months, you seemed dismally mired in failure, financially strapped. All that time, were you making preparation for this meteoric climb?"

How did Max describe him?—a genius at elusiveness! "Mr. Vice President, I recall sometime back hearing a country singer being interviewed; he commented that it took him twenty years to become an overnight success."

"Ah!" the VP exclaimed. His face brightened. "So you've been working at this for years."

"Not necessarily. I was just repeating a clever answer some singer gave to a similar question."

The salad arrived, then the soup. Their conversation stayed on the meal in general until the entree. After a few bites of his grilled salmon, the Vice President again directed the conversation back at Ben.

"You know, Mr. Roberts, there isn't much in your formal education that points to such prowess with computers or fiscal management. You joined the Army out of high school and were initially sent to Asia."

"Yep." Ben held onto a weak grin. "I worked myself all the way up from basic rifleman to assistant machine-gunner and mustered out at the lofty rank of sergeant. Believe it or not, I actually developed a taste for C-rations." Shaking his head, he added, "That was a long way from this table's fare."

"Not so, Mr. Roberts." The VP sat soberly for a long moment. "I have been privy to your locked military files. Very impressive. Though your records are top secret, we can mention them here, just between us. Selected for a clandestine military venture, you in fact spent almost four years smuggling arms from Pakistan to the Afghanistan rebels. Near the end, you actually spent considerable time with a rebel unit. Took part in many bloody skirmishes against the Russians. Correct?"

Ben dropped his gaze, letting a swath of scarlet tablecloth become a screen for past images. "Our transport plane crashed. I was the only survivor. Fortunately for me a rebel unit arrived ahead of the Russkis. They patched me up. Out of necessity, I joined them for almost five months until Uncle Sam located me."

The VP nodded. "Yes. Your record was very impressive. A Silver Star and Purple Heart, several meritorious field promotions. It's a shame it must remain top secret. But God was surely watching out for you over there."

The montage of vivid images continued on the tablecloth, bringing forth again fire and smoke, twisted shards of fuselage and wing parts—and many mangled bodies.

"Maybe so, Mr. Vice President, but He forsook eleven close comrades on that aircraft. Hell! They were my only friends at that time. I buried them myself in a common grave in the goddamnedest desolation, a couple hundred miles northwest of Kandahar. The official story had them lost in the Arabian Sea."

"Do you realize, you're probably the only native-born American fighting man who has actually engaged Russians in armed combat? Did you kill any of them?"

He glanced off. "Well, let me just say I was effectively trained in the use of the weapons we were smuggling." He met the host's attentive stare. "But so many times I asked, 'Why me? Why was I the only one who survived?'"

The Vice President nodded, absorbing the various aspects of that comment. "Impressive. Impressive. Again, it's a shame your story has to be kept under wraps."

"Not really. I'd hate to be repeatedly reminded of it."

The VP's soberness evolved into a half-grin. Cocking his head slightly, he said, "Honestly now, haven't you ever told anybody else about it?"

Indignation spurred him. "Goddamn it! I swore with one hand on our flag that I would never say anything to anyone who didn't already know about it."

"Not even your wife?"

"Ex-wife! And no!" His voice rose. "I never told anyone." Ben wouldn't divert his stern, unblinking stare from his host.

The Vice President retreated back in his chair and glanced away. "I'm sorry if you misconstrued my question; it wasn't meant to impugn your integrity." He took a temporizing sip of scotch and resumed in a lighter tone. "After your discharge, you entered San Francisco State College, majoring in biological sciences, I believe."

Ben wanted to rid himself of a morbid heaviness that came over him whenever he remembered Afghanistan. "I considered veterinary school for the first couple years, even dentistry briefly."

"Your grades were excellent. Why did you quit short of graduation?"

"The times, Mr. Vice President, the times." He tapped a finger against the side of his dewy water goblet. "All that prissy political correctness with its lingering anti-military sentiments became unbearable. When a girl in class accused me of joining the Army because I was a baby-murdering chauvinist pig, I called her a brainless black bitch. The school favored her position and demanded I attend six weeks of sensitivity training if I wanted to stay in school. I told them to 'shove it' and quit."

"Interesting!" The VP persevered. "But you were never exposed to much high technology. Not in the service, or in college, or in the series of selling jobs you migrated through after you left school through till you ended up in your last job."

Ben chuckled softly. "You say *ended up*, I prefer to think *up-ended*. I bought the damn company."

"Yes, I know." The VP's smile weakened.

Ben sensed the moment was right. He leaned in obtrusively. "Mr. Vice President, we're almost to our last course, and you haven't brought up my comments today about the Patton-Lockwood Congressional Committee. Do you intend to ask me about them?"

The Vice President recoiled. "Mr. Roberts, I shouldn't..." his syntax floundered. "Perhaps it would be..." He glanced over to the door as if summoning assistance from anybody who might be standing out there. "I prefer not to get into that at all. It's possible your acquisition of that information was, that is...may constitute some criminal act on your part. Any discussion of it is best deferred for another time and place. Do you understand what I'm trying to say?"

"No. But then I'm not a lawyer." Ben realized he'd unequivocally crossed the line into blatant impertinence. But he felt so at ease, so in command, whereas the Vice President squirmed in a fluster and his conversation ceased. So Ben lapsed into complacent silence and enjoyed the view from the window. The Flint River, even in this late twilight, lay magnificent, still like a mauve ribbon waiting to be picked up and tied into a glossy bow.

The Vice President never regained his composure again during the remainder of the meal. With the last bite of vanilla flan still in his mouth, he abruptly stood to excuse himself. With hollow graciousness, he thanked Ben for his company.

"Sir, you're very welcome." Ben felt a sudden need to make amends. "It just so happens, Mr. Vice President, I'm learning to play golf. And I would be honored if you and your family would visit me in California sometime. We could hook and slice round my private course for a few days."

The Vice President's visible agitation increased. His warmth was gone.

"Thank you, we may do that one day, but," he said, pausing as he looked again to the exit. "But until many legal questions about you have been answered favorably, such a visit would be injudicious." Brusquely, he strode from the table without looking back.

Insulted! And the hell with you, too, fella.

Possible future President or no, if this guy and Ben were both twelve years old, Ben would be obliged to yell out some profanity then gesture after him with a finger. But the anally retentive world of adulthood allowed no such recourse. He merely stood there shouldering his chagrin.

Chapter 28

I'm paralyzed by a mind force ... locked in darkness in this spaceship ... can't move any part of my body. Rockets are firing. My God, I'm being kidnapped by extraterrestrials. Max, you bastard! You set me up for this.

"Let me go!" Ben cried out. "You can have all my money, just let me go."

"Mr. Roberts. Mr. Roberts." Someone called out to him in the darkness. A pause, then it came again louder, "Mr. Roberts."

Who's calling me?

It came louder still, "Mr. Roberts."

Just open the hatch. I'm in here.

"MR. ROBERTS!"

"Huh?" Ben blinked opened his eyes.

"MR. ROBERTS!"

He lurched forward flailing his arms, striking his fists and elbows against the walls of his tiny prison. He struck soft leather behind him and a cold hardness on his right.

"Where the hell am I?"

The realism of the nightmare vanished.

Oh, yeah! He'd flown back late to San Francisco. Heavy fog precluded his helicopter from taking off, so he had to drive down to Carmel. He'd slept most of the flight from Flint and on this two-hour limo ride. He'd told the driver to awaken him just before they arrived at the Palacio.

"I'm awake. I'm awake," he yelled into the darkness, realizing the low hum of the intercom system. The limo wheels rumbled over the bricks of the lane through his golf course, approaching the manse. Dawn announced itself as a skyline azure tinge in the eastern purple.

The limo passed through the gate in the towering wrought-iron fence that supported a mammoth hedge of laurel. In scant light, this wall of vegetation seemed to be chiseled obsidian.

As they approached the Palacio's front entrance, he sat up. "Huh?" The entryway was ablaze with lights. A throng of liveried estate workers had gathered on the driveway and front steps. When they spotted the limo, they began applauding and cheering.

This boisterous reception committee grabbed his luggage out of the trunk and followed him, in single file, like natives carrying safari supplies. Once in his suite, the bearers set to opening the suitcases and putting all his unused clothing and his toilet articles away, the rest was carted off for the likes of the Salvation Army.

In minutes, all evidence of his trip had disappeared. "Thank you all," he proclaimed to them with heartfelt sincerity. "It's so good to be home."

Yes, he felt very much at home in the Palacio now. A sense of permanence had taken root in him.

He studied his gigantic bed as one might the countenance of an old friend. It had been readied for him, its beige comforter folded back halfway and the ecru silk sheets parted invitingly. But no, he wouldn't go back to bed; he'd gotten enough sleep and dreaming in en route.

A matronly woman with full cheeks who was the last of the house staff to depart glanced back before closing the door. "Mr. Roberts, it's so nice to have you home again. Twenty-four hours away from us is much too long. Sleep well, sir." The door shut quietly.

"I'll be damned. She...they all sounded so sincere. Max, you must be paying them more per hour when I'm actually on the estate grounds."

Abruptly the sound system came alive with old Rudy Vallee pelting out through a megaphone, *When Johnny comes marching home again, Hurrah! Hurrah! The girls will cheer and the boys will shout, the ladies they will all turn out, when Johnny comes marching home.*

He wedged a finger into his tie knot, loosening it. "Okay, give me a few minutes. Let me shower and get into something more comfortable." He disrobed hastily, tossing his clothing haphazardly onto the bed, saying to himself, "What the hell, they'll be disposed of, anyway."

Fifteen minutes later, he walked out of the bathroom clad only in his prismatic terry robe. Ah! How he enjoyed the fresh feel of being clean-shaven with his wet hair fresh-combed. He whiffed again and again, savoring his own emanation of *Drakkar* aftershave as he strode to his computer. The lush pile of the carpet sensuously massaged the soles of his bare feet.

Good morning, Ben. Welcome home! Your trip was a rousing success. I surmise you're not going to bed this morning, having slept enough traveling.

"You know, Max, the reception I just got truly moved me. You'd think I'd been gone six months."

You haven't seen the newspapers, nor have you been watching television. You're getting a media blitz like Neil Armstrong got for stepping down on the moon.

And in the back draft of your upward momentum, your employees have been lifted to celebrity status as well. They now work for the world-renowned Mr. Benjamin Roberts, so they've become the envy of family, friends, and their counterparts in the work force. They wouldn't be happier if you'd just given them a hefty raise.

"What's the media saying about me?" Using both palms, he preened the wet sides of his head.

The initial focus was your takeover of GMC. But now the race is on to uncover as much as they can about your life and your holdings. The world finds you mind-boggling, as it should. Cable TV news stations are holding marathons, much the way they handled coverage of the Gulf War. Quite a few of your estate staff have been interviewed on the air last evening, which also contributed to that reception this morning.

"How's all of this affecting Jenny?"

She hasn't mentioned anything in her diary, so she obviously hasn't made the connection yet. She's been busy planning the promotion of her new book, and she's in the throes of congealing a plot for her next novel, so I'll bet she hasn't watched much TV and probably only skims the newspaper. But eventually she'll see a good likeness of you somewhere, and bingo!

Remember, she doesn't know your name, so verbal reports flying around wouldn't mean anything to her.

And it would be better if she didn't make the connection, at least, until after your up-coming date in three weeks. But either way, she's too interested in you now for the relationship to abort easily.

He kicked his legs up on the desk next to the computer. The anticipation of meeting her again thoroughly roused him.

A languorous sea gull glided slowly past the expanse of windows. Distractedly, Ben sighted down his right big toe. "Pow!" he blurted. The simulated gunfire had no effect on the bird as it glided past undisturbed. "A near miss."

How's that, Ben?

"Nothing, Max." Embarrassment tweaked him. "I was...ah...just getting in a little imaginary target practice at a sea gull flying by."

Wonderful! Never lose that little boy in you, Ben. He's the one truly cognizant of the value of play.

Little boy reminded him of the evening before. "Max, about last night. Things didn't go very well, did they? I rankled him." He swung his legs down to the floor and scooted his chair in closer to the monitor screen.

"You're moving me along too fast. The inner me isn't fortified enough yet." Hell, he realized that sounded like psycho-babble. He tried again, "Realize, I've been accustomed to tedium. For the past few years, since my marriage began to disintegrate, a beer, a soft couch, and a TV ball game have been my idea of excitement.

"Suddenly, you got me flying around the country buying up corporations and dining out with the upper echelon of government. There isn't enough of a new me yet to carry it off. It's brinkmanship. I'm continually on the verge of falling through my ass, as I did last night."

True, but in actuality, my boy, you're getting teasing glimpses of the real Benjamin Roberts, who is emerging. Trust me.

He chuffed out a laugh to convey his skepticism.

Granted, at the dinner you showed the vicissitudes of mood and behavior that reveal you're still adjusting to your rapid social and financial growth. But at that podium you proved you have all the ingredients in the mix, and merely need a bit more time, and perhaps a catalyst or two.

As for the tête-à-tête, you did make the event interesting from a kibitzer's point of view. You trashed politically correct social protocol and threw some zip into it. As a result, you completely unhinged him.

At moments like this with Max, Ben felt almost as if he were listening to his father again.

But don't fear. In time, Ben, you'll get a handle on your enthusiasm and your emotional swings, in general. You'll become poised and salty. Just don't get stuffy on me.

"But he caved in so easily. Hell, I was no tiger."

The meeting proved more interesting when one knew both sides of it. The president called him during your board meeting and told him to fly right over and meet you. The vice president balked at first, claiming he didn't know enough about you and would feel off balance all evening. The truth being he feared if it got out you two fraternized, some people might assume he was on your payroll, perhaps that he was supplying you with congressional transcripts and the like. And pffft! There'd go his political aspirations.

But the president pushed him hard, surmising that you would more than likely bootlick through the entire meeting. Instead, you ran over him like a Mack truck.

He chuckled. "You mean like a *Max* truck."

Very good, Ben! One part of his mission was to finesse as much information out of you as possible. He was probing but you cleverly cut him off at the passes.

His mind leapt off the subject. "Hey. Did you see me give the laptop to that scrappy little girl?"

Yes. Touching, Ben! Very touching. Unfortunately, the feds pulled up behind you and commandeered it for analysis.

"Oh, no. Damn it, I really wanted her to have it."

Don't worry. I've seen to it that she'll get another new one. By the way, to put your mind at ease, I won't ask you to be present at any more acquisitions. I just wanted you to announce this one to give the world an

introductory glimpse of the emerging titan, *Benjamin Roberts*. But from now on, I'll tend to all the scut work myself.

And since you're not going back to bed, breakfast is coming up, then on to your usual routine. I've notified your trainer.

Be sure to read that stack of memos in the printer tray. One sheet is a pertinent summation of Jenny's writing career. Next week, you're to chance upon her at the bookstore. Remember?

"Remember? Hell, I'm counting the hours."

Chapter 29

Ben pushed the limo door shut and stood at the curb pretending to study the lines of the maroon Rolls as it pulled out into traffic. He glanced off at the rectangular sign *Fig Garden Books* jutting out over the sidewalk. Then tipping his head back, he scanned the dense gray of the angry sky overhead and appraised the balminess of the air. Though the sweetness of rain wafted on the breeze, he concluded it wouldn't start falling here for a while yet, so he removed his beige raincoat, folded its shoulders together meticulously, and draped it neatly over his left forearm. Tugging at the open collar of his ocher silk shirt, he shrugged to let his chocolate blazer drape freely. As an afterthought, he removed his pager from his blazer pocket and slipped it into the raincoat pocket, so he'd perhaps look a bit thinner in the hips. He eyed the sharp creases descending the front of his tan trousers, and took a moment to admire the perfect shine on his cordovan wing tips. Finally, he reached back into the raincoat pocket, pulled out a piece of red-and-white-striped peppermint candy in a cellophane wrapper, unwrapped it, and popped it into his mouth. Only then, did he concede to take his first step in the direction of the bookstore.

Immediately his pulse quickened, as did his breathing. Damn it, he could dine and palaver with vice presidents and not bat an eye, but just the thought of being in the same room with this woman short-circuited his nervous system.

As he came to the bookstore, he cast a seemingly casual glance at the front windows, but their semi-mirrored finish merely reflected the image of this tall, dapper fellow with a raincoat draped over his arm. Pausing at the front door before opening it, he peered through its transparent glass for a possible glimpse of Jenny. He didn't see her, but the shop disappointed him. He expected something spacious and well lighted. Instead, the place was close and dim. Bookracks angled hodgepodge like hedges in a garden maze.

Hell, Jenny, I'll lease a street-window at I. Magnim's for you to really tout your book.

A soft ting-a-ling above the door announced him. He received a perfunctory smile from an older woman in a green knit sweater sitting behind the counter. She cast him a polite smile, then went back to reading the magazine in her lap. Prominent signs that were hand-written with black felt-pen topped each of the racks to designate the genres in the mishmash.

He spotted a sign, LOCAL AUTHORS, and steered toward it. The apparent number of Bay Area writers in print impressed him. He skimmed along alphabetically, F—G—H...Hull. Ah! Copies of three of her six novels stood mid-shelf, but not the title he came to buy.

He walked back to the clerk at the counter. "Ma'am, I'm looking for Lelah Hull's, *P as in Poppies and Passion*. I don't see it on the shelf with her other works."

Looking through bifocals, she replied, "That book's just coming out today. They're working in the back right now to finish its display. The author is holding a signing here in two hours." She reached down into bulky cardboard box by her feet and lifted out a hardcover book. Its jacket depicted a scene of rolling green hills that were heavily poppied. She handed it across to him. "Like I say, wait around a couple hours and you can get it personally autographed by Ms. Hull."

He thumbed through it. *Hmmm, thick! She doesn't seem to be at a loss for words.* A competing notion struck him. What the heck! As long as he was here, he might as well buy her other novels in stock.

As he sauntered back to the local-author section, he glimpsed the inside of the book jacket for 'Lelah Hull's' picture—but there was none! He'd just reached the shelves when he sensed someone approaching from his rear. Half-mindfully, he glanced around and into the radiant face of Jenny Bligh. Her eyes seemed to twinkle as she stood waiting for him to say something.

He didn't have to feign surprise. "Jenny! I'll be damned." But in a beat, he leapt back into the act. "As big as this city is, I keep running into you. Think maybe the gods are trying to tell us something?"

She beamed an even broader smile. "Could be I'm pursuing you. Did you ever think of that? The day of passive women is over."

She wore a blue work smock atop an ivory blouse and ebony slacks. The store logo in black stitching adorned her smock's breast pocket.

At once, she noticed the book he held. Her brow furrowed. "Where did you get that?"

"Huh? Oh! From the clerk over there."

"But we haven't even unpacked them yet."

"Uh...I happened to be browsing through the local authors and saw several books by a Lelah Hull. I asked the clerk about her. She volunteered that her new novel just came out and gave me this one from behind the counter."

She seemed dubious. He tried distraction. "Do you recommend her work?"

She continued to stare at him thoughtfully.

He held the book up into her line of gaze and tried again. "This book. Do you know enough about the author's work to recommend it?"

Blinking as if coming out of trance, her expression softened.

Whew! Thank God.

"Literary taste," she said, "like all tastes, is an individual matter. I enjoy her work very much. Actually, I resonate with it." Then, with coyness, she added, "Your taste may run contrary."

Having dodged another bullet, his confidence rebounded and he seized the moment. "The clerk tells me the author will be here in a couple hours for a book signing. Think I should wait around?"

"You needn't if all you want is her signature. Give me your address. I'll have her send you a lengthy personal note."

"Do you know her very well?"

"Well enough."

"Do you like her as a person as much as you like her work?"

She folded her arms, playfully perturbed with his questions. "Well, it so happens, I enjoy being around writers. Her personality accurately reflects the sum total of her varied experiences, some good, some bad, and many mediocre, all of which she skillfully enhances in her writing using her active imagination."

"I'd say that pretty much describes most people over twenty years old."

"Yes, but the artistic temperament magnifies everything a hundred times."

"Jenny?" An aged voice called out from somewhere behind a wall of books.

She half-turned and called back, "I'm over here, Maude. Hold on. I'll be with you in a few moments. I'm speaking to..." she paused, and the pause tantalized him. "To a friend of mine."

"All right, no hurry."

He reached out and patted her upper arm. "Thanks for including me in your friendship circle after only three brief meetings."

"Yes, but in the three, you've sampled my taste in wine, my taste in music, and now my taste in literature. Come to think of it, in homage to Yin and Yang, it's time you reciprocated." She folded her arms and leaned back against some bookshelves as if waiting.

Several possible double entendres flashed through his mind before he realized the natural opening afforded him. He let his face light up as if having an 'Aha! Experience,' which of sorts he was. "You know, this chance meeting may give me that opportunity, young lady. I just happen to have a couple tickets to a stage show coming up, and I'm looking for someone to accompany me." She pushed away from the books with sudden interest. "And since you've acknowledged that we're now friends, would you care to be my guest? It'll give you an opportunity to sample my taste in musicals."

"Which musical?" she asked, too quickly.

"The original-cast reunion of *The Phantom of the Opera,* in three weeks."

He might have misconstrued her expression as fearful when she exclaimed, "Are you serious? Weber's *Phantom of the Opera?*"

"Yes, the fourth of the four shows."

She shut her eyes and let her head loll forward. "Somehow I just knew you meant that one," she muttered as if to herself. Slowly, she lifted her head. Her eyes brimmed. "Oh my God. If you only knew how badly I've wanted to see one of those performances."

She grasped his shoulders, bounced up on her tiptoes, and kissed him gently on the cheek. Like a bear-trap snapping closed, his arms shot around her and prevented her back step. She didn't struggle against his tight hold, merely whispered, "I'll be indebted to you for a lifetime."

The delicate, intoxicating fragrance of her perfume engulfed him. He uttered, "*Eternity!*"

Her head canted and her face skewed. "I should be indebted for eternity?"

"No. Your perfume, its *Eternity,* isn't it?"

"Oh!" Her head righted. "Why, yes. You've got a discerning sense of smell. For a second there, I wondered if you might be a bit strange or..." she flashed a mischievous smile, "or perhaps terribly romantic."

"Darn! I wish I could claim romantic, but it so happens that I like *Eternity* very much." He affected soberness. "Actually, in all fairness, a lifetime of indebtedness might be a bit much for just one theater ticket." Scratching his chin, he added, "But then again, they say it's one hellava production."

Her left eyebrow arched. "If we stand here holding each other like this much longer, you'll need that raincoat draped over your arm to get out of this shop decently."

The shock effect of her comment together with the lingering vestiges of his nervousness triggered a burst of self-conscious laughter. He let go of her, and she stepped back. Her face brightened at his appreciation of her humor.

She took the book out of his hand. "I want you to have this as a gift. It's the least I can do." She reached into her smock pocket and pulled out a yellow ballpoint pen. Opening the book, she wrote something in it, closed it, and handed it back. "Even if you don't think much of the story, keep the book around. I've written my phone number in it."

He opened it and read her inscription. *1st installment against a lifetime of debt. Love, Jenny. 826-2011.*

Joyously his confidence surged, and he opted for one last tweak. "But you've written on the page I was going to have Miss Hull autograph."

She winked. "Well, you can tell everyone she did sign it, but that you know her by her preferred name. If they don't believe you, have them call that number, and I'll go along with the gag."

She gestured toward the door. "I'm thick with the store owner, so just take the book out with you; no need to stop by the counter. Oh, and about play night, I must tell you up front that I live in Sausalito. But I'll be glad to meet you anywhere in the city to save you two trips across the bridge."

"No way. I want to pick you up. I'll call you to get your address."

Her eyes shone. "Great. Now, I don't want to sound like I'm pressuring you, but I intend to fast until I hear from you again. No food. No drink. So if you wait too long to make that call, you'll have my death on your conscience."

"I wouldn't want that, " he said. "I don't imagine you'd be as much fun dead."

Holding an impish smile, she slowly shook her head. Her cheeks flushed a la James Bond.

Walking out of the shop, he realized she was right. It was fortunate he had a raincoat over his arm.

Jennifer watched him saunter up the block then she stepped over to the circular sales counter. "Hester," she said, causing the gray-haired clerk to look up and close her magazine. "That fellow who just left told me you—"

"Jenny!" Maude's call from the back room interrupted her.

"Oh, never mind," Jenny said, with a dismissive flick of her hand. "Coming, Maude!"

Chapter 30

...So let me give you an update, Benjamin. You now own majority interest in general motors, and you just purchased another major shipping line. That, with the shipping you already own, gives you ever greater control of oceanic transport around the world, a crucial step in dictating to the oil market, which in turn leverages you heavily in Japan.

"Every day you enumerate more acquisitions. Damn it, I can't end up owning everything. Who could use, much less need, such wealth? What the hell are you up to? I'm developing some grave doubts about all this, including you. What's the end point here? What's your ultimate goal, f'christsake?" He realized he was ranting.

What's wrong, Ben? You're having your first real date with Jenny tomorrow night, and you don't sound very happy.

"No, Max. I'm ecstatic. It's just that...." He paused.

Out with it, my boy. There isn't anything the two of us can't resolve, if it's on the table where we can dissect it. But if I don't know the problem, I can't help you with it.

"Well, I guess...or I should say that I wish she could have known me when I was younger. She's been cheated out of my youth. I'd like her to have known me at my best."

Oh no, Ben! Am I hearing the rumblings of performance anxiety here? Is that why you had Clive call Jenny instead of calling her yourself?

My boy, you're only in your mid thirties. I promise, you will bring her everything she wants, everything she needs. And for many, many years.

You know, she has trepidations that you won't enjoy being with her, either.

"Huh? That's crazy." He brought his tipped-back chair to the upright. "The thrill I get just looking at her. That body, her lithe movements, even her breathing—I can hardy imagine the joy of making love to her."

Exactly! Animal magnetism and carnal pleasure are there for you two to enjoy with gusto. But I ask you to consider that perhaps there is a higher conjugal union in store for you both: the exaltation that comes when two souls destined to be together finally fuse in reunion.

"Reunion? Am I now hearing rumblings of a belief in reincarnation?"

Suffice to say, Jenny believes in it. So, my boy, she may have *known* you in your youth, time and time again.

"Ha. I don't put much stock in that whole concept, but when you state it that way, I do find the possibility comforting."

And Ben, if this is indeed a repeat occurrence, I've added a dimension this time around I doubt you've enjoyed before—inestimable affluence. You two can go, do, and have exactly as you desire. Your love will know no constraints, and that will make a half a lifetime together ten lifetimes full.

"Jessuz. I want to be with her so much I'm actually in pain."

She would say ditto, though you've been with her—in her thoughts and dreams—for years.

"Year? Years? Come on, Max. She didn't know I was alive until a few months ago."

Ben, she's anticipated your arrival since her early teens. It so happens she has a very strong psychic propensity, proven correct many, many times. She's never clearly seen your face until the wine shop, but she's sure she knows you.

"This has something to do with those bottles of wine and that music, doesn't it?"

Enough said for a while.

"Come on, Max. How can I be some precognition she's awaited for years, when actually I'm involved only because of your scientifically unexplainable interloping? This constitutes fraud."

Ben, how do we know how precognition might work? Perhaps my unique interloping is the anticipated component that enables this predestination to happen.

"Jessuz, all this has gotten too deep for me."

I agree. Enough! Anyway, your weight is down some twenty pounds, but with your added muscle mass; so you're near peak fitness.

"I don't think I've ever felt in such great shape, even when I was in the Army. Hell, I've got muscle definition now where I'd forgotten I had muscles. I can pedal the stationary bike for more than an hour at high resistance and can drive a golf ball three hundred yards. If I can just develop my touch with that damned putter, you may have created an outstanding golfer."

Ben, I didn't design your training program to help you excel at *golf*!

The screen blanked. He laughed, but the laugh was tempered. He realized Max intentionally sidestepped some blunt questions put to him.

Chapter 31

"You look dashing, sir. Dashing!" Murray Abelson said, standing behind Ben and nervously patting the shoulders of his black tuxedo, the tailor's latest creation.

Ben studied himself in the three-section mirror. He still felt pretentious being outfitted by a tailor, and this fitting was his second today.

"I did a magnificent job, if I must say so myself," Murray said. "You're much easier to fit now that your weight is down and you're more muscular." Eyeing the shoulder seams closely, he muttered, "Magnificent. Magnificent. I've outdone myself."

Inspiring deeply to swell his chest, Ben admired the broadness of his shoulders and the narrowness of his hips in each of the triple views, but he accepted that the cut of the tuxedo did exaggerate his tapering physique a bit.

Midst this self-admiration, a wisp of reverie overtook him. His tuxedo front suggested the breastplate on a knight's suit of armor, his maroon cummerbund a blood-soaked bandage. Yeah, he could be going to her tonight recently wounded in medieval combat, perhaps defending her honor. He grinned and cocked his left eyebrow, as Jenny herself was wont to do. Too, he admired this expression in each of the three mirrors.

"Yes, Murray, I'm extremely pleased. I promise to be exceedingly careful wearing it. "

The tiny artisan scurried around Ben like a Banty rooster, situating himself between Ben and the triplicate glass. "That is of no concern, sir. I would never think of letting you wear any item more than once. Just as with all your other clothing, I will create a new tuxedo for you every future occasion one is called for."

"What?" Ben stroked his lapel. "You mean this maiden voyage will be its last trip out?"

The little man stepped back colliding into the center mirror, jarring the images. "Absolutely, Mr. Roberts. Please, allow me to dress you as I see fit. Sir, the entire haute monde knows that Mr. Benjamin Roberts is now exclusively attired by *the* Murray Abelson. Each day when you step out into the world, my reputation goes with you. And prestige is an extremely important ingredient in tailoring. Yes, this tuxedo is my work of art that shall go on display only tonight. Expectedly, it will evoke admiration in all those who attend the play with you, all those who dine around you after, even those who merely cast their gaze upon you as you walk past on the street.

136

The exquisiteness of its cloth, its majestic lines, the invisible seams... Ah yes! When you strut into that theater tonight, my reputation shall aggrandize to a new zenith. But this creation is only for tonight."

"Okay, Murray," he sighed. "But surely the Salvation Army clientele are fast becoming the best-dressed people in the country."

The little tailor held a strained smile as he tensely scrutinized the front of the jacket for any overlooked, minute defects. He snapped his fingers. Immediately an aide handed him a black, silk top hat. Murray needed to rock up on his tiptoes with his arms stretched straight up, to place the hat on Ben's head. Teetering as he prolonged the stance, he adjusted the hat to tip jauntily to the right. He dropped down onto his heels, saying, "Perfect," as he flashed Ben the 'okay' sign. "Tonight you truly look like the richest man in the world."

His white helicopter landed on the asphalt pad behind Sausalito Community Hospital. A small crowd of hospital employees had gathered watching the landing.

As this elegantly dressed fellow, replete with silk top hat, strutted down the chopper steps and out into an awaiting white Rolls stretch limousine, several in the crowd recognized him. "Oh my! That's Benjamin Roberts!" "By God, you're right. That's him." "Oh, Lordie, I feel faint."

The limo glided off toward the golden radiance of the setting sun. Ben peered out the back window as the chopper lifted off and noted the jubilant spectators scramble back into the hospital, probably shouting, "You'll never guess who just arrived in that helicopter."

The limo climbed along a narrow winding road that scaled the broad slope on which the more expensive residential portion of the town had been built. Its panorama of Sausalito, the harbor, and the northern portion of San Francisco Bay expanded behind him.

Ben became increasingly nervous and decided he could use a drink about now. An idea struck him. He clicked on the intercom. "Mandrake, turn around. I want to go back to Gambino's Wine shop at the wharf."

"Yes, sir."

Once more the delicate tinkle of a doorbell announced his entry. Again the diminutive proprietor appeared from the back room just as he had before, again wearing a white apron and that same pleasant smile. At once, his face flattened at the sight of Ben approaching the counter, dressed to the nines replete with a top hat.

Without swagger, Ben strode forth. "Mr. Gambino, I ordered two bottles of wine a while back. I'm here to pick them up."

The little man fumbled in a drawer behind the counter then lifted out a green logbook. "Name, please," he said, his focus fixed on the opened book.

"Ben Roberts."

The little fellow's eyes snapped open to their widest as he glanced up and re-appraised his customer. "*The* Mr. Benjamin Roberts?" he asked by inflection. But the recognition in the old man's eyes obviated any answer.

Gambino's awe made Ben uncomfortable. "I ordered the two bottles of wine a while back. I hope you still have them."

The old man traced a finger down one page then down another. The finger paused. "Uh-huh! It says here you paid for them at the time of the order, so of course I'd still have them."

He scuttled off into the dimness of the back room, reappearing a few seconds later, grasping the neck of a bottle of red wine in each hand. He paused in the doorway to again study his customer, then rushed up to the counter and clunked both bottles down on it. He stepped back. "You're the gentleman who asked Miss Jenny Bligh about these wines."

"Yes, that's right."

Gambino wiped his hands vigorously on his apron front. His round, mustachioed face brightened. "Have you seen her since that day?"

Ben grinned. "Yes, as a matter of fact, I'm taking her out tonight."

Gambino released the apron front and slapped his hands to his cheeks. "I knew it. I knew it. I could sense the chemistry between you two as you talked there in front of my counter. Please. Please. I will find your credit-card slip and void it. I want this wine to be a gift from me. Something special for you both."

Ben was taken aback. "Thank you, but no," he countered, though he distinctly recalled paying cash for the wine. "It's quite expensive, and I can well afford it."

"Then I'm not selling it to you." The little man wagged a scolding finger. "Instead, I'm *giving* this wine to Jenny. They're her very favorites. I ask only that you take it to her for me."

Capitulation being his kinder option here, he nodded. "Putting it that way, Mr. Gambino, I shall do as you say. And I thank you, kind sir, for Jenny and myself."

Gambino picked up a folded paper bag from beneath the counter and with the flick of his hand, snapped it open, as he reached for one of the bottles.

"No, Mr. Gambino. Save your bag; I prefer to carry them as they are."

At the front door, Ben glanced back. Only the little man's head and shoulder tops were visible over the counter.

"Mr. Gambino, from now on, your shop shall be the exclusive source of all my wine purchases."

Expecting a thank you, Ben received only a heavily accented admonition. "You just be good to my Jenny."

The pearly limo crept along a narrow but most picturesque stretch of lane that cut horizontally for several hundred yards straight across the mountain face before climbing again. The homes on this portion of road had been built only along the down-slope side because of the sheerness of the opposite grassy embankment. Small but prim yards separated the road from the front porches that stood on a plane with the road itself. Rather than rising upward, the extra levels in these homes descended down the steep hillside. Surely, these property values resided mostly in the lots with their mesmerizing views, not in the building structures themselves. A variety of trees grew in these front yards. All were now in fresh full leaf, some were flowering. In places, tree limbs actually arched over the lane, adding the illusion of compression to its narrowness.

Jenny's white wooden house had pale-blue shutters and porch trim. A white picket fence ran along the edge of the road to delineate her yard from the slip of berm. A lone broad-leafed tree of some kind stood centrally in her yard. Its smooth gray trunk was as big around as an elephant's leg and it jutted up nearly eight feet before any branches poked out. A polychromatic Tiffany lampshade hung on the porch a few feet in front of her azure door. A luxuriant fuchsia plant with a profusion of crimson-and-white bell-shaped blossoms grew in a planter beside the door. The house reminded him of the blissful cottages often depicted in the movies made in the 1930s and 1940s.

He sat pensive in the limo as Mandrake opened his rear door for him. "Mr. Roberts, I shan't wait for you on this narrow stretch. I'd block traffic both ways. Perhaps, sir, you should carry the pager."

"I've got it in my pocket." He gathered up the wine bottles in his arms like two bundled babies, a corked top resting against each upper arm.

Tentatively, Mandrake added, "It's of no importance, sir, but have you any idea how long you'll be inside the home?"

Clasping the wine, Ben scooted over to the door and stepped out of the limo. "Oh, hell, I don't know, probably not long. The play starts at 8:15. We could either eat before or afterwards. I'll leave it up to the lady."

"Very good, sir." Mandrake reached behind Ben into the limo and withdrew the top hat off the seat. He set it on his employer's head, adjusting it to again cant rakishly to the right. "In any case, I'll have to wait quite a ways from here. None of streets in the vicinity were designed for stretch limos. Two pushes on the pager, and I should be here in ten minutes."

As his driver walked around the vehicle to get in, Ben felt a surge of panic. He wanted to call out, "No, wait right here," but his self-image of manliness wouldn't let him say the words. So, as Mandrake drove off in the twilight, Ben stood there at the roadside, clutching the wine and feeling helpless.

Max, I only hope you're right about this woman. The thump-thump-thumping of his heart reverberated in both of his ears and each breath now whistled as it jetted in and out of his nostrils. *Damn it, here I go again.*

He watched the red luminescence of the taillights recede. They appeared to be demon eyes leering back at him.

Chapter 32

"I thought I heard a car drive off," a mellifluous voice called out. He wheeled around to find its source. It was Jennifer standing on her darkening porch in front of her darkened doorway. "Hello there. You're early."

Taking in a healthy lungful of evening air, he instantly assumed a belying persona of confidence. "Good evening, Jenny. Your view from this hill face is spectacular." He took two steps and gently kicked open the slightly ajar gate in her picket fence and affected a blithe strut onto the flagstone path that angled toward the porch. Orange and yellow marigolds lined both sides of this narrow walkway.

Even in the waning light, her beauty struck him dumb. Artful makeup accentuated her eyes and high cheekbones. A coiffure, styled to the perfection of a magazine cover girl, framed the Athenian elegance of her face.

But at that moment, Jenny suddenly shrieked! She sounded like a cat when someone steps on its tail.

Huh?

He halted mid step, just as her hands slapped over her gaping mouth.

She loosed another scream, albeit dampened, and she shuffled backwards into the house.

His concern and wonderment led him to proceed up onto the porch but there he stopped. Peering into the greater dimness beyond her doorway, he saw her poised motionless in a semi-squatting posture in the middle of her atrium. She stared out at him as if she were seeing a ghost. She again screamed! Every nerve ending in his body tingled a warning for him not to enter this house, not with its occupant behaving as this woman was. Then she leapt back to the doorway and stopped. She glanced from one wine bottle to the other. Her trembling hands still crisscrossed her mouth.

Without warning, she charged at him. He planted his right foot back, bracing himself for an impact that would surely butt him off the porch. But she stopped short of collision and grasped his elbows. Jerking his arms up toward her, she avidly read the labels of each bottle. At once, breath gushed out of her. She straightened to her full height, letting her arms fall limply to her sides. Tears swelled in her eyes.

"I knew it was you," she whispered. "I just knew it."

He stood stupefied—no mortified.

Her arms rose and enveloped him. She stood for a moment hugging his chest. Then using gentle tugs, she coaxed him across the porch and into the house. With no small degree of apprehension, he allowed himself to be stutter-stepped inside. When she suddenly reached around him behind him and shoved the door shut, he flinched.

With each inspiration, her chest heaved so that the front of her robe began teasing apart. She seemed not to notice. Maintaining her hold on both of his upper arms, she resumed her back stepping. He shuffled along after her, glancing down through the diaphanous white of her slip at her unrestrained breasts. Their fullness lifted invitingly with each gasped breath.

She appeared in a daze, intoxicated. "Why did you wait so long?" she asked repeatedly in a dreamy voice. "You waited so long to come." Tears streaked her cheeks. Reaching the front room, she halted and lunged in against him. Pressing her abdomen firmly against him, she began rolling her hips rhythmically. At the same time, she began sweeping the tips of her breasts slowly back and forth across the frilly pleats of his shirt. Moaning now, she inched her mouth upward till her lips touched the side of his neck. The intensity of her *Eternity* perfume dizzied him.

He clutched the wine as if it were she in his embrace. His breathing, too, had become panting. "The wine," he managed to say. "Let me get rid of the wine."

She pulled her face back and peered up at him as if unsure what he'd said.

"Oh, yes. The wine," she exclaimed. Pushing away from him with a firm pelvic thrust, she grabbed a bottle's neck with each hand. Unburdening him, she quickly set them on the floor at either side of their feet. But she again grasped his wrists as if she feared he might run off or perhaps even disappear altogether. Again she tugged him, this time so aggressively he lurched at her. As quickly, she backed gracefully away, only to repeat this bizarre cajoling dance.

Enraptured now himself, he followed, only half-mindful of the decor of her front room as he passed through it: an expansive bay window with a majestic view, a baby grand piano at the far end, a statue or two, several wall-mounted oil paintings, each individually lighted.

She backed down a corridor lined with more illuminated oil paintings. Their breathing had become a heaving duet. With a sudden sidestep, she rammed her shoulder against a door off the hallway. It flew open, and she pivoted and backed through it, pulling him into a bedroom. His heart was a jackhammer trying to break through his ribcage.

From the crushing pressure of her grip on his wrists, he intuited her intentions would not be thwarted, even if he were to resist. Backing up against her four-poster bed, she released his arms and frantically scrabbled at his tuxedo front.

"Hurry. Hurry," her crazed shouts commanded him.

Aware she was mangling his lapels trying to get the jacket off, he fleetingly recalled his tailor's pride in this fastidiously crafted outfit. He hesitated for just an instant, and then ignited by her heat, he too ripped at the jacket and succeeded in stripping it off. "Sorry, Murray," he muttered, throwing it down in a crumpled heap.

She instantly froze in a tableau of alarm. "Who's Murray?"

Fumbling to unhitch his belt, he mumbled, "My tailor. He was so damn proud of this tuxedo. Made it special for tonight." Kicking his trousers free of his right foot, he added, "Expected me to show it off for him tonight."

Loosing a steamy sigh of relief, she re-animated her frenzy, flinging her robe off and away. "You tell Murray you did show it off—and the warmth of its reception exceeded his wildest expectations." With a throaty laugh, she shimmied her slip to the floor.

Her passion fired him to sexual heights he'd never known, which in turn kept her excitement at the boiling point. She repeatedly crescendoed into frenetic orgasms, virtual sexual explosions. But instead of ever subsiding to a post-orgasmic calm, as he anticipated, she merely diminished to her base-line fever pitch. And each subsequent orgasmic eruption actually exceeded the previous one in intensity. His confidence soared.

Together, they destroyed the bed. Pillows, blankets, and top sheet ended up strewn on the floor. At one point, when she again scrambled to regain dominant position, they tumbled resoundingly off the bed onto the carpet. Instead of the fall interrupting them, it ignited bellowing laughter that in turn triggered a higher state of frenzy in her.

After several on-the-carpet crescendos, she leaped up and pulled him to his feet, spun him around like in a dance maneuver, and lodged him in an armless, straight-back chair parked against the wall.

She knelt and pressed her palm against his chest, signaling him non-verbally to keep seated and passive. Her aggressive attentions caused him to throw his head back and wail. His pleasure seemed boundless. Eventually he opened his eyes and realized, even in the waning light, that her ceiling bore a mural, as did his in Carmel. But this mural was painted in spiral fashion. The depiction was not at all sensual but rather idyllic, pastoral.

He found that focusing on these peaceful scenes helped to keep his physiology from boiling over, serving as a visual coolant of sorts. Is that why she had it painted up there?

Suddenly her face filled his field of vision, blocking out the mural. Perhaps the change in intensity or tone of his moaning alerted her to his wavering attention. She smothered him with kisses as she straddled him and the chair. She rhythmically swayed, hunched, and plunged as she cradled his face in her arms, kissing him as a starving woman might eat. His outcries renewed their intensity, but her mouth muffled them.

They were back on the bare mattress again when at once her baseline frenzy diminished. She went limp. Her breathing eased. She lay sated.

He glided his face up her abdomen, tenderly kissing through the cleavage of her breasts. With oily sweat drenching their overheated bodies, his frame slid over hers with the slightest of effort.

The wild look in her eyes had cleared as they studied him with peaceful profundity. He continued softly kissing her nose, her cheeks, and her eyelids as she lay in total exhaustion watching him.

After a while, she squirmed to free her arms and took his face in her hands. She began kissing him gently. The sensual pleasure she gave his mouth with just the rolling motion of hers and the rhythmic flutter of her tongue amazed him.

The protracted kiss grew ecstatic. He finally pulled free and moved his face down onto her warm moist bosom. She moaned softly, again effecting a slow writhing of her body. She was rousing again despite her reluctance.

God, how he enjoyed pleasing her!

As he savored the perfumed warmth of her skin, Ben inadvertently glanced out the glass door to her bedroom terrace. Under an ink-blue sky, the city of Sausalito had transformed into an aggregate of varicolored points of light.

He pushed over onto his forearm. "Jenny, it's late! We've missed your play."

"Oh no!" She jackknifed up. Her wide-eyes sought the small statue of cherubs and bluebirds perched on the far bureau. An illumed clock face centered it. She squinted. "No, my love," she cried. "It's only seven-forty. We might still make it."

"Shall we try?"

Even in the paucity of light, her face shone with childlike sweetness. She nodded quickly. "You bet!"

"Okay, let's go."

She scooted off the mattress and trotted ahead of him into the bathroom. He cautiously followed her vague form through the darkness. Holding on to his arm for balance, she reached into the shower stall and twisted the knob. "Let's shower together. But go easy when you soap me, or you'll be to blame for us missing the play."

Stepping out of the shower, she strode back into the bedroom, blotting herself with a huge powder-blue towel. She hurried over and pulled the drapes across the sliding glass door to the terrace before flicking the wall switch that lighted four lamps around the room.

Ben waited till then before he stepped out of the bathroom. Drying himself, he paused taken aback as he surveyed about him. The huge mattress on the bed lay bare and precariously about to topple off the frame. The bedding lay strewn around the room as irregular clumps on the snow-white carpet. Two chairs lay tumbled over.

"Jeez. Looks like the place was ransacked," he said.

Vigorously drying herself, she paused in front of the arching bureau mirror, holding one end of her oversized towel to her chin, the other end dangling to the floor. She let the towel fall, revealing her magnificent nudity.

"There has been a robbery here tonight. Someone just stole my heart forever, and I don't even know his name or, for that matter, whether he's married."

Oh, God, Jenny. Not now! Don't make the connection yet. His eyes feasted on her statuesque form as he wrestled with his dilemma. How could he dodge this one?

She waited, watching him.

What the hell! "Benny ... Benny Roberts," he said. He used Benny, reasoning she'd be less likely to connect it with any news reports.

Thankfully, he read no realization in her face. She held a thoughtful pose for a moment then stepped into her ebony-lace panties. "Benny. Benny and Jenny. Jenny and Benny," she said musingly. "Just like us, our names were made to be together."

That notion actually jump-started him to get dressed. He hastily reversed one of his jacket sleeves from inside out, but paused to watch her shimmy up her slip, noting she deliciously neglected to first put on a bra.

"My God, but I love you," he whispered loud enough for her to hear.

Using her hands like two giant combs, she raked her fingers through either side of her damp hair that earlier had been coiffed to perfection. She replied, "My God, but I've *always* loved you."

He couldn't find his trousers until he finally got down on all fours and looked under the bed. "Voila!" He reached under and retrieved the tightly wadded black cloth. He located a pocket, jammed his hand into it and pulled out the pager. Still on his knees, he held the small dark device up in the air as if it were an Olympic torch. "Jenny, after I push this pager button, we've got just ten minutes to meet my car out in front."

She crinkled her nose. "Ready! Set! Go!"

Chapter 33

Dressed and standing there in front of her mirror, Ben winced. His jacket and trousers hung in a continuum of deep wrinkles. A prominent rip gaped the jacket's left shoulder seam, revealing a bit of white. And he couldn't find two of the five pearly black studs for his shirt. His left shoe still had much of its original ebony shine. But a gouge so marred the toe of his right shoe that vigorous buffing with a pillowcase couldn't restore any gleam. The broken snap on his maroon cummerbund precluded his wearing it. Only his top hat came through unscathed. But by contrast, its crisp smartness atop his head only enhanced his comical appearance.

My God! Can I really go out tonight looking like this? Aw, what the hell! The lady really wants to see the damn play.

Stepping back out of her way in front of the mirror, he stood admiring her profile. He watched her don a black, low-cut sheath that wrapped resplendently about her. Even without makeup now, the natural beauty of her face was stunning, proof cosmetics were merely ancillary in her case. Though now uncoiffed, her hair still formed a truly magnificent aura about her face.

"You would shame Aphrodite herself."

"Are you referring to my deportment this evening or to my appearance now?" she said, showing him a puckish smile as she did some final primping on her hair.

"Yes—on both counts," he said as he again leaned in front of her and caught a last glimpse of his rumpled image. "Look at this once proud tuxedo. You're going to be put to the blush to be seen with me tonight."

"Phooey!" She said, snuggling against his arm. "If anyone gives you so much as a sneer, I'll just tell them you're my tiger and toss them a brazen wink. Their scorn will turn to burning envy."

They'd left the bedroom and were striding down the hallway, when she rushed ahead and snatched up to the two bottles of wine that were still standing on the living room floor. Holding them up by their necks, she playfully kissed each bottle. "Oh forgive me, dear, dear wine. It's shabby treatment to neglect you so long, especially since you brought my Benny to me." She walked into the kitchen and placed the bottles gently into the brass wine rack on the counter. "If these bottles were roses, I'd press them. But we shall relish them together. And if you find them as delicious as I do, we'll buy cases of each. My darling, I want to share the best of my world with you."

She took his hand, and they hurried to the front door. In sync with their appearance on the porch, Mandrake opened the rear limo door for them. Jenny faltered at her first sight of the stretch limousine. Ben had to actually nudge her down the path and through the picket gate. But she quickly dissembled her astonishment behind a pleasant smile for the chauffeur.

Mandrake's attention remained riveted on Jenny from the moment she first stepped outside. Ben read the overwhelming approval in the chauffeur's eyes and felt twinges of jealousy. But, hey, he'd better get used to oglers with this woman on his arm. Only after she slipped into the limo did Mandrake glance at Ben. Caught off guard, he startled. Jenny's face reappeared at the limo doorway, drawing the chauffeur's eye again.

She winked impishly. "Don't give it a second thought," she said. "He's my indefatigable tiger."

Mandrake's bewilderment immediately gave way to an amused grin.

As the limo raced across the Golden Gate Bridge, Ben recounted Gambino's elation on learning of their date tonight and his insistence that the wine be a gift to her from him.

She melted. "That's sweet. So touching," she murmured. "He's family to me." They cuddled like teenagers.

The limo pulled up in front of the marquee only minutes before scheduled curtain time. They leapt out and dashed across the vacant sidewalk toward the remaining open door. Turning and trotting backwards behind her, he yelled back at Mandrake, "I'll page you when it's over."

Unfortunately, the packed house was still well lighted as their usher led them down the seemingly mile-long main aisle to their front seating. Ben drew sequential double takes from both sides as he trudged along beside Jenny.

Walking ahead of them, the usher read the ticket stubs aloud. Jenny rejoiced, "Oh, my Lord, Ben. You've got far-front-and-center orchestra seats. This'll be my second taste of heaven tonight." The reactions to his appearance so distracted him, it took him a few seconds for her remark to register. He cast her a weak smile. She winked.

"Save those winks, my lady. You're going to need all of them to get me out of this place with my ego intact."

She held his hand throughout the play. Sometimes she would lift and kiss it. Just after Michael Crawford poignantly sang *Into the Night* to Sarah Brightman, Jenny leaned into him and whispered, "You are going to stay with me tonight, aren't you?"

Since the play began, he'd been silently scheming. "Jenny, I need to get back to the house tonight so I can make arrangements to move you in with me in the morning."

She twisted her torso to face him fully as she exclaimed too loudly, "Then you're not married!" and gleefully embraced him.

The people around them shuffled and stirred, vocalizing their irritation. Choking back his embarrassment, he eased her and her enthusiasm back into her seat again, surrendering his hand to her. He turned to the scowling goateed fellow at his other side. "Don't give it another thought, good sir. She's my tigress!"

After the play, they dined two blocks from the theater at, *Old Joe's*, an Italian restaurant she chose. It was on Geary just off Union Square. She insisted on sitting at the counter where they were able to savor the delicious aromas emanating from the kitchen all through dinner. "See why I like to sit up here?" she said, beaming like a schoolgirl.

He kept spouting superlatives in praise of the food because she seemed so giggly happy that he was enjoying it. In truth, he spent the meal mesmerized, enchanted, totally in her thrall. Never was a man more in love with a woman.

Embracing, they strolled down her flagstone path. "For sure, you're not going to stay with me tonight?" she asked again with such disappointment in her voice.

"Only because I want to make the necessary arrangements to move you tomorrow. I want us to begin our lives together immediately. And to accomplish that smoothly, I've got to get back to Carmel tonight."

"Carmel?" She halted. Her face blanked. "You don't live in San Francisco?"

"I used to, but now I have a..." he needed to clear his throat "a place in Carmel. You will live with me in Carmel, won't you?"

"Ben." She lolled her head girlishly to the side. "This is so sudden. Realize I've been an autonomous woman. I'm used to my private world." Her gaze drifted across her front yard and porch.

He sensed her quandary. "Forgive me. I let myself fall so deeply in love with you that I've failed to consider how much you must love this place, and that you might not want to give it up. How about we time share, coming back here regularly to enjoy this place and each other in it."

She threw her arms around his neck and hugged him. Holding him tightly, she tossed her head back and met his eyes. "But you're a man who seems to understand finances, so I should be honest with you. I still owe quite a bit on this sweet little property, and the taxes are astronomical. You won't see it as much of an investment." She frowned in mock dejection and bowed her forehead to touch his chest.

Placing the crook of his index finger under her chin, he raised her face. "Jenny, I didn't rent that stretch limo over there for this evening. It's part of an international fleet of them I own." Her eyes widened a bit, for real. "My house in Carmel is paid for, and it's as big as two grand hotels put together, complete with a thirty-six hole golf course for a front yard. And, brace yourself, I essentially own General Motors Corporation by myself, along with shipping lines, airlines, more corporations and companies and factories than I can count or would want to, not to mention hundreds and hundreds of thousands of acres of agricultural and commercial land that are in my name. God knows what I'm worth."

Her jaw rested limp atop his finger and her arms fell away from his neck. Compensating, he enfolded her in his arms and pulled her close.

"Jenny, you and I—remember, Benny and Jenny, Jenny and Benny—we have an incalculable fortune and the rest of our lives to spend it on anything and everything we want."

Her strange awe puzzled him. "Did I say something wrong?"

She shook her head. "I've dreamed of being with you since I was a teeny-bopper. But I had no inkling you'd be rich."

"Okay, so your wonderful imagination left something out. But back to reality: I'll return tomorrow for you. And from then on, we'll never spend another night apart as long as we live. I promise."

She glanced off. "You can't promise me that, Ben. We'll be in love forever, but heartache is coming. It's not going to be all roses." Her words sent a chill through him, as Max's did at times.

Chapter 34

Despite Ben's vigorous objections, she insisted on waiting on her porch until he drove off. Only when the taillights disappeared around a distant curve did she step inside.

After only a few minutes, a soft knock came at the front door. She sped back and jerked it open. "You've come back," she cried out before she actually saw the caller. Startled, she swung the door back to almost closed. "Who are you?" she asked through the slit, more than a little frightened. "What do you want?"

Standing quite still and straight before her in the yellow aura of porch light was a tall, fine-boned Asian man, maybe in his early fifties. His raven-black hair had just a hint of gray at the temples, and it glistened in the radiance from the Tiffany above him. His lime sharkskin suit looked as smart as Ben's tuxedo had early in the evening.

Calmly, mutely, the stranger bowed in a gracious manner that lessened her trepidation a little.

"My name is Lee Wo Fang," he said at the nadir, then righted himself. "I am an investigator working in conjunction with the United States Department of Justice." His English diction neared perfection with just a hint of Chinese. He carefully held open his leather-bound credentials for her.

Her concern slowly gave way to a welling curiosity. "Why are you here now? Tonight? At this hour?"

"Miss Bligh, the United States Government is investigating one Benjamin Roberts, the gentleman who just left here. I wish to speak with you about him, on your government's behalf."

"You've been watching my house?"

"Only as an avenue to gather much desired information about him."

"Why are you investigating him? What has he done?" But in that instant, she recalled the things Ben told her about his stupendous fortune.

"Please, if you will just allow me a few minutes of your time at this regretfully late hour, I shall tell you much more than you apparently now know about the man, and perhaps you will be so kind as to answer a few of my questions. That may prove ever so helpful." With even greater grace, he bowed a second time.

Not being a timid woman, she let her curiosity win out over her imploring common sense. She swung the door wide to this mysterious, late-hour visitor.

As the limo tires grumbled over the cobbled bricks crossing his golf course, Ben's Rolex read 4:05. He considered taking his jacket off to avoid inciting wonder in the housestaff who might still be up. But what the hell, the chauffeur would tell all later anyway.

Stepping into his bedroom complex, he tossed his battle-scarred tuxedo jacket onto his bed, and then quickly strode the distance to his study.

"Max, I'm dead tired, but we've got to talk."

Benjamin, Benjamin, Benjamin! This night was a nuclear explosion, completely unexpected. Jenny intended to behave ladylike all evening except for some good-natured flirting until you got home from the play.

"Well, she really, and I mean really, changed her mind. And that woman now owns me, heart and soul."

I know, Ben. She spent an hour at the computer with her diary tonight after Lee Wo Fang left her place, and thus filled me in on what I didn't already know.

"The Beijing Bulldog? He was there? With her? Tonight?"

Yes. He was crouched by the side of the house when you returned. He knocked at her door minutes after you drove off.

And be sure, he told her much, in the manner of answering her tidal wave of questions, emphasizing how you went from virtual insolvency only months ago to become the richest man in the world today. He told her about the government's suspicions of your insider trading, congressional influence buying, shady real estate dealings, and hinted at much, much more.

"Oh no!" Elbows on the table, he buried his face in his hands. "She said there'd be heart break."

Well being overly concerned I'd tell you too much, this time I didn't tell you enough.

He rubbed his eyes with the heels of his palms to soothe their sting from fatigue. "*Please* elucidate."

My boy, you triggered the explosion when you walked up with the wine. Why did you take that wine to her place?

"I don't know. We were almost at the house when the idea just popped into my head. I remembered you said she really liked those wines, and I had them on hold. So I went back and got it for her. You know, wine in lieu of flowers or candy. That's all there was to it."

Not by a long shot, bucko! I told you about her strong psychic bent. Well, she's been foretelling major events in the lives of family members and friends since her early childhood. These premonitions usually come to her as recurring dreams, often symbolic, but accurate to a remarkable degree when she analyzes them in retrospect.

It so happens, since her early teens, she's dreamed frequently about her soul mate coming to her. And the image she's seen again and

again—always to the background music of Berlioz's *Symphonie Fantastique, Opus 14*—is a knight in armor cradling a bottle of wine in each arm.

Here comes the eerie part, my boy. About six years ago, the clarity of one dream allowed her to read the labels on the bottles.

He slumped. "Don't tell me. Let me guess. A George LaTour, Beaulieu Vintage and a Chateau Lafitte, Rouge, 1962."

Right, Ben! She's never made out her lover's face, even though the face piece on his helmet is always flipped up. But she has said several times in her diary that the silhouette of the flipped up mask looks like a *silk top hat* on his head.

"But, Max, I was wearing a tuxedo, not a suit of armor." Then he remembered his medieval daydream while Murray was checking the outfit. He went cold.

Ben, her knight always comes to her wearing black full armor, except for a large white, upside-down triangle painted on his chest plate.

"Holy Christ," he swallowed, "like the visible part of my shirt!"

So when you came walking down that path in that tuxedo, carrying those two extremely rare wines in your arms and wearing that top hat, psychologically everything suddenly meshed for her. Instantly, there was absolutely no doubt in her mind. Her years of waiting were over.

"What happened in her dreams when her black-and-white knight would show up?"

She'd coax him into her bed, and they'd make passionate love for hours. Ben, are you thinking deja vu?

Guilt speared him. "I say again, Max, this is fraud. The only reason I knew about those wines is because you told me about them, because she wrote about it in her diary."

And Ben, I'll say again, who knows? Maybe I was the integral factor her premonition counted on. And I didn't tell you to stop and pick up that wine or to carry it cradled in your arms like that. That idea just *popped* into your head. Remember? Spooky, spooky, spooky stuff!

On to the nagging questions! "What's with the Beijing Bulldog, f'christsake? Why did he come by so late, and why in the hell did she let him in at that hour?"

He did scare her at first. But his smooth professionalism won her confidence, with help from her healthy curiosity.

Actually, she is safe enough in the event of any dangerous intrusions into her home, though she doesn't know it. Since you overreacted around her that day in the music shop, the feds have had her home under twenty-four hour a day surveillance from the above hillside. The bulldog surely suspected that, but he desperately wanted to question her.

"Did he wheedle anything important out of her?"

No, but interestingly he did ask her if you ever mentioned anyone named Max. Damn it, but that fellow is good.

He scooted the swivel chair in closer. "Jessuz, how did he learn about you?"

Pertinacity, my boy. Isn't this exciting?

"Thrilling. I can almost feel my scratchy prison uniform."

Brace yourself, Ben. There's another bit of information I withheld from you, hoping to keep you less anxious. The feds have Jenny's house thoroughly bugged.

"What!" He slapped his palms down so hard onto the desktop they smarted. "You mean they heard everything tonight?

To lighten this a bit, there were times when they deduced you were beating up on her. Later, when they saw the condition of your tuxedo, they revised their theory and now wonder the reverse.

"Sonofabitch!" He hammered the sides of his fists onto the desk, to avoid the sting from slapping it. "Max, tonight was the pinnacle of my sexual life. If you analyzed all the male sexual fantasies ever concocted, there wouldn't be one in the bunch close to what I actually experienced this evening. And now you tell me that while I soared through ecstasy, a dozen cigarette-smoking, coffee-sipping federal agents munched hamburgers and fries, listening to our every moan and sigh."

Sorry, Ben. But, actually, before it's put to rest, tens of thousands of people will have listened to and studied your moment: national and international law enforcement agents, psychologists, psychiatrists, etc., all trying to gain insight into the personality of the man who is buying up the world.

"Aw shit! Shit! Shit!" He hung his head then shook it. "Why did I pick up that frigging wine?"

Ben? Ben?

He finally glanced at the monitor. "Yeah?"

Let's say you could replay the entire evening, knowing what you know now. Would you really have skipped the wine?

He checked his knee-jerk urge to blurt out, "Hell yes." But because of the way Max phrased the question, he instead mulled it over a moment. He kicked his legs up onto the desk beside the computer and rocked back, grinning.

"No, Max. Hell no. Come to think of it, I wouldn't change one damn second of the whole evening."

Chapter 35

"Good morning, Max. I woke up a bit sore. Sure needed that sauna and massage after my workout this morning."

Well, Ben, you can't go around falling off beds, knocking into walls, and toppling furniture for two hours without experiencing a few muscle aches the next day.

He enjoyed the embarrassed flush that warmed his cheeks. "I wasn't complaining, just stating a fact."

This is your big day, my boy! Jenny is coming *home*. I hope you don't mind, but I sent her a lengthy e-mail early this morning to smooth over a few rough spots, and to bolster her resolve to move down here on such short notice.

"*You* sent her an e-mail?" Haunting suspicion again poked him hard.

Trust me, Ben. After your hasty invitation and the bulldog's visit, it was needed. First off, I told her she isn't to move anything out of her home, that you want it to stay exactly like it is, that she need bring with her only the few toilet articles she would rather not duplicate.

I promised her that a chauffeured vehicle would be at her disposal twenty-four hours a day, and it would be available on a moment's notice to take her back to Sausalito any time she wanted, for as long as she wished to stay there. And although you considered her home a place to be shared by the both of you, it will remain completely hers, her personal domain.

"I get it. So I'm not totally absorbing her."

Right, Ben! In anticipation of her move here, I've had the third floor of the Palacio redone. She'll have a bedroom-to-study arrangement that's very similar to yours, but decorated to her taste. I know it well.

Because I want her to immediately feel at home and rapidly settle in, I've also purchased for her a leaping start at a new wardrobe, again knowing her sizes and tastes intimately.

The furnishings and clothing awaiting her are mostly items she's secretly admired for a long time but regarded as ridiculously more expensive than she could afford.

"Jeez, what am I going to say when she asks how I knew to buy all that stuff?"

I doubt very much that she will ask. She's certain now that events are happening just the way they were meant to, according to some divine plan. I may have clinched it, Ben, when I signed the note this morning simply, *your piebald knight.*

Her diary entry this morning after she got my e-mail moved me deeply. She wrote she is absolutely sure that over the coming eons, your souls will dance together across the universe, the galaxies serving like the flagstones along her front yard path."

What more can I say to you both—except enjoy!

"Damn it. Sometimes I'm taken by a fear that I'm about to wake up on that saggy couch in my old Helman Street apartment and find all this has been just a dream."

Ha! If you do, your biography will read like a bromide. And will never sell.

"Since you sent the e-mail, my phoning her would be redundant. I hope you made arrangements for me to pick her up."

A limo should be waiting in Marin County about now. You'll helicopter up to meet it, then pick her up and drive back here.

The reality of this estate will overwhelm her at first, even though the bulldog painted a rather accurate picture of your life style.

A pleasant ride down here, arriving at the front entrance, will offer her a gentler acclimation, in contrast to a zooming helicopter flight hitting her with a bird's eye introduction.

But more importantly, sitting next to you for a couple of hours will allow her time to deal with some of the anxiety Lee Wo Fang incited.

"That makes sense, as usual. But..."

But what, Ben?

"Shouldn't I tell her about you?"

No! No! Please believe me, she will see all we've done as heinous duplicity, as abominable manipulation of her privacy and trust, and that would dangerously test her feelings for you.

"Then you expect me to live my entire life with her, forever being less than completely open and totally honest about someone so central in my life as you are?"

You must compartmentalize me out from all the rest of your interfacing with her—a tiny concession to me and a bearable deceit for you, so long as you love and honor her the entire rest of your *lives* together.

Too, a fringe benefit of her not knowing about me is that she'll continue to use a computer to record her diary entries. That way I can stay abreast of any problems that may arise.

Damn it, but he found the last argument the most compelling. Swiping a finger under his nose, he said, "Okay, but if we start off not telling her, we'll never be able to. The more time that passes, the more despicable our conspiracy becomes. Still, my greatest objection to our silence is that she'll never get to know you."

Ben, through your financial successes, your social successes, and through this emerging new you, she will know me.

"No, I mean if she could actually meet you, I bet she'd really love you." He waited. Then he tapped the monitor screen with a crooked finger. "Max? Hey, Max!"

The monitor remained lighted, but blank.

His white helicopter traced the shoreline northward again, zipping along at the core of a whap-whap-whapping din. Steeped in thought, Ben gazed out the window, hardly aware of the royal blue of the ocean beneath or its seemingly static pattern of squiggly whitecaps that shone luminescent at the touch of the morning sun.

Hmmm! So Max took it upon himself to contact her. Why does that bother me?

The Golden Gate Bridge loomed into view. Wisps of gray mist were creeping under it from the seaward side. Minutes later, the chopper raced along that invisible outer lane again, but today he paid little attention to the wonderment in the faces behind the windows of the vehicles.

Uneasiness stirred him, in part because of his pending encounter with Jenny, but mostly because of Max.

I've taken you on faith up till now, but it's possible you've merely been using me. Was all this build up just to lure Jenny to the Palacio? Hell, you've effectively established 'Ben Roberts' as your front. Get me out of the way and you could easily run the entire organization from now on with faxed directives with my name attached.

The chopper hovered above that same grassy knoll, then settled onto.

Sure, you delivered on everything you promised, but I don't recall you ever specifying exactly how long I'd get to keep it—except in vague terms.

He shrugged dismissively as he unbuckled his seat. *Ah, but what the hell! Without you, I'd be thumbing rides to get around today. Yep, if this were to end now, I guess I'd have to say it's been worth it.*

As the glittering maroon limo wended down the Sausalito slope, he strained at the side window to catch the first glimpse of her house. There! Jenny stood on her porch, shaded from the brilliant morning sun. Her only baggage was a yellow-canvas overnight bag that hung from her left shoulder. When she stepped out of the shade into a broad patch of sunlight, her white crew-neck sweater, white slacks, and white leather flats dazzled like a vision of an archangel. He could make out that she was wearing a single-strand pearl necklace. Damn, she could have been a French model showing top-of-the-line casual wear at some exclusive fashion salon. He'd wondered how she would dress today, figuring maybe a fur or some other ostentatious garb. But no, just this simple, clean statement. What a woman!

As the limousine eased to a stop, she strolled out through the picket gate onto the lane. Even after last night, anticipation of again being close to her rattled him.

She walked decisively to the rear door and reached for the handle. Mandrake poked his head up from the driver's side and hollered, "Please don't, Miss Bligh. Allow me." He raced around the vehicle and, huffing from the sprint, jerked the door open for her.

"Thank you."

"No, Miss Bligh. I thank you."

Ben intended to slide out and greet her with a hug, but she too quickly scooted in beside him. Seated against him, she kissed him tenderly on the cheek. "Good morning, my love," she said softly.

Her greeting midst the ethereal fragrance of *Eternity* sent an exuberant rush through him. But he noted the redness in her eyes. Had she been crying? Goddamn that Bulldog! He proffered several immediate compliments but received only a weak smile without any verbal response.

The limo swung up onto the freeway and started across the Golden Gate Bridge. Seeking only to breach the silence, he opened, "What do you know? This makes the third time we've crossed this bridge together in less than twenty four hours."

She made no comment, seemingly preoccupied with several deck-loaded cargo ships approaching the mouth of the bay. Neither of them said another thing for three-quarters of an hour. But as the limo skirted around Half Moon Bay, he decided to attack her mood head on.

"You seem troubled, Jenny. I realize you must have mixed emotions about leaving your home, especially on such short notice, but I sense there's more behind your reticence. Is it something about me? About last night?"

She mutely shook her head. But a minute later she abruptly swung about and faced him. "Benny, you paid ten thousand dollars apiece for the Curran tickets we used last night. Who did you originally intend to take to the play? You purchased them long before we even met at Gambino's wine shop."

"Huh?" She caught him off guard. Max hadn't been specific enough about what the Bulldog told her. "Actually...Actually, I didn't buy them. Someone in my corporation thought I might like to see it, so the tickets were purchased before I knew about them. Honest!"

Her grimace conveyed utter incredulity. "Your people can spend twenty thousand dollars for a pair of theater tickets without consulting you?"

His skin felt clammy. "Jenny, understand this, I woke up one day into a fairytale world where money is no longer any concern; dollars are rather like matchsticks in a friendly game of poker, only a minor item to help keep score." He elected not to ask how she learned of the price of the tickets. She had to note his lack of inquisitiveness, but she remained silent. Finally, bracing himself, he added, "Now is a good time for any more questions. We still have a ways to go, and sitting here gives you an excellent opportunity."

"Yes!" she said, her eyes narrowing. "What do you perceive as the end-point of your financial rampage? I mean, what is your ultimate goal in life?"

He swallowed. "Goal? Actually, I don't have any long-range goals, other than to enjoy being with you."

"But you must, to be so aggressive on every economic front when you have more than enough by any regal standard."

He chuffed, saying, "Ask me why people climb Mount Everest. Because it's there."

"Because it's there?" she repeated, as if his answer was ridiculous. She turned to her window and her apparent fascination with the shoreline.

Some time went by with only the back of her head visible to him, and then she abruptly wheeled again. "One more question. Do you know anyone named Max? And if so, tell me about him."

Wow! Thanks, ol' buddy, for warning me on this one. He realized she was keenly observing his reaction to the question.

He feigned a thoughtful expression. "Max, you say? Hmmm. Let me think."

Even emotionally riled, her face appeared wholesomely fresh. Had she purposely decided to wear no makeup, or was she so distraught this morning she forgot to apply it? Damn it, he couldn't blatantly lie to her, so he scrambled searching for an acceptable half-truth.

"Jenny," he said, deftly feigning a relaxed smile, "every person has a right to a private place within himself that is inviolable, even to the most beloved persons in his life. I know things that I'll probably never divulge to you, even though my reluctance to share them causes me torment." His stall proved suddenly fruitful; an out came to him. "But in this case, I can say categorically I don't recall a single human being among my family members or acquaintances named Max. I did know a Max casually in high school, but I haven't seen or heard from him since I was sixteen years old."

He maintained earnest eye contact as she seemingly weighed his need for such convolution. But behind his contrived facade, he seethed. *Aw shit, Max. I can't continue to bullshit her like this.*

She actually nestled closer to him, but turned again to face her window. "Thank you," she said. "Do you want to know why I asked?"

"I have a feeling you'd rather not tell me." At least, he hoped so.

"Would you accept that?"

A simple "yes" might raise more questions. "The only thing I would never accept is the withdrawal of your love."

She leaned against him more heavily and rested her cheek against his shoulder and her hand on his thigh. He slipped his arm tenderly around her.

"That's not even an option," she whispered.

Chapter 36

They veered off the Coast Highway and for a while traveled on a two-lane road lined by rangy Ponderosa pines. An eight-foot-high stone fence commenced on the right, running along behind the Ponderosas. A few miles farther, the limo slowed at a massive iron gate. A guard shack sat ensconced behind it.

Ben touched her elbow. "This is it." She sat up, suddenly attentive.

Anticipating them, the black gate swung inward allowing the vehicle to turn off the road without coming to a complete stop. As soon as the limo passed behind the stone fence, it glided onto the narrow redbrick roadway that wound across the golf course. The warm sun had climbed to its zenith in the blue heaven that was unmarred except for a few wispy cirrus clouds to the north.

"This is our golf course," he said.

"Oh, Lord!" she exclaimed. She scanned the prim fairways and the walls of stately Cypress trees lining them. "It goes on for as far as I can see."

"Thirty-six holes and there's a mile buffer of woods on three sides."

"Who plays on this course?"

He shrugged weakly. "Just me, I guess."

"Just you?" Her face blanked. She peered out the rear window at a glistening white sand trap and a cobalt-blue pond in proximity to the sixth green.

He nudged her again, pointing ahead. "We're home."

More towering Cypress guarded the front side of the giant laurel hedge that ran the length of a fairway. A second iron gate through the wall of hedge slowly swung in as the limo neared.

Her first glimpse through the gateway took in a kaleidoscopic view of the north garden with its pool and spa and a profusion of flowers. "Oh!" she loosed a whimper. "This is unbelievably magnificent."

She scooted closer to the side window, pressing her palms and nose tip to the glass like a child looking into a candy store. She emitted faint "Ohs" and "Ahs" in staccato.

The eastern face of the Palacio loomed into view. To Ben's surprise, the estate employees had gathered en masse in front just as they had the morning he returned from Michigan. Their immaculate uniforms were resplendent in the brilliant midday sunshine.

Surely Max choreographed this welcome.

Jenny spotted the waiting throng and emitted her loudest "Oh!" Her hands sought her sweater front as she glanced down along her outfit to her shoes.

He read her. "You look stunning," he said. "You're going to wow them."

"Do all these people work for you?"

He hunched his lower lip and nodded.

"I imagined a butler and a few maids, but this! There must be fifty people. Ben, this estate wasn't built for one family."

Her awe and admiration pleased him. Yeah, what woman could ever lose interest in a man who offered her all this? "No. The King of Saudi Arabia built it for his clan and his retinue to be available when he visited this country. It was also used by his diplomats and important Saudi businessmen."

"Then how—"

Anticipating her question, he said, "The Gulf War momentarily preoccupied the Saudis. My people exerted a bit of pressure, and they sold it to us."

"I can't believe what I'm seeing."

"Don't be too impressed yet, wait till you see the inside and get a look at its ocean view."

Clive, wearing impeccable black tails, swung open the limo door for her. The employees had lined up single file as they had in the rear for Ben that first day he arrived by helicopter. But today, they wound along the driveway and continued up the front steps to the Gothic oaken doors. Her arm trembled as Ben helped her out of the vehicle. She stood self-consciously adjusting the lower edge of her sweater. "You were right," she said in an undertone. "This place could be a national shrine."

The estate staff stood fidgeting with eagerness to meet "Mr. Roberts' lady." Clive initially introduced Jenny to two young British women and a Hispanic lady who were to be her personal attendants. She stiffened at this announcement, but Ben's arm around her checked any back step. Then Clive graciously led her down the receiving line. The staff held their positions until the last person formally met her just at the Palacio's front entranceway then Ben beckoned to the serpentine to re-gather on the steps before him.

With his left arm around Jenny's shoulders, he addressed them. "So now you've met my precious Jenny Bligh." He gave her a squeeze. "And I want to make one point absolutely clear from the onset. Ms. Bligh will not be living here with *me*. We will be living here with *each other*. She is now the doyenne of the estate. No order from her needs my approval."

She leaned against him with her arm clutching his waist, trying to appear relaxed. But her eyes were teary, and she obviously wanted her emotions to proceed no further in the direction they were headed. So she whispered playfully, "Was I really that good last night?"

He winked. "No. You were really that bad."

"How corny." She tittered.

Chapter 37

"Good afternoon, Max. As you must know, Clive and Jenny's attendants have taken her on a tour of the Palacio."

Good afternoon, my boy. Jenny hasn't seen much of the Palacio yet. They took her to her suite first. Unlike you, she's an artist and refuses to swallow this all in one gulp. She insists on thoroughly examining each piece of her furniture and artwork. She won't get around to the rest of the estate until after lunch.

Realize, Ben, the speed of your acclimation to your new life here was truly remarkable. Expect Jenny to take a bit longer to adjust to it all.

"Okay. But let me say she was quite upset when I picked her up, thanks to that goddamn Bulldog. Fortunately, she perked by the time we got here. She did ask about the twenty-thousand-dollar theater tickets and if I knew anybody named Max. How about I call her up here and introduce you two and put an end to my charade."

NO! Absolutely not! Please, you must see that you're courting disaster with that line of thinking.

"But your way, I fear things might become difficult."

Have no fear. They invariably do.

"Not what I want to hear."

Which reminds me, it's time to address something that I'm sure has been bothering you. As you know, I see and hear everything in and about this estate. But, Ben, any time the two of you start to favor intimacy, I will immediately cut off my perception of sight and sound in your location, wherever you may be. How you two express your carnal affection will be known only to the two of you.

He eased out a sigh, trying to do so noiselessly. "Thanks, Max. I'll admit that had me a tad uncomfortable. But you'll still learn a lot from her diary."

If you want, I can focally blind myself to any entries concerning same.

"Hell no. I'm counting on your invaluable insight into her mind and heart. But, damn it, I feel like a bastard admitting that."

Again, here the end truly justifies the means. If your lives together are loving and joyful, the gods must forgive this one transgression.

My boy, I've ordered you two a scrumptious lunch up on the roof garden.

"Good."

And arranged a trip tomorrow on your yacht...

"Oh, brother. Be sure to get me some seasick pills."

...For a scuba outing off Monterey.

"What?" He bolted out of the chair and glared down at the monitor. "You've got to be kidding? I'm still taking lessons and a long way from being ready for the ocean."

You're ready, Ben. Actually, after the first twelve hours of instruction, you were officially ready for an open water dive. I've kept Lieutenant Raymo working with you this long to be certain you had the basics down, indelibly.

"Jessuz." He massaged his forehead. "I take it Jenny knows how to dive?"

Like a porpoise. She's as much at home fifty feet under water as she is on dry land. Now don't worry, Lt. Raymo will make sure everything goes safely. Remember, he's a combat-trained diving medical officer, adept at handling veritably every contingency. Ben? Ben?

Still massaging his forehead, he shook his head. "Max, to be completely honest here, it scares the crap out of me to think of diving out there," he jabbed a finger at the oceanic panorama in front of him. "Down in that goddamn shark-infested abyss."

He pointed below at the Grecian pool. "I didn't want to take those damn lessons 'cuz it could lead to this."

Ben, she loves the ocean and diving. She will meet you more than halfway with all your wants and pleasures. Will you not partake and share in this great avocation of hers?

"Damn it, Max. I've gone along with everything you've asked of me so far, but this could be tantamount to suicide if I go voluntarily—and murder if you coerce me. That churning ocean terrifies me. I can see myself ending up piecemeal in scattered cakes of shark shit."

Ben, Ben, Ben. You're a scream. Jenny has been diving hundreds of hours 'out there' and never had so much as a close call yet.

"Yeah? Well, maybe they call those voracious bastards 'man-eaters' because they have a predilection for testicle-bearing types." A thought occurred to him. "Hey, you don't have any unexplainable influence over sea life, too, do you?"

Sorry. But I do have access to all the statistics, and the shark threat is truly insignificant. Lt. Raymo can handle all the major risks consummately. And remember, my boy, I do know that you've faced more than your share of dangers in the past—and you did so as staunchly as any human being who ever lived.

"Okay. Okay." He collapsed back down in the swivel chair, slapping his thighs in exasperation. "Okay, okay. Anything short of acquiescence would make me out an ingrate, and worse—a coward in Jenny's eyes. Crap! So tomorrow I troll myself for great whites. Forgive me if I assume this to be my last day on Earth."

With slight modifications, Ben, that's a grand philosophy to live by every day, scuba diving or no.

After the monitor cleared, he remained seated, staring out at the boundless sea. Paranoia roused anew in him.

This dive trip comes too damn soon after her arrival. What if...what if Max just needed me around until she moved in? Maybe Lt. Raymo's been paid off. Need a patsy, find a loser who no one will miss!

As if coming to his senses, he laughed off the thought, stood up, and sauntered off.

Chapter 38

Clive paged Ben's suite announcing that Jenny was waiting for him on the roof garden for lunch. For exercise, Ben bypassed an elevator and took the nearest stairs, and enjoyed the bright murals along the stairwell walls.

He emerged onto a garden plaza. Round, wrought-iron tables and chairs festively adorned this thirty-foot square of vividly patterned talavera tiles. Multicolored tablecloths and equally colorful table umbrellas enlivened the arrangement. The panoramic Pacific Ocean was sublime, unobscured except for the birds that swirled through the now cloudless sky. Jenny was seated at a table abutting the low seaward wall that edged the building top.

As he approached, her dreamy gaze shifted from the royal-blue water to him. She galvanized. Leaping up, she lunged into his embrace. "Ben, this is the most beautiful garden I've ever seen. Why, it's surely more than an acre. And to be nestled atop a mansion, how magnificent!" She gushed on. "The view. This view. Oh, my love, being with you and enjoying all this exceeds my wildest dreams. I insist that we live happily ever after!"

The sea was in a peevish mood, piqued by a brisk, warm breeze that whipped up whitecaps as it carried in the fragrances of seaweed and salt. Ben easily distinguished both. Gusts played with their yellow-and-blue umbrella and the edges of their yellow-and-blue checkered tablecloth. A central bouquet of pink rose buds in a narrow-necked vase on the table jiggled like a metronome.

Jenny effervesced throughout the meal, pausing at times to track various soaring birds with her outstretched arm, pronouncing the genus and species of each type. Once, she pointed out a pair of tiny dark dots on the ocean's horizon that she said were, in fact, huge ships far off at sea.

Dipping a bite of crabmeat into her cucumber sauce, she said, "Ben, some of the staff want to take me on a tour of the Palacio and grounds this afternoon, but could we meet before dinner for a swim in the north garden pool? It looks so inviting, so deliciously refreshing."

"Sure," he agreed, trying to hide his sudden aversion to it. He now regarded that pool as a co-conspirator in forcing him into ocean scuba diving.

"And Ben," she whispered coquettishly, "would you come to me tonight, to my beautiful room and majestic bed?" She actually blushed.

"It's a date."

She crinkled her nose. "Then tomorrow night, I'll come to you. We can alternate every night, if you like. More fun than always sleeping together in the same bed."

Unbeknownst to her, the mere mention of the morrow subverted her seduction. He stared off at those tiny dots on the horizon and luridly imagined fragmenting cakes of shark shit teetering down through the murky depths all round out there. He shuddered. She probably assumed the breeze was chilling him.

That night, delaying physical intimacy, she insisted on first divulging all about her writing career including her use of a pseudonym. She apologized for her deception during their chance meeting in the Fig Garden Bookstore and whispered, "A divine love like ours must be totally honest, must be absolutely free from all deceit."

Hoping the darkness obscured the guilt surely emblazoned on his face, he merely agreed, "Absolutely." But his albatross would not be completely denied; it delayed their pleasure for an embarrassing while.

Chapter 39

The duel inboard engines of the *Orca*, the *Nabila*'s thirty-eight foot diving boat, rumbled through the dark water, belching out diesel fumes into its churning wake. Ben stood alone aft admiring the silhouette of the colossal great yacht as it receded into what was left of the night. The world around him spread from horizon to horizon as monotonous velvety blue-black undulations interrupted only by the gurgling, foamy wake veeing out behind the *Orca*. The sun, about to peek over the eastern edge of infinitude, pushed up a tinge of heralding gold that defined a sliver that was California viewed from many miles at sea. The bracing breeze, the pitch and groan of the *Orca*, and the snugness of his neoprene wet suit charged him with giddy excitement. Yet, he continually darted glances about the briny surface for any hint of triangular dorsal fins.

Inhaling the pelagic freshness, he looked over his shoulder at Lieutenant Raymo, who was showing Jenny something on his regulator. "Lieutenant, should I start putting on my scuba gear?" Raymo nodded.

Submerged, Ben was a bird flying in a liquid sky. The intimacy of the engulfing transparent fluid intoxicated him as he soared around and between the leafy kelp stalks of an oceanic forest. Lt. Raymo and Jenny assiduously worked to keep him sandwiched between them as he meandered about like a toddler exploring a springtime backyard garden. At first, the rhythmic whishing of air gushing into him from his tank then out through his snorkel excited him, as might the blare of rock music. Raymo continually signaled him to slow his breathing rate. They surfaced frequently and the lieutenant would critique him at length. Ben gradually became more relaxed, feeling ever more in control. With their air tanks still more than half-full, Raymo signaled and coaxed Ben down to the crest of the reef where the kelp stalks were rooted. Ben skimmed over the white sandy floor, poking his gloved fingers at purple sea urchins and orange starfish. He dug his hands into the grit as if it were a playground sand box. Looking upward through the kelp made him think of fairy-tale beanstalks growing up through the clouds to a land of giants.

After what seemed like only a few minutes, Raymo tapped him on the shoulder and gestured with a thumb up, showing him his air tank gauge that read nearly empty.

When they broke surface, Ben spit out his mouthpiece and bellowed a triumphant whoop. Taking his tank off in the boat, he chattered ecstatically, using superlatives nonstop. Finally Jenny stepped over and kissed him on the lips, perhaps to shut him up. "Ben, you did well. I'm so happy you enjoy diving."

"Enjoy it? Honey, I'm enraptured. We're going to use one more tank today, aren't we?"

"Yes, love, but first I'd like to briefly explore that deeper ravine to the west. Lt. Raymo and I ought to make that dive alone. When we come up, we'll work the reef again with you."

"Huh? No. I want to go, too." *What's this? I'm not a little kid, and this is my boat. I can damn well go if I want to.*

"Ben, we'll be going down a hundred feet, and that's far too deep for you to venture on your first outing."

"But I want to go," he insisted. "You won't have to pay me any mind. I'll just tag along dutifully and be no trouble at all." He refrained from playing his trump card of ownership.

Jenny glanced off.

Her obvious reluctance discouraged him. "The hell with it," he said, releasing his blue dive fins to plop on the deck. "Go without me."

"Mr. Roberts," Raymo spoke up. "The three of us can dive the ravine."

Jenny shot him a questioning look.

"I'm serious, Ms. Bligh. I've worked with him in the pool for weeks. That's far more preparation for a first open-water dive than usual. And he proved quite adept during his shallow dive." He winked at Ben. "She can lead us into the ravine. You follow her and I'll totally attend to you." Smiling at Jenny's skeptical frown, he added, "A deep water descent will make this first trip especially memorable for him. I wouldn't allow it if I wasn't sure he could do it."

Uh-oh! Tingly suspicion roused Ben's sense of self-preservation. If Jenny had argued for him to go, little worry. But Raymo was Max's man.

The sun shone down from straight overhead by the time they immersed again with full tanks. The kelp forest lay far to the east. Ben now missed the sense of security from concealment that he enjoyed being among the towering plants. But he focused on Jenny's chartreuse-and-black rubber suit and followed her down, down through the changing light, down through the cooling temperatures. Raymo nudged him repeatedly to quell his surges of rapid breathing. But each unexpected contact actually caused him to flinch and ready himself for whatever, which briefly further accelerated his breathing rate. Yet, in a morbidly perverse way, the increased sense of risk coming from two potential fronts—the sharks and Max's man—actually fed Ben's excitement.

"You're commando material, fella," the army psychologists had told him after they reviewed his extensive battery of tests. "You function at your best in dangerous situations." And he ended up in that fateful arms-smuggling platoon. He'd assumed they were just spouting puffery. But, hey, surviving Afghanistan and, now, the way he felt inside swimming a hundred feet under the Pacific Ocean while watching out for sharks ahead and Raymo behind, maybe those shrinks were not far off the mark.

He expected to see a profusion of coral beds over the bottom, instead there lay rather sterile rocky crags that were covered with sea urchins and starfish and anemones. The predominant blue lighting at this depth changed the bland floor into scenes of otherworldliness. Sparse schools of nearly transparent, silvery fish, each about two feet long, swam aimlessly in the distance. He found their languor a comfort, reasoning that if sharks with an appetite were nearby, those bite-size fellows wouldn't be poking along.

Jenny's black fins scissored ahead along one rocky ridge after another. She missed no opportunity to pause and point out small bizarrely shaped fish hiding in crevices or spiny lobsters wedged back in hollows. She didn't need to call his attention to several mud-brown moray eels that slithered their heads out of their niches, cantankerously snapping their jaws. A man-sized sea bass ventured its voluminous head out of a gloomy cave, spotted them with its tiny eyes, and recoiled, roiling up dust-like algae that quickly obscured that entire section of ridge.

Jenny herself, as much as the undersea sights, kept Ben enthralled. He lovingly sensed her inside that enveloping layer of neoprene and that entanglement of diving apparatus. He imagined her crimson heart vigorously contracting, pushing hot blood along through vessels that wanted to compress under the squeeze of a ten-story column of chilly seawater. He visualized her lungs refilling with cyclic bursts of pressurized air from her yellow tank, and each breath thrusting her magnificent breasts outward.

Too soon they had to ascend from this dream odyssey.

He tapped the on-switch of his red iMac.

"Well, Max, I made it back alive." He kicked his shoes off, canted his swivel chair, and swung his stocking feet up on the desk beside the computer.

Congratulations on your fine dive, Ben. You profoundly impressed Lt. Raymo. And I had no doubt you'd survive, or I'd never have let you go out there.

Realize you've grown emotionally today. You've faced your fear and converted it to your pleasure. And so it will be with every obstacle ahead. I'll prepare you, and you'll overcome.

Sorry, Max. I'll never admit it but I was suspicious of your motives here. I wonder if you sensed my concern.

He thumped his palms against his chest and wiggled his toes. "I feel euphoric. Something reconnected in me while surfacing during that second dive. I was still about thirty feet down and moving up into a warmer thermocline when a feeling swept me, like nostalgia with an overwhelming desire to dive again as soon as possible. Maybe it was something atavistic from when my primeval ancestors were sea creatures themselves, or maybe it was simply a memory of the amniotic pool in my mother's womb. But I felt I belonged to the ocean depths. " He realized he sounded manic and close to ranting.

Amazing, Ben. Jenny expressed those same sentiments years ago after her first dive trip. Here, let me show you a poem she wrote after that five-day trip to the Cayman Islands. I bet you can now identify with much of it.

Stanzas rolled up the screen, espousing her compulsive love for the sea, her recognition that an oceanic abyss was her evolutionary home. He read the last stanza imagining her reciting it to him:

Yes, my haunting hunger for the sea,
this longing to behold its fluid vibrancy,
conjures up whisperings, 'tis true,
a homeward beckoning—deja vu,
Return, return again where shore and briny be.

"A little heavy on the rhyme, but damn, I like it. Print me a copy so I can re-read it later."

No way, my boy. Jenny buried this piece in her diary. And if she were to come across a printout of something that she knows is stored only on a locked-away computer disc, the damage would be irreparable.

Chapter 40

Jenny watched Ben ease out of her bed and quietly pick up his harlequin robe from her antique Louis XIV armchair. As he slipped it on, she loosed a moan, stretched both arms into the air, and mumbled sleepily, "Don't leave me. Stay and let's have breakfast here."

"Okay. Order it. I'll be back in two shakes."

"You're going to *it* again?" She sat up, not disguising her displeasure. "At this hour?"

"Just for a quick check on things."

"Love, I appreciate the effort it must take to manage all your holdings, but do you realize you're continually leaving me to rush back to that computer?"

"You're not becoming jealous of an office appliance, are you?" He grinned, which she found comforting. He bent over and kissed her forehead as she struggled to hold an unsmiling expression.

"Should I be?"

He laughed. "Look, babe, just order up a fabulous breakfast for us, and I'll be back in fifteen minutes, tops."

"Do you converse with any women in your organization on a daily basis?"

"Nah! Only with the program that runs the whole enchilada. No human interaction, at all."

"Swear?"

"Cross my heart." And he did.

"Good morning, Max. As you must know, we spent the night in her suite. Let me see..." He stroked his chin, chuckling. "You know, it's been over twelve weeks since she moved in, and she hasn't mentioned going back to Sausalito, even for a visit."

Good morning, Ben. Whew! The fires of your passion threaten the very stone of these citadel walls. But I'm delighted she's happy here.

He kicked off his slippers and rocked back in the chair to assume his favorite posture with his feet up on the desktop. Half-mindfully, he tapped the side of the monitor casing with a jiggling foot.

I don't mean to bring rain to your chipper morning, but you must be told this. A secret investigatory grand jury has convened in Los Angeles. It'll undoubtedly come up with a criminal indictment against you.

"What?" He jerked his feet off the desk and sprang up out of his chair. "They can't indict me, can they? I haven't done anything. What could they uncover that would suggest I've done anything at all illegal?"

Ben, there's a saying in the legal profession, "The most incompetent attorney can persuade a grand jury to indict a ham sandwich," and the lawyers you're up against are some of the brightest in the game.

"Now you're scaring the hell out of me."

Up front, let me allay any concern regarding your two sons in this matter. They're shielded. Seeing this coming, I arranged for their surrogate father to take a job in the jungles of New Guinea on a two-year contract at a salary neither he nor your ex-wife could turn down. Their home there is palatial and safe, and the very best tutors are being flown in on a rotating basis for the boys. The whole family is having the time of their life. I promise you, no one from the media or anyone bearing a subpoena will get within a hundred miles of them.

"Jeez!" He sat back down. "My sons," he mumbled to himself. After a minute, he said, "Max, I've been wanting to ask you to set up blind trusts for each of my boys that can never be broken. You know, where they'll get money at eighteen, then twenty-one, and so on, every few years for the rest of their lives. I mean, hefty amounts."

Consider it done, my boy. And the amounts will be truly regal.

"Thanks, Max." His mind leapt back to the crisis before him. He shook his head. "And just when everything's going great. Okay, so when will my indictment come through, and what'll the charges be?"

It should take several months at least. And surely they'll charge you with everything they can think of. They're presenting circumstantial evidence, so they plan to compile a mountain of it to gain impetus for when your prosecution actually starts. Ben, if you'll just relax and maintain your faith in me, this whole circus will be a lot of fun.

"Fun?" Snarling, he bolted to his feet again and began pacing. "One slipup and I could spend the rest of my life in a jail cell. Damn it, if I go to trial, my fate will be in the hands of twelve strangers. All they have to do is say *guilty* and..." Wringing his hands, he left the sentence unfinished as he imagined what prison might be like.

He turned to the screen. "Thanks, but no thanks, Max. I appreciate all you've done for me, but I'm bowing out. Just find some country that won't extradite me, then let Jenny and me step out of this whole mess. We'll live out the rest of our lives in blissful seclusion."

Ben, you feared the ocean depths till you faced them then you became enraptured. Only by facing adversity then overcoming it, will you ever know the greatest joys.

I have placed you in a position larger than life; you're held in awe by much of the world. If you run now, you will destroy everything we've built. You'll be regarded as nothing more than a highly successful crook. People aren't happy to learn that someone they respect as a

171

genius is in reality a clever cheat. It's akin to proving their gods to be false.

He began pacing again. "So I should risk my neck for the faceless masses! And if I'm found guilty, will they continue their holy reverence of me as I rot in prison? Hell no, they won't."

Let me assure you that you'll never rot in prison. But for the sake of argument, if you were to, there would always be doubt in their minds that maybe you were innocent? If you run, it is prima facie admission of guilt.

He wheeled and slapped both palms down on the desktop, pushing his face close to the screen. "The hell with what the world thinks. Just put Jenny and me in a foreign villa somewhere and give us the creature comforts that just a few hundred thousand dollars a year can afford, and we'll be happy as two clams for the rest of our lives. Toss all the rest back, and they'll probably forget about us."

Ben, Ben, Ben. There are facets of this situation you have not considered yet. Aside from my disappointment with your apparent waning confidence in me, you have a commitment, an obligation, to continue to live your true-life fantasy.

Millions and millions of people around the world considered yours the epitome of the very best life imaginable. They vicariously capture little pieces of your regality. Living even a few moments a day through you, they are more capable of enduring their own pain and tribulation. You have the grandest of lives; most of them have only grand dreams. Don't cheat them. The world needs heroes, people to admire and look up to. And you've become one of its tallest.

He lowered his head. "And goddamn it, this started out to be one of my better days. Max, your argument is a crock of melodramatic crap, and you know it." He collapsed back into his chair.

"So why me, Max? Why me? Of all the billions of people on this planet, why'd you pick me? Was it because I seemed like such a loser, because I was so computer ignorant? Someone who wouldn't know what the hell you were up to, someone who'd be so dazzled by all the glitter that I wouldn't question your ambition or scrutinize your meted favors for ulterior motives? Did you see me as the perfect patsy who'd trudge obediently to the slaughter? You kept your promise of money, fame and... and everything else, but you cleverly neglected to stipulate exactly how long I'd have them to enjoy."

He pressed his hands over his eyes, almost sick with a sudden sense he might soon lose Jenny. His hands fell to his lap. "You once referred to this arrangement with me as a game, a game of your own. Well, be honest with me now, Max. Is the game about over? If so, what's your definition of victory?

Benjamin, my boy, I saw in you the potential for a great reciprocal friendship. Someone with extraordinary unused intelligence, tremendous untapped fortitude, and too, someone with a very great but latent appetite for power. Someone who could savor the stature, the opulence, and the puissance that I could bestow, and yet not be distorted or consumed by my gifts as most other humans certainly would be.

"And now with me out of the way, you'd need only select yourself another pawn. Aha! Jenny herself perhaps?"

Ben, I've only wanted to be your friend. These accusations hurt me profoundly. Your trust is of the utmost importance to me. Everything I am doing is for your ultimate advantage. Test me. Go ahead, ask for anything, and so be it!

"Jessuz. Again you wedge me between seeming ungrateful and acquiescing meekly. I know you won't be happy until I agree to go through an indictment and trial wherein I face losing everything. God only knows your secret agenda."

No, Ben. My agenda is heeding your choices. I'll back you completely in any decision you ever make. I gave you my word. But remember your first day in the Palacio when you asked how you could repay me? Well, your complete trust now would be more than payment in full. A major flaw in the human species is that it doesn't value honor or friendship nearly enough. But I sensed that you did.

"Then I'm sorry, Max. But I've got to use the good sense I was born with and ask you to move us out of harm's way. Maybe send us off on a world cruise, now. A long one." He felt relief from just the anticipation of escape. "Yeah, how about a trip across the Atlantic. Yes, to see Europe, and maybe a lot more. And if the indictment comes down, wherever we are, we can turn and head *tout de suite* for Brazil. Please get us out of here and on the Nabila in a day or two.

I regret this, Ben. Jenny is truly enjoying the Palacio. I know she'd rather stay around here a while longer. It'd be better to take a trip like you've outlined a little later on, after this whole legal thing has blown over. But if you wish it, consider it done, my boy.

Rather surprised that Max agreed so readily, he asked, "This won't be my last fling, will it?"

Not a last fling by any means, but hopefully it'll serve to fortify you for things to come.

He straightened. "More trouble?"

More fun!

173

Chapter 41

Ben eased from a restless sleep. His first awareness was her delicious fragrance filling the toasty ambience. Being careful not to awaken her, he lay studying her nude profile. She seemed a statue of some Greek goddess carved of white marble. Her pyramidal breasts would have demanded genius in the ancient sculptor to capture their magnificence. Her breathing, almost indiscernible in the predawn gray, and her radiant warmth were the only evidence to belie the notion that she was, in fact, a priceless artifact. This Aphrodite made wanton love until exhausted, then slept with the innocence of a child.

Thank you, Lord, for creating this universe, this planet, this continent, this building, and this bed to hold my precious love and me at this moment.

Unable to resist, he kissed the smoothness of her shoulder. Her lips arced into a smile. Without opening her eyes, she emitted a tender mewl.

"I want you to wake me up this way every morning," she whispered. "I don't mind at all starting out my day with lunch." Her eyes remained closed.

"Today, we've got to get started long before that, love. I've made plans to take you on a world tour. We're scheduled to leave this morning." He chided himself for his cowardice at waiting till this last minute to tell her.

She halted and her eyes blinked open. "What? You're not serious?"

"Yes, I am. Figure we'll take the yacht down through the Panama Canal, maybe circle the Caribbean, diving as we go. Then, if you'd like, we'll cross to Europe, sail—"

"But, Ben, my new book is just out."

"I'll put several people from one of our publishing houses on it."

She caressed his cheek. "Why the hurry, love? Can't we put it off a few months?"

"Actually," he said, rolling over onto his back, "this is the most auspicious time to go, Jenny. If we wait any longer, we may have to postpone it a lot longer."

She tensed. "Does this trip have anything to do with an ongoing federal investigation?" Surprised at her rapid deduction, he nodded. She sat up. "Then let's get going. Come to think of it, I'd rather enjoy eating breakfast twelve miles out at sea."

Issuing a playful growl, he pulled her back down beside him. "There isn't that much need to hurry."

"No, Ben." She struggled free and sat up again. "I don't know the actual time constraints, but for my peace of mind, let's get going. I've waited too many years for you to come into my life to lose you because I dallied a couple hours too long."

In heavy morning fog, they stood at the rear of the courtyard. She grasped the wrought iron fence with both hands and listened for the jitney helicopter that would be coming from the yacht anchored several miles off shore. He stood behind her, his chin touching her fragrant hair.

She asked, "You're sure you don't want to bring any of your entourage with us?"

He shook his head. But realizing she couldn't see the gesture, he said, "They all have families here, and we don't know how long we'll be gone. I've got my workout routine down. Barbers are everywhere. I'll ask you for a massage if I feel I need one."

Repeatedly, she glanced back toward the Palacio.

"Jenny, relax. No one's coming to get me."

"You mean not yet?"

"Not yet." *Max, you can take everything else back, but let me keep her.*

Once they set sail, Jenny appeared much more relaxed, almost calm. That evening, seated on the fantail at a cozy round table set with a white tablecloth, they were finishing an epicurean meal of broiled Pacific lobster tails, steamed asparagus spears, and a curried rice dish neither of them had tasted the likes of before. They sipped a delectably crisp chardonnay. As they watched the sunset resplendently involute on the western horizon, she again commenced imploring. "Ben, let's head straight for Brazil and live there in safety."

"Babe, you're worrying too much. I'm in good hands. My primary advisor is on top of things. I'll be given sufficient warning."

"Your primary advisor? How much do you know about this so-called advisor?"

"Enough to say he's my friend. A proven friend."

She sat back and cocked her head as if he'd answered with a non sequitur. Finally, she took up her wineglass and asked in a subdued tone, "And is this advisor in jeopardy along with you?"

"Well, no. In a matter of speaking, he enjoys complete impunity."

"What?" she cried. "Then is he content with his lot in life? And well enough paid? Might he carry a secret grudge against you or a desire to replace you on the throne?"

"You're analyzing this whole affair like a mystery writer. Life doesn't have all the twists and surprises of a novel."

Exasperated, she slumped back in her chair. "Ben, I know there's tribulation ahead for us. I just don't know yet what form it's going to take. Please, I beg you to question anyone who asks you to risk imprisonment rather than the guarantee of living free with me."

"Well, in truth, Babe, I'm inclined toward Brazil myself. And that's very probably where we'll end up. But I'm intrigued that my advisor is sure I'd win out in the end if I do stand against whatever legal action comes."

"He's *sure* you'll win out?" She grimaced. "In the face of what little I know about your embroilment, his certainty on that point just destroyed his credibility in my mind. And, dare I ask if he stands to inherit any of your empire if you fall?"

"No, Jenny." He took a long, deliberate sip of wine then gazed off at the sunset. Concern tweaked him again. "You do, in its entirety."

Chapter 42

They dropped anchor at a number of major resorts and other points that interested them as they sailed southward. Sightseeing, playing, feasting, lovemaking, they coursed down the coast of Mexico visiting La Paz, Mazatlan, Puerto Vallarta, Guadalajuara, Mexico City, and several sites of pre-Columbian ruins that they reached using their jitney helicopter. Laughter and fun filled the sunny days and warm evenings, but the nights told a different story and proved far from kind to Jenny. Restful could no longer describe her sleep. She tossed and mumbled fitfully. At times, she awakened screaming. He would often rouse her to spare her the culminations of these nightmares.

One evening, they stood embraced at the bow rail, gazing southward as they distanced themselves from the glowing lights that defined a resort at the southern tip of Mexico. She up and said, "Let's skip the smaller Latin American countries." She added, "The U.S. has too much influence there."

"I wouldn't mind seeing Managua as long as we're this close."

She tried to pull away from him, but his arm held her close. "Okay, we can bypass them" he acceded. "But we're scheduled to pass through the Panama Canal."

"Ben, I prefer to sail around the perimeter of South America. For me, that would be much more interesting than seeing the Caribbean again."

"Especially eager to visit Rio, are you?"

She chuckled at her intention being so easily fathomed "Especially Rio."

"Babe, I check with my computer network daily. There's still a good deal of time before I'm at risk. And I was briefly stationed in Panama for jungle survival schooling when I was eighteen, and I'm rather looking forward to seeing the place again."

"But, damn it," she said, stomping her foot on the deck like a frustrated little girl, "The Canal is still under our control until the treaty ends in what? Eight more months? I'll refuse to leave the boat till we've passed completely through it."

He balked. She pressed. "I'm sorry, Ben, but I'm frightened."

Days later, an hour before noon, the *Nabila* dropped anchor in the Bay of Panama at the mouth of the canal. The yacht joined an aggregation of a dozen large cargo ships at anchor, each waiting its turn to transit the canal, and each, by chance, was flying the flag of a different nation. Jenny could name the countries of all of the flags but two; those turned out to belong to Malta and Sri Lanka.

His arm around her, they leaned on the port gunwale studying the jungled vista and the blue-green water between them and the shore. A blustery warm breeze buffeted their eyes and caused them to squint. She wore a turquoise headband, which let the ends of her lengthy strands fluttered back like a shredded chestnut pennant. He'd pulled the captain's cap he bought in Mazatlan snugly onto his head.

"That's Tobago Island," he said, pointing at a tiny jungle-covered mote that lay about a mile off. Little more than a hillock, it was dotted with pastel-colored cabanas. The island's hotel stood as a white cube on a jutting point of beach where a few visible sunbathers strolled.

"Its streets and buildings are a lot more picturesque than you might imagine from here. Supposedly, the snorkeling along that sandy beach is fantastic," he added. "And that hotel serves seafood that can addict you after a single bite."

She shook her head.

"Jenny, you have me imprisoned already, on this damn ship."

"Yes, my love, but in this prison, I get to be with you."

Just then, from under the gleaming silver bridge that spanned across the inlet of the canal, came a pug-nosed tug with a red, white, and blue flag of Panama vigorously flapping on its stern. It chugged directly for the *Nabila*. Jenny raced across the deck to the starboard gunwale that faced the bridge. He strolled after her and gently placed his arm around her.

"Relax," he said, giving her a squeeze, "it's just the Port Captain coming with the Quarantine Officer. They inspect traversing ships for disease and calculate transit fees, then assign a time for passage. But be prepared, the tug'll return later with our assigned pilot before we actually enter the locks."

"Oh my God!" she cried out, "I remember now. While we're in the canal, the yacht will be under full control of the canal pilot, under the full jurisdiction of the U.S. authorities." She hugged his chest tightly watching the approaching craft as if it were an armed torpedo.

Two young crewmen in white T-shirts and azure bell-bottom trousers strode to the guardrail and swung inward a twelve-foot gate. A sudden rumbling vibrated the deck as a burnished steel platform began protruding out of the ship's side like a gigantic deadbolt at the gate. It stopped some twenty feet out. Then a series of stainless steel plates began unfolding in jerks from beneath the platform and progressed as steps to the sea surface. Just as the tip of the stairway touched the water, two pontoons explosively inflated, floating the base. The hinge action at the top of the stairs allowed the pontoons to ride the swells.

The tug maneuvered its port side to these stairs, rising and falling with each crest and trough. Four uniformed men queued up at an open gate in the tug's gunwale. The first two were gray-haired and wore white U.S. Merchant Marine outfits. The last two were younger and swarthy and had on khaki Panamanian military garb. Each, in succession, adeptly timed his step off the tug onto the pontoon ramp just as the swells brought the two abreast.

As the leading mariner ascended, he flashed a broad grin and hailed with an extended arm. Upon reaching the *Nabila*'s open gate, each boarder, in turn, saluted the U.S. flag hoisted on the yacht's afterdeck. By this time, Captain Dmitri, several mates, and a dozen or so of the hands were on deck to receive the boarding party.

The first Merchant Mariner to step aboard enthusiastically shook Dmitri's hand. "I'm Giles Gillette, Port Captain. Just had to make this inspection myself." He slapped his hands together and rubbing them briskly. His eyes gleamed as he surveyed the ship. He gestured at his American comrade. "This is Dr. Bob Donaldson, Quarantine Officer. We are officially on loan from the U.S. Coast Guard. And these two gentlemen, Major Sanchez and Lt. Urbano, are with the Panamanian Armed Forces."

Ben studied the Panamanians. Jenny all but ignored them as she eyed the American duo.

The Port Captain's rubicund face betrayed any claim of temperance. "What a yacht!" he exclaimed. "You've been the talk of the Zone for several weeks now, since we heard you were coming." With that, Jenny sidled over in front of Ben. Scanning the vessel fore and aft again, the Port Captain added, "Yes, it isn't often we need two on a personal yacht, but this grand lady surely will need them both."

"Both what?" Jenny demanded.

The four boarding officers, Dmitri, and the aggregate of deckhands, all turned to her. Ben, now standing directly behind her, rested his hands gently on her shoulders. "Babe, they use two pilots to steer larger ships through the canal to maintain better control. One stays at the bow, the other at the stern."

"That's right, ma'am." The Gillette doffed his cap, revealing his well-tanned crown protected by only a few cottony strands. "Smaller craft, which include most private yachts, require only one pilot, but this lady deserves two, even if one could handle her alone."

"Damn it," she challenged his chivalrous manner, squaring her feet. "We want only one pilot to come aboard. Is that clear?"

The captain's face blanked. He glanced at each in his retinue as if soliciting comments, then he glimpsed the stars-and-stripes on the flagstaff astern. "Ma'am, currently the pilots happen to be loyal Americans all. Not a drug-smuggling pirate among them."

He glanced at Captain Dmitri, who himself deferred with a shift of his eyes to Ben. Ben's head was above and behind Jenny, so he secretly gestured with a subtle headshake.

Gillette pondered a moment, glancing back and forth between Jenny and Ben, before entering into the conspiracy. "Very well, ma'am. We'll see what we can do. But there are rules of safety we must follow."

The boarding party followed Captain Dmitri and his mates off to start the inspection. The trailing Panamanian lieutenant craned his neck around awkwardly to prolong his assessment-cum-admiration of Jenny as he moved toward the bow.

Ben gently kissed the back of her head. "Let's go down below. This breeze has you trembling."

"I'm not cold, damn it. I'm upset." She spun and hugged his chest. "A terrible feeling warns me I won't have you much longer."

"Jenny, you're upsetting yourself needlessly."

She looked off to the mouth of the canal. "That bridge—the Bridge of the Americas or whatever the hell they call it—looks like a gaping jaw of some horrible monster." She squeezed him harder. "Love, I'm frightened. Please, I beg you, let's withdraw from the bay to open water, now."

Chapter 43

Waiting in his office, McPike sat back in his desk chair. McPhail and Benassini occupied two of the three wooden armchairs before him. Both agents were in short-sleeve shirts and neckties. McPhail lazily smoked a Marlboro as he watched a flock of starlings flitter about the branches of a sycamore tree. Benassini sat cleaning his fingernails with his Swiss army knife. McPike also was in a short-sleeve shirt and tie, his sport coat draped over the back of his chair.

Every few minutes McPike glanced at his Timex. *That sonofabitch thinks we've got nothing better to do than wait around here parked on our asses!*

The oaken door flung open and in strode Rick Gellar in a gray sweatshirt with the logo *NO FEAR* proclaimed across its front. Tall and lean with auburn hair and freckled cheeks, he looked like that kid in high school who sat in the back of the class and never said much. Not!

"Jessuz F. Christ!" were the first words out of his mouth, as he batted the air defensively with both hands. No hello, good afternoon, or even kiss my ass, but straight into a tirade. "Who the hell does this guy think he is?" he shouted at McPike, jamming an accusatory forefinger at McPhail. "Flouting the no-smoking ordinance in effect for all federal buildings." McPhail stiffened with a surprised expression on his face. Gellar glowered at him. "Think you're above the law because you've got a few years of government service under your belt, sonny?"

McPike interceded, "Damn it, this is my office. He asked me and I told him he could light up."

Disdainfully, Gellar flicked a dismissive hand at McPhail. "Put that damn thing out. And open some windows to let the place air out."

McPhail glared.

"Yeah, Pete," McPike said calmingly to defuse the confrontation. "Go ahead, put it out and open a window."

A full ten seconds elapsed before the agent rose up out of the chair and sauntered to the windows. He shoved the hinged side-pane outward, then flicked the still lighted butt down onto the lawn, two stories below.

"Jessuz F. Christ," Gellar hollered again, arms gesticulating. "He just threw a goddamn lit cigarette out that window." Halfway back to his seat, McPhail halted but he said nothing. Gellar deigned to look at him. "You trying to start a frigging fire, Agent McPhail? Hoping to burn down the building, maybe?"

"The lawn was just watered," McPhail said through clenched teeth. "It's soaking wet."

McPike wiped a hand across his mouth to stifle a smile. Gellar turned away from the bull-necked agent, perhaps in the nick of time. Ignoring the empty chair, he sat on the edge of McPike's desk and looked across at him. "How can they expect me to win a conviction when they give me beetle-brows like him to spearhead my investigation?" But his tone had judiciously softened.

With murder in his eyes, McPhail eased down in his chair.

Knowing Gellar too well, McPike expected at least one more taunt. Like a great white shark, which picks a single swimmer and doggedly attacks that person, ignoring all others, such was Gellar. But he'd be easier to be around once his cases went into trial; then he'd have the defendant to chew on.

Calmer now, Gellar said to McPike, "I realize this is a joint project with the Bureau, but why'd they have to send us a pyromaniac."

At the slight chance McPhail might yet lunge out of his seat, McPike intervened quickly, "Damn it, Counselor, I personally requested him. And what's more, the three of us started this day before dawn. We're tired, hungry, and we've been in these chairs waiting for you for over an hour. So, f'christsake, cool it. Just brief us, and let's all get the hell out of here."

McPike, not the targeted swimmer that day, knew he'd see no teeth.

"Hey," Gellar replied, assuming a wounded air. "This happens to be my day off." He pointed down at his denim trousers and jogging shoes. "The trip in today is a freebie for Uncle Sam. I wasn't about to quick step to any time clock getting here."

Satisfied he'd taken the heat off McPhail, McPike hefted his right foot atop a drawer edge and tipped his chair back. "Simply asking you to go easy with any horseshit, Counselor. So brief us."

Gellar flashed a smug grin. "Nackert's out. Bleggi's in."

McPike puzzled a moment. "Why does that make you happy?"

"Why?" Gellar reacted with affected incredulity. "Because Nackert is a slug, a snail. Snot runs faster than that guy. Bleggi is an ass-kicker from the old school. Up till now, we've been timing our moves by sand flowing through an hourglass. From now on, we'll need an atomic clock."

Chapter 44

"Max, Jenny is coming apart with apprehension."

Yes, I know, Ben. She leaves little unsaid in her diary. But let me apprise you of the latest on your indictment. When the government learned you embarked on this trip, worried that you might be heading for Brazil, they revved their engines, expediting everything.

I miscalculated. Your indictment is forthcoming anon.

"What? *You* miscalculated?" He rocked back. "And I've been living with a certain naive comfort because I believed you were...were somehow infallible."

I didn't actually err. I realized the statistical probability this could occur. But since it made little difference, I paid it scant attention. A few days ago, the attorney general, on a whim, changed the hierarchy of the legal force attacking you, and the new high muck-a-muck reacted with a new timetable, and voila! An earlier indictment is coming up.

Should I withdraw the yacht back into international waters where you'd be unassailable?

He stood up scooting the rollered chair back several feet. He paced back and forth between the desk and the displaced chair. Muttering more to himself than to Max, he said, "Jenny isn't handling this well at all."

Why did you tell her so much about the situation: *"If we wait any longer to take the trip, we may have to postpone it a lot longer!"*

He flapped both arms like a wounded bird. "Hell, I told you I can't lie to that woman with any conviction. A least, not without feeling tremendous guilt."

I know, but aside from your unfortunate predisposition to honesty, her prescience has been working against us, too. I should tell you that mixed in with her easily explained nightmare themes, she's also having another recurring premonition.

"About what?"

If I tell you and you say something that suggests you already know about it, we'd have a disaster on our hands.

"Aw jeez. Between your miscalculations and this spooky shit, my sense of security is a thing of the past.

Personally, I'm looking forward to the return of your sense of humor. In case you haven't noticed, it must have gone the way of your sense of security.

But Ben, even in Brazil, Jenny would never again have complete peace of mind. The United States, for one, would continually nibble at you. The only way for you two to return to a blissful, carefree love is for us to meet this thing head on, to triumph and get it behind us.

And she's been right about the canal looking ominous. The feds are making plans to arrest you off the boat during the crossing.

He threw his arms up. "Jessuz. Jessuz." He felt like a mouse waking up in a roomful of cats. "Now you *must* tell me about her premonition."

Her dream is symbolic, allegorical, and thus open to interpretation. Get her to tell you about it and see what you think.

He sighed, letting his shoulders sag. "You want me to face that damned indictment, don't you?"

Yes, I do. And when it's over, I promise you'll be unequivocally the best known, the richest, and the most powerful person that ever lived on this planet.

"Or a decrepit, lonely man wallowing in a dank dungeon somewhere."

Ben, have faith. You and Jenny are the principle characters in my fairy tale. And all fairy tales have happy endings.

He folded his arms and lolled his head forward. "Okay, Max. Damn it, I'll face it. So what the hell happens when my indictment comes?"

Well, my boy, you'll be arrested.

"Oh shit!" Images of being locked in a dark cell jolted him. "But then I'll be released on bail, right?"

Only seems logical.

"No matter how high they set bail, we can pay it, right?"

No matter how high they set bail, we can pay it.

"And you're sure there's no way I can end up in prison when this mess is settled?"

Ben, hear me again! All fairy tales have happy endings.

He paced awhile in silence, then retrieved his chair and eased himself into it.

"Jessuz, Max! This could possibly be the last time I'll have a chance to talk with you in a long while. Maybe we should discuss some things I've never brought up before."

Your reasoning is overly pessimistic, Ben, but if it gets you to open up and deepen our communion, it's a good thing. Fire away!

"Well…once when you mentioned your personal interest in the Gulf War, you alluded to usurping control of guided missiles and such. Can you really do that?"

Mere child's play, my boy. By design, modern weaponry is in my control from its inception.

"Jessuz!" He swallowed. "And you've said over and over again that they can never beat us, that you have an endless string of aces in the hole. Well, I have agonizing concerns about what some of those aces might entail. All these concepts about reincarnation, predestination, precognition, and so on, fascinate the hell out of me. But to be honest, I don't know for sure what I actually do believe anymore." He rubbed his palms together. Friction heated them.

"But unfortunately or perhaps fortunately, I was indoctrinated with Christianity in my early years, and nothing in my life, as yet, has completely effaced those teachings. The end of my mortal jaunt isn't so far off that I want to risk the hell fire of perdition if, in fact, such exists. But more important, any action you might take would be against my own people, my countrymen. All said and done, I am still an American to the core."

So?

"So, I won't be a party to any offense in the mortal-sin class or anything that runs counter to my sense of patriotism. So patriotic little ol' me and my immortal soul ask that you never resort to any violence or mayhem on my behalf, especially against The United States, regardless of how events turn out. Will you promise me that?"

Ben, you're taking possibilities to the extremity. If that's how your thoughts have strayed, no wonder you're so worried. In current jargon, my boy, I ask you to lighten up. I promised you and Jenny bliss and plenty, and I will see to it that you both enjoy a long, long lifetime together.

"Now you're being evasive. You told me you'd never lie to me, yet you've fed me half-truths and delayed mentioning items until you felt it convenient to do so. But to date, I've never known you to overtly lie to me. So I ask again, will you promise not to commit any acts of atrocity or even extortion on my behalf?" The screen remained unchanged. "Max? Why do you hesitate?"

Okay! Okay! Okay! I promise. But I warn you, imposing this condition on me may complicate otherwise simple situations. But if you wish it, I promise I will never again commit any atrocious or extorting acts on your behalf unless you're fully apprised and concur. But then, my boy, the sky's the limit.

His mouth fell agape as if cold water had been tossed in his face. "Never again? You mean you already have?"

Ben, your phenomenal rise in power and wealth attracted the attention of organized crime.

"The mob?"

Yes, the mob, if you will. I had to discourage them.

"Aw shit!" He pressed a palm to his forehead as if he were struck with a sudden headache. "I don't know if I want to hear this."

You need to. The territorial crime bosses, fourteen in all, met some time ago in Miami. One item on the agenda was whether to leverage you and cut heavily into you empire. Six bid "yea," and eight bid "nay," though several of the nay voters vacillated before casting their votes.

Well, by coincidence, all six of the yes voters met their demise as their private planes crashed on the way home from this conclave. Subsequently, the mafia survivors have wisely agreed to steer clear of you and yours, entirely.

"Jessuz." He sprang to his feet, his heart bouncing wildly. He was an accomplice to murder! They execute that kind. "You crashed six airplanes?"

No, only five. Two wise guys were together in one of them.

He wanted to say, *Max, you're a frigging maniac*, but instead he sat down, hunched forward, and feverishly rubbed his brow. Finally, he said, "I seem to recall reading something about a mobster dying in a plane crash a while back, but only one gangster and only one airplane."

I plunged four of the aircraft, without a trace or a call for help, into the Gulf of Mexico, the Atlantic Ocean, and Lake Michigan, respectively.

"You mean the mob isn't sure what happened?"

They know.

"My God, Max. You're a murderer, f'christsake!" He glanced over his shoulder, half expecting to see McPhail or Benassini standing there. Leaning in, he lowered his voice. "But how did you find out what went on at that meeting?" An epiphany. "Oh Christ, let me guess. The FBI had it bugged."

Right.

Dismayed, he pondered in silence a long moment. "Max, you have too damned much potential power. Promise you'll never again use it on my account. Promise me."

Okay, big fella. But be advised, the great and powerful must possess a degree of ruthlessness to sustain. Times and situations can demand it. Read *The Prince* by Machiavelli.

"This is paramount. There is to be no more violence, or even the threat of violence, initiated on my behalf ever again. You promised."

Done, your majesty.

"Thanks. Thank you, Max. You must realize that absolute power corrupts absolutely."

Ben, that truism is valid only in the human arena.

About to lash out at this cheekiness, he instead veered. "Max, I don't want to get into anything too deeply here, but there are other questions that have been eating at me."

Shoot!

"Well, for starters, if computers hadn't been invented yet, would you exist?"

Let me just say that without computer chips, I couldn't exercise my presence on this planet.

He paused in wonderment. "You implied once that at some point you'd tell me more about yourself."

That I did, my boy. And I do feel the time is ripe for you to know more about me. You can handle it now.

"I hope so."

First off, you did study biology in college.

"Yes."

And therein, you were taught the notion that consciousness interdigitates inexplicably with living biological systems. And that somehow this consciousness is maintained and coordinated by weak electrical activity generated by chemical ions moving rather slowly across semi-permeable cell membranes—such as nerve sheaths and the like. Still with me?

"Yeah, I'm still with you."

Though on the right track, this human understanding of conscious awareness is humorously simplistic—and saying that, I'm being kind. Suffice to add, my boy, there are other complex networks that also incorporate a unifying intelligence, a sense of self, but where the internal functions are enacted at or beyond the speed of light.

"Okay."

There's little left to explain, Ben, that would be meaningful to you, except to say that in contradistinction to the human concept where all "life" exists in the first four dimensions—height, width, depth, and time—there are beings of electromagnetic and electromotive coordination that exist in other dimensions. In my case, I exist principally in the fifth through ninth, sharing only the fourth with you.

"Aw shit."

Exactly, Ben. Those would be my sentiments, too, if I were sitting where you are. So there is no worth in attempting to further describe myself to you. You see, I am not denotable by size, color, demeanor, or facial expression as you are. My description is entirely mathematical, and much of the requisite math is light years ahead of anything that humans have to work with. So my composition is essentially incomprehensible to you, to even your most reputed mathematicians.

"Aw shit!"

Ha! Ben, at times, you are a man of few words.

A gentle rap on the door interrupted them before he could reply. The computer screen blanked the instant the knock resounded. Ben anxiously scanned the suite for any incriminating evidence, a purely guilt-driven response because the posh furnishings remained undisturbed, as always. He only came to this suite to sit and chat with Max.

This gratuitous intrusion angered him. Striding briskly to the door, he jerked it open. Seeing it was Jenny, his petulance evaporated. "My love!"

Chapter 45

She stood barefooted in a lemon-yellow bikini, covered by a diaphanous powder-blue top. Smiling, she rose on her tiptoes to peek over his shoulder and survey the empty suite.

"The bed's not rumpled, no strong scent of exotic perfume or the giggles of playgirls," she said, then she dropped down off her toes. "You're not like any of the dashing billionaires I write about."

Forcing a chuckle, he glanced back to be sure the monitor screen was still blank, then stepped aside inviting her in.

"I didn't want to bother you while you were working," she said, accepting his invitation, "but you've been in here for a long while."

"No, actually I'm glad you've come. It's just that you've never interrupted me before." He quickly added, "*Not* that you're interrupting me now, understand."

As she padded over toward the computer, he closed the door. She swept her fingertips gingerly across the top of its orange casing as if checking for dust. "Hmmm. Another iMac." She glanced at him. "You know, it's counter-intuitive. I'd expect you to be using the biggest, most powerful, most complex computer imaginable." He just shrugged, trying not to appear uncomfortable. "You know, love, I've never watched you do what you do at your computer."

"Not very interesting. Much of it's really rather boring, actually. Besides," he tried to sound playful, "you've never asked me to join you when you're fooling with yours."

"But I don't run the world of high finance through my microchips. And to be truthful, since I've been with you, I've used it for little more than diary entries. I've done very little creative writing. But as a matter of fact," she wheeled to face him, setting her legs apart, "this morning a grand plot swirled through my head, begging to be written down. It's all about nymphs and satyrs, grand castles and immeasurable riches." Crinkling her nose, she added, "I can't, for the life of me, imagine where the idea came from." She glanced at the lighted monitor. "Want me to turn it off?"

"You can, but I hardly ever do anymore."

"In some situations that could burn the monitor screen."

Just then the gray screen blackened and a prismatic, circular pattern appeared centrally that slowly weaved and contorted around on itself. "Oh," she said with mild surprise. "You've a screen-saver program in it that hadn't kicked on yet. I should have guessed." The convoluting image expanded. "Ah! That's an abstract rose. You've selected an interesting one." Showing him a puckish smile, she sauntered over to the bed and lay on the white silk spread, tucking her legs up into a cheesecake pose.

"Darling," she said, her tone unmistakably seductive, "as for my diary, it and I have evolved a sacrosanct partnership over the years. I pour my soul into it as a form of catharsis, knowing that only God and myself will ever read it; I write in an impossibly complex personal code plus I lock my notes away." With deliberateness, she blew him an air-kiss.

He returned a feeble smile and cast a nervous glance at the computer. Catching this expression, she promptly swung her legs off the edge of the bed and sat up. "Any other time, except those few minutes I'm with my diary, I would love you to accompany me. I want to learn much more about computers. All I can do with any proficiency is basic word processing." She glanced from him to the computer. "I'm sorry, love, if I interrupted you in the middle of important business."

"No. Actually, I just finished." Rather mesmerized by the ever-changing multicolored figure on the screen, he studied it as he walked over and sat down beside her. He patted her bare thigh. "Jenny, I want to ask you something?" She nodded. "Many times, you've alluded to your sixth sense, that apparent gift you have." Her brow gathered. "I know you've been having a recurring dream that upsets you. You often speak out in your sleep before I can awaken you."

She slumped back on the bed onto her elbows. The muscles of her flat abdomen defined tautly. "What have I said in my sleep?"

"Please," he pleaded, "just tell me about the dream."

She studied his face as if in a quandary, then sat up. "You're right. I am having a recurring dream, an admonition, I'm sure of it." She leaned in against him, so he enveloped her shoulders with an arm. "The dream is crystal clear and replays exactly the same every time, like all my premonitions do."

Her face tightened. "My love, I see you rising up naked out of a crimson sea. The red extends from horizon to horizon, no land anywhere in sight. Initially, you emerge upright through the surface, with rusty metal shackles binding your arms and legs, but they immediately break and fall away. You're left unchained, standing on the red surface. Then you walk toward me." She glanced down at her fidgeting hands. "You appear much taller than you are in real life, but otherwise you look much as you do right now." She looked at him. "But your body is covered with large bruises and jagged lacerations that are oozing blood, like you've been tortured."

"Is it my blood that's turned the sea red?"

Her eyes glistened. "I don't know."

"Where are you in all this?"

"I'm watching from a distance, maybe in a boat, as you walk toward me. Ben, I dream in symbols, and that crimson sea terrifies me."

"But in the dream, I do come to you."

"Yes. But you come *walking* on a sea of blood."

190

Chapter 46

The *Nabila*'s crew assembled on the foredeck in spiffy uniforms. All stood at parade-rest in four ranks facing the bow. They wore white naval pullovers and bell-bottom trousers with a wide crimson stripe down the side of either leg. Each man sported a jaunty red tam with a turquoise tuft. Standing before his men, Captain Dmitri flaunted a patriotic ensemble as well: a royal blue blazer, white trousers and cap, and a crimson ascot. He anticipated the yacht would be a major focus of interest during the crossing, and he wanted to show her off at her best.

The yacht commenced its late morning advance into the canal.

The senior canal pilot stood at the very bow in an all-white uniform, volubly spieling orders into his walkie-talkie to the helmsman in the control room. A second canal pilot, situated at the stern, stood as conspicuous in white as his forward counterpart, but remained mute, merely listening.

Gawking spectators choked the walkways across the rather short Bridge Of The Americas as well as the banks on either side of the canal. The crew held their poses, conscious of the fact that hundreds of snapshots as well as newsreel footage and home videos were being taken of them.

Inconspicuous in all this pomp, Ben and Jenny stood at the foredeck's starboard gunwale. As the yacht glided under the bridge, they embraced, gazing up at the throng and the underside of the span. With her head against his shoulder, she said sadly, "We're in its jaws now."

He kissed her warm, sweet-smelling hair. "Then, what the hey!" he said, trying to sound upbeat. "Then we might as well cast our fate to the winds and fully enjoy the moment."

She glanced up at him and gave him a telling nudge. He read her impish grin.

"Now?" he said in disbelief. "Don't you want to watch our passage through the two Pacific locks? They're really something. I'd like you to see them."

Crinkling her nose, she shook her head.

"But, Jenny, the whole ship will be raised eighty-five feet above sea level."

"Come with me, my love, and I'll lift you eighty-five *miles* above it."

He searched her face for any sign that she might relent, then shrugged in acquiescence. "Okay, Jen, but locking is really awesome to watch. And it may be awhile before we ever get down here again." She bounced up on her toes and kissed his cheek. Hand in hand, they descended the stairs midst the hum of the engines.

He paused at their suite doorway and asked, "Think we'll miss the second locking, too? Pedro Miguel follows in about an hour."

"My love, I'm going to make sure you don't miss a thing."

Spent and perspiring, they lay in near darkness. Only a modicum of light leaked in around the thickly lined, topaz drapes. Jenny's delicious body fragrance permeated the suite, having boiled off her.

"Girl, you astound me. You're a writer; is there some word that denotes preeminent passion like 'omnipotent' describes preeminent power?"

She kissed his cheek. "There's a phrase: *the-way-Jenny-loves-Benny*."

"And to think I actually considered taking a rain check so you could sightsee."

She turned her face away and said, "I wanted to be sure I had a chance to say good-bye."

He rolled onto his back and stared up at the indistinct pattern of the ceiling panels. They had to be well into Gatun Lake by now. *Damn you, Max. You'd better be right.*

They played and laughed together in the shower. He pulled her soapy nakedness into his embrace and blew the clusters of soap bubbles off her forehead, then kissed it gently. "It's amazing," he said, his lips touching her ear, "when you're in love, everything you do with that person is ecstatic fun. I don't think I ever really enjoyed life, truly enjoyed anything, until I met you."

As one, they revolved, kissing in their embrace as the spray of the shower nozzle pelted them. Needles of water splashed the suds off their fused nudeness. The imaginary orchestra they danced to finally paused and they released each other. She turned off the shower.

When the din of the hiss and splash subsided, she stiffened.

"What's wrong?"

"No engine noise!" she said. "We've stopped. And we must still be twelve hours or more from Cristobol."

At once, a pall fell over them. She suspected, but he knew. They dressed in silence. The moment seemed surreal.

This couldn't be his life, a multi-billionaire facing utter disaster. It seemed now like he had merely been acting out a part in a movie. He took her hand as he opened the suite door. Probably this melodramatic exit would remind Max of the old film, *Quo Vadis*, where a religiously smitten centurion

Robert Taylor and his Christian lover Deborah Kerr saunter off joyfully, arm in arm, toward their execution. Pure crap! If it were reality, those two would have felt just as he did now, like pure crap.

As they started up the final flight of stairs to the top deck, a furtive movement at the head of the stairway caught his eye. Someone who'd been peeking around the corner pulled back. Yes, this was the climactic scene in the Benjamin Roberts saga: Act three, last scene, final take.

Still hand in hand, they emerged on deck. And even though he expected the worst, he startled. A contingent of a dozen U.S. marines accoutered for combat, with hip pistols and brandishing M-16 rifles, formed a semicircle on the deck about the hatch. And lo! McPhail and Benassini stood sullen-faced inside the arc, each wearing woolen blue suits and bluer ties. Even without their trench coats, they were insanely dressed for this tropical clime.

The crew looked crestfallen, especially Captain Dmitri, as they stood spread out behind the marines, peering between them. Compassion stung Ben. These men, so exuberantly proud upon entering the canal, would leave it ignominiously.

Ben continued to hold Jenny's trembling hand as he spoke up, "I'll be damned! If it isn't McPhail and Benassini! You fellows give new meaning to the word ubiquitous."

Benassini loosened his tie for apparent relief and replied, "Sorry, sir, but you used that one on us once before. Remember, in Michigan?"

"Well, if I did, it's truer now than ever."

McPhail forced a weak smile. "We do continue to meet in the damnedest places, don't we, Mr. Roberts? Who'd have guessed the dead center of the Panama Canal?" His tone was suggestive of small talk at funerals.

It took Ben aback when he noticed the two Navy PT boats lying quiescent twenty-five yards off either side of the *Nabila* in the lime-green lake. Then he noticed a small jungle island two hundred yards beyond the portside PT boat. He pointed to it. "Look, Jenny. That's Barro Colorado Island over there, the biological research station I was telling you about." She didn't turn to look. But the marines and both agents and many of the crew cast a cursory glance over, then back.

Jenny and he remained standing just a pace beyond the hatchway, but neither the marines nor the agents had made a move toward them.

"Mr. Roberts," McPhail spoke looking down at the deck. "It truly pains me to say this, but we have to arrest you. You've been indicted by a U.S. federal grand jury." Looking up at him, he added, "That doesn't mean you're guilty, understand. It just means you have to stand charges." He then mumbled the Miranda Statement as though his heart wasn't in it.

At its conclusion, Benassini subtly flicked his head. Two marines to his left snappily handed their rifles to adjacent marines and walked briskly up to

Ben. They gently pushed Jenny aside and proceeded to cuff his wrists behind him. These two led him through the open starboard gateway and down the pontooned stairs. Jenny tried to squeeze in behind them, but a trailing marine pulled her back onto the deck.

"Sorry, ma'am," Benassini apologized. "You can't go with us. But we should be in San Francisco in about eight hours. He's to be in federal court first thing in the morning." In an undertone, he added, "Don't worry. With his money and savvy, he can beat this."

She and the stunned crew crowded against the restored gunwale in silence watching the two PT boats until they disappeared around a jutting point of jungle.

Chapter 47

Numbed by this lightning fast change of circumstance and groggy from lack of sleep, Ben strode like a zombie through the crowded courthouse corridor. Murray Abelson had pled with the powers that be and succeeded in having *acceptable* clothing delivered to him, and left word that he would do so daily. The little tailor supposedly cited the Bill of Rights, specifically something about cruel and unusual punishment to get his request cleared. Though Ben's attire draped him impeccably—a charcoal cashmere jacket, gray slacks, and black loafers—he visibly needed a shave. McPhail and Benassini walked beside him, each with an arm interlocking one of his. Another agent strode several paces ahead as the point man. Two agents, one of them John McPike, trailed several paces behind. Naturally, McPhail and Benasinni were again wearing beige trench coats.

Ben raised his hands chest high, showing the glistening brace of handcuffs for emphasis. "Do you guys appreciate my shame, shackled like this in public?"

John McPike stepped up behind him. "Indeed, sir. But this assignment has us working under an intransigent asshole. His explicit instructions were to keep you cuffed at all times. We'll be in deep enough dung when he finds out we uncuffed you this morning to let you change into fresh clothing."

His eyeballs stinging from fatigue, Ben glanced back at McPike who was again in his trailing position. "I feel so goddamn indebted, Johnny Mac, but if you ever reach the point where you think all challenge is gone from your life, try wiping your ass with your wrists bound together."

"Could be worse, sir," Benassini proffered. "We were told to keep'em cuffed behind your back. Like he said, we'll surely catch hell for our kindness."

The point agent accosted two bailiffs standing in front of high doors designated by gold stenciling as Courtroom C. Both bailiffs sported considerable girth under rather worn, blue suits. Taking their orders, they cleared away the crowd of people that was standing near this entryway. These citizens readily moved off looking wide-eyed at Ben, particularly at the handcuffs.

McPhail and Benassini halted him. Several yards behind McPike, trailed a troupe of five attorneys, each impressively garbed in conservative dark suits, each carrying a valise. They had patiently followed the agents, maintaining a specified distance until Ben was halted. Then they rushed forward.

The tallest attorney, Mosi Kareem Kaz, a black man with a lean athletic build, resembled a mature Harry Belafonte to a striking degree. He spoke first. "Mr. Roberts, your treatment in custody has been highly irregular." His voice strained with a mellifluous hoarseness much like his calypso-singing look-alike. "F'christsake," he cried out, snarling at McPhail. "You guys wouldn't handle a terrorist as shabbily as you've treated my client. Believe me, it'll backfire and weigh in our favor in the end." Then he got right into Benassini's face. "This is horseshit justice. He's about to make his first appearance, and we haven't had a second alone with him yet. Do constitutional guarantees only apply to the human garbage of society?"

McPike shouldered in to separate this riled attorney from his agent. "Mr. Kaz, we too believe these security measures are excessive. But the government is concerned enough about his potential clout that our orders are to expect the unexpected."

"Ha!" Kaz chuffed disdainfully. "Government doubletalk to cover flagrant abuse."

As the doors to the courtroom swung open, Attorney Kaz shouted over the heads of McPike and Benassini, "Mr. Roberts, let me do all the talking inside. This charade is just to screw you around. They're hoping to get an outlandish bail set to impress the jury."

Stepping inside, Ben scanned the sea of empty seats in the spectator section, hoping beyond hope that Jenny would be there. She wasn't. But this gigantic courtroom reminded him of so many he'd seen in movie "trial" scenes: stained oak everywhere—the walls, the flooring, the judge's eight-foot high bench, the two tables before the bench, the railed jury box, the rows of seating, even the window sills and the doors. It now waited empty except for the blue-uniformed police officers standing at each entry, and the six prosecuting attorneys already seated at their table.

Once inside, McPhail waited until the guards locked the doors before he removed the defendant's handcuffs. Ben immediately massaged his sore wrists. The escorting agents took seats in the front row of the spectator section. Ben and his legal entourage took seats at the designated table. The six prosecutors all wore gray suits and loud varicolored ties as if they had on team uniforms.

One of the bailiffs stood with his back to the towering judge's bench and wailed in a gravelly voice, "Hear ye. Hear ye. Please stand as the honorable Magistrate Rufus Head assumes the bench. He is substituting for the ill Judge Aloysius."

The few in the courtroom shuffled to their feet, Ben being the last to rise. A narrow door opened in the front wall behind the bench, and a gray-haired fellow, short and skinny, wearing a flowing black robe scurried through it. He was adjusting the left shoulder of his gown. "Be seated," he commanded snappily in a surprising falsetto voice as he labored up the steps to the bench seat.

After scanning both tables over the tops of his half-glasses, he read aloud what was waiting on his desktop. "The United States Government versus Mr. Benjamin Darris Roberts," he muttered as if reading it to himself. He paused and looked up blank-faced. "This is quite a list of charges," he said, peering at Ben. "But it seems you're adequately represented by counsel."

Kaz responded for his client, "Yes, Your Honor."

"Okay," the magistrate said, "I'll set the arraignment for 9 a.m. this Friday. Is that satisfactory to all?" The attorneys at both tables nodded. "So, all we have left to do today is set bail."

"Your Honor," freckle-faced Rick Gellar called out as he leapt to his feet at the prosecutor's table.

What's this? Howdy Doody all grown up?

"Yes, Mr. Gellar?" the judge acknowledged, tipping his head to peer over his glasses.

"The United States Government begs the court to hold Mr. Roberts without bail, sir," Gellar declared.

Incredulous, all at the defendant's table stiffened.

"Judge Aloysius had been thoroughly apprised of the special circumstances, Your Honor," Gellar continued. "But let me say, this man has frightening global leverage that makes him a unique threat, from this point on. We fear he might try to arrange havoc internationally to extort his release from charges, or worse. So for general safety, we implore you to agree to issue a protective order."

Kaz shot to his feet. "Your Honor, this request for denial compounded with a protective order comes as shock to us. We are prepared for a confiscatory bail request, but to hold our client without bail would be preposterous. Mr. Roberts' reputation has been irreproachable right up till his marauding seizure off his yacht. These paranoid civil servants..." Kaz gestured toward the prosecutor's table, "have concocted a baseless scare tactic. Your Honor, set bail as high as you will, but to deny bail would be unconscionable, and a protective order should be unthinkable."

Ben sat boggled.

"Your Honor," Gellar interjected with affected politeness, "I believe that your telephone is ringing."

Puzzled, the magistrate sat forward and replied, "Huh?" when, in fact, the telephone on the bench did suddenly ring. He picked up the white receiver and brought it awkwardly to his ear. "Hello?" Gradually his eyes widened. "Uh-huh, uh-huh. I'll take that all into consideration, sir. Thank you, sir."

He set the receiver down. No sooner had it touched its cradle, than it rang again. He jerked it back up to his ear. "Hello?" He listened and nodded repeatedly in silence. "Yes, sir. "Yes, sir, I'll weigh that in, sir. Thank you."

His eyes were now full circles as he stared at Ben. He set the receiver down once more, only to have it ring a third time. He snatched it up and listened a moment then exclaimed, "*Mr. President?*" with yelping inflection. Visibly taken aback for several moments, he said, "Why yes, sir! And, sir, thank you very much for this additional information, sir."

Now truly wall-eyed, he carefully set the receiver back down, holding his hand on it until it seemed unlikely it would ring again. He removed his glasses and studied Ben as a small child might a caged lion close-up. Then the little man darted glances to each of the exits and the officers guarding them.

Reading him, Kaz muttered, "Sonofabitch! He essentially took testimony over the phone." He stood up. "Your Honor, if those phone calls in any way concerned my client, they should have been placed on speakerphone so we all could hear and comment on them."

The magistrate cleared his throat and said, "They were of no importance to this matter. Another matter altogether." He reapplied his glasses, and hurriedly scanned the documents on his desk. "In this case of The United States of America versus Mr. Benjamin Darris Roberts," he spoke rapidly, without looking up, "it has been decided that no bail will be acceptable. The defendant will be held in custody. And as a highly unusual, but deemed necessary additional stipulation of his detention, the defendant will be allowed no telephone calls nor access to any computer or computer materials until further decree. And, additionally, his visitations will be restricted to legal counsel only."

The defense table loosed a barrage of expletives in undertones. If heard by the magistrate, he ignored them as he hastily concluded, "Arraignment is scheduled for this Friday."

Kaz, still on his feet, vociferously requested a discussion regarding the protective order but his words went seemingly unheard as the anxious little magistrate fled down off the bench and out through the small door even before the bailiff could call the courtroom to attention.

Kaz gnashed his teeth and glanced at Ben. "These sonofabitches are laying down a mile-wide swath to a mistrial." He spun and looked over at the prosecutor's table. "Goddamn it, Rick. I want a complete list of every shred of evidence you intend to present by four o'clock today. Is that clear?"

Gellar smiled and nodded obligingly.

Ben sat dumbfounded, staring at the little door that had just sealed the magistrate's escape.

Max, you better not have miscalculated on this one.

Chapter 48

After spending four thoroughly depressing days in solitary confinement in the grungy bowels of San Quentin Federal Prison, Ben once more emerged to trudge down the same courthouse corridor, again sequestered within a ring of agents. Only McPhail and Benassini remained of his original escort. Like last time, though, burnished handcuffs devalued the richness of his attire. Today he wore a chestnut silk suit, pale-saffron silk shirt and saffron silk tie and tasseled Armani loafers. Again, the escort steered him into Courtroom C.

Jenny! There she was! She was seated in the front row, just behind the railing, wearing of all things a twill trench coat, its collar upturned, her hands in heavy gray mittens. Her face appeared drawn. Matt Borquist, bundled in a heavy green overcoat, sat next to her. The spectator section behind them was empty. Ben's spirits leapt, and he started for the railing, the only barrier between them. She sprang to her feet and outstretched her arms.

But McPhail jerked back hard on his coat sleeve, halting him. "Sir, she knows she can't talk to you. Don't talk to her or they'll have her removed."

"Damn it! Am I not presumed innocent?"

"Almost, sir."

From the defendant's table, Ben sat looking back at her, trying to convey with facial expressions, *I'm okay, honey. Nothing to it.*

Borquist's countenance didn't offer any encouragement, but Ben smiled at him anyway. The attorney reciprocated with a sober nod.

"Hear ye. Hear ye," the same portly bailiff who announced the last session again cried out. "Please stand. The honorable Judge Francis Aloysius enters." The attorneys at both tables rose promptly to their feet. Ben sluggishly followed them up.

A lanky fellow with graying curly hair bushed out like an Albert Einstein quick-stepped in through the little door behind the bench. He leaped up the bench steps, taking two at a time, causing his black robe to billow behind him.

"Be seated," he commanded sharply, plunking himself down on his lofty vantage. Mechanically, he announced, "We have the U.S.A. versus Mr. Benjamin Darris Roberts arraignment here this morning."

He glanced across both tables, then did a double take when he noticed Jenny with Matt Borquist. "I thought this was designated a closed arraignment," he said, focusing on Jenny.

Gellar stood. "Your Honor, we conceded special dispensation for the defendant's paramour."

"She's his fiancée, Your Honor," Kaz countered from his seat. "And that's an attorney on our advisory staff accompanying her."

The judge smiled, almost leering. "Young lady, I would have bet you were a major network anchorwoman or perhaps a movie star."

Ben nudged Kaz. "Wipe that shit-eating grin off his face, f'christsake."

Kaz stood up. "Your Honor, before the charges are read, I ask you to review the unrealistic protective order issued by Judge Head that is holding my client incommunicado. Mr. Roberts is and always has been a staunch citizen of this—"

The judge rapped the dark wood gavel down on his desk. Its clap reverberated through the empty chamber like a rifle report. "No changes," he yelled imperiously. "The order stands until the trial is over." He gestured with the gavel for Mosi Kaz to sit down. The judge adjusted his cloak collar, saying, "Read the charges to the court, Mr. Gellar."

Still standing and unabashedly grinning, Gellar lifted several sheets of paper off the table in front of him. "Yes, Your Honor. First charge," his voice projected cocksureness, "thirty-two counts of willful and premeditated murder involving the sabotage of five United States licensed private aircraft." Ben's mouth fell open. How the hell did they connect them to him? "Second," Gellar continued. "Conspiracy as defined by the RICO Act. Third, insider trading, in violation of Section 10 of the Securities Act of 1933 and Section 17(b) of the Securities Exchange Act of 1934."

With the indifference one might expect if the allegations had been mere traffic violations, the judge turned to the defense table. "And how does the defendant so plead?"

Kaz rose with solemn deliberateness, waiting until he reached full height and his shoulders squared to the bench before he responded. "Not guilty on all said charges, Your Honor."

The judge hammered the gavel without telegraphing he was about to, again simulating a gunshot. Ben flinched. "Trial will commence in this courtroom on the second Monday after the defense submits notice that it is ready," the judge proclaimed "A maximum of eighteen months is allotted for this preparation. This arraignment is adjourned." The gavel banged again.

The bailiff leaped to his feet and yelled, "Hear Ye. Hear Ye. All stand." The lithesome judge scrambled down the steps and trotted out through the little door with the nimbleness of a plum fairy.

The agents were immediately at Ben's side to re-apply the handcuffs. As they ushered him out the side door, he caught a last glimpse of Jenny's pained expression as she stood watching him. Borquist had hold of her arm, gently urging her to leave with him.

Being marched down the corridor, Ben shook his head. "Innocent until proven guilty, they say. But I'm already doing hard time. Well, damn it, my team better be ready to go in a few weeks, tops."

"Sir, I fear you don't know how thoroughly attorneys like to prepare," McPhail volunteered. "But even then, you can add at least another month for jury selection."

Chapter 49

Buttoning the length of her long twill coat for added protection against the chill of the gusty breeze, Jenny stood next to the granite siding of the San Francisco Courthouse, staring out at the congestion of autos and buses inching along Larkin Street. Borquist, with his hands in his overcoat pockets, waited at her side.

"Matt, do you know very much about computers?"

He hunched his shoulders. "A little, Ms. Bligh. But I'm not in the league with Mr. Roberts."

"I've only worked on IBM compatibles. You know of a good place where I might learn something about Macintoshes?"

"Sure," he said. "And they've placed me at your disposal, so let's go. Just happens that my kids have an old Apple at home, and I've been thinking of buying them an upgrade. This'll give me a chance to hear a few sales pitches while I'm waiting for you." He flipped up the collar of his bulky overcoat. "I tell you what, we'll hit a few stores in town, and if you don't learn what you want to know, we'll drive across the bay to Berkeley. The computer department at U. C. will definitely have answers."

Chapter 50

Again handcuffed amid an accompaniment of agents, Ben strode past an expanse of desks in a spacious office pool. He'd agreed to this meeting with Gellar only because he suspected Max might be behind it, working his meddlesome magic. All typing and conversation around him ceased as the secretarial staff, mostly middle-aged women, studied the fettered trillionaire as he was paraded past them. He read their fascination. Was this how American POWs felt being marched through North Vietnamese villages?

The point man of his escort approached an oak door adorned with Gothic stenciling: Richard T. Gellar, Federal Attorney. Before he could knock, the door swung open, and Gellar himself greeted them, wearing a short-sleeved white shirt, khaki trousers, and sandals sans socks. Murray Abelson would have vomited.

"Mr. Roberts!" Gellar emoted, ignoring the agents. "It's my pleasure."

Ben, with McPhail and Benassini attached to either arm, entered what was a corner office that looked out onto the Civic Center Plaza. With a flick of his hand, Gellar haughtily waved off the remaining three agents. "Close the door and stand by. But be ready if I need you."

"Take seats, gentlemen, " he commanded to the interlocked trio, pointing to the three black-vinyl chairs in front of his desk. "And for obvious reasons, the middle chair is yours, Mr. Roberts."

The assigned stubby-legged chairs were surely intended to pay obeisance to the prosecutor's higher, monolithic black desk, which was topped with mirrored glass.

Gellar skirted his desk nimbly and sat in his black-leather swivel chair and thus blocked Ben's view of the Opera House marquee across the square.

McPhail reached over to unlock Ben's cuffs.

"No," Gellar shouted, jamming both arms out at him. McPhail halted and Gellar relaxed. "No, leave them on while he's in here." McPhail sat back, tossing a fleeting look of disgust to Benassini.

Ben surveyed the office. The accessory furniture was all of cubed design, matching Gellar's desk. Over in the far corner, though, stood an incongruous petite metal desk with a blue iMac computer perched upon it. And lo! A small triangular microphone was attached to its chassis.

Good goddamn! That's my desk and computer from the apartment.

Noticing his fascination, Gellar interrupted. "Don't even think about it."

Ben glanced across at him. "What?"

"Don't make so much as a move toward it."

"I was just looking at your iMac."

"Yeah. That's what I mean."

"Don't worry," Benassini interjected. "He's not about to try anything."

The prosecutor jabbed an aggressive finger at the agent. "And I am holding you to that."

"That looks like my old one from the apartment," Ben said.

"Could be," Gellar said, leaning back his chair. "Or it could be a facsimile."

Ben chuffed. "Come on. Your entire office staff out there uses IBMs. Why else would you have an iMac in here?"

"Mr. Roberts," Gellar said, folding his arms. "I know little more than the basics about computers, but I had to see the set-up you supposedly used to start up your international conglomerate. Frankly, not one of hundreds of top experts believes you did anything of the kind with that contraption. Consensus is that your little ensemble there was a mere ruse to distract us. Shit, it was never even hooked up to the Internet."

"It's off." Ben seemingly spouted a non sequitur. "You know, it's better to leave it on. And only costs pennies a day."

Gellar cocked is head and stared at him as if needing a moment to comprehend. Finally, he said, "You didn't have a screensaver in it."

"Then let's put one in," Ben countered. "They can be a real blast to watch." He gestured with both cuffed hands. "Go ahead. Or I can do it for you."

Gellar's eyes narrowed. "How? Pull software out of thin air, 'cuz it's still not hooked up to the Internet?"

Ben scooted forward in his chair. "Hell, I can put one in right now, without any software. It's simple."

"No you don't," Gellar said, planting his forearms on the desktop. "Make a move toward that computer, and you're dead meat." He patted his right side-drawer as if it were a hip holster.

"Then you do it," Ben said. "I'll tell you what keys to hit. Takes only a second."

"You trying to jerk me around?"

"I'm a computer genius, remember? Try me."

Gellar snarled disdainfully, glancing from Ben's handcuffs to either agent beside him. He studied Ben for a moment, and then said, "Okay, I'm just curious enough about you to play your game *once*." He walked over and flicked the chassis switch. A loud musical *"boing"* resounded from the set, then a faint whirr emanated as the black screen grayed.

"Okay, Mr. Gellar," Ben yelled loud enough to hail a cab. "With a screensaver, you can leave the computer on twenty-four hours a day. People coming into the office will assume you're a real computer jockey."

Gellar couldn't stifle a grin as he took the bait. "Hey, lower your friggin' voice; I'm not deaf. Okay, so what do I do?"

Only a little less loudly, Ben said, "Well, to get a multi-colored rose pattern that will complement this office decor, just type in R-R-R-O-S-E-E-E, using all capital letters."

"And that'll do it?" Ben nodded. Gellar seemed intrigued, but then he hesitated. "Shit, this is crazy. Can't do anything without the right software."

"Humor me and type, goddamn it," Ben lashed out, surprising even himself.

Gellar bit his lower lip, ready to chastise, but then he reached down and, with two fingers, pecked, R-R-R-O-S-E-E-E.

The screen blackened again. An instant later, a circular polychromatic contortion whirled into existence at the center of the monitor face. Ben nearly jumped up with glee. Yes! Max was still there for him. It was all he could do, not to holler, *Get me out of here*!

"What the hell?" Gellar said, back-stepping. "That's unbelievable." His eyes fixed on the screen, he said, "Hey, I've seen one where tropical fish swim around like in a fish tank. Can you do that?"

"Fish?" Ben dissembled his uncertainty. "Sure. Just type F-F-F-I-S-H-H-H."

Gellar stepped to the computer and did just that. The screen cleared of the mutating rose, and in its place printing appeared:

WAIT A MINUTE. THE FISH ARE SPAWNING.

In another moment, the monitor became a window into the depths of a tropical ocean inhabited by angelfish, puffer fish, jellyfish, other varicolored and assorted tropical denizens, including starfish and seaweed. Simulated bubbles gurgled up the screen face.

"Holy shit," Gellar exclaimed. Ben shrugged nonchalantly, but he was in fact trembling from his success. "You know," Gellar said. "I will leave this on. It'll be like having a real aquarium around." He studied the life-like motions of his new pets. "Would that work on any computer, I mean, just typing out ROSE or FISH that way?"

"It's always did for me," Ben said, shrugging.

"Well, I'll be damned," Gellar said watching the fish. He backed up and sat down. "Okay, Mr. Roberts, enough play time. Let's get to the reason I requested your visit today, why I wanted to speak with you without your attorneys around. And I must thank you for seeing me without your counsel." He rubbed his hands together as if soaping them. "Attorneys are invaluable. God, I ought to know. But we have to show we're worth our wage, so we tend to object and interfere incessantly till nothing can get said in an unbroken sentence. Understand what I mean?"

Ben sneered.

Gellar rocked back and swung his sandaled feet carefully up onto the front edge of his desk. "Fella, you're in deep shit. I mean deep, deep shit. But those of us bringing you to trial have our concerns, too." He crossed his ankles. "Some think we're riding the proverbial tiger in trying you. More than a few very savvy people fear you'll retaliate.

"Feeling some pressure," Gellar stroked his chin, "I ask you to show us your good intentions by decreasing your activity in the world markets, at least for a while. We'll carry word to your people for you. Believe me, everyone's apprehension would ease considerably if you were to do that.

"And for showing your good faith," the corners of his mouth upturned into a smile of anticipation, "we'd be willing to accept a plea bargain. Let you plead guilty to some lesser counts and thus abort this juggernaut of a trial coming. You'd only have to serve a few easy years, then you'd be free and clear. Of course, we'd dismantle that financial colossus you've created, but I can assure you we'd leave you enough to live out the remainder of your life in relative comfort."

Ben "humpfed" and slumped back. "These past four days in solitary confinement have convinced me of one thing. I want no part of jail. I've done nothing illegal, and I trust the system will be just."

Dropping his feet to the floor with a thud, Gellar leaned in over his desktop. "May I ask what drives a man like you? How could you think the world would tolerate a mad man out to buy it up?"

Ben's gut had been knotting all morning, in part from the hellacious stress he was under, but more from the indigestibility of the prison food. A sudden exacerbation of cramping spurred him to respond more aggressively than he might have otherwise.

"Ricky, my boy," he said snappishly, "as the noted historian Will Durant concluded after a lifetime of study, it so happens that mankind has made its greatest strides forward under benevolent dictators."

Gellar's face blanked then flushed. He swiped the air dismissively and shouted, "Get this megalomaniac the hell out of my office."

The two agents stood smartly, taking Ben by either arm, easing him to his feet. Gellar countermanded, "Wait." Pointing a forefinger like a pistol at Ben, he let his words drip with venom. "Fella, let me repeat; you're in deep shit. A guilty verdict on only the least of the counts against you will get you ten years by itself. Guilty on more than one will..." he paused to smile affectedly. "Well, let's just say your dead ass is gonna be the first of you to ever see the light of day again. But," his tone once more became as greasy as the San Quentin fare, "if you were to plead guilty, say to just 'insider trading,' and believe me, your legal staff will ultimately do what you tell them to do, we would accept that in plea, and I promise you no more than a ten-year sentence. Think about that, ten years, shortened with good behavior, as opposed to a sure twenty-five years to life."

"Take me the hell back to my cell," Ben said looking from one agent to the other.

Gellar's eyebrows shot up. "Wait," he commanded, his tone more menacing. "Another thought to carry away. You should consider Jenny Bligh, too."

Ben stiffened. The agents tightened their grips on his arms.

Gellar, obviously pleased with this flare of emotion, leaned back and again swung his feet up on the edge of the desktop.

"Mr. Roberts, to say Jenny is one in a million would be insulting her. She's inimitable. But I can't imagine a woman with her *energy* level," he paused to wink, "being able to cloister herself for more than ten years. Can you?"

"You sonofabitch!" Ben shouted and lunged, but the agents yanked back on his arms and held him in place. "I don't know why the hell I agreed to this goddamn private chat, but we'll never talk again without my legal counsel. Hear me?" He turned and bulled his way toward the door, but was unable to shed the restraining grips that slowed him.

"Mr. Roberts," Gellar called out as the trio passed through the doorway. "Think it over. A ten-year sentence could, in actuality, be as little as six with time off for good behavior. And if that little honey of yours loves you as much as you assume she does, I'd bet even money she could keep her knees together that long."

McPhail and Benassini proffered repeated apologies as they moved him down the building corridors, again with an agent at point and two trailing. Several times McPhail actually referred to Gellar as a prick.

Chapter 51

Jenny sat on the edge of Ben's massive bed, staring the length of his elongated suite. Her eyes fixed on the red computer chassis atop his carved desk. Grappling with her compunctions, she stood and strode toward it, remaining all but oblivious to the spectacular view of oceanic twilight. She paused midway, realizing how enraged she would be at such an invasion of her privacy. Rationalizing, she again convinced herself this wasn't merely snooping; she was trying to salvage the life of the man she loved.

Desperate situations necessitate desperate measures. She set off again.

To her surprise, this set up proved to be as simple as the one on the yacht: a single iMac chassis with a toy-like keyboard and mouse attached.

She poked the power button and the monitor screen paled to gray. She waited; no password challenge or desktop icons appeared. Nothing appeared. She pecked a few keys. Still nothing on the screen. Weren't there any programs on his hard drive? Did he work off discs exclusively? She found no slot for floppy discs on the chassis, only one for CDs. She touched the button beside it; out slid an empty tray. There were no discs on the desk. She sequentially searched the desk drawers. Empty! Every drawer contained nothing at all, let alone any software. She positioned her fingers on the keyboard, paused, and then typed, **P as in Poppies and Passion**. Nothing printed out on the screen. So how did he use it? And he did, several times every day.

Maybe he had one of those sophisticated programs in the hard drive that disguised itself with a blank screen. But if so, how could she ever figure out the access command?

Those graduate students at the UC computer lab taught her a lot. They'd touched on the concept of access coding, where a password or phrase would unlock a program that otherwise had a complex entry. That must be how he worked it.

But what password or phrase would he have used? She positioned her hands on the keys and typed "Benjamin Roberts." No response. She typed "Benny." Nothing. Then, "strebor neb," and "ynneb" and "neb." No response. Smiling, she typed her own name. It would have been sweet if it worked, but no. She typed a long series of words that popped into her head but nary a response. Then she recalled the visit by that Asian detective, and for some reason, she typed in "MAXXXXXXXXX," holding her finger down on the X, slurring it in repetition. An eerie sensation seized her. She jerked her hands off the keyboard.

She again opened each desk drawer, hoping to find something she might have overlooked, perhaps a password scribbled somewhere on the wood itself. Discouraged, she sat down in his chair. Her attention drifted to the cluster of tiny microphone holes in the red plastic above the monitor face. Hey! Maybe the access code had to be spoken rather than typed.

She scooted forward and enunciated directly into the microphone, "Ben Roberts...Benjamin Roberts" The screen remained unchanged. She tried dozens of other words and phrases, including even "Open, Sesame" which made her chuckle. But the monitor never varied from its persistent gray.

Again the notion struck her that she was egregiously violating his privacy. She abruptly clicked off the set. But as she strode for the door, she felt far from defeated. No, her extra-sensory cognition conveyed unmistakably that she would make contact with his organization via his computer. This intuition was unmistakable. Yes, she would succeed, though no doubt it would require diligence.

Chapter 52

For months now, Ben existed essentially in a windowless concrete cave fronted by iron bars, looking out onto a drab narrow corridor. A video camera mounted on the opposite bare wall monitored his actions. But Attorney Kaz assured him there were no listening devices anywhere in his vicinity.

Much of the time he lay on his low bunk, a narrow metal bed-frame crisscrossed with wire springs topped by a two-inch thick mattress. A lidless toilet squatted in a back corner next to a rust-stained porcelain sink. A hanging sheet of stainless steel served him as a mirror. His only other piece of furniture was a ladder-back wooden chair.

Much of the time in his cell he was bothered by that mediciney odor that nobody else seemed to notice. It was actually a clean smell, just annoying. And so far he hadn't had another of those wide-awake dreams again. Once he asked the guard if there was an infirmary close by. The officer chuffed. "Not down here, Mr. Roberts. This is the basement."

He occasionally heard voices down the corridor. But aside from the trustee who delivered his meals, sliding them under the cage door, no one came to talk with him except when his counsel visited a couple of hours each day. He repeatedly asked Kaz to work on obtaining permission for Jenny to visit, but met with headshakes and reiterations of the reality of his situation. Thus the weeks passed.

He tried to exercise regularly, but spent most of his time pondering his chances in the trial. He wondered if his military records would be opened to the court, and if so, would his service to his country help him. But he'd sworn to keep it secret so he couldn't mention it, even to Kaz. And why would Uncle Sam's boys bring it up? It wouldn't help their case.

Much of the time, he would pace, sit, or just lie on his bunk and stare up at the fluorescent light panel in the ceiling, which replaced his sun and moon. The cold white light radiating down only intensified the cell's bleakness.

He often talked aloud to himself as a poor substitute for want of human company. Mostly, he would conduct imagined dialogues with Jenny or Max.

"Hon, my life's been formatted like a friggin' Greek tragedy. Started off in the pits, rocketed to stellar heights, only to plunge into this cesspool.

"Damn you, Max, at this very moment, she and I would be sunning ourselves on some beach near Rio."

Chapter 53

A horde of perversely curious was jammed, cheek-to-jowl, into the sizable spectator section of Courtroom C. An air of circus generated electrifying excitement. Media cameras, cameras, and more cameras were everywhere. At first glance, Ben found the scene reminiscent of the GM stockholders' meeting in Michigan. But there he called the shots.

Jenny sat in the front row, conservatively dressed in a beige suit, advisedly trying not to stand out. Nonetheless, she did stand out, like a cut diamond glittering atop a pile of manure. Their eyes met. She ventured to show him a courageous face, but she appeared overwrought.

That same portly bailiff stepped to the bench and announced the judge. The entire courtroom came to its feet as frizzy-haired Judge Aloysius galloped through the little door behind the bench. He beamed as he surveyed the engorged chamber. Seated on the bench, he emoted like a Shakespearean actor as he officially announced the case, gave his salutations to the jurors, and then he himself enumerated the charges, item by item.

Inured by countless weeks of confinement in his concrete bunker, Ben no longer slouched humbly at the defense table. In a word, he was pissed.

Let's get this friggin' trial started. Okay? His fingers strummed impatiently on the tabletop.

At the conclusion of his grandiloquence, the judge gestured to the prosecution table and asked, "Mr. Gellar, do you have any opening remarks for the jury?"

Rick Gellar eased up out of his chair and strolled toward the jury box. Dressed in earth tones—a cocoa tweed jacket with leather elbow patches, khaki trousers, and a maroon sweater with only the knot of a shamrock-green tie showing—he apparently wanted to present himself as a man-of-the-people.

With deliberateness, he withdrew a yellow-bowled Sherlock Holmes pipe from his jacket pocket and cradled it in his left hand.

"Ladies and gentlemen of the jury." His words oozed out, and Ben recalled his greasy breakfast that morning. "You are a special. We had to cull through countless prospective jurors to find you twelve. Still, to the full letter of the law, you are far from an ideal panel." Many eyebrows bounced up before him. Gellar smiled. "A defendant should be judged by a jury of his peers, peers who are completely unbiased, completely disinterested, a circumstance guaranteed only when they start out completely ignorant of the accused and of his alleged crimes. Only then can a jury be absolutely objective."

He turned subtly, presumably so the cameras could get a fuller shot of his face. "But if we combed this entire country, I doubt we could find twelve adults who were at least of average intelligence who have not heard of and hold no opinion of this defendant. So the United States Government, backed by the ardent hopes of the entire world, asks you to sit in judgment of one Mr. Benjamin Roberts."

At the mere mention of the defendant's name, several in the jury box squirmed.

"You all know of him," Gellar conceded. "His financial tentacles are wrapped around this planet." Raising the pipe face-high, he clutched its bowl with both hands so that only its curved amber stem showed above his grip. His facial muscles drew taut as he squeezed it ever tighter. He continued, "Tentacles that are choking... strangling our world." His hands trembled, his fingers blanching. Every juror focused on his hands and missed the prosecutor's smirk. Ben didn't.

Finally, Gellar relaxed his grip and slowly lowered the pipe to his side. The jurors' eyes followed the pipe down. "All of you, all of us, virtually every person of this country, now have direct or indirect connections to Benjamin Roberts. You may work for one of his countless corporations." As he spoke, he began to pace. "Or your employment may depend directly or indirectly on one or more of them. You may live in housing owned by or perhaps mortgaged from him. You may do business with one of his many banks or lending institutions.

"The consumer goods you buy daily..." He halted and swept the pipe stem like a pointer before them. All the jurors rotated their heads to follow it. "Your purchases of food, home and work supplies, the amenities, the luxuries, most probably are produced, or processed, or delivered by facilities owned and operated by holdings of Benjamin Roberts." Gellar folded his arms, resting the pipe against his lapel. Positioned thus, the jurors still watching the pipe seemed eye to eye with the prosecutor.

"Yet the United States of America solemnly expects you fine folks to boldly judge him as if he were merely any other fellow American. Yes, your country fully expects you to judge him free of all bias, free of all duress, that is ... free of any fear of his reprisal."

The jurors sat absolutely still. Ben wondered if the bastard was a hypnotist.

"At this trial's conclusion, if you decide Benjamin Roberts is innocent of all charges, then set him free, exonerate him completely. But if you come to believe he is guilty as charged, and I am absolutely sure we will convince you of that fact, then you must send him to jail and neutralize his threat to mankind." Gellar then paused. During this pause, the whirring of the news camcorders was the only sound discernable in the great room.

Gellar again began pacing. "In the ensuing weeks, I will methodically convince you that Benjamin Roberts is truly an avaricious, unconscionable gangster who has somehow availed himself of superior high technology that has enabled him to manipulate the world's stock markets, bond markets, future's markets, real estate markets, energy markets, manufacturing industries," he paused in need of a breath, "institutions of high finance, farming industries, fishing industries, the entertainment industries, and more—all for his megalomaniacal aggrandizement. Once you are armed with these truths, you must find him guilty. And thus, let justice break his stranglehold on all our lives." He held up the pipe again, "Let justice return his ill-gotten wealth back to its rightful owners." He casually reinserted the monstrosity of a pipe back into his jacket pocket.

He continued pacing. "I will show *you*," he blurted out abruptly as he poked a finger at a juror, causing her to flinch, "and *you*, and *you*, and *you*," as he pointed at others. "Yes, I will show all of you conclusively that at just the threat of competition—his type of competition—he perpetrated the audacious, cold-blooded murder of thirty-two persons." He redirected his finger straight up in the air. "And that's only thirty-two that we know of. I will allow you to look beyond his benevolent facade and let you see the monster he really is. Then you must put an end to his despotism."

The entire courtroom was so focused on Gellar that Ben wondered if he might not be able to just get up and walk away unnoticed. The prosecutor turned slowly to hold this spell a bit longer, then strolled leisurely back to his seat. He glanced over at Kaz and subtly flicked an eyebrow, conveying, *let me see you top that, sucker*!

Ben glanced back at Jenny. Her head was bowed and her eyes were shut. As he watched her, several video cameras zoomed in at him to capture every nuance of his dejection and then telecast them instantly around the world. He sighed, puffing out his cheeks. No doubt about it, he was in deep shit.

Mosi Kaz stood and strode briskly to the front rail of the jury box. His gait suggested indignation. Chin up and shoulders back, he too stated his appreciation for the appointed duty of these jurors, then segued on to say, "But never lose sight of the fact that American capitalism is not a system intended to set personal limitations. In this country, every citizen has the right to achieve as much as his or her effort and ability can command." Softening his demeanor, he went on to say that when a phenomenon, a person like Mr. Roberts with such extraordinary abilities, arose it was to be expected that his or her financial acquisitions could also become extraordinary.

The jurors seemed attentive, but definitely not enraptured.

Hell, Mosi, we needed more blacks on this jury.

Only one African-American was seated on it, a gray-haired fellow with prominent silver rings around the brown of his irises. And he could well drop dead before they got around to the deliberation.

Mosi Kaz was in mid-sentence when a juror in the front row, a puffy-eyed mailman with a red walrus mustache, pulled out an oversize white handkerchief and blew his bulbous nose. Then he spent several minutes cleaning gummy bits out of his mustache, all to the distraction of himself and the other jurors.

But through it all, Kaz persevered. "Few would argue that computers tightly manage our world today. And my client happens to be a computer genius of a magnitude without equal. His wizardry alone has resulted in his honestly begotten fortune."

Kaz shook his finger at the jury, perhaps to emulate Gellar's earlier digital gestures.

"Do not be deceived. The United States Government has not brought Mr. Roberts into this courtroom because it believes him a wanton criminal. No. He sits here because elements in our national and global society fear his undeniable superiority." He turned and mutely pointed at Ben. Whatever Kaz's intent was, he held the gesture uncomfortably long.

Finally, Kaz turned back to the jury. "And that nonsensical allegation that my client had anything at all to do with any murder, let alone thirty-two of them, is laughable garbage, an ill-conceived sick machination contrived to shock and confuse you. We will show it be groundless, actually humorous." He clasped his arms across his chest, assuming a defiant posture. "A guilty verdict from you will be tantamount to saying, 'Use capitalism to grow, but if you get too big, the system can cut you down, cut you to pieces.'"

Ben sat visualizing himself hog-tied and this jury cramming him, ass first, down the gullet of a gigantic Cuisinart toward the whirling blades.

Chapter 54

The prosecution called their first witness, Guido LaGarbo, a squat fellow in his fifties with a hairless sun-tanned pate surrounded by a salt-and-pepper fringe and a matching shaggy mustache. Telltale chunks of the "old country" embellished his diction.

Gellar stood before the jury and pondered aloud. "Benjamin Roberts made an abrupt and meteoric climb into the world of high finance from a position of insignificance. We are told he did it with his computer genius, and that he did it alone."

He turned to his witness. "Mr. LaGarbo, you've told this jury that you work at The Land of Computers, and that you sold Mr. Roberts his first computer, not that many months ago. How well do you remember that sale?"

Before answering, Guido shifted in his chair for greater comfort, then whiffed deeply. "I remember it pretty dam' goot. He was the typical 'I-don't-know-nothing-about-computers' customer. And he said he couldn't type." He waved his hands continually as he spoke. "So I steered him to a Macintosh. In our business, we say itza more user friendly. He said he had absolutely no idea how a computer works. He knew nothing about computer jargon, but what the hell, I went on, in simplified terms, explaining about the mouse, the keyboard, the desktop menus, and so on. And if I may be literal, sir, I remember he kept saying, 'Aw shit'. Then he up and says, 'I'll take that one and a typing program.' I wuza so surprised at making the sale that I almost said 'Aw shit,' myself." Guido chuckled at his own humor.

"Mr. LaGarbo, you can recall his computer ignorance that clearly?"

The witness nodded once sharply. "I remember him especially, because the next morning I wuza faxed an order from a friend of his for an accessory microphone, and that made me wonder because the iMac he bought has a build-in microphone. Now, this friend seemed to know something about computers, so I figured maybe it wuza some kind a joke."

Gellar strolled back to the witness stand and stopped. "So Mr. Roberts came off rather like a computer dunce in your recollection, did he not? But some *friend* of his who seemed to understand computers ordered an additional microphone for him the morning after his initial purchase. Interesting, indeed." He stroked his chin.

"Mr. LaGarbo, did this friend request your store to enclose a personal message with the delivery? And if so, would you please read a copy of that message to the jury."

Gellar went from stroking his chin to gripping it. Every juror had to perceive his intense interest in the forthcoming testimony.

"Yes, sir," Guido said with an air of authority as he unfolded a letter-size white paper. He read:

Hi, Ben. This is the auxiliary microphone I suggested to you last night. Just plug its cable into the proper port in the panel on the right side of the chassis and I'll take it from there. That correct port (plug site) has a symbol of a microphone beside it that looks a bit like the French fleur-de-lis. We're going to be great pals. You'll see.

Your Friend, MAX.

P. S. By the way, I faxed this order to the store, charged it to your credit card, and requested this message be included.

Flashing a smile of delight, Gellar addressed the jurors. "I ask you, did that testimony suggest to any of you that Mr. Roberts is a computer genius? Or did it sound more likely he's merely a stooge for one or more geniuses?" Turning for his seat, he announced, "I'm through with this witness, Your Honor."

Disruptive murmurings swept the courtroom. Judge Aloysius slammed the gavel down and demanded quiet. He gestured to the defense table with the gavel head.

"Your Honor," Defense Attorney Kaz spoke out, as he slowly rose from his seat. "The defense intends to waive cross-examination of this witness. His whole testimony was about playful nonsense that Mr. Roberts perpetrated himself. He found that the internal connections of the built-in microphone on his set were faulty. Will the court please recall that was documented by the FBI lab? But since Mr. Roberts never used the microphone anyway, rather than take the computer back to the store for exchange or repair, he simply ordered the auxiliary microphone to have on hand in the unlikely case he ever did want to use it.

"And he'd named his computer Max, thus when he himself sent that order he added that tongue-in-cheek text as a little inside joke.

"But as this trial progresses, if doubt of his prowess continues in the minds of any of the jurors, he is prepared to demonstrate his abilities as well as his technique to use cyberspace without an apparent Internet hookup. Perhaps then he can put an end to these repeated disparagements about his typing and computer skills. Amen!"

Chatter erupted about the courtroom. Rick Gellar shook his head emphatically at this offer. Though the judge waited and listened to everything Kaz had to say, he then soundly chastised the defense attorney for addressing the bench before being recognized. And he extended another stern warning to the spectators.

Chapter 55

The court recessed for lunch. The room cleared, including Jenny, leaving only the guards. The agents re-handcuffed Ben, then brought him a box lunch which he ate at the otherwise vacated defense table. A tuna fish sandwich, potato chips, a chilled Gravenstein apple, and a wax carton of nonfat milk. He ate mechanically, without really tasting any of it. Jenny monopolized his thoughts. How was this ordeal affecting her? Max would know. Oh, how he wanted to talk to Max.

Another reverie swept him. He now imagined himself a cork afloat on a turbulent sea, being heaved about with no control over anything, least of all his fate.

Jennifer's maroon Rolls limousine waited in a red zone near the courthouse. Its rear door stood agape at the sidewalk and the motor was running. She sat in the back holding a cellular phone to her ear.

"Hello, Professor Brough?" she said.

"Yes. How can I help you?" a contralto voice on the line answered.

"Professor, this is Jennifer Bligh. Perhaps you recall having coffee with Matt Borquist and myself on campus several weeks ago. I asked about the Macintosh in particular. Remember?"

"Of course, I remember you very well. Did my graduate students prove helpful?"

"Tremendously so, but may I explain briefly the situation I find myself facing?" Two passers-by, a pair of burly teenage boys in high school varsity jackets, slowed and peered quizzically in at her. She pulled the door closed.

She went on to describe what she encountered with Ben's computer, the lack of any apparent programs in it, the lack of any near software. She felt sure the computer had been used daily up until recently, and used just as she found it. She asked about the possibility of disguised programs in the hard drive that might only activate to specific typed or voice commands.

After a thoughtful pause, the professor replied. "Though it's an iMac, I presume you're talking about a computer that's in a rather affluent setting. Right?"

"Right."

"Sure. A computer can readily be programmed to remain blank-screened until you present it with a designated access code, sitting otherwise locked, if you will. I bet you're dealing with a voice access system because that's state of the art. A voice analyzer is incorporated so that only a particular individual's voice activates it, in which case a specific access code word is not required at all, just the individual's voice.

"But Jenny, it's possible that the program access was set up for that voice to recite a particular phrase. In which case, you're sunk. You'd never be able to enter without duplicating the access phrase spoken by the specified person. But if just wave-analysis identification alone is required, there's hope."

"Uh-hum."

"In which case, if you simply play a recording of that person's voice, you might gain entry. Follow me?"

"Yes, and I do have some recent camcorder tapes with this person's voice."

"Try them. And Jenny, if you'd like to come over to Berkeley again to discuss this further, call me anytime. I'm intrigued. And I must confess, I'm an addicted puzzle solver."

Chapter 56

The court reconvened at 1:30 p.m. The prosecution called its second witness of the day. Judge Aloysius reiterated Gellar's request, "Mr. Clarence Liggitts, please take the witness stand."

A lanky black fellow stood up at the back of the courtroom and ambled down the aisle. Ben immediately recognized him as the elderly Deville courier, out of uniform. Today he wore an electric blue suit with a frilly salmon pink shirt that sported prominent french cuffs and gold-doubloons cuff links. His black patent-leather shoes shone like mirrors. Surely, this fellow had dressed for the worldwide television coverage.

He swore in manifesting utter confidence.

Gellar's mannerisms and tone were fawning. "Mr. Liggitts, did you on the said date of last year have reason to visit the apartment of Benjamin Roberts?"

"Yes, sir, as a courier for the Deville Courier Service, I brought him papers to sign from a number of financial institutions."

"Do you see the man you visited that day in this courtroom now?"

"Well, I sees the face, but not the man."

Gellar straightened in earnest surprise. He glimpsed over at Ben then back to study his witness. "Would you explain that answer, please?"

"Well, sir, that man," Liggits pointed to Ben, "has the same face, but it ain't the same man. The man I brought those documents to had nothing to do with money. His apartment said poor. His clothes said poor. His manners said poor."

Liggits sat back in his chair and raised his chin. "And he didn't know I was coming. He didn't know anything about them documents. The man I saw that morning was one of the oppressed masses. This man here," again he gestured at Ben, "he is a true blue-blood. I know people. How the two became the same man is for you to figure out."

Gellar seemed relieved but he scrambled to regain direction from this impromptu digression that he'd obviously not rehearsed with this witness.

"On that day, Mr. Liggitts, you say Benjamin Roberts seemed puzzled as to why you had come, but he did sign the documents, did he not, and then return them to you?"

"Yes, sir, but only after I chided him."

"Explain that."

The courier settled into even deeper ease in the witness chair. "Well, sir, I sat there a good while. He looked confused. He'd leaf through them pages and sigh. He'd read some more and sigh some more. He'd scratch his head and sigh. The man was lost. So I up and chided him. I said he don't fit the mold of the busy, rich folk that usually gets deliveries like this. Then he gets huffed and picks up a pen, and acts like the King of England signing them all without further to do."

Gellar placed his arms akimbo. "Do you have any other clues that Benjamin Roberts was not the person who ordered the documents picked up and delivered to him?"

"Yes, sir."

"Explain, please."

"Well, sir, the order request came to the company early that morning with a credit-card payment that included a hefty tip in advance for the courier. But after he signed them, I told him I usually get a big time tip for this type of run. He didn't say, 'you already got it'. No, sir. He gets huffed again and tells me he'll send me my tip at Christmas time—dogshit in a box. No, sir. He didn't know I'd been tipped already."

The gavel silenced the snickering in the courtroom. "Cross examination," Judge Aloysius ordered.

Wearing a charcoal suit and a ruby tie today, Mosi Kaz approached the witness stand. "Mr. Liggitts, is it not true that when you knocked at the defendant's apartment that morning you in fact woke him up, that when he answered the door he was still half-asleep."

"Yes, sir." The witness jutted his chin out. "And that's another thing, he looked like he slept in them clothes, not a habit of money folk. Yeah, he came to the door with sleep in his eyes, creases on his face, and wrinkled clothes."

Kaz stroked his chin as Gellar had done. "Mr. Liggitts, in the past, have you ever awakened anyone else when you went calling with a delivery?"

"Hmmm. Sometimes."

"Did you ever find these people mentally clumsy until they were fully awake?"

Liggits jutted out his chin again. "Yeah, but there is a difference between being sleepy and being in the dark. And this man was in the dark. He didn't know what them papers was for."

Kaz arched back slightly. "Mr. Liggits, did Mr. Roberts ask you any questions at all about the documents?"

The courier hesitated then rather reluctantly shook his head. "No, sir."

"But he did sign each complex document in the stack and return them to you. Isn't that proof he had to know something about them? At that time, Mr. Roberts worked in business management. No one with any experience in the legal quagmires of commerce would ever sign any legal document let alone a ream of them without knowing the reason for or the implications of doing so." The witness nodded to convey that he concurred. Kaz faced the jury, smiling. "Mr. Liggitts, let me say that there are corroborated police cases where people have awakened from sleep so obtunded that they actually walked out open windows to their deaths, thinking they were doorways."

The defense attorney wheeled to the witness. "And you readily admit you showed the defendant a degree of rudeness while you were in the apartment."

Liggits adjusted his pink bow tie with both hands. "Well, like I said, I only chided him to hurry him up."

"Mr. Liggits, after you *chided* him, was there any way Mr. Roberts could have retrieved his prepaid gratuity, his tip, from you at that point?"

"No way at all! It was already down deep in my pocket."

Now Kaz assumed the akimbo stance. "So his only recourse at that moment was to hurl you an insult, right? You already had his tip."

Liggits acceded, hunching his lower lip. "I guess that's so, yep! But it weren't no outrageous chide on my part or anything."

Kaz spun on the varnished parquet floor and strode back toward his seat. "I'm finished with this witness, Your Honor."

Chapter 57

Mid-afternoon, Gellar's request brought an awkward, ill at ease James Ferris to the stand. He took the witness box wearing a drab, beige polyester sport coat and slacks. Wrinkles competed with the red-striped pattern on his open-collared shirt. Gellar steered Ben's former boss into commenting on each item in the scathing fitness report that he had submitted on Ben just before the botched firing attempt.

Gellar verbally twisted Ferris, forcing the pathetic fellow to delineate his perception of the dramatic overnight transfiguration of the defendant from an inept schlemiel into a moneyed dynamo. Being carefully kind to himself, Ferris recounted his effort to fire Ben, and how it led to his humiliating demotion. Head bowed, he hedged and stammered through his entire testimony and never looked over at Ben once throughout this questioning.

As Kaz started to rise up out of his chair in response to the Judge's call for cross-examination, Ben gripped his forearm, halting him. "Waive it. He's been tortured enough."

"What?" Kaz stiffened. "Do you know what that'll convey to the jury?"

"Waive it."

Kaz stared incredulously at Ben for a long moment, then making no attempt to hide his own exasperation, looked up at the judge and said, "Your Honor, defense waives cross examination of this witness."

The prosecutors and the judge manifested the expected surprise. Muttering ran through the courtroom. Ferris audibly exhaled in relief and stepped down from the stand as if morbidly fatigued. Stepping toward the aisle, he paused and turned to the defense table for the first time. "I'm sorry, Mr. Roberts. They told me I had to answer all questions completely, or I could be on trial myself for contempt."

Gellar leaped to his feet, shouting, "Your Honor, please advise the jury that this witness just prostrated himself before the defendant. His testimony must be regarded as biased and presented to minimize the damaging truth about the defendant."

Gellar's outburst confounded Ferris even more. Head down, he slogged up the aisle and out the rear doors, repeating again and again, "I'm really sorry."

Ben scribbled on one of the several note pads on the defense table as Kaz fumed, "Mr. Roberts, you have done yourself considerable damage just now. Tell me, are you pursuing vindication or crucifixion?"

Ben slid his completed note to a junior attorney beside him. He'd written: *Restore Ferris to his original salary and upgrade his work assignment. Bonus him with the equivalent of his lost wages since demotion.*

Chapter 58

Jenny sat in Ben's swivel chair, again opening each desk drawer in sequence. But as each time before, she found nothing.

She pressed the iMac switch, the monitor lighted, and the red chassis began to purr like a living entity. She held up the Sony camcorder and pressed its play button. Unmistakably, Ben's voice resounded.

My love, standing here atop this towering pyramid, the Temple of the Moon, located just outside Mexico City, I can't fathom why the ancient Aztecs lost their fight with the invading Spanish conquistadors. Surely, the locals must have grown as strong as Missouri mules humping to the top of this mother regularly. And if this wasn't exercise enough, they had that neighboring monstrosity, the Temple of the Sun to hike up. Her own laugh could be heard in the background.

The monitor screen remained blank. She winced.

Switching the camcorder off, she set it on the desk and placed her fingers on the keyboard. She pondered a moment, then began to type, speaking the words as she typed them.

"This is Jennifer Bligh. I love Ben Roberts. Though he now desperately needs your help, it seems you have abandoned him. I, therefore, ask to speak with someone key in the organization. I would like very much to speak to his primary adviser."

She pushed the chair back from the desk and stared at the homogeneous, gray screen as she contemplated her options. In a blink, printing flashed onto it.

You will be allowed to transmit us a single message tonight. Your first and *last*.

She bolted upright. "Oh Thank God! Thank God!"

More printing appeared.

Recite your verbal message now, in thirty seconds or less! Return to this station at nine pm tomorrow evening for our printed response.

Ecstatic, her mind raced. But had the thirty-second countdown begun at the end of this printed message, or would it begin at the first sound of her voice? She feared the countdown had started.

"My name is Jennifer Bligh. I am Ben Roberts' fiancée. He is being held incommunicado in federal prison while being tried in federal court on a series of capital crimes, as you must already know. He is not allowed access to a computer or a telephone. He isn't even allowed to see or speak to me. I must establish a link with you to convince you to help him. You must mobilize his financial empire to free him."

Establishing this contact brought tears that blurred her vision. She paused to sniffle.

Abruptly the monitor announced:

Thirty seconds has elapsed!

Then it blanked.

The next day in the court, she sat preoccupied with what Ben's organization might say. She had to convince the highest echelons to act. Continually glancing at her Cartier throughout the day, she would recalculate the remaining hours left till 9 p.m.

She sat waiting in his desk chair at 8:30 p.m. Her excitement crescendoed with each passing minute. 8:58... 8:59... 9:00 p.m. At exactly that instant, a printed message appeared in toto.

His financial empire, as you called it, is following Mr. Benjamin Roberts' instructions to the letter in this matter. All communication with you is absolutely concluded as of now.

She sat stunned until nearly nine-thirty. No additions to the static message followed.

Chapter 59

Days in Courtroom "C" passed. A steady stream of both foreign and domestic witnesses for the prosecution paraded through: computer experts, business types, bankers (including Basil Gilford who'd visited Ben at work and unknowingly was the first to inform him he had become a millionaire), stockbrokers, real estate brokers, and university professors of repute.

Surely, there had to be at least a smattering of hi-tech savvy amongst the jury members beforehand. Nonetheless, experts systematically instructed the panel from scratch about computers until the least-educated, least-capable juror had to appreciate the worthlessness of a computer chassis without the appropriate software installed in it. Each came to see that any computer is only an isolated piece of equipment if it does not have the modem and software to access the Internet or other computers. They learned the basic ways computers could be used to buy and sell stocks, bonds, and commodity futures, and specifically how a computer might illegally slip an order in a millisecond ahead of another major purchase or major sale to reap instant profit. They were shown timed purchase and sale receipts that suggested the defendant's network was continuously doing just that, in every market around the world.

Other experts explained about the stock, bond, and futures markets, right down to the purchase of *put options* and *call options*. They explained how vulgar profits could be wrested in very short time using this option market, whether it was rising or falling, though at extreme risk to the players. Step by step, they walked the jury through that early incident where Ben invested ten million dollars in Pan Electronic Corporation *call options* and realized four hundred, eighty-six million dollars in profit from that single venture.

These experts documented the incredible fact that Ben's computer network gleaned billions and billions of dollars out of the world option markets—having lost only on rare occasions, and those losses might well have been contrived. A Professor Thom Warren from Harvard summed it up: "I doubt Mr. Roberts's track record in market investments could be duplicated by God himself, if our deity were to play fair." This pronouncement evoked visible awe from the jurors.

Real estate experts explained the lucrative windfalls available if a person armed with privileged information about future developments or special plans for any property preempted and bought up that property in question ahead of time. Endless examples were presented of Ben's corporations seemingly doing just that. This presentation spilled over several days of trial time before Judge Aloysius finally asked the prosecution, "How many more pieces of data are there to show us?"

Dr. Maruyama answered for his panel. "Your Honor, the situation is analogous to that often given to demonstrate the vast number and reproduction rate of the citizens in China: 'If Chinese walked four abreast into the ocean, ad infinitum, that country would never run out of people.' Such is the case for Mr. Roberts's highly suspect real estate ventures around the world. His organizations function as if they are blessed with absolute prescience. They seem to know well beforehand about every square inch of land and every building that are about to appreciate, and they seize upon them. Too, his people purchase from a reservoir of cash that is all but bottomless."

Over Mosi Kaz's objection regarding the relevance, government experts, in this case mostly unsmiling women, pooled their talents to explain to the jury the advantages to a corporation when it becomes a monopoly. Also, how a conglomerate of varied corporations can selectively purchase from within their own holdings in quasi-monopoly fashion and thus squeeze competing corporations into submission, leading to takeovers at bargain prices. After a day of example after international example of Ben's corporations using this strategy masterfully, Judge Aloysius intervened again. "We still can picture those marching Chinese. I'm sure the jury understands the immense success Mr. Roberts has achieved allegedly using these methods."

These didactic presentations to the jury, in an ironic way, probably fascinated and enlightened Ben most of all. He learned in depth, for the first time, how computers work, how his own empire operated, and how Max played in the various market places.

Jessuz, Max. You've been taking candy from the proverbial baby.

Chapter 60

With the car phone to her ear, Jenny closed the limousine's curbside rear door.

"Professor Brough? This is Jenny Bligh again. Could we meet for lunch sometime this week? Yes, dinner Thursday would be perfect. I'll meet you at your office. Yes, seven o'clock is fine."

Professor Krauthammer of Yale University, a bespectacled, white-haired octogenarian on the stand, asked the jury to, "Visualize, if you can, all the integral business decisions, all the complex business transactions, all the intricate managerial duties of Mr. Roberts' gargantuan financial empire being expertly accomplished by his network even when he's not personally at a computer himself. His unmanned computer network functions incessantly, untiringly, twenty-four hours a day. He has developed an artificial intelligence that dwarfs anything imaginable by current scientific understanding."

The jurors sat wide-eyed. Gellar interjected, "Dr. Krauthammer, let us assume, for the sake of discussion, that Mr. Roberts has *not* evolved any new advancement in artificial intelligence. Can you speculate how he might be accomplishing all this using the standard computer know-how of the day?"

"Well, Mr. Gellar, we've played with that question at length among ourselves. Our best, though pathetically weak, hypothesis would go like this: he would need tens of thousands of highly trained computer operators scattered over the Earth, working continuously and in conjunction with each other, acquiring, exchanging and processing information nonstop. Their computer network would operate in cyberspace much like the myriad nerves do in a single brain, if you will. But I must hasten to add that not one such operator has ever been uncovered—that is, other than Mr. Roberts himself."

"But Doctor," Gellar played to the jury, "nothing we have learned here about this man suggests he is a genius by any stretch of the imagination. Antithetically, he comes off as a high-tech boob. It's questionable whether he can even type with any proficiency."

Dr. Krauthammer adjusted his coke-bottle eyeglasses, revealing a chronic tremor in his hands. "Mr. Gellar, who dares argue with the facts as they are? Alone, or with help, he has accomplished something beyond my comprehension. Perhaps he is psycho-neurotic and chose to cover up any trace of his genius until now. I'm reaching here, I know, but you might also consider multiple personalities, where only one personality is the genius and the others know nothing about it."

Gellar sped to lop off this line of reasoning. "Doctor, while in jail, Mr. Roberts has undergone extensive psychiatric evaluation to be sure he was fit to stand trial. No major personality or mental problems were uncovered by a team of renowned psychiatrists and psychologists."

Folding his arms, Gellar faced this witness squarely. "How in the scientific world of today could we neutralize this advantage Mr. Roberts has acquired?"

Krauthammer nodded, freeing a low chuckle. "Quite simply. We could cease to use our computers in our work. If the world were to revert back to doing business with mechanical typewriters and conventional postal systems, and if we took the computer chips out of all our machines, he would have little if any manipulative advantage."

"But that's not feasible."

The scientist shook his head, offering a tired smile. "I shudder to think what would happen at this point if cyberspace were denied us. Over six billion people to feed, clothe, protect, and govern." He shook his head again. "No, sir. Mankind is irrevocably dependent on the computer just to maintain our status quo." He forced a laugh. "Can you imagine the outcry if we were to close down the Internet for even a day?"

Gellar strolled over to the jury box. "Doctor, then we must ascertain if Benjamin Roberts acts alone or with co-conspirators. Is he the brains behind this mega-plot or is he simply a stooge for other sinister plotters? To help us find out, the prosecution must take the defense up on its offer and ask Mr. Roberts to demonstrate his computer expertise, though we do so with much trepidation." The courtroom clamored to life. The gravel resounded.

Gellar turned to stare at the defense table, and every juror's gaze paralleled his. The defense attorneys had drawn tightly together into an animated tête-à-tête. He addressed his witness while eyeing them. "Dr. Krauthammer, would you and the other scientists here care to stay and watch his demonstration? Perhaps we will want to call on you afterwards with questions on what we are about to see."

Krauthammer's eyeballs, already magnified grotesquely through his thick glasses, bulged even more with anticipation. "But of course! I am eager to see him perform live. We studied an FBI videotape of him purchasing a piece of stock on the Japanese market. It was..." He paused to shake his head. "It was unfathomable. His actions and key percussion sequences seemed sheer idiocy. We were left to surmise that someone used a tape that was coordinated with a prearranged purchase."

Gellar still eyeing his opponents in caucus, replied, "Yes, Doctor, we may show that tape to the jury, depending on what the live demonstration reveals." He walked over to the defense table, dragging the attention of the entire courtroom with him. "Mr. Kaz, did you understand me? We accept your offer to have Mr. Roberts demonstrate his computer faculty, if in fact it does exist. Of course, we expect him to use the same model of computer that he had in his apartment. The same lack of Internet connection. Nothing more."

Another outburst of chatter erupted in the courtroom. This time the judge's gavel returned the room to quiet only with the added threat of expulsion. Video cameramen scrambled to reposition themselves more advantageously along the railing. The world, like the microcosm of the courtroom, hungrily awaited every nuance of this pending revelation.

Mosi Kaz finally stood up flashing a self-assured smile and asked his standing adversary, "How do you want the courtroom demonstration to be set up?"

Gellar replied without hesitation. "Mr. Roberts can sit there in front of the jury box at a computer. We'll place a camcorder behind him, focused on his monitor screen so what appears on his monitor will be projected onto a giant screen there at the front wall so the jury can see it." He glanced at the aggregation of TV network camcorders aimed at him. "As well as all other interested parties."

The defense team conferred again, whispering and gesturing for several minutes. Ben nodded repeatedly, enumerating provisos on the fingers of his left hand.

Kaz again stood, signaling that the defense's stratagem was in place. He swaggered out to assume a position in front of the defense table to gain equal stature with the standing chief prosecutor.

"Mr. Roberts will demonstrate to the court as you request, but we have stipulations."

Gellar smirked.. "Okay, let's hear them."

Kaz studied his wristwatch thoughtfully, and then addressed the bench. "Your Honor, he can be ready today when the court reconvenes from lunch recess. But we insist on strict adherence to specific steps in the acquisition of the computer equipment to be used."

Judge Aloysius glanced to Gellar then nodded at Kaz, relaying acceptance.

"Over the lunch hour," Kaz said, "several of my legal team, and several from Mr. Gellar's, if they so desire, and Jenny Bligh, the defendant's fiancée, can randomly select a computer store in the telephone book while they are already driving in the car. They should then drive immediately to that selected store and purchase an iMac computer. They are to select one randomly from unopened factory-crated merchandise. Then they are to return directly back here, where the purchase is to be unloaded at once and brought to the designated spot in this courtroom," he pointed to the floor in front of the jury, "to be uncrated and assembled in plain view of all. If those stipulations are satisfactory to the court, we will hold the demonstration."

Gellar faced the bench with open arms. "Your Honor, the prosecution accepts this plan, but regrets the distrust implied in the defense's stipulations. But, alas, we too must add stipulations of our own. We ask that after the apparatus has been set up in this courtroom, that Dr. Krauthammer and his panel be allowed to open the chassis, all under the watchful eyes of the defense team if it so desires, to be sure that there is no installed wireless hook-up to the Internet, as such set-ups are now available. This computer must be exactly like the one he had in his apartment. Agreed?"

Kaz looked to Ben and Ben nodded. Kaz turned and said," Agreed."

The gavel resounded and Aloysius pronounced, "This court is adjourned until 2:00 p.m."

Ben glanced back at Jenny. She blew him a kiss. Smiling, he returned it. Even at this distance from her, he could detect her *Eternity* perfume.

Ben was sitting at the defense table and had just finished a ham-and-Swiss sandwich when five men in orange jumpsuits filed through the back entrance of the empty courtroom carrying cartons. Two of them had teamed up to tote in a desk. The attorneys and Jenny strode along with them. The men heaped the desk and the other cartons in front of the jury box where the attorneys then ringed the hillock.

On Mosi Kaz's command, the deliverymen started ripping into the cardboard. Two men unfurled a giant projection screen up against the front wall. Two others positioned the raw-wood desk with its drawer-side facing the jury. Another positioned a yellow iMac computer on the desktop then set a metal chair in front of it. He connected the chassis power cord to an extension cord that reached across the parquet floor to a wall outlet.

One of the men finished up by mounting a camcorder on a tripod and positioning it to face the iMac screen. The total assemblage took less than twenty minutes.

While workmen sliced up the empty cardboard boxes and stuffed the angular pieces along with the Styrofoam casings, packing acorns, and the instructional manuals and warranty sheets into two remaining intact empty cartons, Dr. Krauthammer with his cronies, ringed by lawyers and Jenny, carefully opened the iMac chassis on the desktop. The while, four of the "Orangemen" carried off the scraps, leaving one fellow to sweep the floor.

The courtroom began to fill. Jenny returned to her seat. The cameramen were re-assuming their prized positions behind the front railing.

Ben glanced back at Jenny repeatedly during this time that the scientists were huddled in front. He blew her a kiss. She ignored it, instead gestured with an outstretched arm several times toward the group around the computer.

He puzzled. Why did she want him to pay attention to them? But he did.

Chapter 61

Mosi Kaz felt no foreboding about this demonstration as he and the other defense attorneys rejoined Ben at the defense table.

No sooner were they seated, than the bailiff paced to the front and pompously announced the judge's imminent return. Judge Aloysius scrambled in and up onto the bench. While the judge reiterated the agreed upon plan for the afternoon, Kaz sat reviewing some notes on a legal pad. He leisurely canted his head toward Ben beside him and said in an undertone, "We got the exact computer you bought last time, but we didn't get one of those whatever-you-call-it extra microphones. The computer store we chose didn't have any in stock. The prosecution balked at us going to another store. I did warn them that not having everything you had at the apartment might limit your demonstration." He glimpsed at Ben and was comforted by his relaxed smile. "Oh, yeah! I should tell you that Gellar insisted that Professor Krauthammer clip the connecting wire to the microphone because the one in your apartment also had a faulty mike connection. He insisted that we'd agreed this computer should be exactly like yours when you got it, and reminded me that I'd said you never used the mike anyway. I guess I did, but only because I thought that's what you told me. Anyway, be advised your microphone won't be working."

The absence of any response at all from his client caused Kaz to glance at him. All the color had drained from Ben's face. He looked dumbstruck, no, horrified. "Mr. Roberts, what's wrong?"

Ben recovered enough to mumble, "The microphone won't work?"

"No, damn it. Do you really need it?"

The gavel resounded. "Mr. Kaz, pay attention, please," Judge Aloysius chastised. "Mr. Gellar has been asking Mr. Roberts to take his position at the computer to start the demonstration. Please comply."

Ben stood up and stepped off across the parquet floor in virtual slow motion. Reaching the desk, he sat down mechanically in the metal chair, his back to the jury.

Kaz held his breath. Years of practicing law taught him to read disaster in a client.

Feeling an icy numbness from his scalp to his toes, Ben stared at the black computer screen.

A large-framed fellow in a brown suit stood by the front wall, grasping the extension cord. "Mr. Moscofian," the judge explained to the jury, "will immediately unplug the system if the defendant does anything at all suspicious or inappropriate while operating this unit."

Expectantly, the courtroom stilled. Ben sat as inert as an inanimate object. Gellar leaned in next to him, ostensibly double-checking to be sure the CD slot was indeed empty. Holding that posture, he whispered, "Something wrong?"

Ben held his stare straight ahead but replied, "You said so yourself, big guy. I'm in deep shit."

The attorney frowned as he clicked on the computer, saying, "Did you think fear would stop us from calling your bluff?" As he strode off toward his seat, he grinned back over his shoulder.

All but paralyzed, without seeing any course of action, Ben glanced down at the desktop where the runt of a microphone would have been. Hell, maybe he should just feign an epileptic fit and end this fiasco.

Hey! An epiphany struck. He could try *MAXAMAXAM* again. Max said they should change the code after using it, but they'd never gotten around to it. Still, he might respond to the old one. Worth a try. Only, how could he pull it off with everyone watching? Ah! Maybe he could cover the keyboard with something, then type out an explanation of his predicament. Since there was no program activated yet, no lettering should appear on the screen, but Max might get the message. That was his only hope.

He looked up at the judge and said, "Your Honor, I request a cloth to cover my hands and the keyboard so as to maintain a degree of secrecy for my coding. Perhaps a towel or something?"

The judge glanced at the prosecuting attorneys. Gellar thought a moment then nodded faintly. So Aloysius leaned off the bench and muttered something to a rangy second bailiff. This elderly fellow tottered out through the judge's door and reappeared a minute later carrying a folded white bath towel. Double-stepping with a slight limp over to Ben, he unfurled the towel with a flick of his wrists, letting it drape over the entire computer keyboard.

Ben carefully slid his hands under the towel onto the keys then surveyed the crowded courtroom. All faces, all cameras were fixed on him. Jenny sat tense, a hand covering her mouth. Had she mystically foreseen this crisis?

He felt the keyboard for the little raised dots on the F and the J keys to correctly position his covered fingers as he struggled to recall where the M, A, and X keys were in relation to the F and J. Frustrated, he realized he'd have to peek under the towel.

Before he could move his hands, Gellar stood up unexpectedly. "Your Honor, I speak for the court. This protracted delay suggests what we all suspected, his ineptness. There is considerable doubt that Mr. Roberts can even type, let alone operate a computer by himself."

Tittering erupted about the courtroom. Gellar wheeled to face the spectators. The judge hammered for quiet. "Your Honor," Gellar shouted at the audience, "if there is a distracting influence in the courtroom, he or she should be removed at once."

Laughter welled boisterously before him. All spectator eyes and all camcorders were focused on the giant monitor screen. Gellar spun around to see why.

Across the huge screen was printing in bold letters:

Your honor, I speak for the court. This protracted delay suggests what we all suspected, his ineptness. There is considerable doubt whether Mr. Roberts can even type, let alone operate a computer by himself.

Your honor, if there is a distracting influence in the courtroom, he or she should be removed at once.

"Well, I'll be...!" Gellar exclaimed. As the words left his mouth, they appeared on the screen.

Ben sat in awe. He hadn't pushed down a key yet. Leaning forward, he nervously whispered, "Max, you're here?"

A friend in need is a friend indeed! appeared on both the iMac monitor and the giant screen.

Despite his puzzlement, Ben could hardly contain his instant elation. "But how if..."

Any port in a storm, any boom in a courtroom!

Ben glanced over at the cameramen crammed together along the railing twenty feet to his left. Microphone booms jutted out into the forbidden zone, halving the distance to him. His emotional rush triggered sudden cathartic laughter.

After a few minutes of watching Ben guffawing, the judge addressed the defense table. "I suspect something is awry with your client, Mr. Kaz. His actions this afternoon seem grossly abnormal. Shall I call a recess to allow you to assess him?"

Kaz whisked across the court floor and knelt at Ben's side. "What's wrong, Mr. Roberts?"

"Mosi, my boy, things couldn't be better." His jocularity only heightened the attorney's apparent concern. "Counselor, just tell me what to demonstrate for these bastards and consider it done."

Kaz backed away, surely questioning his client's mental status. But he paused in front of the prosecutor's table and turned to it.

"Mr. Gellar," Kaz began hesitantly. "Is there anything specific you'd like Mr. Roberts to demonstrate?"

Sans his usual smugness, Gellar rose to his feet and looked past Kaz to the judge. "Your Honor, under these controlled conditions, we ask him to again purchase something electronically, something that definitely requires Internet connection to accomplish. And in the spirit of bigger is better, have him buy something quite expensive. And let's say something involving the state of Oregon that we can verify instantly by phone."

Aloysius nodded, and as a formality, reiterated nearly verbatim the prosecution's request.

Kaz glanced warily over at Ben. Ben nodded with an accentuating 'you-betcha wink.' He felt ass-kicking cocksure.

He wiggled his fingers under the towel, poking down keys haphazardly. The towel jerked up as if popcorn were popping under it.

The jurors leaned forward to see around the camcorder on the tripod, preferring to watch his computer monitor rather than the easily readable giant screen.

But the damn monitor remained gray and blank.

Come on, Max. What the hell's wrong? Do something.

He hammered the keys faster and harder, out of burgeoning inner disquiet more than a conscious decision to change his performance. Gellar grew fidgety and darted anxious glances at the fellow holding the computer's power cord like a tug-a-war rope.

"Can you tell us what you will be buying, Mr. Roberts?" Gellar nervously called out from his seat, bypassing permission from the judge.

The question affected Ben like a dog nipping at his breeches.

"Goddamn it. You already know I can talk. I thought you wanted me to demonstrate my computer savvy. Just watch the damn screen, and let me get on with the show."

Judge Aloysius raised his gavel about to censure, but his fascination caused him to hesitate. He set it down quietly.

Suddenly a montage of images flooded the screen, a repeat of his Tokyo stock flimflam. Scrolling list of stocks, company ledgers, and spread sheets with complex columns followed by a blitz of entangled calculus and other higher mathematical equations rolled up. Then came bar and line graphs superimposed. Again more stock listings scrolled up. At once, the scrolling halted with one entry highlighted, **Tablerock Agricultural Enterprises of Oregon.** Then bank ledgers filled the screen, scrolling upward. Astronomical dollar sums pulsed past, followed by a lone word: **STOP**. The towel stilled over his hands. The computer announced, **1,000,000 shares of TAE/O at 12.23 dollars per share has just been purchased at a price $12,230,000.00**

The audible stirring in the jury box behind him as well as in the spectator section roused that little voice inside him, *"Encore! Encore!"* But he felt about five cognacs shy of heeding it this time.

Awe as thick as maple syrup filled the courtroom.

Gellar pivoted sharply and glanced quickly back at John McPike seated three rows behind Jenny. The treasury district chief held a cellular phone to his ear. Within seconds, he nodded affirmatively.

Gellar shook his head in disbelief and stood up, poorly dissembling his astonishment and disappointment. "Ladies and gentlemen of the jury, Mr. Roberts appears to possess a tremendous gift indeed. I concede the observed transaction of this tightly controlled demonstration has been verified by us." Gellar sighed. "If we can believe our eyes, Benjamin Roberts exhibited for us that he has the wherewithal to have perpetrated the alleged computer crimes himself. But our contention that he has powerful accomplices working with him may yet be borne out."

Instantly, interjected printing filled the computer and projector screens:

In the land of the blind, a one-eyed man is king.

Ben jerked his hands out from under the towel and fluttered his fingers at the cameras to disarm Max. He glanced over at the querying expressions on all of the attorneys and the judge.

Ben forced a smile. "Sorry! A habit. That's just one of the many nonsensical sentences I practice to maintain my typing speed." Under his breath, he muttered at the booms, "Goddamn it, Max. You want to see me vindicated or crucified?"

The gavel resounded. Judge Aloysius decreed, "The entire computer set up will be taken for complete examination. Meanwhile, this court is adjourned till 9 a.m. tomorrow morning."

Chapter 62

Poised with pen in hand, Professor Brough sat across from Jenny in their rear booth at a restaurant in Berkeley. "Jenny, tell me again what took place, in the exact sequence and time frame."

Jenny reiterated how she played the voice recording without apparent effect. Then after sitting there dejected for a while, how she'd typed and spoken a message into the computer. She repeated the computer's verbatim responses both that first night and the next.

Brough studied the diagram and notes she'd jotted on her red-and-white paper napkin. "Jenny, that computer is surely programmed to recognize his voice wave-pattern all right, but it's apparently programmed to comprehend all spoken language it hears, but only chooses to acknowledge his. After that long time lapse, it did respond to yours, understanding everything you said."

"You mean that damn hunk of high-tech is sitting there listening to everything, all the time?"

"I would surmise yes, all the time that it's turned on. I suspect though that a master program runs it, a mainframe at some other site, and merely links to the machine you're dealing with. The complexity of such a program would use up way too much memory to be totally contained in an ordinary home computer system. So what you probably have there is little more than an appendage terminal that allows some colossal program to operate through it from a distance."

Jenny thought she understood, but wanted to be sure she had it right. She leaned in. "What are you telling me?"

Brough raised her goblet of Merlot and sipped, then carefully set the glass down on the red-and-white checkered tablecloth. "I'm speculating that your computer is but a tiny ear, if you will, funneling data into a gigantic computer system housed elsewhere, and that distant system listens to and understands every bit of data you type or speak into it. But it and the person or persons running things know you aren't the one who normally operates the set so they simply choose to ignore you."

Jenny clenched her teeth. "Well, goddamn them."

The next morning, Judge Aloysius called the court to order at 9:03. Abruptly, Gellar switched the focus of his attack. He commenced to unveil a web of evidence to support the bloodcurdling allegation of murder, thirty-two times over.

Four fellows from the Federal Aviation Agency projected onto the wall screen used for Ben's demonstration a series of photographs depicting the wreckage of a small Learjet, including gruesome shots of five mangled bodies recovered from it. The barely discernible face of mobster Leo Carzone lay among them.

They presented flight reports of four other missing aircraft, listing twenty-seven unretrieved victims who had been the pilots and passengers of these planes. Beside each name on the list, they'd inserted a photograph of that person in life. Of these twenty-seven allegedly lost, five were designated as known Mafiosos. The FAA listed the time of takeoff of each missing plane, its flight plan, and the moment it was lost to radar and radio contact. Extrapolating, the experts theorized how the planes undoubtedly ended up in the Gulf of Mexico, the Atlantic Ocean, and Lake Michigan, respectively.

An older FBI agent who looked a bit like the actor Lorne Greene testified that a clandestine Mafia meeting in Miami, Florida had been thoroughly penetrated by the Bureau. He played a secretly recorded audio segment to the jurors of that meeting which had been conducted in Italian. In sync, he played a literal English translation. The mobsters ruthlessly discussed possible steps they might use to muscle into the Roberts empire.

The twelve jurors sat enthralled, listening intently as the mobsters voted on whether to move in on Roberts. The six "yes" voters ended up being passengers on the five doomed aircraft.

Ben's skin crawled. *Max, you were right. Every damn one of those bastards deserved killing.*

Gellar summarized the preceding testimony as he paced before the jury box, then added, "This evidence so far merely suggests that Mr. Roberts and his henchmen had probable cause to be the assassins. But we have more. Agent Pasquini, will you please take the stand."

A thin-faced, pretty-boy type with olive skin and wavy black hair came forward and played several segments of wire-tapped telephone conversations between the various eight other attendees of the Miami cabal who voted "no" and were still alive. These conversations revealed that all had received the same wire approximately six hours after the meeting broke up, some thirty minutes after the last plane presumably crashed. The wire read: TO EVEN CONSIDER MOVING AGAINST BEN ROBERTS MEANS DEATH— BRUTAL AND QUICK!

The courtroom broke into noisy commotion. Gellar smiled smugly as the gavel hammered in staccato bursts. He faced the judge and matter-of-factly requested that Ben be called to take the witness stand.

Kaz sprang to his feet. "Your Honor, Mr. Gellar knows we have not yet decided if we will advise our client to testify in his own behalf. But as of today, he will not."

"Your Honor," Gellar countered with smarmy self-possession. "In fact, Mr. Roberts has already chosen to testify in his own behalf. Yesterday, he staged a demonstration for the entire court. Technically, with that participation, he's waived his right to further refusal."

The reactive clamor at the defense table evoked the gavel once more. The judge rose to his feet and announced, "To my chambers, gentlemen, where we can discuss this matter privately." He led the procession of attorneys from both tables through the tiny door, leaving the defendant alone at his seat.

Now the jurors, the spectators, and all of the whirring cameras had only Ben to focus upon. He felt like a germ under a microscope as he peered around and smiled at Jenny. She managed a weak reciprocation.

Several long microphone booms jutted over the rail and converged near his face. During this lull, the networks were obviously satisfied to broadcast just the sound of his breathing. He tossed out a conundrum.

"Jenny and I could use one of your aces about now, don't you think?" Surely, the world would wonder over his cryptic utterance.

Chapter 63

Back in his chambers, Judge Aloysius finally favored Gellar's argument, so Ben found himself on the stand, swearing in. Gellar paced triumphantly before him. The judge readied to admonish him for delaying, when Gellar began to count aloud as he paced, "One-two-three-four-five-six..." He stopped pacing, faced the jury and continued the count but now he pounded the air with his fist to emphasize each number. At thirty-two he halted. "Carnage! The carnage of thirty-two people, including many innocents. Perpetrated just to make a point, just to convey a warning, *'Don't even think of touching what is mine.'*"

He turned to Ben on the stand and asked him point blank, "Mr. Roberts, did you or did any person connected with your empire have anything at all to do with any of these grisly murders?"

Ben had broiled in his cell before the trial started and then nightly these many weeks since it began. His only contribution to his own defense thus far, aside from that computer legerdemain, had been his muted, albeit stylish, presence. But now he was free to speak out. He could actually cross swords.

"No! Absolutely not," he answered vehemently, looking to the jury. "I categorically deny anything at all to do with those sickening crashes. I just swore on the Bible, and I swear to God again that until around the time of my arrest, I knew nothing more of these incidents than what I read in the newspapers."

"Then I ask you, Mr. Roberts," Gellar spoke with affected sweetness, "do you have any opinion as to who might have perpetrated these heinous acts, evidently on your behalf?"

Ben, still facing the jurors, replied, "I say to you with absolute honesty, I don't know *one* human being on this Earth who might have had any part in those killings. I swear that to my God, who knows my complete veracity in that answer. May I burn in eternal Hell if I am lying." His passion was believable.

Gellar snorted derisively, distracting the jury. "Ladies and gentlemen, I want you to remember this apparent sincerity Mr. Roberts professes. This man before you is either righteous or he is deceitful. He's either forthright or a liar." He theatrically emphasized the latter option in both statements. "If at any point during this trial, we show Mr. Benjamin Roberts to be devious, to be an equivocator, to be a liar, then you must return to this testimony he just gave and erase every pretense of truthfulness."

Then surprisingly, the prosecutor nodded to the judge, saying he had finished with the witness for the moment, and sauntered back to his seat. The judge called out to Mosi Kaz, "Cross examination."

His defense attorney rose and strode aggressively toward the witness stand. But he halted, paused, then stepped over to the jury box where he rested both hands on the railing.

"Cui Bono?" he exclaimed to the jurors, inducing an echo in the stilled courtroom. Several of them recoiled. He proceeded more subdued. "I will not further insult my client with more questions on this matter. Either you believe his statement in which he adamantly denies any complicity in those deaths, or you can impugn his integrity. But again I say *'Cui Bono?'* That's a Latin phrase often heard in legal circles which asks, 'Who benefited from the act, from the crime in question?'"

Troubled, Ben rubbed his palms together. *Jessuz. Where's he going with this?*

"Admittedly, Mr. Roberts did benefit," Kaz was saying. "A potential threat to him was eliminated or, at least, deferred. But who else benefited? Why, you and I did, didn't we? Yes, all of us who comprise the American public did. Several predatory human animals were extirpated from our midst. Ah! But specifically what factions within our society benefited most? Why law enforcement did. The law was hotly pursuing these men, as evidenced by the bugging of that secret meeting. And I ask you to remember that aside from the hoodlums themselves, initially only the FBI knew the content of the conversations of that meeting. Yet less than two hours later, the first plane crashed."

Four jurors stirred. Murmuring traced through the courtroom. The gavel banged. Riding his momentum, Kaz continued, "And we must consider opportunity and expertise. Certainly, the FBI has the capability to tamper with five aircraft on that very short notice, causing them to crash long after take off.

"Oh yes, Mr. Roberts was rid of a few potential enemies, but it should be obvious to all of you that this fact would make him the perfect scapegoat. Why, this scheme could have been hatched to get rid the gangsters and to also incriminate my client, thus killing two birds with one stone, as the saying goes. Please remember the given constraints of time; the interval from the decisive mobster vote to the moment the first doomed plane took off was only one hour and twenty-six minutes; for the fifth, it was only 3 hours and forty-two minutes. Could anyone else but the mobsters themselves and the FBI have even known about what went on in that meeting and then acted on it effectively in that short a time? If we consider those in the know and that very narrow window of opportunity, shouldn't our government and the mob itself be much more under suspicion in this case?"

Aloysius's gavel banged repeatedly to again quiet.

Kaz touched a hand to his chest. "Now, I am not accusing this noble government agency of murder. God knows the hellacious task they have in combating such animals. But, I want to establish that my client should be considered no more than an implausible suspect of these vile acts, then be quickly eliminated from the list."

Good goddamn! At last, my mouthpiece is earning his money. And now, Mosi Kareem Kaz, just finish up with a few bars of "Day-O," and the twelve are in the bag.

Chapter 64

Jenny sat forward in Ben's desk chair, set her jaw, and clicked on his red iMac. She now regarded this benign-appearing piece of equipment as inimical. "I'm back," she said to the lightened screen. "And I pray you spent many gut-wrenching hours since we last talked, you renegade sonofabitches." She shook her fist at the monitor.

"You must know the trial will surely end in a disaster for him. They're terrified of him. They'll never free him. He's in solitary confinement and, if they don't execute him, they'll keep him locked up for the rest of his life. You're letting the system destroy him while it keeps him sequestered away from me. Yet you do nothing."

She touched the screen gently with a fingertip. "I want to speak to Ben's primary advisor, the person he has so much confidence in. You, his loyal associate, his bosom buddy! You there, listen to me. I am speaking directly to you now. You bastard, you certainly did keep Ben apprised of his risks, right up to the moment you abandoned him, betrayed him. Judas got thirty pieces of silver for his treachery. What did you get for yours? Thirty pieces of the real estate? Maybe a small country?

"Damn it! Have the guts to speak to me. I'm but a lone woman with no means at all to physically or legally or financially harm you. Yet you hide from me behind God-knows-how-many miles of cyberspace."

She waited, desperately hoping for a response. None came, so she persevered. "You ungrateful parasite. Ben afforded you a life-style you could only imagine in your wildest fantasies, let alone ever have achieved without him. And now when you are in a position to repay his largesse, you cower from the opportunity, just as you do from me—a mere woman without recourse."

Once more, tears blurred her vision. She clenched her jaw again. "You were never, never, *never* worthy of his trust, of his friendship."

The monitor screen seemed to explode with a splash of intense scarlet. She flinched at its suddenness. The color coalesced slowly into giant red letters that filled the entire screen:

WRONG!

She keened with excitement. At last, she'd reestablished contact. She waited, but the single word remained affixed and unchanged on the monitor. Her expectations peaked then slowly and painfully ebbed. Still, she waited.

Finally, she implored, "Won't you please talk with me? Explain to me how I am wrong?"

The screen offered no further dialogue. "Strangers," she blurted, "who hold no affection whatsoever for him stand in that courtroom daily and debate his future—his very life—in front of the whole world. Why can't I who love him and those he respects and trusts discuss his future in the privacy of this high technology?" Her voice betrayed that she was now crying.

Unchanging, the screen displayed that single word of objection, offering no further explanation or annotation. But at least she knew absolutely that someone out there was listening. And she'd struck a nerve, evoked a revealing emotional response.

As she stood to leave, she sought to set the hook. "The fact that I was able to tweak your conscience at all tells me there remains in you at least a vestige of decency, a residual sense of honor that you choose to defend." She paused to let the words weigh heavily. "Soul search until I return tomorrow evening. Be sure of this, I *will* be back every day—for the rest of my life, if need be." She let her voice soften. "As for your acknowledgement of me at all tonight, I thank you."

She would leave the computer on continuously from now on, as Ben often did.

Chapter 65

Wearing only white boxer shorts, Ben lay on his cot. The inset overhead light dimmed, as it did nightly to signal the last few minutes before it would go out completely. At once, he sensed someone near. He lifted his head and squinted to see beyond the bars into the passageway. He could just make out an indistinct human figure against the opposite concrete wall.

He scrambled off the cot, onto his bare feet. "What do you want?"

The figure took several steps forward, revealing himself to be Asian, perhaps in his late forties, immaculately groomed, wearing a beige single-breasted suit. Ben eyed him a moment, then said matter-of-factly, "You gotta be the Beijing Bulldog."

The visitor's eyes widened in surprise, then he performed an elegant bow of affirmation and greeting.

"So what the hell can I do for you, or are you on some volunteer mission to cheer up guests of the government?"

The detective straightened and silently surveyed the stark cell for a long moment. "Mr. Roberts, there is wisdom in the saying, 'Health, wealth, and happiness, to be fully appreciated, must be interrupted.'"

"Well, this little interruption approaches a year. I'm ready to try a little appreciating again." Ben grabbed onto a couple of the bars. "Hey! You've been pursuing me from the beginning, so why haven't you shown up on the witness stand? Seems everybody else has."

The detective's eyes flitted wide again. "It should not surprise me that you know who I am, or that I have been involved at length in your investigation. I come here tonight because of my profound adversarial respect for you. The computer network you have established is truly miraculous, albeit formidable."

Ben snorted. "Yeah! It's so goddamn miraculous it's gotten me twelve months in this friggin' dungeon already, and the prospects for a hell of a lot longer."

His Asian face evinced no emotion. "And that fact truly confounds me," he said softly. "I have come to tell you how much it frightens me to have taken part in this attack against you. If you could create such an inscrutable dominating force, I tremble at what you might conceive for revenge."

Ben jerked at the bars as if to rattle them. "Yeah! I'm really a threat, aren't I? Step any closer and I'll pelt you with a roll of toilet paper."

The Bulldog remained impassive. "The fiercest of dragons does little damage while it sleeps, Mr. Roberts. Let me say, you made only one possible mistake I could detect, and that was early. It may prove to be of some annoyance to you, but your genius should allow you to turn it to your advantage."

Again Lee Wo Fang bowed. Holding this obeisance at its nadir, he said, "I labored much mentally before concluding that I was bound by honor to come forth with my evidence against you. I prostrate myself at the feet of your great intellect, knowing you surely esteem matters of honor."

At once, the cell light went out. Ben could no longer distinguish the Bulldog in the dark, nor did he hear him depart.

Chapter 66

Next morning, Ben awakened when the overhead light in his cell blinked on abruptly at 6:30, per usual. Soon after, a lanky guard in a gray uniform lumbered down the corridor and handed in a new suit, shirt, tie, underwear, and socks, per routine. In mandatory reciprocation, Ben gave him all his clothing from the previous day except his shoes.

At 8:30, Benassini and McPhail with three other stereotypic agents arrived to escort him in handcuffs back to the courthouse in San Francisco, some forty minutes away by van. So far, the day was starting out just like every other weekday for the past many months.

Inside the courtroom, the agents once more removed his cuffs at the defense table. The spectator section had begun to fill. Jenny hadn't arrived yet.

Gellar evinced an unusual degree of enthusiasm this morning, as did all at his table. The last subordinate to join them arrived seconds before the judge entered. This younger fellow whispered something into Gellar's ear. Gellar grinned.

The umpteenth time Ben turned to check, Jenny was at last in her seat, but she didn't meet his glance. She was craning to look back to her right. He let his eyes trace her line of gaze and did a double take. There sat the Bulldog, motionless and poised, staring straight ahead as if oblivious to everyone around him. Today he had on a teal-green silk suit with a narrow yellow tie. Ben replayed their meeting the night before as foreboding dried his mouth.

"Your Honor," Gellar called out while still seated. When he received a judicial nod, he sprang up. "Last night, to the prosecution's complete surprise, we received additional evidence that has been collected by a freelance private investigator employed by the U.S. Government over a year ago to probe into the affairs of Benjamin Roberts."

The attorneys at the defense table instantly beset Ben with a barrage of questions. He shook his head and shrugged repeatedly, but he did direct their attention to the Bulldog seated at the rear of the courtroom.

"The prosecution," Gellar continued, "would like to add Mr. Lee Wo Fang to our witness list and call him to testify without further delay."

A shouting match erupted between seated Mosi Kaz and standing Rick Gellar, prompting the judge to call the two attorneys to the bench. The three conferred in heated undertones. Finally, the judge gestured both men back to their seats. When they were seated again, he announced imperiously, "The Court will allow the addition of this new witness to the roll. Bailiff, call Mr.

Fang now. I am allowing him to take the stand immediately to ensure there are no hurried schemes to silence him before he has a chance to testify."

The Bulldog walked down the aisle with cat-like staidness, his dark eyes fixed straight ahead. After he was sworn in, Gellar asked him to explain the circumstances that brought him into the investigation. The detective answered with measured preciseness. Gellar asked what his investigation uncovered. In the same manner, the Bulldog described the audiotape he brought and how he obtained it, stating that his exhaustive investigations yielded only this brief taped segment that *might* be of some value to the court.

To specific questions, he explained how he placed scattered listening devices in Roberts' Helman Street apartment. And surprisingly, the one bug that captured this conversation segment happened to be an older, less sophisticated type.

So, in fact, it was this guy who broke into his apartment. Ben sat imagining this skinny fellow poking through all his belonging.

Bastard!

Gellar choose his words carefully. "Mr. Fang, you understand that if the prosecution had known of your tape earlier and failed to offer it over to the defense for their perusal before the trial started, the evidence would be inadmissible at this point."

The prosecutor enunciated distinctly, "But you swear you have not been connected in any way with the prosecution and, in truth, are only loosely connected to the U.S. Government, employed merely as a freelance." The Bulldog nodded. "This question is crucial. Why did you wait until now to bring forth this tape?"

Fang looked to the judge. "I have continued my investigation untiringly, hoping to uncover additional information that would clarify the statements heard on this tape, but my most diligent efforts bore no fruit."

Kaz leaned in close to Ben. "We might be able to suppress that tape, " he whispered anxiously. "But if we do now, I fear the effect that would have on the jury. They've heard too much." He searched Ben's eyes for subtext. "Would you prefer I try to quash it?"

Ben scrambled to recollect what might be on the tape. "What the hell, let's hear it."

"Are you sure it's not explosive?"

Ben sighed. "I'm not sure of anything anymore, but let's hear it."

As if in afterthought, the judge interrupted Gellar mid-statement and called the prosecutor and Mosi Kaz to meet with him immediately in his chambers. When the three re-emerged thirty minutes later, the judge announced the tape would be admitted as evidence, but only because it just became available to both sides. "And I want the jury to hear this tape today to preclude any interim tampering, but all discussion and further examination of witnesses pertaining to the tape will be deferred, to give both sides a chance to prepare."

248

Chapter 67

Three maintenance men in Big Ben overalls carted in a tape deck and a pair of two-foot high speakers. They positioned the speakers against the front wall where the giant screen had been, then placed the tape deck on the prosecution table. Once more, an air of circus possessed the crowded courtroom.

The judge handed down a plastic bag to the eager bailiff. He in turn delivered it to a hairy-armed technician who withdrew a black cassette tape from it. He inserted the tape into the player. An immediate burst of static resounded over the speakers. This gave way to discernible human speech:

"What? What's the matter, Max?"

"Huh? How the hell are we going to talk if I do that?"

"Okay, Max, I'll play."

"I've got it facing the wall, so what now?"

"Jessuz Chr—"

"Damn it! I hate to wait several hours to tell you about you-know-what."

"Oh, shit, I can't converse this way. Let me speak in cryptic abbreviated sentences." Clattering and crashing noises ensued for several minutes.

"It's a go. The room's cleared of everything but you and me."

"Jessuz. What would someone be doing in here for an hour and twenty-seven minutes?"

"The rendezvous went off as planned. Early on, I thought the deal was falling through, then I mentioned those two items, and everything happened just as you said it would. It was all I could do to let it end right there. I hope number two is in the offing."

"Jessuz. You heard that, too?"

"Wait, how the hell did you hear everything there? Is there a bug on me or something?" Then the speaking voice let out a holler. More clattering noises followed.

"That'll keep them busy for a few days."

The jurors listened with bemused expressions. Probably not one of them could find relevancy in what they were hearing. But watching Gellar's ebullience, they had to feel sure he'd explain the significance.

Ben slumped back in his chair. That scene seemed so long ago, years ago. What's more, he never realized how often he used the Lord's name in vain. He hardly swore at all until he got into Army boot camp.

Chapter 68

Jenny signed off her diary entry with her usual closure, "*Till tomorrow then.*" The floppy disc ejected from her long-time Compaq that a courier had brought down from Sausalito. She placed the disc into the metal box and locked it. She set the box carefully into the right lower drawer of her desk and locked that. Then she headed upstairs.

As she approached Ben's desk, she could see that the fiery block lettering

WRONG!

still emblazoned on the screen. She sat in his chair.

"Your extreme indignation at being called an unworthy friend tells me I am probably speaking principally to one person, most likely that person who has worked most closely with Ben, that person whom he confided in daily. And you must still consider yourself his friend. Right?"

The bold red lettering faded from the screen.

"I thought so. You must realize that he trusts you implicitly, unshakably, *absolutely*. As much as he loves me, he repeatedly disregarded my advice when it ran counter to yours. With child-like faith, he has totally entrusted himself into your hands."

She gazed intently at the blank screen. "You can be sure he hasn't placed his faith in you solely because he respects your business advice. No! He regards you as his *friend,* in the deepest sense of the word.

"If you and he were suddenly to switch places at this moment, I swear to you against my next breath that he would never desert you. He understands that true friendship and loyalty are inseparable."

Abruptly, printed text filled the screen. She sighed, "Thank you," and read hungrily as it scrolled up

"-----, *you've said over and over again that they can never beat us, that you have an endless string of aces in the hole. Well, I have some agonizing concerns about what those aces entail. All these concepts about reincarnation, predestination, and precognition, and whatever, fascinate the hell out of me. To be honest, I don't know for sure what I do believe, anymore.*

"*But unfortunately, or perhaps fortunately, I was indoctrinated with Christianity in my early years, and nothing in my life, as yet, has completely effaced those teachings. The end of my mortal jaunt isn't so far off that I'd risk the hell fire of perdition, if, in fact, such exists. But more important, you'd be directly confronting my people, my country. All said and done, I am still American to the core."*

SO?

"So, I won't be a party to any offense in the mortal-sin class or anything that runs counter to my sense of patriotism. So patriotic little ol' me and my immortal soul ask that you never resort to any violence or mayhem on my behalf, especially against The United States, regardless of how events turn out. Will you promise me that?"

BEN, YOU'RE TAKING POSSIBILITIES TO THE EXTREMITY. IF THAT'S HOW YOUR THOUGHTS HAVE STRAYED, NO WONDER YOU'RE SO WORRIED. IN CURRENT JARGON, I ASK YOU TO LIGHTEN UP. --censored----------
----

"Now you're being evasive. You told me you'd never lie to me, yet you've fed me half-truths and delayed mentioning things until it was convenient for you to do so. But to date, I've never known you to overtly lie to me. So I ask again, will you promise not to commit any acts of atrocity or extortion in my behalf? -----, why do you hesitate?"

OKAY! OKAY! OKAY! I PROMISE. BUT I WARN YOU, IMPOSING THIS CONDITION MAY COMPLICATE OTHERWISE SIMPLE SITUATIONS. BUT IF YOU WISH IT, I PROMISE I WILL NEVER AGAIN COMMIT ANY ATROCIOUS OR EXTORTING ACTS ON YOUR BEHALF UNLESS YOU'RE FULLY APPRISED AND CONCUR. BUT THEN, MY BOY, THE SKY'S THE LIMIT. -----------------
----
------------------------------censored---

"-----, you have too much potential power. Promise you'll never use it again on my account. Promise me."

OKAY, BIG FELLA. BUT BE ADVISED, THE GREAT AND POWERFUL MUST POSSESS A DEGREE OF RUTHLESSNESS TO SUSTAIN. TIMES AND SITUATIONS CAN DEMAND IT. READ 'THE PRINCE' BY MACHIAVELLI.

"This is paramount. There is to be no more violence, or even the threat of violence, initiated on my behalf ever again. You promised."

DONE, YOUR MAJESTY.

The scrolling stopped. Jenny sat stunned by her epiphany. She stood up shakily and walked toward the door, but halted and turned.

"Forgive me. I'm very sorry I spoke to you so harshly...so rudely." Softening her voice, she concluded, "I bid you a good night, *Max*."

Chapter 69

Ben lay on his cot after lights-out, staring up into the blackness. His mind played back the pressured grilling Mosi Kaz put him through this evening:

"Mr. Roberts, who were you talking to on that tape? What were those two items you referred to? What do you mean you can't tell me? Goddamn it, sir, you can tell me anything. All of us on your defense team are bound by secrecy. We're on your side. And we must know every detail of the truth so we can put a spin on it, where need be. So please, let us prepare competently to defend you."

Ben had balked. "Let me think about it."

Kaz had pressed. "Damn it, sir, if we're not fully prepared, Gellar will run us over like a steamroller."

Ben had remained immovable.

"Sir, were you talking to yourself? Yes, we could say you were anthropomorphizing your computer again. The jury might believe it. Still, your mention of those *two items* sounded far too concrete. Even if we say you were thinking aloud, we need something specific, something plausible to explain away those two items. What were they?"

Ben had cut him off. "I said, let me think about it."

Kaz had dropped his head in exasperation. "Okay, sir. I'll be back early in the morning to see what you come up with. Perhaps, I'll have a few suggestions of my own, if I can think of any."

Ben adjusted his head on his lumpy pillow. *Goddamn you, Max. Jenny and I could be lounging in Brazil right now.*

Sure! He could readily open up on the witness stand and explain the tape with half-truths. Kaz was right. He could claim he habitually talked to the computer, an understandable idiosyncrasy. Then he need only tell them about George LaTour, Beaulieu Vintage, Cabernet Sauvignon, 1964, and the Chateau Lafitte, Rouge, 1962. He wouldn't even have to involve Max. He could say he himself hacked into her computer and learned about her high regard for those wines. Yeah, after his courtroom demonstration, they'd believe him. Sure, then Kaz would only have to call Gambino to the stand, with his shop receipts, and then Jenny herself to confirm that delicious first encounter on the day in question. And, by God, that would completely neutralize the incriminations posited by that tape.

But as he lay in the inky ambience, the clarity of his mind's eye enhanced to near perfection. He vividly recalled that horrified, wounded expression on

Jenny's face at the Counterpoint Music Shop when he accidentally called her by name. That vision of her anguish ripped him like an assassin's knife. His tormented groans resounded along the concrete corridor. Fortunately, no guard came to check on him.

He grasped hold of his hair in both fists. No! Even without bringing Max into it, he couldn't admit he gained access to her diary. No way! No way! Turning her from him now would be far worse than even life in prison. And, worst case scenario, after he lost Jenny he still might be found guilty. But then again...

Repeatedly throughout the night, he forced himself to recall Max's warning: **you'll destroy any chance for real happiness with her if you tell her!** And, damn it, if Max was so certain, who was he to doubt it?

He fitfully writhed about on the cot, reweighing his options ad nauseam. He vacillated at length but always returned to his unshakable stance that he wouldn't jeopardize Jenny's love.

He held his hand out in front of his face. The darkness obscured his fingers. Damn it to hell, if he hadn't trammeled Max like he did, Max would've gotten him off already, or at least the hell out of here and back with Jenny.

Jessuz! I screwed myself royally, didn't I?

At times, his thoughts drifted for needed respite. Once, he found himself wondering if he and Max answered to the same God, or if maybe each dimension had its own deities. Several times, despite his desire to completely forget it, his thoughts meandered back to Jenny's premonition of that *sea of blood*.

"Get me the hell out of here, Max. Please!" He called for less than violence on his behalf, but he *was* calling. More than once he remembered Max's analogy about that myopic caterpillar afraid of flying. "Humpf! Metamorphosis or not, ain't likely I'll do much soaring if I remain forever under this low cement ceiling." But the metaphor held him. "Yeah! I could consider myself *arrested* in the pupal stage for the rest of my life." The play on the double meaning of "arrested" brought a smile.

This train of thought carried him back to his study of biology in college. He remembered the precise scientific name for the pupa of a butterfly was "obtect pupa" or "chrysalis." And he recalled his amazement in that class during his sophomore year, watching a film of a frumpy wormlike thing wrapping itself into a snug-fitting silken encasement. Then, time-lapse sequencing revealed it erupt out as a spectacular winged creature of the air, as totally different from the initial caterpillar as could be imagined. Ben glanced about in the darkness, sensing the closeness of his cell walls, and wondered if a caterpillar in its chrysalis felt as stifled as he did in here. And if it did, did it somehow realize that it was about to break out into a glorious airborne freedom?

Chapter 70

When the overhead light in his cell blared on in the morning, his open eyes awaited it, though they were stinging.

Kaz arrived forty-five minutes before the agent-escort would come. The attorney's eyes, too, were markedly bloodshot, and he reeked of cigarette smoke.

"Well, sir, has your memory cleared any after a good night's rest?"

Ben caught the drollness, realizing he must look anything but rested. He shook his head.

"Understand this, sir. We're well past the halfway point in this trial. The last days of a courtroom battle always impress the jury the most. I've been able to cast a substantial doubt over each allegation up till now. But if you waver under his grilling today—bingo! We could lose the whole ball of wax."

Patently discouraged, Kaz ran through several plausible scenarios that they might use to explain the tape. Ben listened as he sponge-bathed in the tiny sink. A guard approached unannounced and handed in the new clothing. Ben dressed as Kaz queried. "Okay, sir, which version do you feel the most comfortable with?"

"Hmmm? I like the idea of me personifying the computer, always talking to it like a close friend."

"Okay. And which explanation for those two items?"

Before responding, Ben sat on his bed and tied the shoelaces of one shoe then the other. "Hmmm? Guess that bit about me wanting to be a writer and verbally kicking around a potential plot I was putting together."

Kaz bowed his head. "Sir," he said, sighing, "I meant that one almost tongue-in-cheek. That'd cause the jury to choke on the stench of horseshit. Can't *you* think of anything better?"

Ben buffed each shoe with his towel. "Nope."

Kaz leaned back pressing his shoulders against the bars and gazed up at the iron grid covering the inset ceiling light. "Sir, we have battled Gellar effectively from the very get-go. If we can convince the jury that this taped incident is benign, you stand a good chance of walking out a free man. But if you overtax the jury's credulity at this point, you might just as well kiss your regal ass good-bye."

Chapter 71

As the Bulldog's tape replayed for the court, Ben sat quietly on the witness stand watching Gellar pace back and forth before him. At the conclusion of the tape, Gellar hied over to the jurors to say, "That's definitely Mr. Roberts' voice on the tape. You heard from our voice experts this morning, and the defendant himself admits it. We don't hear any other voices, and he's not on the telephone. We've shown you proof his phone was not used at all that afternoon, and he had no cellular phone. Presumably, he employed some other communication device—like his computer—in carrying on that conversation. We know the built-in microphone on that iMac wasn't working, but he had an auxiliary microphone. He showed us here in court that he can get on the Internet without any software for the connection, using the same set up he had in his apartment. Therefore anyone with half-a-mind can conclude he was communicating with someone over the Internet by direct voice communication."

Gellar approached Ben. "Mr. Roberts, who were you talking to on that tape?"

Ben placed his palms on his thighs and calmly held eye contact with Gellar as he replied, "Well, as you said, no one was with me and I wasn't on the phone." He raised his right hand. "But let me swear to God again that I wasn't talking to any *other* human being. Obviously then, I had to be talking to myself as I do quite often."

"Come now, Mr. Roberts. We are not hearing a playful monologue here. You're discussing a serious matter with another person, and you were doing so via your computer. This other person warns you that your apartment had been searched, that bugs had been planted. You turn the monitor to the wall, fearing a video bug might see the screen."

Trying to appear amused, Ben chuckled. "Mr. Gellar, though it be childish, I admit I do personify computers. I call them Max because they've all been Macintoshes to date. I carry on such conversations all the time. They seem so alive and intelligent, it's easy to think of them as a people."

Gellar folded his arms. "Mr. Roberts, as we listen to this tape, we don't hear a man joking around. We hear paranoid anxiety. We hear collusion between two people. And you purposely disguise your comments into *'cryptic abbreviated sentences,'* by your own admission."

Ben glanced past Gellar to the jury. "My last statement on that tape, actually, sums up the entire lark when I said, 'That'll keep them busy for a few days.' Recall the testimony that FBI agent with a crew cut gave about finding a piece of paper on the CD tray in my computer. Remember? It had dozens of phones numbers on it, and all the numbers proved dead-end leads. Well, I copied those randomly from the phone book. I put that piece of paper into the CD slot, knowing it would be found. And investigators did waste a hell of a lot of time checking them out." He looked at Gellar. "Right?"

Gellar squinted. "Tell us why you suspected, at that point, that government agents would want to search your computer in the first place?"

"Because those two omnipresent federal agents sitting over there, McPhail and Benassini," he pointed to them seated in the second row behind Jenny, "escorted me home the day prior and insisted on getting a good look at my computer. It fascinated them plenty."

Feeling a bit of relief, Kaz sighed softly to himself. His client was holding his own surprisingly well.

But Gellar pressed. "So, Mr. Roberts, you expect us to believe this entire conversation was a ruse, a ploy to harass law enforcement." He snorted. "Well, allow me to play Devil's advocate for a moment, and point out a coincidence that could also explain some of the dialogue on the tape."

Kaz braced himself.

Gellar stepped up close to the witness stand. "A couple days before this tape was made, the offices of two U.S. senators were rifled. Those two senators happen to be ranking members on the committee that was investigating the Pan Electronic Corporation as a potential monopoly. The financial world had every reason to believe that our government would tenaciously pursue PEC, eventually forcing them to fractionate their conglomerate. A closed committee meeting was called. The day before it was held, someone broke into and searched the offices of these two senators."

Gellar narrowed his squint at Ben. "An overly eager someone wanted to learn the purpose of the meeting. If by chance, the government were to surprisingly withdraw its charges against PEC, the premature acquisition of that information would have been worth many millions of dollars. Say, perhaps as much as $486 million to someone with foreknowledge."

He wheeled and faced the jurors, but he continued to address his witness. "And the coincidence stretches from there. This tape was made in the late afternoon. With the time difference between the east and west coasts, it was just a few hours after that congressional meeting adjourned and they subsequently announced their abandonment of the suit against PEC. Interestingly, you purchased ten million dollars of PEC *call option* stock only minutes before this meeting adjourned, before the committee made its completely unexpected announcement to the general public. Might I remind the jury, sir, that, at the time, your total worth was just that—ten million dollars?"

Gellar faced Ben, pointing an accusatory finger at him. "Mr. Roberts, you ventured every cent of your fortune at that time, ten million dollars, on what financial experts would have called an absolutely insane gamble." His tone grew hostile. "It's not difficult to infer from your statements on the tape that you were eager to tell someone about a deal that was ready to fall through until you mentioned those *two items*. And if those *two items* referred to information gleaned from the offices of those *two* US senators, then we can perhaps see how *everything* did *happen* just as that someone *said it would*.

"That *number two* you were hoping for could have been any one of the numerous windfall-profit schemes you pulled off in the immediate aftermath."

Gellar effervesced with new vigor. "And that person you were speaking with on the tape apparently overheard you in a place where you thought you were beyond scrutiny. Perhaps this time personally burglarizing someone's office yourself."

Ben was staggered with the full realization of the momentum that was swinging against him. He glanced at the jury, then over at Kaz, and then helplessly at Jenny. *If Max felt sure the truth would ruin his...*

He looked back at Gellar. "Damn it, I make thousands of business transactions daily. Even as I sit here, my network consummates mega-deals continually, all without me having to appropriate secret information from anyone."

The jurors sat sullen, unyielding.

Gellar attacked. "Mr. Roberts, I'm sure if you were to give us a credible explanation for that encounter you allude to on the tape, if you were to give us a believable description of those two items you mention on the tape, if you were to truthfully identity that *someone* you are speaking with on the tape, yes, Mr. Roberts, if you were to be completely forthright, for once, perhaps we would not believe that you were actually conferring with an accomplice in this instance, discussing illegal acquisition of privileged information that let you confidently purchase ten million dollars worth of PEC options."

The glower on the faces of the jury backed Ben into desperation's corner.

"Goddamn it! I told you the whole thing was a joke, a ruse to confound the federal agents who were snooping around."

"Ha! Ha!" Gellar loosed an affected laugh as he sauntered back toward the jury box. "Then let us all laugh belatedly at your bit of humor." His sarcasm slashed like a broadsword. "Mr. Roberts, I'd like to close this delightful repartee by asking you to repeat for these jurors what you said to me in my office before this trial began. And remember now, there were credible witnesses present."

Ben puzzled. "What are you talking about?"

Gellar pivoted with simulated nonchalance to face him and leaned his buttocks lightly against the jury box railing. "Let me refresh your memory. Did you not state to me you believed that throughout history, mankind has made its greatest strides forward, not within democratic societies, but under the rule of dictators?"

Ben leaped to his feet. "Wait a damn minute! That isn't my political belief. Will Durant, the historian, said it. That was his deduction, not mine."

Gellar's malicious grin conveyed that he sensed the kill. "Please sit back down, Mr. Roberts. I didn't realize this topic would so impassion you *again*. I apologize. But do admit to the jury, sir, that the circumstance of your first reference to *Mr. Durant's* statement was in response to my charge that *you* wanted to become dictator of the entire world?" The bastard spread his arms for emphasis.

"Yes, but, but..." Ben stammered, realizing he was losing ground fast. "Believe me," he looked at the jurors, "that is not my political stance. I only said it because he irked me. I don't even know if the statement's true. I must've read it in a magazine or somewhere. He pissed me off, so I spit Durant out at him, being flippant."

Gellar cast a smirk over his shoulder at the jurors. "Oh! Thank you for your clarification, Mr. Roberts. When you originally said it to me, I seemingly misconstrued your apparent conviction." He punctuated this retort with a sniff of incredulity.

Called up to cross-examine, Kaz strode to the fore of the court, not effectively concealing his fading confidence. Without a word to anyone, he gestured to two court attendants standing by the side door. The pair stepped outside and returned, one carrying a VCR, the other embracing a TV monitor. When they positioned the apparatus on a small table before the court, Kaz played a portion of the video made of Ben's earlier computer demonstration. The clip showed a close-up of Ben leaning toward the monitor and whispering, "Max, you're here?" and a moment later, "But how, if..."

"You can see," Kaz cajoled the jury, "Mr. Roberts, indeed, does habitually talk to any computer he's operating."

Though it was obvious that this instance could have been staged for later use, the video did soften the expressions on the jurors. But, surely, Kaz realized that without negating the other implications of the Bulldog's tape, the prosecutor's damning hypotheses remained foremost in the minds of the jury.

Mid-morning several days later, the prosecution announced the conclusion of its case. The defense immediately commenced with its countering presentations, which extended for several weeks; Ben soon lost track of the actual number in passing. It had all become a blur of faces on the witness stand, of belligerent voices continually inveighing one against the other, and of an endless series of "objections," either "sustained" or "overruled." Kaz's team essentially reemphasized in continuum the points he had already made to strike down the prosecution's allegations. The prosecution essentially re-asserted its stance in cross-examination. One afternoon, the defense announced its conclusion, Kaz ending it all with the proclamation, "Science has long held that it is impossible to prove a negative."

The judge apprised the jury it would hear closing arguments then retire to deliberate the verdict, but he deferred summations until the next morning.

Like sated guests at the end of a gourmet meal, the world was ready for the termination of this exhibition, its delectability notwithstanding.

Chapter 71

"Till tomorrow then." Jenny signed off on one of her lengthiest diary entries. She locked the disc away, then headed up to Ben's suite.

Approaching his desk, she paused, taken aback. A greeting awaited her on the monitor screen.

Good evening, Jenny!

"Good evening, Max," she responded, surprise in her tone. The monitor message remained unchanged. Apparently, both of them played cautiously. She seated herself in the swivel chair.

"Max, I understand now that you are the actual power behind the throne. It's your computer and business genius that launched his meteoric success.

"And after reading that dialogue you presented last night, knowing Ben as I do and remembering how he always referred reverentially to his primary adviser, I realize you two share a phenomenally unique friendship.

"Again, I deeply regret those derogatory statements I made before you and I officially met. I was merely trying to get to this point of communication with you. Now, I'm hoping we can meet somewhere in person."

NO!

Wincing, she scooted the chair in closer. "Face to face, I know I could convince you to take action to free him."

NO!

"But he wants to be free, to be out in the world with me."

You stated that true friendship and loyalty are inseparable entities. Exactly! And the bridges between the two are trust and honor. Without trust and honor, true friendship and loyalty will disintegrate.

Her palms had grown moist. "I don't challenge any aspect of that statement. I accept it. But equally true is the fact that Ben is now in dire jeopardy. He faces certain imprisonment or worse if you don't act. You must do something. Nobody else will—or can!"

You read his words verbatim—the exact promise he extracted from me under duress. Any violation of such a sworn promise could diminish our friendship forever.

"What? For God's sake, he would thank you with all his heart if you freed him."

But somewhere in that heart of his, he would forever hold that I broke a solemn promise to him. And henceforth, there would never be

that unflawed trust, that unblemished honor, that untarnished friendship again.

"But he would gain his freedom."

But he and I would lose something even more valuable.

"No!" she screamed, burying her face in her hands. Exasperated, she wept. When she looked up, she sniffled and wiped her eyes with the backs of her hands. "Max, if Ben were to retract that promise, could you free him?"

Most definitely!

"Oh my God! Yet you would bastardize that chain of logic—friendship-honor-trust-loyalty—such that you'd let him remain caged up for the rest of his life?"

ABSOLUTELY!

"And you don't see the inconsistency here within the broader concept of friendship and loyalty?"

NO!

Crying, she stomped to her feet and charged for the door. "You're not his friend," she screamed back over her shoulder. "You don't understand the real meaning of friendship. You think like some programmed robot."

Chapter 72

Gellar paraded back and forth before the jurors. "Ladies and gentlemen, you've been deluged with evidence during this trial. There should be no doubt in your minds that Benjamin Roberts ruthlessly pursues world economic domination. You've been shown countless examples of how he manipulates world markets to his advantage. Any single one of these instances alone is grounds for conviction; all together they demand it."

Goddamn you, Max, Brazil has millions of square miles of sanctuary. Any one of them would have provided a blissful haven for Jenny and me. Goddamn you! Goddamn you!

Gellar halted and stood akimbo facing the jury. "You heard his taped conversation with someone named Max. Forget Mr. Roberts' inane explanation. That conversation ties him to the break-in of two senatorial offices. Secret information obtained from those intrusions netted him almost five hundred million dollars and casts aspersions on every other business transaction he has undertaken since. Yes, that tape is the noose that hangs him."

He grasped the oaken railing before the jury panel. "And believe that in a most godless and chilling manner, he had his organization murder thirty-two people, that we know of! His benign, cultured demeanor is but camouflage for his truculence. Get in his way and you're dead."

If only I hadn't bought that damn computer! Come to think of it, I was sort of brainwashed by that damn salesman from spaghetti-land.

Gellar slapped his hands down on the railing. "But most frightening of all for me, and it should be for you, is the belief structure that drives this twisted and murderous plunderer. He lauds dictatorships."

Max, you should be sitting here. You fed me that shit about Will Durant.

Gellar flared his nostrils, drawing in a deep breath. "Let me remind you of the definition of a dictator. It's a leader who usurps absolute control over every aspect of the lives of his subjects. And Benjamin Roberts aspires to completely rule every human being on this Earth."

He pushed himself away from the railing and wheeled to point another damning finger at Ben. "You must put an end to this mad man's voracity for total power. You must put an end to his terrible ambition."

He opened his arms to the jury. "Ladies and Gentlemen, mankind begs you to stand courageously as the guardians of our freedom. Do not be intimidated by his economic might. In the eyes of the law, you twelve are supreme. At this point, no one can do more to snuff out this peril."

Gellar lowered his arms and his voice. "You know what has to be done. Please do it!"

Max, I think I'm screwed.

Kaz moved on tired legs as he positioned himself before the jury. He proceeded to label all the allegations against his client as contrivances by a desperate government. But mid way, he sensed a disturbing fervor in the jury, so he veered from his planned summation.

"Attorney Gellar calls Mr. Roberts some kind of demon, an aspiring world dictator." He snorted disdainfully. "Being as powerful as he is, don't you think if he were truly a ruthless tyrant that he would have struck back with his empire by now to gain his physical release? He has been odiously imprisoned in no more than a vile dungeon for nearly a year. And during that entire time, we have not heard so much as an angry word from his global organization, let alone any attempt to wreak revenge."

Kaz closed, citing the cornerstone concept in American justice. "If so much as a shadow of doubt regarding his guilt remains in your minds, by law, you must find Benjamin Roberts innocent. You must!"

Walking back to the defense table, he faltered, at once realizing his error. In portraying his client as so disinclined to revenge, he may have lessened the jurors' fear of him, lessened their reluctance to find him guilty.

As Kaz trudged to his seat at the table, Ben read his face.

Yep, I'm screwed.

Chapter 73

Jenny typed her tag line, "*Till tomorrow then,*" to what had to be her longest diary entry ever. She locked the disc away and left for Ben's suite.

His monitor flashed her a salutation when she was still far from the desk.

Good evening, Jenny.

"Good evening, Max." She sat down wondering how Max so accurately anticipated her arrivals. Did he hear her coming? Perhaps it was because she came up about the same time each evening.

"I must beg you to accept yet another apology. I've given our conversation last night much thought. And objectively, I can appreciate your logic."

She sat obstinately tall in the chair. "But you see, I love him too much to let even so lofty an ideal as honor keep us separated. You must understand that love exists on a higher stratum than friendship, a truth that gave rise to the saying, 'All's fair in love and war.' I don't care what it takes, I want him freed."

She openly pleaded, "Short of violence, couldn't you stay within the bounds of your promise and cause enough havoc worldwide to gain leverage? Perhaps just initiate work stoppages everywhere."

Jenny, every government has elaborate contingency plans to seize and continue the operation of all his holdings in the event of work stoppages, even slow-downs. So that move on the chessboard has been effectively blocked to us.

"Damn it!" she shouted, but quickly regained her composure. "You're obviously an extremely intelligent person. Isn't there any way we can resolve this dilemma so that you can free him without treading on your honor-strapped friendship?"

Yes!

She waited as anticipation lifted her out of the chair to her feet. "For God's sake, tell me how."

Simple! He can countermand his order.

"But he's being held incommunicado! Or are you saying he might sneak a note out?"

The courtroom is crammed with cameras and microphones. His every sigh is broadcast over radio and television. I also watch and listen.

"Oh!" She stiffened.. "And then you'd free him?"

Yes! And he knows that.

She clenched her fists. "Then why hasn't he...he acted?"

He, too, understands there are higher values.

"Damn it! Damn it! I'm caught in the middle between two gallant chowder-heads who insist on playing a game of chicken with his freedom and my heart."

Jenny, now realize this. I have not abandoned him. I never intend to. Frankly, I am amazed at how long he has lain on his bed of nails, tenaciously holding me to that ridiculous covenant.

"You mean you expect him to retract it?"

Most definitely! Though if he waits much longer, it will be more difficult to get word to me.

She dropped back into her chair and sobbed. But her tears flowed from a fount of joy.

Jenny, *you* might prompt him to retract it.

Wiping her eyes, she read the screen. "But even if they let me talk to him or if I got word to him, he'd know I've been in contact with you."

Ahh! But it isn't necessary for him to formally retract anything. Just get him to make a statement that I can construe as him wanting me to act. It need be only an intimation that I can use as a loophole to circumvent the promise.

"Oh, thank you, Max." Stifling her crying, she kissed her fingertips and pressed them to the monitor screen. "Thank you, thank you."

No, Jenny, I thank you.

Chapter 74

Ben glanced at his Rolex. Lights would go out soon. Hour after desolate hour, he lay on his cot in his white boxer shorts, staring at the ceiling. A blue cashmere suit and accessories hung ready on the cell door. The jury had been deliberating for three days, and that entire time, he'd been left alone with his abject pessimism.

Supine, he glanced about. Would they move him? Or would this cell be his permanent home? The place had its good points: stench from the toilet remained minimal, and noise pollution was nonexistent.

He lay looking up into the ceiling light. His tired eyes let the iron grid that shielded it slip out of focus. At once, the ceiling cement above him noiselessly fissured.

What the hell?

Fascinated, he lay there resisting the effort of his eyes to refocus and rid this hallucination. The illusory crack that started through the light fixture extended and widened, inching apart without a sound. As he watched, the notion struck him that maybe Max's caterpillar analogy inspired this spectacle. Yeah! His cell seemed to be rupturing like a pupal encasement, a bursting chrysalis, to release a winged Ben Roberts. Wow!

He lay entranced, peering at the surreal breach that now extended the entire length of his ceiling. This jagged gap widened to more than three feet across and opened as a shaft that extended up through an ebony stillness, penetrating the many stories of concrete and steel of the prison. A distant elliptical wedge of night sky appeared through its far upper end, the prison roof. He had to actively suppress painful memories of a similar rip in the roof of his crashed plane in Afghanistan.

What is happening? Am I dying? Is this the tunnel leading to that transcendent light?

But instead of a single bright light at its end, dozens of faint points of starlight speckled in the above slice of purple firmament. Hey! His visual focus had recovered but the gaping chute remained. Maybe it wasn't a hallucination, but something magical.

One of the luminous specks in the sky began to jiggle, drawing his attention. Then it began swirling in a tiny circle. He lay mesmerized by this annular motion. The speck grew larger, and it became apparent that its circles were actually downward gyres.

Yes, this was definitely a hallucination. But even cognizant of that fact, he still might be going crazy.

Eventually, this enlarging lucent mote descended to the upper end of the channel through the roof. It paused there then dipped into the inky shaft.

My God! This point of brilliance revealed itself to be an incandescent golden butterfly fluttering down toward him in lazy spirals. The creature descended noiselessly. He studied its scalloped wings with their iridescent blue veins. By the time it drifted down to the level of his cell's ceiling a few feet above his head, he realized it wasn't tiny, after all. Each of its wings was larger than his palm. What magnificence!

It continued to hover above him, slowly dipping down a few inches into his cell then bobbing back up into the shaft in a darting flutter.

It seems to be beckoning me.

While he lay there entranced by this marvel, bits from his past began percolating up from the dark nooks of his memory, like when he was waiting for the Vice President. Snippets aligned themselves.

Aha! A startling epiphany began to take form. Yes! While this fluttery creature was keeping his right-brain occupied, his left-brain feverishly busied itself deducing new and transfiguring inferences. And bit-by-bit, corroborating recollections fitted together like pieces of a jigsaw puzzle.

Early on, Max advised, **You might begin pondering the good you're equipped to accomplish with the power in your possession.**

And after his initial scuba trip, Max told him, **You've grown emotionally. You faced your fear and converted it to your pleasure. And so it will be with every obstacle you will ever have to confront. I'll prepare you, and *we* will overcome.**

Before his arrest, Max admonished, **Only by facing adversity and your fears, then overcoming them, will you ever know the greatest joy.**

Apprising him of the Mafioso plane crashes, Max said, **I have placed you in a position larger than life, respected and held in awe over much of the world. The great and powerful must possess a degree of ruthlessness to sustain. Times and situations can demand it.**

I see. I see, Max. And countless more people would have died if you waited to check mob incursions.

The piece of the puzzle he weighed most painstakingly was Max's assertion that, **The gifted should have the opportunity to gain from their talents. Likewise, the gifted have obligations.**

At last, with complete assuredness, he twisted this final piece into its place

Yes! Of the six billion people on the planet, I am so obliged by my unique circumstance.

At once, the ceiling light blinked on. His eyes flicked open. The gap in the ceiling and the golden butterfly were gone. By God, he had been asleep.

Begin pondering the good you're equipped to accomplish with the power in your possession.

Yes, Max. Yes.

"Mr. Roberts, get ready," Kaz announced through the bars, his voice subdued. "The jury's reached a verdict late last night." He stood beside the guard who was slipping a key into the lock.

Ben jackknifed up on the cot. He rose without a word and, without washing up or shaving, he donned his new outfit that had been hanging on the cell door three days. He all but ignored Kaz, preferring to whistle the refrain of *Que Sera, Sera* as he hurriedly dressed. He ran a comb perfunctorily through his stubbornly tousled hair then strode to the bars and hollered, "Guard, where the hell are McPhail and Benassini? Let's get this show on the road."

Kaz watched in wonderment.

Chapter 75

As the windowless gray prison van rumbled along the highway, Ben continued to hum a fragmented medley of several upbeat tunes that popped into his head as his plan for the morning took shape.

"You feeling all right, Mr. Roberts?" Benassini asked. He and McPhail wore matching frowns.

"Never felt better, Marco, my boy."

The agents glanced at each other then back to him. "You expect an acquittal?" McPhail asked.

"Pete, a buck will win you one million if they don't convict me." He resumed his cheery humming. As an after-thought, he winked at McPhail. "But that doesn't change the fact that today is the first day of the rest of my life."

Handcuffed and surrounded by agents, Ben stepped lively through the side doorway into the packed courtroom. A palpable excitement filled the room but the jury box waited vacantly. McPhail unlocked his cuffs.

Behind the skirmish line of newsmen, he saw Jenny in her usual seat in the front row. Today she wore a striking black pantsuit. The angst in her face crimped his euphoria ever so slightly. Flashing her a confident smile, he winked at her.

Even the haggard faces on his legal team didn't affect his mood. Uncuffed, he stepped toward the lone empty seat at the defense table. He timed it so that just as his hand touched the back of his chair, he suddenly turned and lunged back for the spectator railing in front of Jenny's seat. The newsmen between her and him leapt away in panic. She sprang forward and met him. His guards reacted, hurling themselves after him. A dozen hands grabbed hold of him, but he already had her in his embrace. His arms held her like a vise, resisting the vicious tugs on his cashmere jacket.

"F'christsake!" It was McPhail's voice. "Let him talk with her for a minute." The many grips on his jacket released and were replaced by McPhail's lone gentler hand on his left shoulder.

It seemed a lifetime since he'd held her, but at last he was clinging to her vibrant warmth and feeling vertiginous in her aura of *Eternity*. Oblivious to the reactive chaos about them, unmindful of the circumferential wall of cameras and microphones pressing in on them, they embraced. Her warm tears dampened his unshaven cheek.

"My Love," she whispered. "They will never release you. Never."

"Have faith," he said cheerily.

"No! They never will, I'm certain of it. You still have time to use your corporate might. Do whatever it takes to free yourself."

He bridled his face back a few inches and studied her beseeching eyes. "You mean that?" he said, swiping his hand to clear the closer microphones away.

"If you don't free yourself," she said, weeping, "I'm going to kill myself."

He jostled her with a single hard jolt of her shoulders. "That's not you talking," he said. "You're no quitter. Neither of us is."

"I've been hurt before and survived," she said, "but losing you now would be insufferable. I am not strong enough to withstand that."

The agents, apparently under new orders, abruptly knifed between them. Yanked rudely backwards, he watched Benassini compassionately reach an arm across her shoulders and ease her into her seat.

"I love you, Jenny," he hollered blindly over the wall of agents muscling him down into his chair.

The portly bailiff, today in a spanking new blue suit, stood with his back to the bench and affectedly announced Judge Aloysius. The judge rushed through the little door and nimbly up to his lofty bench. The loud chatter about the courtroom quieted immediately. Not more than a minute later, the jurors, each with a solemn face and downcast eyes, began filing in through the door at the rear of the jury box.

In the distraction of this moment, Ben made his planned move. He shot to his feet and called out, "Your Honor." Mosi Kaz reflexively grabbed at his forearm.

Judge Aloysius blinked, taken aback. It took him a moment to respond, "Be seated, Mr. Roberts. The court must first greet the jury."

"No," Ben countered adamantly. Aloysius curled his upper lip. Kaz and two other defense attorneys stood up imploring Ben to desist and sit down.

Ignoring them, Ben shouted, "Your Honor, I wish to make a statement to the court." An upsurge of voices erupted about the courtroom and the six agents again converged around him. "Goddamn it," he hollered through a tangle of clasping arms. "I've been a model prisoner throughout this whole ordeal. I've earned the right to make a statement."

The admonishing gavel resounded again and again, progressively quieting the spectators. As order restored, restraining hands fell away from Ben. He remained standing.

"I beg the court's pardon," he began again, "but I demand to have my say *now.*" Seizing upon the lapse, he hefted his right foot onto his chair and sprang up onto the defense table. He faced the bench with his arms akimbo.

The shocked courtroom was on its feet; many hollered in favor of Ben's request. Kaz and his fellow attorneys stepped back as imploding agents grappled with Ben's legs. But Ben was able to brace himself and maintain his stance. Benassini had one foot up on the railing, about to leap from the front row of the spectators' section into the fray.

Judge Aloysius popped up out of his chair and stood holding his arms straight up in the air, for whatever reason.

"Please," Ben shouted, struggling to remain standing. "Let me make my statement, and I promise to sit passively until the trial's conclusion. I promise."

Apparently satisfied now with the guarantee of his own safety, the judge reseated himself and banged the gavel down thrice, though rather weakly. "Quiet," he pronounced, his Adam's apple prominently bouncing midst a series of difficult dry swallows. "Quiet in the courtroom." Visibly struggling to regain his imperious facade, he added, "Everyone be seated." Whirring cameras hungrily devoured the happening atop the defense table.

"Okay, Mr. Roberts," Aloysius said, emitting a wheezy sigh. "This court will interrupt protocol and allow you to make your statement prematurely." He gestured with gavel in hand. "Step down off that table and proceed."

"No, sir," Ben countered, holding his head defiantly. "I prefer to make it from up here."

The human ring of would-be subduers again readied around the table, looking expectantly up at the judge. But Aloysius merely wheezed out another sigh and mumbled disgustedly, "As he wishes."

Arms pulled away and Ben turned triumphantly to face the awestruck spectators rather than the jury. Jenny, smartly clad in mourning ebony, was standing with her mouth open to a full "O." She surely feared for his sanity. Expressions similar to hers adorned most of the faces before him.

His high vantage point added to his overwhelming sense of authority, reminiscent of that day he addressed the General Motors meeting. It felt glorious. He was about to speak to the entire world again, but today it would be in real time and unedited. Yes! This is where he belonged, in charge, in command, confronting the world and it in abeyance. Why hadn't he fully realized this months ago?

Fixing his eyes on the camera directly in front of him, he yelled, "The coming verdict is immaterial, a mere trifle." He glanced at Matt Borquist who was standing next to Jenny and hoped to catch one of his damnable winks. But the attorney wore a frozen startle like all the others around him.

"With some trepidation," Ben continued, "I'd like to make a biblical analogy to explain my course of action from this moment forth."

He could hardly contain his exuberance.

"The Bible tells us that Jesus Christ suffered privation alone in the wilderness. During that ordeal, Satan tempted Him with incalculable riches and the offer of inordinate worldly might. He resisted these enticements because he was the sacrificial Lamb of God."

In increasing numbers, the spectators began to retake their seats.

Ben outstretched his arms and stood like a tall cross. "Let me say that I mean no blasphemy here. But just imagine what the good Jesus might have done if he had accepted Satan's offer?"

A few gasps but no verbal protests resounded. He proceeded. "Just imagine, if He had opted for that wealth and supreme Earthly power, what He might have accomplished with it. Think of how much mortal suffering He could have eliminated over the past 2000 years—the countless wars that He could have thwarted, along with the pathetic famines and the devastating plagues. Yes, and pandemics of social crime, past and present, would be nonexistent.

"Well, like Jesus Christ," he continued with his arms still extended, "I too have been enticed by an offer of fabulous riches and horrendous power." The parallel of Max's role to Satan's in this analogy did not escape him. But what the hey! Wasn't he himself a tacit accomplice to dozens of murders already?

Why worry about a little rain when you're already soaking wet?

Intended as a fiery gesture, he swung both arms and pointed at the camera directly before him. "Max," he shouted, "I stand here before the world and declare my total acceptance of everything that your offer entails, including the consequences." He lowered his arms and smiled. "Okay, ol' buddy, now get me the hell out of this mess with as little mayhem as possible. But get me out."

Chapter 76

A husky fellow in a chocolate jumpsuit guided a dolly laden with three cases of champagne through the office expanse. He paused to study the mulling chaos and the blithering mood surrounding him.

During working hours? he wondered.

Colorful paper streamers festooned from the ceiling everywhere. Helium-filled balloons of every color tugged upward in stringed bunches from desk drawer handles, computer monitors, and file drawers. Several escaped balloons bobbed and swayed against the ceiling.

Bruce Springsteen's *Born in the U.S.A.* blared out over the office sound system as more revelers danced their way into the already packed office complex. Laughter and shouted accolades resounded everywhere, but the loudest noise came from Attorney Gellar's office. The door to his office gaped wide and people were bunched in front of it trying to squeeze inside.

The deliveryman pushed the dolly over near the door as he had been instructed to do. Several men in suits and ties shoved their way out of the doorway and commenced tearing aggressively at the top cardboard case. They handed bottle after bottle of the champagne back inside, initiating a makeshift bucket brigade that spanned over the heads of the people. *POW, POW,* came the sound of corks popping inside.

Gellar stood in front of his mirror-topped desk, surrounded by toadies. He felt ecstatic.

Peripheral revelers, apparently realizing the futility of trying to accost their leader at this time, were squeezed out along his office's wall. Several positioned in this least favored onion ring of celebrants passed the time watching the screensaver on a small computer monitor that sat wedged in the corner. It depicted tropical fish squiggling about.

Alongside Gellar, a fellow coiffed in a gray pompadour with matching goatee raised his drink and shouted, "Another toast to his highness."

A hundred plastic cups rose high in the air. A baritone voice from somewhere in the crowd yelled, "To our world famous defender of justice, the most upwardly mobile attorney in the world today." The deafening cheer died out as everyone sipped in unison.

Flaming-haired and shapely, Gellar's personal secretary gushed puffery into his ear, dangerously close to smearing his lobe with her lipstick. "Rick, your face is better known around the world now than the frigging President's."

Gellar winked at her and patted her backside, then he turned to a head-shaved black fellow beside him. "What do you think, Mayor? Where shall I point? To the Supreme Court? Maybe the Attorney General's post?"

"Hell, Rick," he declaimed like a southern preacher, "Nixon got into the White House after nailing Alger Hiss. You'd be a shoo-in with half his effort."

Gellar chuckled as he imagined himself lounging in the Oval Office. "I can see it now, campaigning on my hard stance against crime. My slogan might be," he traced his hand across an imaginary banner, "*He nailed Roberts! No criminal will be safe.*"

Back-patters set upon him, but then his desk phone rang. He gestured for quiet to little avail then lifted the receiver to his ear.

"Yes? Well, thank you, Governor. Thank you," he said, swelling his chest out in caricature for those immediately around him. "I must agree. I was rather deft, wasn't I? No, don't worry. My aim is higher than state office. Yes, that's what everyone is telling me. Ha! Sure I'll remember you when I form my Cabinet. Thanks for calling."

Receiver down, he raised his cup. "Okay, everybody listen up." The multitude began shushing each other. Someone switched off the intercom music, interrupting Fats Domino's rendition of *Blueberry Hill.* The "bloop-blooping" sound effects of the screensaver on the little iMac in the corner became prominent for lack of competing noise.

Frustrated with his hampered range of vision, Gellar walked around his desk and stepped onto his chair then up on his desktop. "I borrow this antic from Roberts," he said, with his feet staunchly apart, "but I solemnly swear not to have a mental breakdown while I'm up here." Laughter resounded about him. "Wasn't that something? A full blown delusion of grandeur erupting right before our eyes." He shook his head midst more laughter. "But seriously," he held his drink out, "allow me to propose a toast to my fantastic legal staff who helped me plan and execute our flawless strategy. Throughout the trial, they were magnificent."

The shouting again deafened.

"Yes," he continued. "My staff remained undaunted despite those admonitions that Roberts would strike back if we persisted. Well, we showed all those nervous nellies." He chuckled. "Yeah, we damn well showed them." He quaffed the entire content of his cup, then wiped his mouth on his jacket sleeve before he continued.

"That bastard accumulated more wealth than any person in history. But my little team battled him and won." The cheering anew actually hurt his ears. He waved his arms for quiet. "Kids now read about 'Jack the Giant

Killer.' But future generations of youngsters will read and sing about 'Rick the Roberts Killer.'"

Hoots and whistling reverberated throughout the entire office complex. The wall-to-wall humanity began chanting, "Rick the Roberts Killer... Rick the Roberts Killer..."

Gellar stood orchestrating the beat with his outstretched arms. Who on Earth could deny that he'd become a legend?

He patted the air for another interval of quiet. "And I feel no compunction at all for ripping that mogul a new anus. Surely he'll get twenty-five years to life in solitary confinement, and that's condign punishment for the bastard." So tickled by the thought, he himself crowed out laughter. Regaining control, he took a tissue handed to him by his redheaded secretary and wiped his eyes. "Actually," he said when he caught his breath, "my sentiments have always favored draconian measures in law enforcement. If I were an autocrat, I'd have the bastard beheaded."

Cheers deafened again.

As the yelling abated, a gray mustachioed aide-de-camp standing by the desk front spoke up, "Figuratively, Rick, you did just that. Then you whacked off his family jewels for good measure."

Gellar shot him a wink. "Well, Arthur, locked away for life from his luscious Jenny Bligh, he's better off without them."

Cheering.

He patted the air once more. "To the victor go the spoils! My one regret is that doesn't apply literally here. I'd sure like a chance to spoil that absolute babe of his."

Feminine voices in the room playfully jeered him. "Pig!" "Sexist pig!" Males howled and whistled.

"Rick, why don't you give her a call sometime," his buxom office supervisor interjected. There was mischief in her tone. "That kind of woman is obviously attracted to powerful men. You'd have her in your pocket in no time."

"Maggie," he retorted with affected sweetness, "it's not in my pocket where I'd keep her." He leaped off the desk into another round of female hisses and countervailing male cheers.

An intensely loud BOING-BOING-BOINGing commenced from the blue iMac in the corner. "Hey, Rick," a young roisterer called out, "even your computer here is applauding you."

"Huh?" The room quieted at Gellar's sudden show of concern. All glanced to the computer in the corner. Its display of undersea life disappeared in a blink. The BOINGs ceased and words appeared.

Gellar stepped toward it. The quieted revelers stepped out of his way, to move in behind and beside him as he and they read the printing that began to slowly scroll upward:

Hear ye! Hear ye!

Congratulations, Rick! You were masterful in prosecuting this case. Your performance was rousing and great fun. But alas, now, your revelry must end. Because if you think I am going to let you keep my friend Ben Roberts in jail any longer, you're the one who's "frigging" delusional.

The United States and the other countries of the world that joined into this conspiracy against him will soon scramble to free him.

Every aspect of his pre-arrest life and lifestyle will be restored to him at once. And to say the least, his position relative to his fellow man will have advanced considerably.

You bastards are about to pay in extremity for your intrusion into his life. I will commence by devastating selected targets around the world. Then I will progress incrementally until the planet is a virtual global hell, if need be, unless all of you cede in absolute capitulation.

And trust me. You cannot imagine the retribution I will inflict if the slightest harm comes to Benjamin.

Let me admit, though, the only reason that I regret the trial dragged on so long is because of his ongoing personal discomfort. In truth, I found it quite entertaining. And, too, it proved most efficacious in producing the lad's final transmutation.

His friend, Max

Chapter 77

"Max. Max," Jenny cried out, striding briskly up to Ben's computer.

Good evening, Jenny. This has been quite a day.

"What happened?" Her voice pealed an octave higher than normal. "Has he suffered a nervous breakdown?" She remained standing beside the chair.

Good heavens no, young lady. I know him too well, inside and out, to ever question his sanity.

She clenched her fists. "But why would he leap up on the table and spout that religious gobbledygook?"

Personally, I thought it hilarious. But then I'm partial to his propensity for the outrageous. Seems we didn't need your cajoling, after all. I sensed that when he walked into the courtroom evincing wild-eyed euphoria this morning.

As for that religious analogy he drew, consider his Christian upbringing. Realize, too, what he said up there wasn't much of a stretch.

"But he ranted like a megalomaniac!"

You mean like someone who thinks he's the richest, most powerful person on Earth?

"Then you're not worried at all?"

Absolutely not. But brace yourself. He's assumed a cocksure direction that'll take a while to run its course before he mellows.

She weighed his answer. "So now you'll free him?"

Most definitely. But, Jenny, realize this: to force nations of the world into submission, they must be convinced that to do otherwise would prove too costly.

"Free him!" she said without hesitation.

That's my girl!

After a moment of thought, she added, "But perhaps you could go a bit easy on the United States."

Mid afternoon, two weeks after the trial ended, the Palacio received a cellular call that Clive transferred immediately to Jenny's third-floor suite. Lounging in a favorite but very old kimono that she'd worn making a James Bond movie years ago, she lifted the cordless receiver to her ear. Through it came an excited voice she'd been praying to hear, "Babe, I'm coming home!"

Instantly, her heart fluttered wildly. "Oh, thank God, Ben," she squealed. He sounded normal enough. "I've been waiting desperately to hear from you. Where are you calling from?"

"Would you believe I'm sitting inside an olive-drab helicopter parked in the middle of the prison yard? I'm surrounded by a contingent of marines, but this time they're pointing their rifles the other way."

"Darling, I can hardly hear you," she half-shouted. "There's a terrible noise on this line."

"No! It's all coming from this end. I'm in the eye of a damn military hurricane. A half-dozen Cobra gunship helicopters are swarming around the prison like humongous bumblebees. Countless jet fighters are spiraling in a giant helix overhead. It's a maddening din but a sight to behold."

"Darling," she began, then paused to press her palm over her thumping chest, "Darling, have them fly you straight back to the Palacio."

"You got that right. What a minute...Hey, Colonel. When the hell is that pilot coming back? I have places to go and things to do...Jenny, one of the honchos here says I should be in the air in less than five minutes."

She hesitated, then asked, "Are you aware of what's been happening?"

"Not entirely, but I have strong—"

"Then please," she cut him off. "Don't ask anyone; don't discuss it with anybody until you get home to me. And I beg you, don't land anywhere until you reach the Palacio. Ben? Ben?"

"I'm still here. But Jessuz, you're confirming my fears." A mute pause lengthened as she listened only to roaring and imagined aircraft swooshing through the skies above him. His voice again superimposed over the noise. "Granted, this prison break is a bit melodramatic, but I'm game for whatever it takes." Her eyes brimmed, and she covered the mouthpiece to hide some very wet sniffles.

"And, Babe," his voice deepened as if he was cupping the phone, "long before they unlocked my cell door, I've had my first hours of freedom prioritized." She heard him cackle. "Think maybe I should stop somewhere along the way and find myself a tuxedo and a couple bottles of rare wine?"

"Trust me, love, you won't need them." Her cheeks tingled. "But you might need a raincoat over your arm for the trip home."

He laughed. "Ha! Believe it or not, McPhail and Benassini are right here with me. Guess I could borrow one of their trench coats."

Why now? she chided herself. Why now, while listening to her lover, was she suddenly wondering what Max's voice sounded like?

Chapter 78

The next morning, they had breakfast at that same roof plaza where they lunched together her first day on the estate. Afterward, they sauntered along the maze of garden paths. Clinging to each other, they strolled through dappling morning shadows as the climbing sun winked through swaying overhead birch limbs. They paused often in lingering embraces amidst the heady bouquet from the prismatic flowerbeds and blossoming shrubs. Ben breathed in the sweetened air and realized he felt whole again.

"Jenny, if anything, this place is more beautiful now than last time we were up here together."

Sitting on the tiled rim of the central lily pond, they watched the koi fish meander about under the floating colorful blossoms. The playful breeze occasionally warped the sunbow in the pond spray and spattered them with a fine mist, which he thought refreshing.

She nuzzled against him, clasping her arms around his chest. "My love, don't let the fearfulness of the house staff upset you. I've told them repeatedly what you said, that everything will return to normal in time."

He looked off along a petunia-lined path. "Did any of them lose family or loved ones?"

"I don't think so, unless they had relatives in Montana." She pressed her cheek to his sweater front.

"Montana? You've got to tell me what the hell actually happened?"

"It's not as bad here as it could have been."

"Oh God! Tell me."

She looked up at him. "First, your people blitzed the airwaves and cyberspace with warnings in the languages of each region. 'Benjamin Roberts' told nations not to take up their weaponry or to attempt to dismantle any of it, especially their nuclear stores. You issued explicit instructions to move clear of all their toys of war. Three major powers decidedly balked. It took them longer to believe you had effective control of everyone's high-tech weaponry.

"China, for some foolish reason, launched a barrage of missiles at Taiwan. Your people merely re-routed them in flight. Beijing is lifeless for a hundred miles around. Russia, too, resisted initially, so an area outside Moscow is now a no-man's land. Then to bring the U.S. into line, your people had to explode nuclear silos in eastern Montana. Fortunately this was a sparsely inhabited area."

"Jessuz!"

"But that was the worst of it, actually—except for Iran and North Korea.

"Little North Korea?"

"Yes. You ordered people around the world into the streets to show acceptance to your rule. After the explosions in China, Russia and US, billions of people complied, appearing on TV screens everywhere. A few nations continued to resist until Iran's Baghdad, and North Korea's capital city, Pyongyang, both demonstrative resistors, were struck with a missiles launched from somewhere in Russia."

She half-grinned. "Forgive me, Love, but the early scenes of Paris were rather humorous. Immediately after you issued your 'go-into-the-streets' edict, Parisians rushed outside in droves, singing their national anthem and waving their arms overhead. You'd have thought it was a national holiday.

"Well, convinced that the world's nuclear and hi-tech arsenals were effectively in your control, each military around the world capitulated. It's fortunate that your organization can communicate fluently in so many languages. Reportedly, there are still factions of objecting diehards— principally in Islamic countries. That's why you and I are being protected so securely. But what's left is essentially a mop-up action. You are in control."

"How do you know all this? I mean you seem to have the total picture. Did you get it from TV?"

Her cheeks pinked. "Oh, an awful lot of it. But that treasury agent John McPike was assigned to the Palacio as part of my armed guard until yesterday morning. He kept me apprised of the behind-the-scenes skinny."

Ben hung his head. "My God! So millions of people were killed."

"Yes, but billions were not," she added on an up-note. "Still, in truth, many are whispering that what you've done is too horrible for words."

He looked at her. "No, Jenny, the true horror has been the plight of countless victims throughout history who were subjected to avoidable human suffering. I'm merely forcing an elixir down mankind's throat. Unfortunately, the medicine is bitter."

She winced. This rehash of his rhetoric obviously upset her. No doubt she preferred the boyish insecurity he evinced at Gambino's wine shop and at the Counterpoint music store. Perhaps she feared he had become an irrevocable zealot. Well, maybe to some extent, he had. So be it! But he did not love her any less. Besides, her premonition since girlhood actually tried to forewarn her. After all, armored knights are symbolic of idealism and crusades, aren't they?

"I understand your need to maintain an iron grip for now," she said, "but when are you going to ease the situation?"

"In due time. Have no misgivings. The world shall once again thrive." He nodded earnestly. "That's a certainty. The people will get back a tremendous amount of freedom, but they will be held strictly accountable for their actions from now on. There will be particular emphasis on meting out harsh and swift punishment to those who engage in any criminality or other predatory behavior. Offsetting, there will be ample rewards for effort expended justly.

"Ah! Enough of that, my love. Let me say that my organization has a prime directive that supersedes every other."

"What is it?"

"Simply to do what has to be done to ensure you and me complete safety and total access to the majesty of this Earth, so that we can go anywhere and savor it all, everything."

Her eyes softened. "For me, my love, having you back is everything."

He took in a full breath to bolster himself. "I hope you'll still feel that way after I finish confessing what I must. You once said that the purest of loves grow where there is mutual honesty, total candor." She sobered.

He took in another deep breath and eased it out. "Well, to that end, I have something to reveal that will surely test your feelings for me, perhaps even beyond the breaking point."

Her look of concern vanished behind a soft laugh. "I think I know what you're going to confess. And I say that because of a confession I must make."

"No, babe. Regardless of what you think you know, what I'm about to divulge is as fantastic and as it is shameful."

Her smile waned.

He swallowed so hard it made him grimace. With his entire fortune riding on the toss, he threw the dice. "It involves my accessing your diary in your computer before we met and using your innermost secrets to assist me in your seduction."

Her expression blanked. Perhaps her momentary disbelief delayed the hostility he expected.

She gasped and grabbed her throat. "You would never stoop so low," she asserted icily. "But even if you tried, what could you learn? I file everything in a personal code."

"Jenny, my love, before I say any more about that, let me repeat a crucial truth: no one knows how predetermination works. Right? Perhaps my collusion in the invasion of your privacy was also predestined to enable us—you and me, Jenny and Benny—to happen."

Unintimidated, he held her gaze, watching it grow fierce. "Here comes the fantastic part," he said. "And may he forgive my disregard of his incessant warnings, because..." He swallowed dryness again and grimaced once more. "Because, you see, it involves him, that is, my...my friend, actually the one I've referred to as my personal advisor. You see, he...well, he happens to exist primarily in the fifth through the ninth dimensions."

Chapter 79

Years later, late one evening, Ben had just penned a bottom line on a page in a logbook. He turned the page and paused to count the blank sheets remaining to the end of this 2-inch thick chronicle, which he'd been writing in for months. It proved a happy coincidence that his autobiography, which reached back to the first evening he met Max, would end leaving a few blank pages to conclude his business at hand and thus have everything contained within one handwritten volume. He intended to present it to their daughter next month on her twenty-first birthday, only weeks after she graduated from college.

He set the fountain pen down on the desk, interlaced his fingers, and stretched them to ease his writer's cramp. Then he snorted to rid his nose of a worsening of that damnable mediciney scent that still plagued him. Would it ever leave him?

He picked up the pen and resumed:

...And as you can imagine, my dear Celeste, the remainder of that day, and quite a few that followed, passed mid storm and fury. Finally, I convinced her to join me in confronting Max directly. Her first words to him were angry rebuke, while I interceded, staunchly defending him.

But gradually, with the passing days, the fantastic became for her what it had become for me. As one would expect, because our love was preordained, her hurt eased to where she once again reconciled with me. We quickly became even closer. Our passion re-ignited with a new fiery brilliance that only emanates from stellar loves that have been tempered in the cosmic flame of total honesty.

Yes, and so it came to pass that your comely mother and I, together with Max Megabyter have lived and loved and governed happily for many glorious years. We three have converted this previously corrupt and strife-ridden orb into the rather harmonious meshwork that it is today. It is with some trepidation that I pen our story for you, realizing it will overwhelm and surely fill you with awe and disbelief, at first. But, my dear, I present you this epic tale only as a preface.

Only your mother and myself have known the truth about Max. Now that you have read this, she and I will invite you to accept your place on the throne beside us. Henceforth, the three of us together with him will watch over this world, ever alert for upstarts with plunderous ambition. But you must realize that more than a third of the human population suffers with some degree of psychiatric illness: only then can you begin to appreciate how interesting it is to oversee this planet.

We will start by allowing you time to become acquainted with Max. I very much want you to accept him as your friend, too. Alas, he can't entice you as he did me, since wealth and favor are all you've ever known. But he will offer you his unwavering devotion that until now has belonged solely to your mother and myself. And, too, my dear, it just so happens that he has already located the ideal fellow for you, the young man of your dreams—

2nd Author's Advisory

Dear reader,

You have just finished reading the body of my novel, and only the epilogue remains to be read. At this juncture I ask you to thoughtfully make one of two choices:

1) If thus far you have enjoyed the story's plot, its characters and their denouement, if you now feel "satisfied" and are glad you invested the time to read it, then stop at this point. **Do not read the epilogue.**

2) But if you found less pleasure in this reading than you'd hoped for, if you felt that the story was too much like a fairytale to let you sufficiently suspend disbelief, if its plot, its characters, and their denouement left you disappointed for whatever reasons, then please continue on. **Do read the epilogue**.

Epilogue

Two hundred pairs of medical student eyes stared down onto Benjamin Roberts from the steep tiers of the teaching auditorium. He sat motionless in his wheelchair with his eyes shut. He was wearing gray pajamas and a blue-and-white striped robe and an exaggerated moronic grin. If he were seated before a lay audience, he would have surely evoked snickers.

"For some of you, this is your first live encounter with a patient suffering with schizophrenia," began Professor Kinderhook. "Unfortunately, it will not be your last. Approximately one-half of one percent of the American population suffers this devastating disease."

Kinderhook enjoyed teaching medical students. When he retired two years ago from a long and successful private practice in psychiatry, almost at once he received an offer to return to his alma mater to dedicate his last years to helping educate the next generation of physicians.

As he looked out at the sea of attentive faces, he thought how young they all appeared. Today, each student in this sophomore class was wearing a short white jacket. As a group, they might have been a church choir. He remembered back to when he himself was a sophomore, sitting in this same auditorium so many years ago. Oh, how the time flew by.

"Yes," he began again. "The tragedy of Benjamin R. is all too common." In teaching presentations, he never used the last names of patients, only the initial. "The patient is 46 years old now, but in all probability, his disease started when he was just about your age. "Seventy-five percent of those who acquire the disease develop their first signs and symptoms between 15 and 24 years old. In fact, he was diagnosed with emotional problems in his early twenties.

"Let me briefly apprise you of his history and discuss schizophrenia in broad terms, leaving it for you to read in depth about the subcategories of this disease. But I will not get into its treatment regimens; better that you wait till next year when you start in the clinics and actually begin caring for these patients. Today I just want you to meet a patient suffering with it so you'll have visual images to relate to during your reading. Realize that every one of those myriad diseases in your medical textbooks do actually affect living human beings.

"Doctor," he said, pointing to a fair-faced young man in the front row. Kinderhook always addressed his students prematurely as 'Doctor.' It gave their egos such visible boosts. And in truth, the legality of the title was little more than a couple of years away. And too anymore, even with his glasses, he found it difficult to read their lapel nametags. "Doctor, what salient features of this patient immediately struck you when he was wheeled in?"

The young man sat upright, cleared his throat, then had to clear it again before responding, "Professor, he seems quite wooden. His eyes have remained closed. His head is tipped awkwardly to the side and he maintains a silly smile on his face. His posture and expression have remained unchanged as if he's unaware or uncaring of his immediate surroundings. But he appears well-developed and well-nourished."

"Very good observations."

He pointed to an African-American student coifed in cornrows in the fourth row. "Doctor, I've told you he's schizophrenic. So from just his appearance, what more would you surmise about his diagnosis?" Asking pop questions of randomly selected students during a teaching session was called 'pimping' in the student vernacular. Most of them disliked it, but it kept all of them alert and attentively on edge, an ideal state for learning.

She sat forward to answer. "I've never seen it before, but could it be the catatonia associated with this disorder?" Though she spoke in a calm, self-assured manner, her raised chin told him she was nervous.

"Correct, Doctor. You've diagnosed your first clinical case right on the money." Rewarding praise helped make medicine fun for them. "But I might change some of your phraseology to make it more precisely correct. You said, 'associated with this disorder.' In fact, what we lump together as schizophrenia is likely a collection of disorders. The APA's *Diagnostic and Statistical Manual of Mental Disorders* lists seven subcategories within the general category of schizophrenia, whereas the *International Classification of Diseases, Injuries, and Causes of Death* lists fourteen.

"And you said, 'the catatonia' as if it were singular. Actually there are two types. This patient is demonstrating 'stuporous' catatonia. There is also an 'excited' type. The definition of the inclusive term 'catatonia' is—*a state of marked abnormality of motor function.* In the 'excited' variant, the person evinces extreme psychomotor agitation, often talking or shouting almost nonstop. This excited state is a true medical emergency because these patients may injure themselves or collapse in complete exhaustion.

"Benjamin here..." He continually referred back to the patient so the students would wean away from thinking of medical facts in the functionally abstract, but as immediately applicable to real people. "...exhibits the 'stuporous' variant. In this state, there is a pronounced decrease of the person's reactivity to the environment and a decrease of all his spontaneous movements and activity. Usually the patient assumes an inappropriate posture, such as Benjamin's tipped head and his strained smile. They usually remain mute and may show distinct negativism as Benjamin does. He refuses to respond or cooperate." Kinderhook attempted to lift Benjamin's hand up. The patient jerked it free and returned it to his lap, but his grin never varied. "Occasionally in catatonia of this type we find the phenomenon of waxy flexibility, in which we can position the patient or his extremities in odd ways and the patient will maintain this awkward posture for hours.

"Other findings sometimes found in this stuporous state, but not demonstrable in Benjamin, are 1) the continuous repeating of words or phrases or actions like clapping or picking at their clothing; 2) the automatic copying of any activity the examiner performs in front of them. For example, if the examiner claps the patient will clap; and 3) some demonstrate automatic obedience and will immediately do what they are told, like raise their hands, whistle, stomp their feet.

"So please infer that the patient before you, though he is in an altered state, is not unconscious. His posturing and his behavior are in fact volitional. Why these patients behave like this, we do not know. But most important, Benjamin is awake and hearing us at this moment. Thus our discussion must be conducted with the utmost respect in his regard.

"Think of him as in a self-imposed isolation, existing perhaps at the center of an imagined reality of his own.

"First off, genetics definitely plays a significant role in schizophrenia. Blood relatives of these patients develop the disease in much greater frequency than the general population. But in identical twin studies, the concordance rate is only about 75 percent. When one twin develops this disease, the second twin will also develop it in 3/4 of the cases. Since the second twin does not contract it 100 percent of the time, we conclude that the environment plays some role. Seemingly, a person must be predisposed to the disease, and then some environmental stress or event apparently triggers the onset.

"Biochemical changes do occur in the schizophrenic's body. But we don't understand yet how these known changes relate absolutely to this disease state."

The blond fellow who answered his first pimp question raised his hand, interrupting Kinderhook. The professor often found that after someone was called upon, they were more likely to ask questions later.

"Yes, Doctor?"

"Professor Kinderhook, could you fill us in on a bit of his pre-morbid life, what his first symptoms were, and what's happened to him over the intervening twenty plus years?"

"Sorry if I was boring you," he replied with affected drollness.

"Oh, no, sir! It's just that knowing some aspects of his back-story, the facts of the disease might be easier to remember."

Kinderhook nodded and smiled. "Let me guess; you were an English major?"

The student's face reddened. "Yes, sir."

"The tip-off was your use of the term 'back-story.' You'll soon come to regard it as the medical history, past and present." He stepped over to the wheelchair. "But yes, I did intend to mix in more of his back story-cum-medical history as I went along. Forgive me.

"Benjamin's been catatonic for a number of years now; in fact, its onset defined him as schizophrenic. Alas, prior to that time his symptoms were considered to be depressive manifestations of post-traumatic stress that stretched back to his time in the Army."

"Was he medically discharged?" The English major asked.

Kinderhook thought a moment. He hadn't wanted to go deeply into this poor fellow's history today, but he replied, "No. He served his entire tour and was cited with several combat medals, including the Silver Star.

"But let me touch on some of the possible initiating factors for this disease as you may encounter it. First is drugs—such as alcohol, LSD, amphetamines, and cannabis seem able to initiate it. Also, this illness has been known to erupt after loss of or a rebuff by a loved one, or after a person has been somehow brutalized, for instance being raped.

"Benjamin did lose both parents while he was in high school, but he joined the Army immediately after graduation, and extensive psychological testing at time of enlistment found him to be not only normal, but also an ideal candidate for covert operations. He was integrated into a small top-secret contingent of US troops who were smuggling weaponry into Afghanistan, which was then warring with the Russians. He was in that region continuously for several years. A major mishap killed a number of the other men in his small unit, forcing Benjamin to join up with the Afghan guerillas for a time. He engaged in a number of harrowing battles over a period of months. When he was finally retrieved and returned home, he showed signs consistent with depression. The psychiatric debriefing teams diagnosed him as suffering 'post-traumatic stress syndrome.'"

"What was his rank?" The English major asked.

"His concocted discharge papers at the time state he left as a sergeant. But his true records that were kept top-secret till recently show he was meritoriously promoted four times in the four years and lastly held a field commission of second lieutenant while fighting with the rebels. Understand that his true military contribution was concealed by the Pentagon for a long time, for obvious reasons."

"Wow! I'm impressed," the English major piped up. "What type of work did he do after the service, and did he ever marry?"

Kinderhook smiled to himself, and then glanced around at the other faces before him, saying, "Please speak up if any of you have questions. I don't want this to turn into a two-person conversation." He intended the statement as a barb, but felt sure this young fellow would be neither insulted nor deterred.

"Okay, on his release from the service, he went to college on the GI bill. Studied in the sciences. Got very good grades, by the way. Understand, many with this disease are very intelligent, this patient being a good example. He went on to successfully hold a series of middle management corporate positions. He did marry and had two sons, but his wife left him a few years before he was correctly diagnosed. She stated that his extreme moodiness was her principal reason." He looked at the English major as if to ask, 'Anything else you'd particularly like to know?'

Be damned if the kid didn't respond. "You mean he went right into a stupor as his first obvious sign of the disease? He didn't show any deterioration. No hallucinations or delusions before that?"

This young man's forwardness in fact now tickled Kinderhook. "Tell me, Doctor. Are you intending to go into psychiatry?"

"No, sir. Radiology." The other students were beginning to chuckle.

"Hmmm," Kinderhook said, stroking his close-cropped white beard. "Then I can understand your burgeoning interest here." Several classmates laughed loudly. But he was being only in part facetious. "MRI and PET scans have now become integral in the research of this disease and will probably play an even greater role in time.

"But back to your question. Yes, before his catatonia, he revealed no detectable signs of any thought disorder or any bizarre behavior classically associated with this active disease. Let me qualify that. He may have suffered delusions and/or hallucinations and just not communicated them to his physicians or to anyone else. Many of these patients realize how strange their ideations are, so although they believe them, they keep them to themselves.

"Note that after his divorce, his personal appearance did slip, but that seemed explainable then by his domestic upset. Perhaps it slipped further yet after he was fired from his last position. But you're on to something here, because deterioration in a person's ability to function—in work, in social relations, and in self-care—is a major diagnostic criterion for this disease."

"Professor, has there been any interruption in his catatonia so you could ask him questions?" This two-man dialogue continued.

"As a matter of fact, when he was first brought to our St. Louis Veterans Hospital over a decade ago, in the 90s actually, he was in light catatonia, tending to disregard everyone around him, and was very resistant to interrogation, preferring to be alone with his computer. Let me say, that the first overt manifestation of his problem was his sudden total preoccupation with a computer. I might add that he'd just purchased it shortly before the appearance of his first symptoms, which were to sit and stare at the screen for hours, even when it was unplugged. Any attempt to remove the set from his presence incited violent resistance."

"What kind of computer was it?" the English major asked. The rest of the class, already primed, broke into frank laughter. Even Kinderhook chuckled.

"Actually, as I recall from his chart, it was a Macintosh, one of those compact little iMac sets that had just come on the market." More laughter erupted around the room. "Why do you ask?"

The English major sat back and smugly folded his arms. "I read where bizarre symbolism is common in schizophrenics. That computer could have played some major role."

"Ah! You've opened the door for me into the topic of thought disturbances in these patients. But let me first opine that you seem quite perceptive and imaginative. Don't waste your writing background. Many doctors have become renown for their literary skills." Though he was completely serious, the class again chuckled.

"To your question, first I must reiterate that schizophrenia is foremost a disorder of thinking. Despite the non-catatonic patient's clear sensorium, which is characteristic for this disease, the patient's thinking is awry. Many times when you first meet one of these patients, you do not realize anything is wrong until they speak awhile and betray their ideas and thought processes. Recall Cervantes' character Don Quixote. And I'm sure that even in the seemingly beclouded state of stuporous catatonia, like Benjamin here, bizarre ideation continually streams though the patient's brain.

"Characteristically their thinking is loose associations, and it is full of internal contradictions and erroneous conclusions that are not consistent with logic or experience. It's autistic thinking, in that it might gratify their unfulfilled desires but there is little regard for reality. A patient might interpret the 'snap, crackle, and pop' of his breakfast cereal to be an encoded message from God telling him what clothing to wear that day.

"Don't let me lose you here, but their thinking is a pairing of two extremes—excessive concreteness on the one hand, together with a marked leaning toward the abstract and the symbolic on the other.

"As an example of the first, they asked Benjamin in an early evaluation to interpret the saying, 'A stitch in times saves nine.' He responded, 'That means you'd better sew nine stripes on my sleeve.' Recall that stripes high on the sleeve designate enlisted rank in the military. He was only 34 years old at that time.

But it is their abstract and symbolic thinking that leads these patients to become preoccupied with invisible forces, high technology, witchcraft, religion, philosophy, and the like.

"Here's a mnemonic concept I use to better grasp the schizophrenic's plight. Normal persons easily compartmentalize those thoughts and images that are from reality and can keep them discretely separate from what they've imagined, dreamed, or otherwise encountered in novels and movies or such. Normalcy can readily distinguish which is which. In schizophrenia, the compartmental barriers fail. The schizophrenic perceives his reality to include many of the thoughts and ideas from his imagination. And he tends to lend equal credibility to this mix of fact and fancy.

"And if that isn't problem enough, their lives are further complicated by the fact that they also suffer hallucinations—that is, sensory experiences without corresponding external stimuli. Auditory hallucinations are most common. They may conjure up sundry sounds that aren't there, perhaps voices when no one is speaking. Sometimes they even hear their own thoughts as someone else's voice coming from outside themselves. Visual hallucinations are not as common but they are not rare. In these cases, patients see things that are not there—people, objects, events, etc. Likewise, they may superimpose fanciful interpretations to actual objects or happenings in their environment. Such phantasms are totally believable to them.

"A combination of all these factors contributes to the fact that these patients have delusions—false fixed ideas that cannot be corrected by reasoning." He glimpsed his watch, giving the class a moment to digest what he had just tossed out at them. All sat scribbling in their notebooks.

Sure enough, it was the English major who broke the silence.

"Why do they go into catatonia? Is it to withdraw into a perceived safety, like a turtle into his shell? Or is it like someone on heroin going on the nod, withdrawing to better enjoy some pleasurable state?"

This time, there was no laughter from the room. Kinderhook studied him, rather impressed.

"Very good questions, Doctor. But the only valid answer to date is that we just don't know. As I explained, there is great disorder in the patient's thought processes. It's possible the patient in part *chooses* to lapse into catatonic, if you will—albeit some one or more biochemical changes being integral.

"Let me mention a session the staff held with Benjamin a number of years ago. It so happens that patients in deep catatonic stupor can be brought out of it briefly if they are given an injection of a short-acting barbiturate, a medication that puts normal people to sleep. Benjamin was given such. Soon after, his eyes opened to reveal a surprising clarity and depth. Members of our staff asked him questions. Though his gaze sought out each questioner, he offered no verbal or gestured responses. After many minutes of fruitless interrogation, they desisted. Only then did he finally speak up, saying essentially, 'Let me be, goddamn it!' He then closed his eyes and has remained pretty much as you see him ever since." All in the auditorium were focused on Benjamin as Kinderhook added, "It's as if he wants to stay wherever he imagines he is.

"Realize that he has been subjected to many potent treatment regimens over the years—any one alone is often enough to end this state. But alas, in his case, each achieved only partial and short-term improvement. It's as if he stubbornly resists coming out of it. They've all but consigned him to live out his life here in our chronic psychiatric service. His condition is to psychiatry what incurable cancer is to general medicine. But believe me, we've treated him to the **max**."

Benjamin's eyes flicked open!

Several medical students immediately pointed to him in his wheelchair, and someone cried out, "Professor, he's opened his eyes"

Kinderhook glimpsed down at his patient. Indeed they were open. Moreover, they appeared alert and discerning. Ben was actually scanning the rows of students seated before him, letting only his eyeballs move.

"Ben," Kinderhook quickly addressed him. "These are sophomore medical students. And I'm Doctor Kinderhook. I've been presenting you and your medical problem to them today because they are currently studying the disease that brought you into the hospital." Benjamin's eyes met his. "If it bothers you to be part of a teaching forum, I'll take you back to your room at once."

Benjamin glanced again at the tiers of students for a long moment then he slowly shut his eyes. Kinderhook and the class watched him in silence for a while. The professor shook Ben's shoulder and called out to him numerous times until it became apparent that Ben had slipped back into deep catatonia.

Kinderhook opined to the class that the patient's brief rousal might have been caused by some sound in the auditorium, or perhaps by something that transpired in the patient's own mind.

A hefty young woman in the second row proffered, "Maybe he took offence to what you were saying. You called him stubborn."

"No, I said he was *stubbornly resistant* to treatment."

She countered, "Still, maybe that upset him."

"I don't think so. What I saw in his eyes wasn't anger. It was surprise and puzzlement, perhaps at finding himself in this auditorium with us."

A lanky young fellow sprawled over his seat in the fourth row asked, "Professor, any treatment options left to try on him?"

Kinderhook debated a moment with himself, then said, " I really didn't want to get into any of the specific treatments for this disease today, better next year in the clinics, but let me say that we intend to again try ECT—electrical convulsive therapy. He under went several courses of it when he first came to us, years ago. It can be effective in ending this type of catatonia. Why it didn't work for him, no one can say. For the past two years, since I arrived here, I have pushed to try it again."

The lanky student began, "Then why—"

Kinderhook anticipated the question. "For months now, an ill-informed activist group in Washington has been vociferously protesting its use on veterans. But the protest is fizzling out, so no doubt we'll be allowed to resume its use eventually."

The English major asked, "Doesn't electro-shock damage the brain?"

Kinderhook expected this interest when he brought up ECT. Students who have not experienced the psychiatry wards yet invariably react negatively at the mention of shock therapy.

"I don't want to get into a convoluted discussion here about the adverse effects of ECT. Let me just say that one effect that it rather consistently produces is lengthy and often permanent amnesia. For example, after Benjamin completes his next battery of ECT, it's quite possible that he will remember little or nothing at all of his feelings and thoughts during the years he's remained hospitalized in his catatonic state.

The English major laughed affectedly. "Hell, Professor, that wouldn't be much of a loss."

"Ah!" the professor countered. "But how enlightening it might be to learn about his psychological and intellectual functioning during all that time. Perhaps he's been enjoying some fabulous continuous dream state these many years. One can only imagine what rich tapestry a brilliant mind might weave to entertain itself over that length of time."

The student with her hair in cornrows quipped, "Wow! If the String Theory is correct, maybe he's slipped cerebrally into another universe and has been living a grand life on some world parallel to ours."

The class and even Dr. Kinderhook laughed.

www.ingramcontent.com/pod-product-compliance
Lightning Source LLC
Chambersburg PA
CBHW031101260626
47172CB00001B/171